Volume 14

Secrets

Satisfy your desire for more.

Soul Kisses by Angela Knight

Beth Chase learned vampires weren't all bad when Cade McKinnon Turned—and married—her sister, Valerie. But some vampires are evil, and to Beth's horror, she finds herself kidnapped by the worst of the bunch, Joaquin Ramirez, an immortal sadist. Luckily, she's rescued by handsome vampire cousins, Morgan and Garret Axton, who are locked in their own war with the killer. Can she find happiness with two vampires—and can they break Ramirez's vicious hold on her very soul?

❈❧☙❈

Temptation in Time by Alexa Aames

Ariana escaped the Middle Ages after stealing a kiss of magic from the dark and sexy sorcerer, Marcus de Grey. When Marcus kidnaps and returns her to the 14th century, they begin a battle of wills and a sexual odyssey that could spell disaster for them both.

❈❧☙❈

Ailis and the Beast by Jennifer Barlowe

When Ailis agreed to be her village's sacrifice to the mysterious Beast she was prepared to sacrifice her virtue, and possibly her life. But some things aren't what they seem. In a time of ritual and mystery, Ailis and the Beast are about to discover that animal passions are just the beginning, and the greatest sacrifice may be the human heart.

❈❧☙❈

Night Heat by Leigh Wynfield

When Rip Bowhite leads a revolt on the prison planet called the Velopit, he never anticipates that the Inter-world Council would abandon the planet, leaving prisoners, guards, and even the administrative personnel struggling to survive against the monsters that rule the night. With their lives at stake, Jemma, the prison's Healer, won't allow herself to be distracted by the instant and overpowering attraction she feels for Rip, until that passion flares to dizzying heights. As the stakes are raised and death draws near, love seems doomed in the heat of the night.

Reviews from Secrets Volume 1

"Four very romantic, very sexy novellas in very different styles and settings. ... The settings are quite diverse taking the reader from Regency England to a remote and mysterious fantasy land, to an Arabian nights type setting, and finally to a contemporary urban setting. All stories are explicit, and Hamre and Landon stories sizzle. ... If you like erotic romance you will love *Secrets*."

— *Romantic Readers* review

"Overall, for a fan of erotica, these are unlike anything you've encountered before. For those romance fans who turn down the pages of the "good parts" for later repeat consumption (and you know who you are) these books are a wonderful way to explore the better side of the erotica market. ... *Secrets* is a worthy exploration for the adventurous reader with the promise for better things yet to come."

— Liz Montgomery

Reviews from Secrets Volume 2
Winner of the Fallot Literary Award for Fiction

"*Secrets, Volume 2*, a new anthology published by Red Sage Publishing, is hot! I mean *red hot!* ... The sensuality in each story will make you blush—from head to toe and everywhere else in-between. ... The true success behind *Secrets, Volume 2* is the combination of different tastes—both in subgenres of romance and levels of sensuality. *I highly recommend this book*."

— Dawn A. Long, *America Online* review

"I think it is a fine anthology and Red Sage should be applauded for providing an outlet for women who want to write sensual romance."

— Adrienne Benedicks,
Erotic Readers Association review

Reviews from Secrets Volume 3
Winner of the 1997 Under the Cover Readers Favorite Award

"An unabashed celebration of sex. Highly arousing! Highly recommended!"

— Virginia Henley, *New York Times* Best Selling Author

"*Secrets, Volume 3* leaves the reader breathless. Each of these tributes to exotic and erotic fiction offers a world of sensual pleasure and moral rewards. A delicious confection of sensuous treats awaits the reader on each turn of the page. Sexy, funny, thrilling, and luscious, Secrets entertains, enlightens, and fuels the fires of fantasy."

— Kathee Card, *Romancing the Web*

Reviews from Secrets Volume 4

"*Secrets, Volume 4*, has something to satisfy every erotic fantasy... simply sexsational!"

— Virginia Henley, *New York Times* Best Selling Author

"Provocative...seductive...a must read!" **4 Stars**

— *Romantic Times*

"These are the kind of stories that romance readers that 'want a little more' have been looking for all their lives without crossing over into the adult genre. Keep these stories coming, Red Sage, the world needs them!"

— Lani Roberts, *Affaire de Coeur*

"If you're interested in exploring erotica, or reading farther than the sexual passages of your favorite steamy reads, the *Secret* series is well worth checking out."

— *Writers Club Romance Group* on AOL

Reviews from Secrets Volume 5

"*Secrets, Volume 5*, is a collage of lucious sensuality. Any woman who reads *Secrets* is in for an awakening!"

— **Virginia Henley,** *New York Times* Best Selling Author

"Hot, hot, hot! Not for the faint-hearted!"

— *Romantic Times*

"As you make your way through the stories, you will find yourself becoming hotter and hotter. *Secrets* just keeps getting better and better."

— *Affaire de Coeur*

Reviews from Secrets Volume 6

"*Secrets, Volume 6* satisfies every female fantasy: the Bodyguard, the Tutor, the Werewolf, and the Vampire. I give it Six Stars!"

— Virginia Henley, *New York Times* Best Selling Author

"*Secrets, Volume 6* is the best of *Secrets* yet. …four of the most erotic stories in one volume than this reader has yet to see anywhere else. … These stories are full of erotica at its best and you'll definitely want to keep it handy for lots of re-reading!"

— *Affaire de Coeur*

Reviews from Secrets Volume 7

Winner of the Venus Book Club Best Book of the Year

"…sensual, sexy, steamy fun. A perfect read!"

— Virginia Henley, *New York Times* Best Selling Author

"Intensely provocative and disarmingly romantic, Secrets Volume 7 is a romance reader's paradise that will take you beyond your wildest dreams!"

— *Ballston Book House* Review

"Erotic romance is at the sensual core of Red Sage's latest collection of short, red hot novels, *Secrets, Volume 7.*"

— *Writers Club Romance Group* on AOL

Reviews from Secrets Volume 8

Winner of the Venus Book Club Best Book of the Year

"*Secrets Volume 8* is simply sensational!"

— Virginia Henley, *New York Times* Best Selling Author

"*Secrets Volume 8* is an amazing compilation of sexy stories discovering a wide range of subjects, all designed to titillate the senses."

— Lani Roberts, *Affaire de Coeur*

"All four tales are well written and fun to read because even the sexiest scenes are not written for shock value, but interwoven smoothly and realistically into the plots. This quartet contains strong storylines and solid lead characters, but then again what else would one expect from the no longer *Secrets* anthologies."

— Harriet Klausner

"Once again, Red Sage Publishing takes you on a journey of sexual delight, teasing and pleasing the reader with a bit of something to appeal to everyone."

— Michelle Houston, *Courtesy Sensual Romance*

"In this sizzling volume, four authors offer short stories in four different sub-genres: contemporary, paranormal, historical, and futuristic. These ladies' assignments are to dazzle, tantalize, amaze, and entice. Your assignment, as the reader, is to sit back and enjoy. Just have a fan and some ice water at your side."

— Amy Cunningham

Reviews from Secrets Volume 9

"Everyone should expect only the most erotic stories in a *Secrets* book. ...if you like your stories full of hot sexual scenes, then this is for you!"

— Donna Doyle, *Romance Reviews*

"*Secrets 9*...is sinfully delicious, highly arousing, and hotter than hot as the pages practically burn up as you turn them."

— Suzanne Coleburn, *Reader To Reader Reviews/ Belles & Beaux of Romance*

"Treat yourself to well-written fictionthat's hot, hotter, and hottest!"

— Virginia Henley, *New York Times* Best Selling Author

Reviews from Secrets Volume 10

"*Secrets Volume 10*, an erotic dance through medieval castles, sultan's palaces, the English countryside and expensive hotel suites, explodes with passion-filled pages."

— *Romantic Times BOOKclub*

"Having read the previous nine volumes, this one fulfills the expectations of what is expected in a *Secrets* book: romance and eroticism at its best!!"
— *Fallen Angel Reviews*

"All are hot steamy romances so if you enjoy erotica romance, you are sure to enjoy *Secrets, Volume 10*. All this reviewer can say is WOW!!"
— *The Best Reviews*

Reviews from Secrets Volume 11

"*Secrets Volume 11* delivers once again with storylines that include erotic masquerades, ancient curses, modern-day betrayal and a prince charming looking for a kiss. Scorching tales filled with humor, passion and love." **4 Stars**
— *Romantic Times BOOKclub*

"The *Secrets* books published by Red Sage Publishing are well known for their excellent writing and highly erotic stories and *Secrets, Volume 11* will not disappoint. "
— *The Road to Romance*

"*Secrets 11* quite honestly is my favorite anthology from Red Sage so far. All four novellas had me glued to their stories until the very end. I was just disappointed that these talented ladies novellas weren't longer."
— *The Best Reviews*

"Indulge yourself with this erotic treat and join the thousands of readers who just can't get enough. Be forewarned that *Secrets 11* will whet your appetite for more, but will offer you the ultimate in pleasurable erotic literature."
— *Ballston Book House Review*

Reviews from Secrets Volume 12

"*Secrets Volume 12*, turns on the heat with a seductive encounter inside a bookstore, a temple of naughty and sensual delight, a galactic inferno that thaws ice, and a lightening storm that lights up the English shoreline. Tales of looking for love in all the right places with a heat rating out the charts." **4½ Stars**
— *Romantic Times BOOKclub*

"I really liked these stories.You want great escapism? Read *Secrets, Volume 12*."

— *Romance Reviews*

Reviews from Secrets Volume 13

"In *Secrets Volume 13*, the temperature gets turned up a few notches with a mistaken personal ad, shape-shifters destined to love, a hot Regency lord and his lady, as well as a bodyguard protecting his woman. Emotions and flames blaze high in Red Sage's latest foray into the sensual and delightful art of love." **4½ Stars**

— *Romantic Times BOOKclub*

"The sex is still so hot the pages nearly ignite! Read *Secrets, Volume 13*!

— *Romance Reviews*

Reviews from Secrets Volume 15

"*Secrets Volume 15* blends humor, tension and steamy romance in its newest collection that sizzles with passion between unlikely pairs—a male chauvinist columnist and a librarian turned erotica author; a handsome werewolf and his resisting mate; an unfulfilled woman and a sexy police officer and a Victorian wife who learns discipline can be fun. Readers will revel in this delicious assortment of thrilling tales." **4 Stars**

— *Romantic Times BOOKclub*

"This book contains four tales by some of today's hottest authors that will tease your senses and intrigue your mind."

— *Romance Junkies*

Satisfy Your Desire for More... with Secrets!

Did you miss any of the other volumes of the sexy **Secrets** *series? At the back of this book is an order form for all the available volumes. Order your* **Secrets** *today! See our order form at the back of this book or visit Waldenbooks or Borders.*

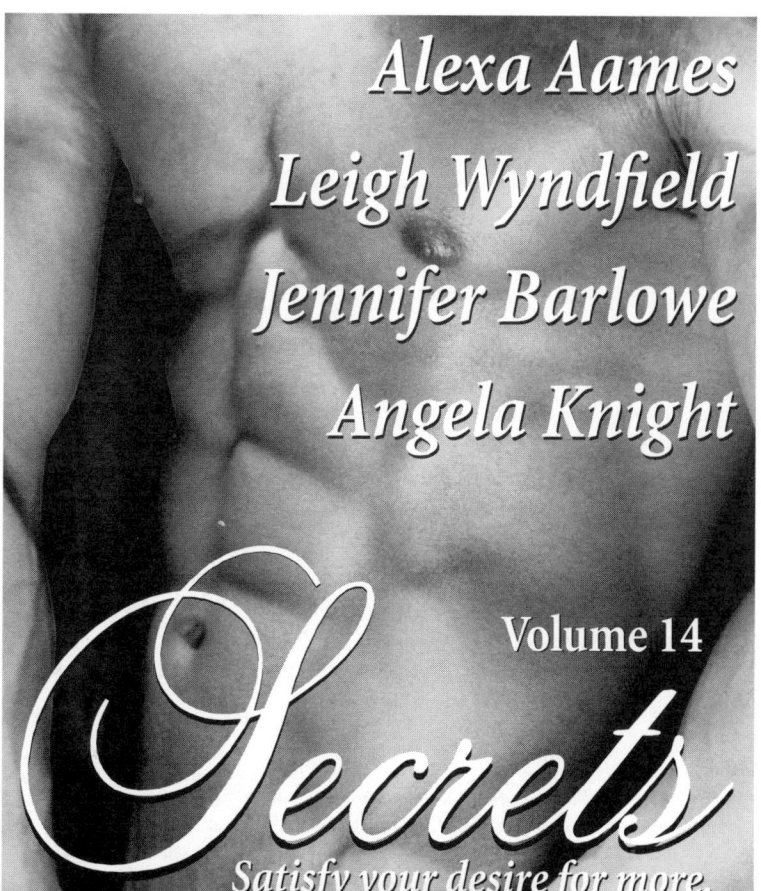

Alexa Aames

Leigh Wyndfield

Jennifer Barlowe

Angela Knight

Volume 14

Secrets

Satisfy your desire for more.

SECRETS Volume 14
This is an original publication of Red Sage Publishing and each individual story
herein has never before appeared in print. These stories are a collection of fiction
and any similarity to actual persons or events is purely coincidental.

Red Sage Publishing, Inc.
P.O. Box 4844
Seminole, FL 33775
727-391-3847
www.redsagepub.com

Published by arrangement with the authors and copyright holders of the individual works as follows:

TEMPTATION IN TIME
Copyright © 2005 by Alexa Aames

NIGHT HEAT
Copyright © 2005 by Leigh Wyndfield

AILIS AND THE BEAST
Copyright © 2005 by Jennifer Barlowe

SOUL KISSES
Copyright © 2005 by Angela Knight

Photographs:
Cover © 2005 by Tara Kearney; www.tarakearney.com
Cover Models: Diana Peterfreund and Will Scheid
Setback cover © 2000 by Greg P. Willis; email: GgnYbr@aol.com

Printed in the U.S.A.

Book typesetting by:

Quill & Mouse Studios, Inc.
www.quillandmouse.com

Contents

Temptation in Time

by Alexa Aames

To My Reader:

As a great fan of magic, history, and sensual romance, I loved writing this story, and I hope you'll enjoy reading it.

Ariana purred softly. She was being stroked just where she needed it most. She stretched, spreading her legs.

She wanted his mouth. He had such delicious, sensual lips.

He smiled, and his eyes, black as kohl, glinted with passion. "Ariana."

She woke with a start and sat up. Fear stabbed her heart. She was alone in her bed, but his touch had felt so real. She shivered. Was he getting closer? She pushed aside her panic, and, for a moment, the memory of his fingers caressing her sex, thrusting inside her came back. Her belly contracted with a throb of lust. She drew in a frustrated breath and exhaled audibly.

She climbed from the bed, marched over to the walnut dresser, and pulled out a pair of sweats. She yanked them on over her damp panties, thinking about the owner of the dark eyes and sensual lips... Marcus. They'd only met once, but he'd made an indelible impression on her. Sorcerers didn't come any sexier—or more infamous—than Marcus; he would be difficult for anyone to forget. She, on the other hand, probably wouldn't have made much of an impression on him if she hadn't vanished after stealing a kiss and, with it, some of his magical power.

It was hard to hide from him now. Even as far as she'd traveled, he could reach the landscape of her dreams. The slightest sexual arousal seemed to draw him to her subconscious like moth to flame, which was why she avoided the intimacy she craved, tried to suppress the passion he stirred. Even now, when the dream had faded, his molten power pulsed through her, linking them, his invisible presence still nearly palpable.

It had been eight years since she'd stolen that kiss. He'd already been dangerous. Just how powerful was he now? She shuddered to imagine.

Celibacy was the only way to stay concealed. Unfortunately, celibacy left a lot to be desired.

Ariana swayed her hips to the reggae beat that thrummed through her coffee shop as she stirred a couple of drops of coconut extract into the oversized black cup. "The Witch's Brew" was printed on the mug in pearly white letters.

"Here you go," Ariana said, smiling at the customer.

The customer winked at her and dropped a dollar into the tip jar without missing a beat in the conversation he was having on his cell phone.

Simon, owner of the reggae music and the longest, neatest dread locks in Ohio, danced out into the middle of the floor. He sashayed behind the counter, twirling her around. She laughed as the customers hooted with approval at the sight of her dancing with the Jamaican.

"Good news, boss lady," Simon said, after spinning her in another twirl.

"What's that?"

"Dr. Bob called from St. Luke's Hospital. He said to tell ya, leetle Angela is in remission."

"That's wonderful." Ariana said, beaming. Modern medicine was truly a marvel. Of course, a healing kiss never hurt either. As she danced, she glanced over at the calendar. She'd wait at least three weeks before she visited St. Luke's pediatric oncology ward again. This week, she'd volunteer at the Columbia burn unit. She'd heard on the news about a firefighter who'd been badly burned. The report had said he wasn't doing well, but she knew he still had a chance to recover. She would see to that. She puckered her lips and kissed the air. Life could be wonderful.

Ariana awoke twisted in her sheets and gasping for breath. She was wearing gray terrycloth short-shorts into which her fingers had apparently found their way. Damned erotic dreams. What was she supposed to do about them? Tie up her hands before she went to bed?

"Ariana."

Her breath caught in her throat. The whisper in her head had sounded far too real. She sat up, shaking off her unease. She would make herself a cup of chamomile tea and think about what to do. Maybe she could wear mittens to sleep.

She turned on the light and climbed from bed. Sighing slightly in annoyance, she pulled down the ribbed tank top that had ridden up during her nighttime exploits. She padded across the beige carpet, watching her feet as she made her way to the kitchen.

Then she saw them and froze. Black boots. Men's boots encasing a man's calves. Her heart began to hammer a protest in her chest.

Her gaze rolled up his body, muscular thighs in black tights gave way to a hard naked torso where two scars slashed their way up from his navel to his left nipple. A cloak the color of midnight hung from his broad shoulders and met with black wavy hair.

She knew whose face it would be, but she hesitated for a moment before looking. Dread and dizziness surrounded her. *Let it be a dream. Nay, a nightmare.*

His mouth was curved into a slight sneer. "Hello, little thief. It has been a very long time."

She reeled backward, turning from him. There was nowhere really to run to, but her body sprang toward even a momentary escape. He caught her shoulders, and she fell back against him. The shock of being pressed against his hard, hot body was compounded when he slid an arm around her torso and his hand cupped her breast. She gasped a protest, but he ignored it. He squeezed firmly and ran his thumb over her nipple, which pebbled into a firm bead at the erotic command of his touch. Her body suddenly felt heavy with need.

"Wait," she said breathlessly.

"Longer than I have already waited? I think not." His free arm coiled around her body like a snake.

"What do you intend to do?" she asked, swallowing hard.

"I intend to exact payment, my lady."

She opened her mouth to speak again, but fell silent at the sound of his deep rumbling voice speaking an ancient language. She didn't even have time to decipher the words before she felt the air rustle.

The breath was sucked from her lungs as a maelstrom claimed them. She felt her body twisted and pummeled by invisible forces, and her eyes could see nothing but blackness. *I'm dying. Please! Help me.*

A moment later, there was silence. She drew in her breath in hungry gasps and felt something hard and cold beneath her palms and knees.

"I'm blind," she said in a hoarse voice.

"It will pass."

"What have you done to me?"

He didn't answer.

She had a very bad feeling. The damp, chill air. The frigid stone. But no, going forward had been peaceful and smooth. Why should coming back have been so rough?

A blurred shadow of light began to form. She blinked several times. Then the room began to come into view. There was no mistaking it. He had dragged her through time. She shivered and then felt his magic swirl around her, warming her shoulders and arms. Physically, she felt more comfortable, but emotionally she wasn't reassured.

She sat back, buttocks resting on the bare soles of her feet. Her eyes darted around the huge bedchamber. The furniture was crude, made from sturdy chunks of wood that were fashioned into bed frame, table, chairs, and bench. "What year is it?" she asked, still clinging to a last bit of hope. Perhaps they were in a castle made to look like the days of old.

"1349."

"No," she whispered, putting her face in her hands.

"Aye."

She had never expected to see this time again. She had been beckoned to the future by a sweet witch, Lucy, who had determined that Ariana was the key to saving her daughter's life. Lucy had offered to send her back after the healing, but Ariana had been enthralled by the future and had chosen instead to live with Lucy and her family until she'd learned to manage on her own in the new time. In truth, she had always felt restless in the fourteenth century. It had been a relief to escape the weak role to which women were confined.

Ariana heard a door swing open behind her and looked up. An old woman shuffled in, eyes flicking over her.

"But who is this, my lord?" the servant asked. "And how did she come to be here?"

"Her name is Ariana, Joan. She's our guest."

"What strange garments are those that she wears?" the woman asked, crossing herself. She hurried over to the bed and pulled the fur coverlet loose.

A moment later it was draped around Ariana who smiled gratefully at the woman.

"My lord, whoever she be, she'll catch her death in this chamber. It is ice itself in here. I will fetch Morgan to light the hearth."

"Nay. I will build the fire. Just tell the cook I will want venison stew in a few hours."

"Aye, my lord. But I forgot meself for a moment. I will have Morgan build a fire in the lady's chamber. We will put her in one that overlooks the garden—"

"Nay."

"The water then—"

"For as long as she is here, the lady will stay in this bedchamber... with me."

Joan pursed disapproving lips and looked over at Ariana for some reaction. Ariana huddled in the soft fur. She agreed with Joan. Marcus proposed a scandal by insisting they share a room, but who was there to object? Her family certainly must think her dead after an eight-year disappearance. She and Joan could object, but anyone who could cross time of his own power would not let the protests of a couple of women stop him from doing exactly as he pleased. Ariana was well and truly trapped... until she could think of a way to escape.

"A trunk then. Leastways so the lady has some proper clothes."

"Joan," Marcus growled.

"A trunk, at least," Joan said firmly, pounding her gnarled fist into her small palm. "You can change me to a toad if you will with that cursed magic of yours, but better that than being damned to hell for leaving a girl without clothes. Morgan will fetch a trunk." Joan turned and started toward the door.

"I would not bother to change you into a toad, Joan, for I fear the difference would be too little," he teased.

"Black devil," she grumbled, shuffling out.

Marcus tossed his head back and laughed. It was like warm rich cream spilling over her skin. She couldn't help but smile a little herself at the exchange. Despite the insults, there had been real warmth between the lord and his servant.

"And what do you have to smile over?" he mocked, leveling a black gaze on Ariana.

Defiantly, she tipped her chin up and ignored the question. She was afraid of him, but she wasn't going to let it show. She thought for a moment about his reputation. When most lords simply hired knights to fight for them, Marcus de Grey rode into battle himself, leading the attacks. He'd killed many men in hand-to-hand combat and was considered lethal and skilled with a sword. He'd also won a critical battle once when a terrible thunderstorm drove both armies from the battlefield long enough to allow for the timely arrival of reinforcements. There had been a lot of whispers that Marcus, whose own forces were outnumbered tenfold, had conjured the driving rain.

Ariana's father and his friends had certainly been bitter over the amount of land Marcus, despite his relative youth at the time, had been able to accumulate. His holdings were large indeed. Most men, it seemed to her, envied Marcus' wealth, feared his sword, and dreaded his magic, though they only half believed in the latter.

Marcus cleared his throat and drew her attention back to the present.

"You stole a kiss from me, my lady. I would have it back...with interest."

Her body tingled. She knew he wasn't simply expecting a few kisses. He stretched out his hand and a fire roared to life in the hearth. *Show off,* she thought in annoyance, but was amazed at his power in spite of herself.

He walked over to a small wood table and poured some wine from a pitcher into a cup and drank. She realized she was thirsty too.

"I'd like some of that," she said, standing up.

"Come," he said with a beckoning wave of his hand.

She walked over, watching him warily. She tried not to be rattled by the full effect of his height. He loomed over her, dark and sinister. She held her hands out for the cup, but he ignored them. He put the rim to her mouth, a symbolic gesture, no doubt, to serve as a reminder that she was under his power now, and had no control beyond what he gave her. She fought not to roll her eyes in defiance of the power play. He tipped the cup and she drank, feeling oddly self-conscious under his gaze. The red wine was rich and sweet. She took a few swallows and wondered if she was going to feel less thirsty or more when she was done.

"Good," she said, trying to sound cheerful. She took a couple of steps back from him, despite the fact that she was starting to feel more at ease around him. "So I suppose you've been wondering why I stole that kiss and some of your magic." *A direct approach,* she thought, *will be best.*

He arched an eyebrow.

"Well, there was a very good reason, actually. A witch summoned me to the future. Her child was dying. It was a call into my dreams that I couldn't refuse, but my healing powers wouldn't have been enough. I needed stronger magic than my own."

"So you stole mine," he said wryly. He unhooked the emerald and onyx encrusted brooch at his throat and let the cloak slide off his shoulders.

Firelight flickered over his huge muscles. She tried to remember how men in 1349 built such bodies. It wasn't as if there were Gold's

Gyms on every estate.

"I suppose you may be wondering," he said, mimicking her, "why I would continue to pursue you after such a long time."

"Well, yes. I do wonder about that."

"It is because I grew tired of the constant injury you do me when you wield my magic."

"Injury?" she echoed.

"Aye." He traced a line down one of the scars from his nipple to the place where it disappeared under the black fabric of the tights.

"Those? They're not from me. I couldn't have done that."

"A finger's span at a time. You did not stop your mission of healing at one child, did you? You drew on my power many, many times. The proof of it is carved quite deeply into my flesh."

Oh, no. "I never meant to do that. Honestly, I had no idea," she said, crestfallen. She suddenly wished desperately that he'd found her sooner. The idea that she'd been the cause of that sinister pair of scars on his otherwise perfect body left her bereft of the joy she'd had from her healing.

He studied her expression. "Aye. Even magic in the name of good has a price."

"But—"

"I did, however, learn a great many things over the years. I learned that when I imagined your pretty face and the things I would one day do to your beautiful body…the pain was less troublesome." He hooked his fingers into the fur and unwound it from her.

Her body shivered at the cool air and the words that lingered on the air. *The things I would one day do to your beautiful body.* She wondered how fear and arousal could coexist within her so neatly.

Again, she felt his power sliding over her skin, warm, sensuous and dangerous. He walked over and flung the fur back down on the bed and then sat on the edge of it. He looked her over. She was quite aware of the fact that she was very nearly naked.

"Come here." It was a command, not a request.

She glanced around. She was in the middle of a powerful sorcerer's castle in the year 1349. Defiance wasn't really much of an option. There was no 9-1-1 service. Hell, there weren't even any telephones. There was just him and her and a few servants who were probably too terrified to defy him.

"Making me wait shows poor judgment, Ariana."

She took a deep breath and let it out slowly, trying to compose herself. "I'm nervous. That's why I hesitate."

He waved a hand toward himself. "Come. I will not hurt you."

"Look, there's something you should know," she said, walking reluctantly toward him.

"Aye?"

"I've never been married." Saying she'd never been married would imply that she was still a virgin. Maybe he would be more careful if he believed that. Of course, she almost was still a virgin in the classic sense. She'd had one encounter where she'd "gone all the way" with a boyfriend. During the act, Marcus' power had roared over her and she'd actually seen his face in place of her boyfriend's. She'd gasped Marcus' name and had really felt as though he were about to materialize in the room. Her boyfriend of the moment had barely finished what he was doing before he'd had a jealous tantrum. Looking back she couldn't blame him, but at the time, she'd been so shaken that she hadn't even been able to reassure him that she didn't prefer the phantom Marcus to him. That relationship had ended quickly, but it had taught her an important lesson. Marcus' energy was fixated on her sexual arousal.

From then on, she'd used her mouth on various boyfriends, who'd assured her she was quite adept at performing oral sex, but she didn't allow them to reciprocate or to sexually arouse her. At first many of them had liked the arrangement, but over time, they came to realize that she was holding a part of herself back. Now, the cause of many of her failed relationships was standing across from her, his face completely unreadable.

She took a deep breath. "I know by the standards of the day I'm rather old to still be a maid, being twenty-four years old, but the future is different."

When she was within his reach, he pulled her forward so that she was standing in front of him. His knees flanked her. His powerful chest filled her vision and his nipples were dark brown and delicious-looking. The two scars did nothing to detract from how gorgeous he was. In some ways, the contrast of perfection and imperfection made each more pronounced.

"This garment is unnecessary," he said and smoothly pulled the tank top up and over her head. She blushed in shock and tried to step back, but he gripped her with his thighs, trapping her. He dropped the shirt on the floor and his eyes locked on hers. Desire tightened in the pit of her belly when his hands cupped her breasts. He glanced at her chest as he fondled her. "I suppose you have heard far too many times that these are perfect. It bears repeating unless your vanity will make me regret it." He looked back at her eyes.

"What?" she mumbled, feeling flushed and dazed, feeling like prey.

He brushed his thumbs over her nipples and sensations rippled through her. She arched her back slightly, jutting her chest forward.

"You are a brazen little thing," he said with a smirk.

She wanted to throttle him for smirking. His grip on her with his thighs had loosened, and she took a step backward. "Well, if you don't want me."

He laughed and pulled her back to him with an iron grip. "You need have no fear on that account." There was a feral light in his dark eyes as he studied her. "I think I like that you are bold. Offer me a kiss like the one you offered eight years ago."

"Aren't you worried that I'll steal more of your power?" she challenged, hoping she sounded confident and perhaps even a little dangerous in her own right. He would have no idea that her power was still as slight as it had ever been.

"Nay, I am not worried. At present, altogether different emotions have my attention." He bent his head and plucked at her nipple with his teeth.

"Oh," she said weakly. She should have been protesting loudly, but the moment was surreal and delicious, and it tampered with her good sense. He'd been a spirit, a presence, pursuing her through erotic moments for years. It seemed somehow right that she should finally be facing him, and that the lust that was always swirling should finally take form.

He sucked her entire areola into his mouth. It felt *very* good.

"Oh, my." She shifted her weight, rubbing her thighs together trying to create some friction. She could feel a throbbing pulse deep between her legs. She squirmed uncomfortably. She wanted him. "Marcus," she rasped.

"Aye, vixen," he whispered in a throaty rasp all his own. He moved her, slipping a knee between her thighs. He raised his leg so that she was straddling it. Solid pressure collided with her swollen sex.

She groaned softly. He'd taken her other nipple in his mouth and was suckling her. Then he started to bounce her on his thigh.

"Oh, God," she whispered, grabbing his shoulders.

He held her hips, controlling the movements of both her body and his. She rode his leg, leaning her pelvis forward so that every time she bounced back down, her troubled clit banged against his solid thigh. She came hard, gasping his name and collapsing against him. He bit her nipple a little too sharply, making her cry out and pull back. "Easy. Those are only on loan to you. I need them back," she said, panting.

Dark desire was blazing in his eyes as he looked over her face. "So little vixen, you recover from pleasure so quickly that you can tease again already? I believe that I am glad of that," he said, catching the flesh of her mons in his hand and squeezing a little roughly.

She gasped and backed off his thigh and away from his hand. "Be nice," she chided and retreated on wobbly legs.

"Was I not nice to you?" he mocked and caught her arm, stopping her from escaping his reach. There was danger rolling off him now in waves.

She felt the need to placate him and quickly. "Look, I know you didn't get your cookies, but just give me a minute to catch my breath, and I'll take care of you."

"My cookies?" he echoed quizzically.

She chuckled. "Just an expression." She would beat him at his own game. He lusted after her. She lusted after him. They would simply get it out of their system and then he would get bored and send her back home. He'd be happy to be rid of her when he saw how ill suited she was to his time. She'd show him she was too bold now for the 1300s. *Show him bold*, she thought. "Take off the rest of your clothes and I'll blow your mind... and the rest of you."

"What?"

"I'll suck you." She would never normally have allowed herself to make such an offer to a stranger, no matter how attractive he was, but doing so gave her a heady kind of feeling, as though she were powerfully uninhibited.

She stole a glance at Marcus. If he was amazed by the brazen statement, he didn't show it. He stood and, without hesitation, stripped.

She stared at him. "Of course," she muttered derisively. His cock was monstrous.

"Does something trouble you?" he asked without guile.

He was thick and ten or eleven inches long, and his balls hung heavy and full below his majestic cock. Her jaw was going to get quite the workout. Too bad it was 1349; he could have been the envy of any male locker room. "Your body is amazing," she murmured absently.

"I am so glad you approve. I conjured it especially for you," he said dryly.

She laughed softly and wondered for a moment if he really had magically enhanced himself. Was that possible? She glanced over the rest of him. He was probably six-five and covered in thick muscles that looked like he could take down an ox. No, probably no enhancement, she decided. His genitals were the same scale as the rest of him. She took a deep breath. "Okay. Lie on the bed, and we'll see what happens."

He didn't move. "You seem to doubt your skill suddenly," he said, seeming hesitant.

"No, no, I'm very good at this, but you're sort of super-sized." *I can't exactly whip out my tonsils and set them aside to make more room.*

"What?"

"Never mind, medieval man, just lay back."

"What did you call me?"

"You realize," she said, looking him up and down slowly, "if I weren't so sure that it would be silly, I'd say you were stalling. Don't tell me the big bad sorcerer is afraid of a girl half his size."

He chuckled at that. "Let us say that, to my mind, you are known as someone who takes more than is offered. Perhaps having your teeth around something that I value does not put me at ease."

"Well, if I got carried away, you could just magically reattach it, right?"

His face fell.

She roared with laughter. "I'm kidding. Joking. Really."

He grabbed her arms and flung her gently onto the bed. "It turns out that I am not interested in your mouth anymore."

"Wait," she yelled, wrestling with his strong hands as they slid her shorts off. Jesus, he was strong. She lost the battle and was nude. "Wait, Marcus, please," she begged.

He had pried her legs open, but he paused there. "What am I waiting for, vixen?"

"I'm not ready. If you do it like this, you'll hurt me."

"No more than you deserve," he grumbled, but his index fingertip slid over her cleft carefully. He held up the finger and rubbed it against his thumb, demonstrating the glistening moisture on it. "You seem ready to me."

She *was* wet, dammit, but she wasn't mentally ready for a full assault by the battering ram between his legs. She bucked away from his hand and scampered toward the far bedpost.

The lust blazing in his eyes said he wouldn't let her escape very far. She needed to maintain some control over the situation to keep him from unleashing his inner predator, which seemed to be lurking just below the surface. Given their relative sizes, should he decide he'd waited long enough, no amount of resistance on her part would slow things down.

He held out his hand to her, like a cat stretching a paw slowly toward a mouse. She realized she'd been holding her breath and exhaled shakily.

"I just need a few minutes to warm up," she said quickly. "I promise not to bite you... at all. Just lie back."

He narrowed his eyes, but then sighed heavily and let his hand fall to the bed. "The slightest nick, I warn you, and I will not show an ounce of mercy."

"Trust me."

He frowned, but lay back.

Thank God, she thought.

Marcus settled back onto fur and studied Ariana through partially lowered lids. This game of hers where she used her mouth would never work, but he wouldn't bother to tell her that. Since he'd been a teenager, women had, on occasion, tried to pleasure him thus. Whenever he became excited, he thrust too hard and gagged them. At which point, he would have to pull out, raise them up and bury himself in their tight channels.

He looked down the line of Ariana's body. She had a very pretty mound. Light brown curls that matched her long hair. The skin of her long legs was the color of sand and so supple. His phallus throbbed. He had wanted her forever. Having her in the flesh was almost too intense.

She had moved to her hands and knees. He groaned at the picture that made. Her breasts so ripe and full dangled tantalizingly from her chest. With one hand she nudged his legs further apart making more room for her to settle between them.

He cooperated without comment, preferring to concentrate on memorizing the lines of her body. For years, he'd had only glimpses of her in his mind. How many times had he felt that searing pain as she drew power from him, only to have it followed by an aching erection as he felt her phantom lips on his mouth or his cheek? Those lips, soft as rose petals. Sweet as apples. How many times had he soiled the sheets spending his erections into them while imagining her naked body? But there was no longer any need to imagine. She was in his grasp. His will was that she would never escape it again.

The rose petal lips were close to him now. A bead of moisture had formed on the head of his phallus, and she was licking it clean with soft strokes from her velvety tongue. The perfect globes of her bottom had risen above the rest of her body as she bent over him. His mouth was hungry for that bottom and for what lay beneath it. She could play her little game of licking him and then he would devour her. By morning, she would belong to him in ways she could never refute.

She moved her mouth lower. Feather strokes of her tongue over his sac made his muscles twitch. He was intensely aroused and grew restless in his desire to be satisfied. Just as he was ready to growl for her to get on with things, she took half the sac into her mouth and sucked on it. She squeezed the other half between her left hand's fingertips. Her right hand came up to grip his erection firmly at the base. She stroked up and down.

The combination of sensations was maddening. He groaned deeply. More cream was leaking from him. It dripped down and ran over her delicate hand. She rubbed the moisture back along the length of him.

Every muscle in his body seemed to be tensing at her command. His hips even thrust up a fraction as she teased him. He tried to stay calm and in control. He wanted to savor this. Trying to distract himself, he studied her back and bottom, but that only made the flames inside him lick higher.

"Mmm," she purred. The sound she made in her throat as she licked the fluid from him made him want to roar. She was kneading his sac with both hands now and sucking on the head of him, pressing the tip of her tongue into his slit and soaking up the juice as it leaked. She sucked, making noises as though he were some delicacy that she was enjoying.

He moaned loudly, clutching the fur in his fists.

She released him for a moment, dropping a few sucking kisses along the sides of his member. When her mouth was positioned over him again, she licked once and murmured almost absently, "Beautiful."

Death. She thinks to tease me 'til I be dead. What other reason could there be for the way she approached his member? Women, he suspected, never enjoyed fornication in the same way men did, and certainly not while using their mouths on a man's phallus, but she seemed to relish it. It excited him to near exploding.

She took him deep into her mouth and created a sensation like none he'd ever felt. He groaned uncontrollably. She slid up and down, caressing him with her lips and tongue as her head moved.

He could not stand another moment. He began thrusting wildly. It was exquisite. Wet, hot, and tight. He roared and suddenly his seed gushed forth. She never released him. She kept sucking and swallowing and milking him until he was completely spent.

'Tis certain. She means to kill me. Oh, happy death.

Ariana was pleased with herself. She had slain the monster and its owner in one. Marcus lay sprawled on his back, looking as beautiful as anyone she'd ever seen. She was tempted to drop a kiss on his gorgeous cheek, but she dared not touch him.

I dare not touch him? Careful, Ariana, you're starting to sound like you belong back in this century, and you don't. Let's not forget about cappuccinos, dark chocolate truffle balls, and hot and cold running water. For heaven's sake, Pride and Prejudice *hasn't even been written yet. You've got to get back to the 21st century.*

Ariana pulled on her tank and short-shorts and then one of Marcus' big shirts that hit her at the knees. Now what she needed was to find Marcus' books. Somewhere in the castle, he probably had a place where he wrote down notes and spells. And somewhere in those notes was information about how he'd zipped to the year 2005 to capture her.

She sighed at herself. She had talked extensively with the witch who'd brought her forth the first time, but she hadn't revealed the details of the spell once Ariana told her she wanted to stay in the future. Even if she did find the spell, she wasn't sure she could make it work. Her only true magical talent was healing. She had had only limited success with other spells she'd tried over the years. Of course, she had to try.

She walked softly to the door and opened it carefully, stealing a glance back at Marcus. He was safely unconscious. Something tender in her chest tugged at her. Since the kiss, he'd always been a part of her life, more vivid than any of her memories. And now that she had him in the flesh, she found that she was anxious to leave his time, but not so anxious to leave him. *Stop it. He's dangerous. And that was just sex. Nothing more.*

The entire hall was silent as a tomb. She moved as quietly as she could. Minutes passed as she peeked into various chambers, but none of them looked remotely like a library or a study.

"What are you looking for?" Marcus' deep voice demanded. She jumped and turned to find him directly behind her, still naked. How had he gotten so close without her hearing him? Magic? Just how powerful was he? Well, he'd come back and forth through time. That probably made him pretty powerful. *Damn.* "Nothing," she lied, widening her eyes to look as innocent as possible. "I was just exploring."

"Not much of an exploration if you keep to the corridor," he commented, catching her arm in his hand and turning her back toward his bedchamber.

"Um, listen, I'm kind of hungry. I know you're probably tired. If you just point me toward the kitchen, I'll find it."

He slid a hand over her stomach. "Hard to believe you could be hungry this soon with a belly full of me."

She blushed. Damn him for making her blush. She wasn't some little maiden. She was a modern woman. For 1349, she was supposed to be scandalous and unflappable.

Maybe he hadn't noticed her blush. She slid her eyes over to check him out in her peripheral vision. He was grinning. He'd seen. *I may have to hate him.*

They returned to his huge bedchamber again. She flopped down on the bench near the fireplace and folded her arms across her chest. She bolstered her resolve to be outrageous and then announced, "You know, semen is full of carbohydrates. That's why it doesn't keep one full for long. I would like something substantial to eat." Surely *that* would shock him.

He drew his brows together. "What?"

"I'm hungry."

He waved off her reply. "Food is coming. Before—what did you say?"

"Semen, your seed, it's full of carbohydrates."

"What is a carbo-hydrate?"

"They're, well…" She suddenly realized she didn't know exactly how to explain. Invisible components of food? Microbiology and a host of other scientific discoveries reeled through her mind. He was looking at her expectantly. *What am I? A biochemist?* she snapped silently in frustration. "Never mind," she said. "It doesn't matter."

He studied her.

"A lot of things have been learned. There's too much you don't know.

It would take too long to explain."

"I see."

She winced, realizing by his tone that she'd insulted him. She supposed that she *had* called him ignorant, but she'd been just as ignorant before she'd gone forward. "It's just that a lot of things have changed in the future."

"I am sure of it," he said and walked over. He pulled her to her feet and then yanked the long shirt that she was wearing up and over her head.

"Hey," she protested.

He hauled the tank off too, exposing her breasts.

"I *said* HEY!"

"Now is not a good time to shout at me, Ariana," he said casually.

She tilted her head quizzically. "I'll bite. Why not now?"

"You will definitely *not* bite," he said, walking her toward the bed.

"You know, I'm not really in the mood to have relations with you."

"I would not expect you to be," he said, casting a predatory sideways glance at her breasts, which were bouncing as she walked.

"But you're so virile, you're going to put me in the mood?" she asked as derisively as possible. Actually, just looking at him did put her in the mood, but she wasn't going to admit it.

"Nay," he said.

No? "Great, so you're going to rape me?" she snapped. *Fat chance with his yummy body.* Maybe she could act all weepy afterward to make him feel guilty. Treacherous to be sure, but it might give her leverage and get her back to the future. Could she be a cruel deceptive bitch to regain her life and her freedom? Unfortunately, something inside her said that no, she would have to find another way.

"Rape? Nay."

Well, that's a relief.

"I'm going to punish you."

She whipped her head to look at him. "What?" she stammered, immediately trying to apply her feet to the floor as brakes.

He simply lifted her off the ground and carried her the rest of the way.

"Wait a minute!" she yelled as he dropped her on the bed.

A moment later, she was struggling in earnest. It was entirely undignified. Yelling, kicking, rolling about. When he finally pinned her underneath him with his crushing strength, she realized that he'd been letting her fight, probably to wear herself out. Damn him.

"When I left, I was just looking for books! I wasn't going to set fire to anything or kill anyone. I was looking for a library," she said between gasps of breath. She hated the fearful pleading note in her voice.

"Calm yourself," he said soothingly.

Recovering, she narrowed her eyes. *Just catch your breath and reason with him,* she told herself.

He bent his head and kissed the bounding pulse in her neck. She could feel his rock-hard erection against her belly.

"You excite me so much, vixen, I worry for your safety," he whispered.

"I worry for it too," she grumbled.

He chuckled, licking over her pulse. Hot tendrils of lust curled inside her.

"Can you please not do that while we're trying to have a conversation?"

"Why not?"

She frowned, knowing that he was purposely toying with her. "Because I'm trying to concentrate and..." she trailed off as his teeth bit her skin gently. Flames licked up between her legs. "And you're not helping."

"When did I ever claim my intent was to help you?" he asked in a low teasing tone.

"Never," she agreed softly, twisting a hand free so that she could run her fingers through his hair. It was softer than it looked. "Such silky hair," she mumbled absently.

He moved down to suck on her breast. She sighed. It felt great when he did that.

Without warning, he rolled onto his back, panting, and stared up at the ceiling.

She looked him over. "Problem?" she asked.

"I have finally realized your true identity."

"Ah."

"Mistress of the devil."

She smiled. She rather liked being considered cool enough to be *that* wicked. "But I thought *you* were the devil," she teased.

"So did I," he said with a slightly bemused tone.

She giggled. "Don't worry. I won't turn my evil powers on you."

"Too late," he said, running a hand down one of his scars.

Her smile faded. "That was an accident. Really."

"I believe you."

"You do?" She liked the curve of his mouth, sensual yet strong.

"If I did not, you would already be dead."

She shivered. He really was as dangerous as everyone said. She couldn't let herself forget that, no matter how handsome he was. "You thought about killing me?"

"Nay. Sometimes during the pain I wished you dead, but I never thought about killing you. That is a different thing entirely."

"I'm sorry I hurt you," she said, trailing a finger over the scar. Why did she feel like tracing it with her tongue? Why did she feel like soothing away any hurt she may have caused him? "Very sorry, Marcus."

"Good." He moved so that he was sitting up and then gestured to his lap.

"What?" she asked, thinking his intentions could be a couple of different things. She was game for a lap dance. The alternative... no.

"Lie across my lap."

Dammit. "Why?"

"Because I have told you to do so."

Her heart was fluttering like a caged bird's wings. Why did he have to look so dangerous and gorgeous at the same time... and so damned resolute, like no matter how long it took, he was going to do exactly what he wanted to her.

"How about if I suck you instead?" she asked, crawling toward him with a seductive smile. No man could resist the magic of her mouth.

He caught her arms and slid her across his body too far to do what she had in mind. "Perhaps afterward," he said.

"Damn you!" she snapped. She tried to push herself up and couldn't. His hands held her in place. One hot palm on her back, one hot palm on her backside.

"It is the prerogative of lovers to spank their women when they have been wicked."

"That is not true!" she argued, pressing up onto her elbows. She had to arch her back just to get her shoulders off the bed. She turned her head to look at him, feeling ridiculously helpless.

His hand started to knead her buttocks intimately, which caused sharp pangs of lust in her lower body. "You look very beautiful with your face so flushed."

"Husbands and fathers and sometimes brothers have the right to beat their women. You are none of those things to me," she protested breathlessly.

His fingers delved down so that they were caressing her sex through the shorts. Hot juices started to pool.

"I am the lord of this castle. My word is law on this land. You stole from me. You injured me. If my justice is to simply warm your backside with my hand, you should be grateful."

Things were getting very foggy. Her mind wanted to argue. Her body wanted to submit to touching or spanking or whatever his hands had in mind.

"Marcus, please." She'd wanted to make one more attempt at reasoning with him, but her voice had sounded entirely too breathy. She couldn't even convince her own ears that she wanted to escape.

He slid the hand into her shorts and a finger stroked her wet cleft. Her labia twitched anxiously.

"Put your head down, Ariana." His voice was so smooth.

She let her shoulders fall back down, her forehead resting on her forearms. She felt him sliding the shorts off. The cool air teased her exposed backside. She wiggled nervously and heard a very low groan from above her. Good, let him be as excited as she was... then he would take her rather than spank her. She was hot and sticky, and suddenly she didn't want to wait any more.

She heard rather than felt the first slap. Two more fell before she could even react to the hot stinging pain. When she did try to push herself up, he simply put a hand between her shoulder blades and forced her back down.

She gasped a protest.

His voice was calm, not angry. "Every time you cause me to stop, I will begin again from one."

She garbled an angry response. And the sting came again. Damn him to hell for the devil he was! Smack. She struggled to be still. There was no one to rescue her from him. Smack. She didn't want him to start over hundreds of times from one. Smack. She was utterly helpless.

Warmth suffused through her buttocks and down between her thighs. With her face and breasts buried decadently into the fur, she started to sink into the rhythm. Her soft cries came from deeper in her body.

Then the cadence of the swats slowed. Her buttocks were scalding and she writhed against his lap. His erection was as hard as ever. The terrible thing was that even in her humiliation she didn't know what to feel. She was as aroused by it as she was furious. And all the tumultuous emotions were tangled up inside her.

Marcus's hand stopped and slid down so that he gently cupped her sex. Her whole body was shaking with fury and desire. "Easy, love," he said, rubbing a finger back and forth over her, sending shockwaves coursing into the swollen wet vortex of her sex.

She moaned between quiet sobs. Then he repositioned their bodies so that she was on her knees with her forehead on her arms and he was directly behind her.

He kissed her buttocks softly while fingering her damp curls. "Come now, do not cry, lest you make me think that I really hurt you."

Being spanked had hurt, but the pain was lost now in other sensations. His fingers agitated her clit until her hips began to jerk back and forth.

"Such sweet tender meat," he groaned, biting the swollen right cheek of her ass.

She cried out, moving forward. She was too sore for him to bite her there, even though it forced the sexual tension in her body somehow higher.

Then she felt him dip his head and nuzzle her sex. Inhaling her scent and licking and suckling her. She moaned from deep in her knotted belly. He licked back and forth between her legs, coming closer to her sex with each pass. *Oh God! It's too much. Please.* His tongue became increasingly demanding, delving into her. It was like being devoured alive.

She became frantic, pushing back against his mouth, pumping her hips. "Please, Marcus," she begged. "Please let me..."

He took a tender cheek in each hand and spread her open. She shuddered uncontrollably. His ravenous mouth plundered her until she was weeping at the exquisite torture of it.

Finally, he moved so that he was lying next to her, one arm under her body, one behind her back. Fingers from both hands pushed into her sex. She cried out, but then she started to move again almost instantly and with twice as much fury. She was driven by a lust the likes of which she'd never felt before. She shuddered at the penetration. His fingers were forcing her open. The moisture of her excitement seeped out as she ground her sex forward, the hard aching knot pressing against his palm. One of his wet fingers slid to her back hole, testing it. She was gasping so hard that she couldn't object, and somehow she didn't want to. Her body was his. He could do whatever he pleased. She would submit. His finger pushed into her bottom. Pleasure ripped through her.

Sensations exploded. She heard herself screaming, felt her hips bucking. And all the while, his fingers thrust into both tight openings, overcoming the hard spasms to continuously invade her. She rode crashing waves of orgasms for what seemed an impossible length of time then she collapsed onto the bed, his fingers still buried inside her. Full body trembling overtook her.

His fingers glided out and she twitched a few times trying to get used to being empty again. When she'd caught her breath, he kissed her shoulder.

"Does my lady love me or hate me?" he asked gently.

"Both," she gulped.

She twisted onto her side so that she was facing him. She looked up into his dark eyes. "And what of my lord? Does he love me or hate me?"

"He has loved you since the day he met you. Why should this day be any different?"

She smiled slowly and pushed a damp lock of hair back from her face. "You exaggerate, but it was a good answer anyway."

"I never exaggerate." There was a remarkable tenderness in his eyes now as he looked at her.

She arched a sardonic brow. "You wished me dead some days," she reminded him.

"Aye, because I loved you and could not have you. And because you raped the power from me and, in so doing, ripped my flesh open. But more than all that even, I wished it because you hid from me constantly…day and night for eight frustrating years I searched endlessly. Plague is kinder to its victims than you, Ariana."

"If I'm so horrible why do you claim to love me?"

"For the same reason all men love women. Because they can not help it."

She leaned forward and bit his nipple gently. "Poor besotted men," she teased.

"Aye."

Exhaustion seemed to descend as nightfall might, coming on slowly then suddenly complete. She closed her eyes.

Ariana woke to the sound of voices. She realized that a servant had entered. She also realized that when Marcus had climbed from bed he had not bothered to cover her up, or perhaps she had slid from under the fur while she slept. The result was the same. She was lying on her side, the front of her curled against the soft fur, but her back and buttocks were completely exposed.

"She has a pretty backside," Marcus said in a conversational tone.

"Aye, my lord."

"That pink color you see is because I tenderized it with my open hand before I made a meal of it."

Bastard! Smug, arrogant bastard!

The boy chuckled.

"She makes a tempting morsel," Marcus added with slow thoughtfulness. She could imagine the young servant giving him a conspiratorial grin. *Damn them both to hell!* She was going to kill Marcus.

"But anyone who fancies a piece will lose his life for his trouble if he acts on that impulse." Marcus' tone was low and ominous.

"My lord, I would not," the boy said soberly.

"Nay? Well, others might. I do not wish to spill blood where it might be avoided. Pass the word, Morgan. She belongs to me and none other."

"Aye, my lord."

She listened to the soft footfalls and the opening and closing of the door before she let out her strangled cry of frustration. "I'm awake!" She twisted under the cover onto her other side and propped up on an elbow so she could glare at him properly.

"Aye."

"How could you leave me uncovered in front of a stranger?" she snapped.

He simply smiled at her. She sat up, right onto her "tenderized backside."

"Ouch," she complained indignantly, moving back onto her side.

He grinned, glancing at her buttocks. "Sore?" he asked innocently.

She straightened up onto her knees, putting her hands onto her rump. "Yes. Is the barbarian pleased with himself on that account?"

"Most," he said with a smile.

She jabbed the air toward him with her index finger. "Well, I hope you got that out of your system. It was the first and last time."

He shook his head and folded his arms across his chest with smug amusement. He could not mean to spank her again!

"When you are strong enough to stop me from doing it, then you may be the one to say it will not happen again."

"You've had your revenge," she said, lips pouting.

"The ghosts of my enemies will be quick to point out that my revenge feels quite a bit different than that."

She drew her brows together, considering. "Well then, why did you do it, if not for revenge?"

"So many reasons," he said with a wicked smile.

"You made me cry."

His smile faded and he looked, for a moment, wholly contrite. "You are not hurt. Not really." He sounded a little like he was trying to convince himself as much as her.

"That is not the point. You spanked me against my will and then let some servant boy see me naked. That's pretty close to unforgivable."

"I had my reasons for that."

"Let's hear them."

He strolled over and sat on the edge of the bed.

"They will see, at some point, that you have a little magic of your own. So it is necessary that they understand who masters whom lest they make a mistake with their allegiance."

"You let that boy know that you spanked me and you left me exposed like some sex toy to show him that you dominate me? So that he wouldn't be confused about whom he serves?" she asked incredulously. "I don't believe that. Like you said, you're lord of these lands. No one here will ever side with me over you."

"People are soft-hearted. If I were a boy and a beautiful lady magically appeared and then asked for my help to escape a castle, would loyalty win over infatuation? I can not say. I might be particularly tempted to help her if I thought the master were under her spell, and, as such, less of a threat. Also, if I thought the lady might fall in love with me, she would be hard to resist. Let us not forget how innocent you can look, Ariana. I was already a man, twice as wary as the next, when I let you steal that kiss. I felt the trouble of it before I ever lowered my head, but lower my head I did."

"If you knew, then why did you?"

"Because the kiss mattered more than the trouble."

"It was just a kiss," she lied.

"Nay." He shook his head slowly for emphasis.

It gave her a strange thrill to hear him acknowledge that the amazing kiss, born of deception, had been something special to him too, despite its terrible consequences. She remembered that moment. He'd been half in shadow and breathtakingly gorgeous. And even though he was dangerous, and even though she doubted her enchantment would work, she had had to kiss him. Something in her soul had demanded it. The feel of those supple lips, the taste of him, were things she had never forgotten. They had haunted her dreams for years.

He spoke, drawing her from her reverie. "And you are every bit as dangerous to that boy as you were to me. More so, because I had no dangerous rival to vanquish as I pursued you. Others, however, have me to cast aside, for I am a deadly impediment to any who wants to claim you."

"I am not dangerous to young boys," she said furiously. But even as she'd been about to say that she didn't use people, the words froze in her throat. How could she say that when she'd used him?

I only use people for very good reasons, she thought, trying to rationalize.

Like getting your freedom back? a small voice queried in her head. She pushed it away. She wouldn't have used the boy and put him in danger of incurring Marcus' wrath. Not even to get her freedom back.

"You could have been dangerous to him. Now, it is less likely."

"Because you let him see that you had beaten me?"

"Nay, because I let him see that you'd allowed it."

Allowed it! Like some wanton whore? She gasped and flew from the bed. She snatched his shirt from the floor and pulled it over her head. She ran to the door, but he got there ahead of her and stood in front of it.

"I didn't let you do it!" she fumed. "As you said, it's not like I could have stopped you."

"Nay." He smiled slowly. "But you have a very strong voice. You could have screamed loud enough for them to hear and wonder what I was doing. Instead you were quiet, except for the screams of passion. And afterward he finds you sleeping in my bed, sweetly sated, not cowering in the corner weeping."

Her face scalded with humiliation. She struck him with all her might and tried to drag him away from the door.

He was as immobile as a mountain. She rained down blows on his chest. "Let me out!" she screamed. She grimaced at the growing pain in her fists.

He frowned and caught her wrists, effectively stopping her violent tirade. "Take care before you hurt yourself."

"You will let me out!" She was shaking with rage, but she stood where he held her without trying to break free.

"Nay. I have waited many years to talk to you. You will not escape so easily."

"Easily? You call this easy?" she spat. "You kidnapped me from my apartment, dragged me back to a past that I don't want, flaunted me as your whore to the servants, and plundered my body and reputation so that I'll never be sought as a wife if I'm forced to live in this wretched time." Boy, she had really thrown in the kitchen sink. As if she wanted to marry a man from this century anyway. Still, she had known that it was a good accusation to throw at him. Women had value as wives. Men didn't want wives who'd dallied with other men. Marcus knew that.

His face clouded, and his voice softened. "Was it all done so badly? If you despise me, why do you call to me in your dreams?"

"I don't." Even as she denied it though, she wondered. She'd let herself believe that he was pursuing her and that she didn't like it, that she was forced to endure it, but on some level she knew she wanted him too.

"You do. Most nights. Sometimes you even speak to me."

"I do not." Tears of frustration pooled in her eyes. "I have a different life than this. I don't want this." Her voice had started strong, but finished weak. Had she unknowingly reached across time for him through their magical connection? She blinked the tears away.

"I will not presume to tell you what you feel, Ariana. That is for you to unravel for yourself."

The anger leaked out of her. His hands rubbed her arms comfortingly.

"Let me explain something. If I took things too far today then it is because I have had eight years to live alone in my fantasies of you with no one to temper them. And if I let a boy see too much then it was probably partly to protect him, but also to show you off to him."

"To show off my nakedness?" she asked, bewildered.

He shrugged. "I have not taken a lover in a very long time. And I never took a wife. This castle has been waiting for a mistress since the day you ruined me for other women. Perhaps, I wanted to show off the body of the woman for whom I had been waiting years."

A little part of her heart soared at hearing that she had ruined him for any other woman. It was a wildly romantic thing for someone to say, especially someone like him who had never been known for anything but danger. Still, there was no getting around the fact that he'd gone too far.

"But don't you see what you've done in the process? You've made me your whore. No one here will ever respect me now."

He scowled. "No one here will ever dare disrespect you. Whether you are wife or mistress, disrespecting you will be a punishable offense, and the punishment will be severe. I will make it clear to them."

She shivered. There was the danger again, emanating from him. She put a hand on his arm. "No, Marcus. I don't want you to threaten them. That will make me even more of a pariah." She drew her hand back and took a slow deep breath, wondering if it were ill advised to command him on the treatment of his own servants. "And no more talk of killing people over words or stolen kisses. You are entirely too violent."

"I am not violent toward you."

She arched a brow. "Shall I show you my backside?"

"Aye, as often as possible."

She rolled her eyes.

"That was not violence," he said stubbornly.

"What, pray tell, was it then?"

"Loveplay."

"Then after dinner I will get Joan and Morgan to get me some rope and a horsewhip. I'll tie you up, and we can see how you feel about violence as foreplay."

Marcus walked over to a basin to wash his hands.

"What do you think, Marcus? Is that a good idea about the horse-whip?"

He didn't bother to look up. "Nay."

She couldn't help but smile to herself, glancing at his muscular arms. Of course, the game was only fun for him if he got to be the one who dominated it. She thought about men knocking each other down on football fields and beating each other in boxing rings. Strong men liked to show off their strength and power. In 650 years, they hadn't changed.

Marcus sat down at the small table and uncovered the serving bowl of stew. He ladled it out into their dishes. She washed and then sat down gingerly across from him. He poured wine into goblets and set one next to her. He lifted his, drinking.

"So, it took you eight years to get me here. Other than beating me and showing off my naked ass to the servants do you have any other plans?"

He choked down the wine in his mouth and grimaced at her. "For someone who claims dissatisfaction at having been laid across my lap and spanked, you bait me as though you would prefer it to eating dinner."

She pouted and then wondered at herself. In 2005, she *never* pouted. Of course, in 2005, men who made her angry were dumped or fired as the case may be. What could she do but pout in 1349?

They ate quietly, each lost in thought. The venison stew wasn't bad, but she found herself craving enchiladas. *Shame about the new world not being discovered yet,* she thought wryly.

She put her head in her hands, suddenly overwhelmed at the loss of her life in the future. Had she ever been a part of Marcus' time? Cognitively, she knew that she had, but it was so difficult to feel anything now but that she was out of place. Out of time.

When she looked up, she found he was watching her. She cleared her throat. "How is my family?" she asked.

"Your father is well. He has a new wife."

Her mother had died in childbirth with her younger brother when Ariana had been four. Sometimes she tried to remember what her mother looked like, but it was difficult. As for her father, they had never been close. He thought girls were silly creatures, useful only in creating alliances through marriage.

"Plague swept through and claimed both your older brothers and their families."

She digested that for a moment, feeling sad, but also oddly detached. They had not been part of her life for a long time. In the future, she'd come to terms with all her family being long dead.

"Marcus, there's no plague in 2005."

"There's no plague here either, right now."

"And women don't die in childbirth anymore, at least not in the country where I was living. Well, once in a while…but only very rarely. Never as often as they do now. And if a babe is born too soon, they just put it in a little warmer and do everything for it until it gets big enough to go home. By the end it's as good as a full-grown one."

"If the healing powers are so good in the future, why did they need you to steal magic from me?"

"I'm not saying people don't ever get sick. But it's different there. Everything is different; it's better." There she'd said it. She waited for a response. None came. "Marcus, did you hear what I said?"

"Aye."

"Well?"

"If you think to go back, you had best get working on your magic because the power it takes to get there is considerable."

"You did it."

"Aye."

"So you could take me back." *And even come with me if you wanted to.*

"What I could do and what I will do are separate things, Ariana."

"I knew it," she said, pushing the stew away and standing up. "This is why I hate it here. Women are a cross between property and prisoners."

He sighed. "This is our time. We were born to it. We belong here, for good or ill. It was unnatural for you to live there."

She shook her head. "If you really loved me, you would want me to be happy."

"I do want that."

"Then take me back."

"Nay. I just brought you here. You will grant me time to make you happy here."

"It won't work."

"Perhaps not, but I would have the time all the same." He reached out a long arm, catching her and pulling her onto his lap. She struggled a moment and then settled, sighing deeply at her defeat. The solidness of his body felt good to her, and she rested her head against his shoulder. All the changes were too overwhelming. Leaning against him made her feel better, more anchored. "I have only ever had two really great days in this century," she murmured absently.

"Tell me about them," he urged softly.

"There was one day eight years ago when I snuck away from home to find a young earl with black hair and black magic. I tricked him into an enchanted kiss."

He smiled. "And the other day?"

"The other day was today." She wondered immediately where that answer had come from. Somewhere in her subconscious?

"That is good news. On the morrow, I do not intend to let anyone see you naked nor to spank you," he said in a gentle teasing voice. "So it promises to be a third good day for you."

She smiled though there was a lingering trace of melancholy in her mood. He stroked her breast through the fabric of his shirt. She didn't encourage him, but she didn't pull away either. Marcus kissed her cheek and continued to touch her softly, coaxing her toward desire.

"All will be well," he murmured hypnotically.

Moments passed. His hand cupped her breast more firmly. Liquid lust formed between her thighs. She kissed his shoulder and moved her hip against his erection. He pulled the shirt off her, bending his head to swirl his tongue over her nipple at the same time his fingers went down to play between her legs.

Within moments, she was arching her back and spreading her legs apart to give him better access. Dark need shone in his eyes.

"I liked the whimpering kitten who let me spank her and feast on her flesh. But I also like the vixen who arches her back and spreads herself open for me."

He pulled his slick fingers free and slid an arm under her knees, then stood up and carried her to the bed, setting her down gently.

She let her legs fall apart, awash in sensations. The soft fur under her, the ache in her buttocks, the hot, tight anticipation between her lower lips. She could feel moisture seeping out of her and down the crease of her buttocks. The smaller hole hidden there twitched, and she recalled the way he'd violated her there so deliciously. She had always been shy to even think about being penetrated that way, but he'd claimed that part of her as easily as he claimed her everywhere else.

Marcus crawled on the bed and over her. She felt the swollen tip of him between her lower lips. He rubbed her slick entrance a few times, lubricating himself. Then with delectable pressure, he pushed the head inside. It stretched the inflamed tissue, but the sensation of searing pain was immediately overcome by the warm pulsating penetration that she realized her body desperately craved.

She gasped and arched, reaching, wanting more of him. He let himself glide deeper and deeper into her body until he was tucked against her womb, and it felt strange yet amazingly intimate to her. She liked the sensation, but knew he wasn't all the way in.

"I'm hurting you," he murmured, pulling out.

"No," she cried, trying to draw him back.

"Ariana, I can see the pain on your face. The morrow will be soon enough."

"Not pain. Just soreness." It was almost inexplicable how much her body wanted his. She stroked him with her fingers. "Please, Marcus. I want you. Come back."

He slid inside her tentatively and not as deeply as the first time. She lifted her hips, but didn't succeed in taking more of him inside. He was bracing himself so that he couldn't get too deep. The way he held himself back was making her insane. He slid in and out slowly. With his thick cock, he did hit a sweet spot, and she started to purr, but she wanted more.

"Marcus?"

"What, my love?"

She ran her hand along the sweat-slick skin over his ribs. "Where is the...oh. Where's the man who spanked me earlier?"

"Locked up so he does not hurt you."

"But, Marcus—" She panted. "That's who the vixen wants."

His eyebrows shot up. "She—you do?"

"Not to get spanked. Just let him loose to take us... me."

"You mean you want me to be rougher?" he asked incredulously.

"Just a little. Can you do that?"

"Aye, angel. As rough as you like." As if to prove it, he shifted his weight, grabbing an ass cheek in each hand and pulling her down onto his big cock. The triple sensation of him squeezing her sore backside, driving deep through aching flesh and striking deep inside her, made her wail and writhe.

"You want me to stop?" he asked.

"Nn-not if you value your life," she stammered.

That unleashed the beast. He dropped her to the bed and hoisted up her legs, which allowed him to thrust deeper inside her.

"Oh, God. Oh, please. Ooooh!" Pleasure exploded, flames igniting inside her. As her spasms greedily sucked him, his cock continued its relentless battering. She dug her fingers into the flesh of his back, trying to hold on. A second orgasm gripped her hot on the heels of the first.

"Oh, Marcus. Oh, yes." She moaned long and loud.

"Aye, vixen." His handsome face was a mask of determination.

Sweat rained down on her and she felt every ounce of his male power concentrated inside her. And then it burst out of him like a dam had broken. He poured a molten river into her vault, thick wet heat pooling and then running down from where they were still joined.

Her rosette asshole puckered and unpuckered at the teasing sensation. She eased her shaking legs down to rest on the bed and felt the damp matted fur under her.

"We ruined the fur," she mumbled absently.

His breath came and went in quick rushes. "What do I care for a fur when I am dead and in heaven?" He lowered himself to rest on the bed, sliding free of her. He lay on his side, looking her over, then reached down and lifted her right leg, crossing it over the left.

"What are you doing?"

"Closing your body."

"Why?"

"So my seed can take root in your womb."

Oh boy. "Now, you want a baby?"

"Aye. It is an idea that I have lately considered a good one."

"Uh huh."

"It came to me while I was inside you."

"So, you've given it long and serious consideration then," she said sarcastically, though a part of her was strangely tempted by the idea.

"When a man's loins are so strongly inspired by a woman's, the thought comes quite naturally I assure you. Suddenly, I would like to swell this belly," he said, running his hand over her stomach possessively. "And these breasts," he said, kissing the lower curve of the breast closest to him. "There is time for at least five or six fat babies to come of us."

"Five or six," she echoed incredulously.

"Aye," he said, his tongue sliding over her nipple. "And having your belly big with child will save you."

"From what?"

"From being laid out over my lap and being spanked."

"We already decided you weren't going to do that again."

"I do not recall having said such. Even if I had, I would have thought better of it now."

"Why?"

"Any innocent who can tell me to use her more roughly can surely handle a few measured swats on her rear."

"That's different. When I wanted more earlier, I was caught up in the moment."

"Aye? So, that is the difference?" he asked rhetorically with a wicked grin. "I will remember to get you excited then before I begin next time. Now, let me have a look at my afternoon's work," he said, flipping her onto her stomach. He trailed a finger over each cheek. "Not even pink anymore. Earlier they were blushing like roses. And I noticed that there was plenty of dew between the petals right after I gave them their color."

She blushed in spite of herself and was glad he couldn't see her face. He dipped a finger down between her legs and into her vagina.

"Marcus," she growled in warning.

A second finger slipped into her. She bit her lip as the wave of excitement started to rise again. Without meaning to, she pushed back against his fingers. She exhaled in a sharp whoosh as pleasure flicked through her. His fingers stroked her slowly until she started to grind her hips. Then he pulled them out unexpectedly. She whimpered a protest, but he ignored it and went about the task of bunching the fur up under her belly and repositioning her so that her knees were fully bent and turned out on opposite sides of her body.

She moaned out load at the feeling of being left completely open by the position he'd posed her in. She was aware that he was somewhere behind her, looking her over.

"If there be a more succulent piece of fruit than you, I do not know it," he said in his rich baritone. He dipped his head and began sucking moisture from her.

She gasped, pushing back against his mouth. He bit gently on her swollen labia. Then his fingers played inside her for a few moments.

"Marcus," she pleaded.

"Aye." His fingers slid out and up to her bottom. "You have only been a little stretched here," he said.

Her heart hammered in anticipation. She was moving her hips and his fingers were slippery, but surprise still bit at her when he pushed those fingers inside. All her sensations concentrated directly on the ring he was violating. It was more uncomfortable with two fingers, but the penetration was also more intense.

He slid the fingers in and out slowly. The rosette gripped them hungrily, puckering and unpuckering like a greedy mouth. Then his tongue went back to work below, licking her dripping slit from clit to hole.

"Marcus. Oh God, Marcus. Please."

His tongue lapped at her opening. The fingertips of the hand that wasn't fingering her ass moved to vibrate against her clitoris. He played her body like an instrument, and for him, it sang.

She cried out as she came, shuddering all over. Afterward, when he left her clit and cleft alone to the cool air, she started to move her knees in.

"Nay," he said, pushing down firmly on her lower back, causing her knees to buckle and slide out and her belly to come to rest back on the lumped up fur.

She was wide open to him still and his fingers started to slip in and out of her ass again, but this time more roughly and with more pressure. She gasped repeatedly, juices dripping again from the front. Then she felt the monstrous bulb of his cock bumping her vulva. Her whole ass contracted in anticipation, and she moaned.

"Aye. Again." Then the bulb bored its way into her inch by stretching inch.

She could feel him impaling her on both sides of the septum that separated the lower parts of her. She was laid desperately open to him and he was using it to his full advantage.

In and out. In and out. Both holes throbbing. Her whole body exhausted, sweaty, and trembling, trying to be obedient to him as he beckoned her to the ultimate pleasure again.

And then his cock thrusts got rougher, deeper. They shook her from the inside.

A hard and unrelenting orgasm grabbed her, gripping her sex and ass first and then every other part of her. It took him a few more minutes to spill inside her. Again he came with a geyser of seed drenching everything.

He pulled out finally and she rolled onto her side, trembling. She'd never known that anything could feel so intense. Her body was so tired and yet part of her wanted to stay awake, to wrap her arms around him and to hold him close to her all night…or maybe forever. It was so hard to sort out her feelings and harder still to stay awake.

He kissed her neck and shoulders before he disappeared from the bed. Her breathing slowed to normal and she drifted in and out of sleep for a while before she realized he was lifting her up.

"Rest. I need rest, Marcus." She tried to focus her eyes on him.

He chuckled. "I know, angel. Close your eyes."

She felt herself being set into warm water.

"Look at the poor thing. What have ye done to her?" Joan's voice clucked at Marcus in the distance.

Ariana wanted to smile, but she was too tired. She was floating. Soft bristles were scrubbing her and then she was cold, but Marcus' chest was warm against her.

Ariana woke in the morning and stretched languidly. The bed smelled clean and fresh and the fur, which had been soiled by so much sex was gone. She looked around the bedchamber. The fire was roaring, but otherwise it was quiet and still. Her only thought was…*where is he?*

She climbed from the bed. She paused when she found that clothes had been laid carefully over the bench for her. She smiled at the old-fashioned garments. No thong silk panties in 1349. She dressed in the yellow gown, which was a bit too large, and brushed her hair quickly. She wanted to see Marcus.

Just as she was walking toward the door, it opened. Joan hurried in. "He said you were awake. And already dressed, I see."

"How did he know I was awake?" she asked, looking around.

"He knows things," Joan said, then dropped her voice lower. "Black devil, 'e is."

Ariana smiled, which caused Joan to look her over suspiciously.

"And ye, plucked from God knows where, to be to him I know not what." Her eyes flickered around the bedchamber with disapproval. "He says we must be kind to ye or be punished, but I say—"

So he had threatened them even though she'd told him not to do it. Ariana shook her head in annoyance. "You do not have to be nice to me, Joan. I am not his wife and therefore not your mistress. You will treat me as you think I deserve, and I will not get you into trouble with him for it."

Joan looked her over and sniffed. "He sent me to help ye dress, but you being already dressed, we go to the next. He would have ye have this key."

She widened her eyes. "What does it open?"

"A book chamber for ye. Though why a lady be wantin' books I could not say."

"Show me," Ariana said, clutching the old woman's arm in excitement.

Joan nodded and led her out. The old woman was surprisingly spry and moved quickly. They came to a door at the end of the corridor.

Ariana unlocked it and pushed it open. It was a beautiful, richly appointed little room, cozy with tapestries, a fireplace, and a desk. And on a stand near the hearth there was a small box shaped like a chest.

"What's that?" Ariana asked, strolling over to it.

"He goes too far," Joan grumbled.

Ariana opened the lid of the box and gasped. Jewels to make Harry Winston green with envy.

"Is it not enough that he makes the men drag all this in here this morn so ye can have a book chamber? Now he gives ye her jewelry."

"Whose? Whose is it?"

"His mother's," Joan snapped.

"Is she dead?"

"Aye, but her jewelry were meant to go to the new mistress of this castle."

Not to some harlot he conjured up, Ariana thought, adding in her mind what Joan did not say. For some reason, she didn't mind Joan's disapproval. She liked the woman and thought that they might eventually become friends. "So, Joan, this chamber was created today? There is another library or study that Marcus uses?"

Joan clucked at her use of Marcus' given name. Ariana simply waited.

"Aye."

"Where is the lord's room like this?"

"If he wants ye to know, he will tell ye."

"All right," Ariana said with a dismissive wave of her hand. She wanted to be alone in the study to look at what volumes he'd loaned her. Books in 1349 were extremely rare and valuable.

"Will ye break your fast soon?" Joan asked.

"Yes, soon."

Ariana shivered at the coolness of the chamber and instantly the little hearth roared to life. Joan shouted with fright and ran from the chamber. *Marcus*, Ariana thought and smiled. It wasn't only the fire's warmth that surrounded her, so too, did Marcus's power. She basked in the heat for a moment, liking the feel of his magic. She shook her head at herself. She couldn't let herself get too cozy with him. It would make it too hard on them both when she left.

She sunk down with a book on philosophy. She wasn't sure how much time had passed when she felt him nearby. She looked up and found his tall frame leaning against the doorway, studying her. He looked deliciously handsome as always.

"Hello," she said with a smile.

His eyes scanned the books that were arranged around her. Then he cast a glance at the ornate box.

"I knew you would prefer the books."

"I can use the books while I'm here. The jewelry is lovely, but it must go to your wife."

"I agree. The jewelry must go to my wife."

She folded her arms across her chest. "I am not resigned to staying in this century. I promised you some time, but it won't be forever. Then I'll be gone again."

"Let us presume that you do go back. Then, by your time, I will be long dead and of no consequence. It will not matter that you were married to me in this time."

"That's true."

"Now let us consider the opposite, that you never go back. Is there anyone in this time that you would prefer as a husband?"

"Well, I haven't met everyone yet," she teased.

He folded his arms across his chest and gave her a stern look. "Let us save time. Is there any man from this time that you think you might seek to marry who could survive me trying to kill him, as I surely could not stop myself from trying to do?"

She chuckled. "No, you're certainly the most lethal person that I've ever met in either century." He was altogether too dark and too possessive, and what she really wished was that she didn't find that so damn attractive.

"And do you think, barring my interference, that any would have you after the way I have been with you in my bedchamber, the way I've claimed you as mine?"

She couldn't stop the heat from rising in her cheeks at the recollection of all the ways he'd had her in that bedchamber. "No. Through your body's use of mine, you have seen to it that I am totally without value in this society."

His eyes snapped angrily. "Do not repeat that... ever."

"What?" she asked in surprise.

"That you have no value. I will not tolerate that sentiment from anyone, not even you."

"I didn't say I believed that I have no value. I said that, as I am now, this society would consider me without value."

"I am of this time. And I find that I value you more than my riches, my title or my land."

"Do you? Truly?" she asked slowly.

"Aye."

That thrilled her in ways too numerous to name and it occurred to her that maybe the small part of her that was in love with Marcus might not have to be without him. What if she could convince him to come with her to live in the future? If he really wanted her more than anything, he might do it.

"You want me to marry you?"

"Is that not what I have just been saying?" he demanded.

"I have terms," she said.

"What terms?" he asked suspiciously and widened his stance as if he were about to face some physical threat.

"I want you to teach me your magic."

"So that you can leave me? Nay," he said, shaking his head.

"Marcus," she said, getting up and walking over to him.

"Nay."

"If I marry you, it will give you total power over me. To do that, I would have to trust you a great deal."

"You should trust me. I will love and protect you like no other could."

"I would like to, but love, to my mind, shouldn't be a selfish thing. If you love me then you may try to tempt me to stay here, but you won't keep me prisoner. I'll give you time, and you'll give me knowledge. And one day, I'll choose between this time and the future. And maybe, if we care for each other enough, you will decide to be with me in whatever time I choose."

"If we care for each other enough? Do you admit then that you care for me some already?"

She glanced at her hands and then back up at him. "I'm not sure. I only know that it feels right to be near you. Even when I woke this morning alone in your bed, I found that I did not like to be separated from you."

"But you stayed in this chamber. You did not come looking for me."

"I didn't need to leave here to look for you. You were here. All around me. Besides, I knew you would come for me when you were ready."

"I came for you long after I was ready," he admitted.

She smiled, liking to hear that he had longed to see her. She poked her head into the corridor and looked both ways. Then she took a step back and pulled him into the room. She closed the door and locked it.

"Tell me your thoughts," Marcus said, appraising her with a look.

"I was thinking that it's very nice and cozy here with the fire. If no one is around, we could lie down on the rug and let our bodies say good morning to each other." She smiled at him seductively, and, by the way he licked his lips, she knew they would be naked soon.

"I would have something first."

"What?" she asked curiously.

"A gift from you."

She narrowed her eyes. If he was thinking about spanking her, she was going to be furious. Not that the idea didn't have a certain allure to it, but that definitely felt like a night game.

"Tell me then," she said.

"A kiss."

As soon as he said it she realized that she had not kissed him yet…not really. She had caressed his body with her mouth, but she had neglected his lips. She studied his face and suddenly understood that he'd been waiting for her to kiss him. It pricked at something tender inside her that a kiss from her was so important to him, that he elevated it as a gift above the sex that she offered on the rug.

"Sit," she said, blinking the tears that inexplicably burned her eyes.

He sat down and she moved to him. She sat on his lap, putting her arms around his neck. His eyes never left her mouth. It made her heart beat quicker. She licked her lower lip to moisten it and then moved her mouth near his. They were so close that she could smell the spices on his breath, mint and cloves.

She put her mouth to his, brushing his lips with hers. Her fingers slid into his hair and gently urged his head forward. And then she was kissing him, their lips pressed together, her tongue caressing him slowly. He relaxed, as though he'd been tense, preparing himself in case she withheld what she'd promised.

She kissed him tenderly and was glad that he let her. His arms were draped around her, warming her, but he didn't grip her as though to toss her on the floor and ravish her. He was content with what she offered. And a thought came to her, of a real gift she could give him.

She drew back so that their lips barely touched and she whispered words very like the ones she'd whispered all those years ago…only different. And when she pressed her mouth into his again, the power rose. The golden tendrils of her fragile magic uncurled and released the midnight strands of his. Marcus' power retracted back across her lips and into him. She felt suddenly empty and lost. A cold hollow place in her chest cried out for his power to be put back, but she only had a second to register her own reaction before Marcus reacted.

He broke the kiss, breathlessly. His hands clutched her arms tightly, making her wince. "Why? Why did you do that?" he demanded. There was something that sounded almost like anguish in his voice.

"I…I wanted to give you a gift…like the kiss," she said hesitantly. She didn't understand what she'd done wrong. "To give back what I stole from you," she added softly.

He loosened his grip, tipping his head back and shaking it. Finally, he laughed mirthlessly.

"What?"

"Ariana," he said, looking back at her face. "Is it possible that you still do not understand?"

"It is possible and quite probable," she snapped, not liking the implication that she was dense.

"The strength of your magic is like the strength of your body when compared to mine. You could never take what I did not yield."

She drew her eyebrows together skeptically. "But I tricked you. Your magic was stronger, but I distracted you with the kiss so I could steal a little strand of it."

"When you were but fourteen, you used your magic for the first time. I was hundreds of miles away, but I felt it. I was aware of you from then on. On the night you finally came for that kiss, I felt you approach when your horse could not even be seen. I waited for you. When you were too scared to seek me out, I sought you out and found you in the garden. I answered your smiles and put you at ease whenever your nervousness threatened to make you back away from me. You stole nothing. You were not capable of it. You kissed me and I gave you what you wished for."

"Why? Why would you do that?"

"Because, in all the world, I love nothing so much as you."

His words thrilled yet terrified her. "I was a stranger to you," she said. He shook his head. "I was," she whispered. "And you understood magic very well by then. You must have known it would fracture your power and leave you vulnerable, that I could hurt you by using it as I did unknowingly."

"Aye, I understood the risk…though I could not have anticipated how far you would journey with it."

She stared at him thoughtfully. She wanted him to love her, but she dreaded it too. Marcus wasn't the sort of person to prove that he loved something by setting it free. He would use his power to try to keep her, and his power was considerable.

"Now ask me if I regret my decision," he said.

"Do you?"

He stared into her eyes, soul bare. "Nay."

The walls she'd been trying to build around her heart came crumbling down. He was there, everywhere at once. She couldn't keep him out. "Why not?" she whispered, thinking of the vicious scars on his chest and abdomen.

"Because just as my body wants to be connected to yours, so does my soul. Putting my magic inside you connected us."

She knew he was right, but there was more to it than that. She shook her head slowly.

"Aye, it did," he said.

"Yes, I know that, but it doesn't explain why you wanted to bind us together through your power. Something connected us before you gave me your magic. Or else how could you have been aware of me years before we met? Were you aware of anyone who cast a spell?"

"Nay. Only you."

"Then there was something between us, even before the kiss." She thought of the way she'd known who he was before he'd told her. She'd watched him approach her in the garden and she'd recognized his magic as if she'd already claimed a piece of it. It should have seemed strange to her at the time, but it hadn't. His presence had been too overwhelming for her to notice anything else.

"Fate then," he said with a shrug.

A chill ran through her, and she shivered. He wrapped his arms around her more tightly.

"You can not be cold."

"No. Just scared."

"What frightens you? Fate?" he asked.

"Yes."

"Why? We can have love and passion, and I will always protect you. What is there to fear?"

"Because if fate means us to be tied together and I can never convince you to go forward with me again, it means that I will be trapped here for the rest of my life…that I'll never again see the amazing world of the future that I loved so much."

He sighed. "Let us concern ourselves with this century for the present. I have had word that the king requires my presence in London. You will come with me, and we will marry there."

She slid away from him and took a step back. It was all happening so fast, too fast. Marcus stood. He reached for and caught her. She took another partial step back, but he held her arm firmly.

"You have nothing to fear from me, Ariana. I would as soon have the heart cut from my body as see harm come to you."

"That is what I fear," she whispered, looking at the place where his hand held her arm and then back to his face.

He raised his eyebrows in question.

"Don't you think I see what you're doing? You'll bind us together in every way possible so that my will has no significance at all."

"Your happiness means something to me. I offer you more than obsession. If I only wanted to imprison you I could do that without taking you to the king. No one even knows you live. I could keep you with me forever without marriage."

"Maybe you want marriage to legitimize your children, the ones you've already told me you want me to give you."

He smiled and brought his free hand to her face, ran a fingertip along her jaw, drawing an involuntary shiver from her. "Perhaps you are right." His voice was soft and low, with a dark sensuous edge. "Love should not make me thus. I find that I have intentions that go beyond reason." His hand dropped, and he held her by both shoulders. "Understand me though. I love you and will have you for a wife. Tell me if you are willing yet to try to tame me through marriage because I must go to London. If you are not ready to accept a betrothal, you may stay here and await my return."

The room was spinning slowly around her. His power hung on the air and weighed down on her more heavily than his hands on her shoulders. "I don't know what to do."

"Well, you can think about it while I make love to you. Whether you come with me to London or not, I need you now, once more before the journey."

She blinked as he took a step forward. "I'm sore," she mumbled. She didn't really care about the soreness. The emotions of the situation were what gave her pause.

He pulled off his shirt and smiled. "And if I thought that you were troubled by it I might reconsider, but that is not what troubles you." He reached over and grasped the fabric of her gown. "Also I find that I want you to feel the effects of my hard use of your body so that you will think of me while I am gone."

She trembled as he undressed her, half from wanting to flee and half from wanting to stay.

Moments later she was lying naked on her back, legs splayed. The hearth was crackling with heat, but that wasn't the main reason she felt such overwhelming warmth. Marcus' tongue licked her nipples slowly. When he bit down gently she undulated slowly beneath his body. She heard his sharp intake of breath and felt him move. His glorious cock pushed slowly into her damp folds.

He held himself still and stared down at her face. She shifted her hips wantonly, encouraging him to move. A faint smile played at the corners of his mouth. He pressed deeper into the wet cavern of her sex, bumping against her womb. She gasped and dug her nails into his lower back. A hot knot of desire had formed in her belly and answered the pressure of him inside her.

"Marcus," she pleaded.

"Deny that you belong to me," he challenged.

She wrapped her legs around him and pushed her heels against his taut buttocks.

"Nay?" he teased. "If you will not deny it, then acknowledge it, and I will give you what we both want."

It was almost impossible not to scream in the affirmative. Every cell in her body from the neck down was begging her to bend to his will and admit the truth…that she belonged to him and always had. She bit her lip to keep herself from answering. There was still a small part of her that wanted to resist him, to resist this century, this life.

His palms were flat on the floor on either side of her and he held himself up so that he could study her face. His gaze fell hungrily on her mouth.

"Marcus," she said very softly. She wanted him to strain to hear her so that he would get closer.

He lowered his upper body until their chests were pressed together, soft breasts against hard muscle.

"What, my love?" he whispered.

She slid her arms around his neck and ran the tip of her tongue over his earlobe. She felt his low growl vibrate through his chest.

She ran a fingernail lightly over the skin of his neck from the base of his skull down to the start of his back. She felt his body tense at the sensation. "Does it feel good to be so deep inside me?" she asked.

She gasped at the power that roared from him and broke over their bodies. Instantly, he withdrew and thrust deeper. She lost her breath over and over as he ravaged her, teeth against her throat, hips slamming forward. Only his arms protected her. He had wrapped them around her so that she didn't bang against the floor.

Waves of orgasm crashed over her, cresting unmercifully, such intense pleasure, it bordered on pain. Finally, he spent himself in her plush passage, the thick heat of his body filling her and bathing his organ as she pulsed around him. He held her to him, and twisted and rolled so that she was lying on top of him.

Her body rose and fell with his deep breaths, and he reached down, cupping a buttock in each hand possessively. Neither of them made any move to separate their lower bodies.

"Are you…"

"What?" she asked, lifting her head from his chest to look at his face.

"You are not hurt." The words were spoken as a statement, but she felt the question in them nonetheless.

"No, I'm not hurt."

He sighed with relief. "I knew that you were not. You did not try to stop me."

She placed a gentle kiss over his ribs and then looked back at him. "I'm not hurt," she repeated and felt some of the tension leave him.

"I confess I do not understand how you escape it. You feel so soft. You have such fragile, delicate bones." He ran a hand up her spine. "I worry that I will crush you beneath me." He took a deep breath and blew it out. "And you are no help to me. In the moments when I am fighting the hardest to maintain control, you taunt me and tempt me. 'Does it feel good to be so deep inside me?' How can you say such things to me?" he asked with mock disgust.

She smiled. "I wanted you to move."

"You wanted to break my control," he observed dourly.

"Yes, and it worked quite nicely."

"Aye. You would do well to exercise caution, Ariana. Such violent couplings as come from unleashing me thus could one day leave you hurt."

"I don't think so."

"Why not?"

"Because I trust you. And instinctively your body knows how much mine can take."

He snorted skeptically. "All my body knows instinctively is that it wants to pound yours into submission." He lifted his hand and slapped her bottom playfully. "Only my mind shudders at the possibility that you might be injured. To really hurt you would make me miserable."

"Well, I'm not hurt, so it's a moot point."

"You know a good wife should temper her husband. She should be a comfort to him, not a vixen that turns him to a beast."

"Then it's lucky that I'm not your wife." She bent her head and nipped his nipple with her teeth. She felt his cock stir.

She moved so that she was sitting upright, his powerful body stretched below her. She took a deep breath and reached her hands toward the ceiling, arching slightly as she stretched. She knew he was watching her and felt his body's response inside her to the tantalizing image she made.

She lowered her arms and looked back at him. His eyes were hooded with desire. She ran a nail over his hard belly, tracing a line around his navel. She leaned slightly forward and then moved back and forth by fractions over his groin. The movement ground her clit into his pelvic bone and made her purr.

His cock lengthened and turned rigid. She caught her breath and moved forward to partially ease him out of her. In her current position, full penetration was too deep. She glanced at his face, but didn't find anything smug in his expression.

She slid slowly up and down, watching him. The connection between their eyes was as intimate as the connection between their bodies. He held himself still, but she could feel the tension building. She rode up and down on his cock, gaining confidence with each stroke.

He closed his eyes finally and fisted his hands at his sides. She loved the illusion of power that it gave her, and she moved more frantically. Soon, she felt her insides jarred as she came down completely on him.

She breathed rather than said his name. "Marcus." His eyes fluttered open.

"Let me...oh!" she gasped, feeling the shudders start. Her inner walls clutched and sucked him as she rose and fell back into position.

As the orgasm eased, she slowed her movement.

He moved restlessly beneath her. "Come now," he said in a soft rasp. "If you raise a beast to ride it, you should do so until he can be ridden no more." He moved his hips so that he slid in and out by small degrees.

She leaned forward to lie on his chest. "I just need a moment."

"So do I," he said with a harsh chuckle. He grabbed her hips and rolled them so that she was under him again.

She grimaced at the first powerful thrust. She actually was very sore now that she took a moment to consider how she felt.

"Marcus," she whispered.

He looked down at her.

"Gently."

He immediately slowed his movement. It took several long moments before he spilled his seed, and it was the most careful joining they'd had so far. Afterward, he slid out immediately and lowered himself to press a kiss on her mons. She squirmed at the ticklish sensation.

He moved to lie next to her and kissed the side of her face. "Ariana, we must be wed."

She didn't answer.

"I would give you time if I could," he said and ran a hand over her belly. "But there are two reasons we should not wait. The first is that it can only be a matter of days before you are with child, if you are not already."

She knew he was right, but wasn't ready to think about that yet. "And the second?"

"Postponing what is inevitable is a proposition that begs trouble. We will be married, and you will come to accept the idea afterward. Postponing will only give you more time to be torn between your differing desires."

"And what if I never come to accept it? What if, over time, this passion we have cools and I'm left with a marriage that I wasn't ready for and didn't want? What then?" Her voice had started at a normal volume, but had risen by the end.

"You must trust me to make you happy," he said calmly.

"Why should I?" she snapped as she sat up. "All you're interested in is keeping me with you. If you really cared about what I want, you'd give me the choice of going back to my other life in the future."

He sighed heavily and rolled away. He stood up and retrieved his clothes. "Get dressed, Ariana. We go to London to see the king."

❧☙

The London of the 1300s was certainly nothing compared to the staggering technology of the twenty-first century, but Ariana felt intimidated nonetheless. It wasn't so much the crowded streets as the fact that she felt like an alien creature, isolated and lonely even among the bustling people.

Marcus had been on horseback during the journey. When they'd first started out, he'd put her in front of him on his mount, and she'd reveled in the intimacy. They could speak quietly to each other and even steal a kiss when the rest of the retinue was focused on other things. Once they'd left his lands, however, he hadn't let her ride with him anymore. She'd had to alternate between being on horseback in a lady's mount or riding in the wagon. The increased distance between them shouldn't have made her uneasy, but it did. He was like a touchstone for her now, the only person who shared in the knowledge of who she was and where she'd been. Anyone else that she told about her experiences would think her mad. In addition, her body longed for his. The warmth and strength of him reassured her when she was nervous.

Inside the confines of the city she had to concentrate very hard not to reach out for him. At the moment, she stood frozen on the steps that led into the dressmaker's shop she was to visit. Marcus had explained that he was going to see the king first and would ask for a private audience to introduce her.

"Please take me with you. I can wait in the hall while you speak to him," she begged.

He smiled at her gently. "It pleases me that you hesitate to leave my side, Ariana, but that borrowed gown will not suffice. You are in need of something finer for an audience with the king. Madame Traineau will see to clothing you and then Morgan will take you and your maid to the inn to rest."

"And you'll rejoin us there as soon as you can," she said firmly, as if trying to convince herself.

Marcus inclined his head.

She took a deep breath and nodded. She needed to pull herself together. She'd been shy when she'd left this century, but she wasn't that teenager anymore she reminded herself. She wondered for a moment if Marcus had put some spell on her to make her not want to be away from him. She narrowed her eyes and appraised him. No, she realized, it wasn't that sort of power that drew her to him. It was more subtle. It was the way the sunlight made his jet hair gleam, the gentle but firm way he handled his horse, the unflagging masculinity he exuded in everything he did and the unguarded smiles he offered her when no one else could see him. There was a part of her that didn't want him just for a half an hour of great sex. There was a part of her that wanted him for always.

The door opened and a woman, shaped like a little white pigeon, clapped her hands together in delight at the sight of them.

Marcus introduced the dressmaker to Ariana and gave Madame Traineau instructions on the sort of wardrobe he would be purchasing on her behalf. Immediately thereafter, Marcus rode off and the group broke up with Morgan directing one of the men to the inn while he secured the horses for himself, Ariana, and her silent young maid.

Madame Traineau hustled her inside and the time passed quickly. The dressmaker and her assistants were extremely efficient. Alterations were made on one of the gowns while she waited so that she could wear it to the inn. The soft blue wool gown was lovely, but the undergarments were a bit stiff and uncomfortable compared to the satin and silk that she wore in the future.

Back at the inn, she had some supper and then retired to her room. The maid Joan had assigned to her, Agnes, was terribly shy and only said "Aye, my lady" or "Nay, my lady" as Ariana asked her questions while she attended her.

"Well, it's—" Ariana stopped herself from saying, "It's getting late." She was having trouble policing her speech. "It grows late. Let us retire."

They had no sooner begun their preparations when there was a knock at the door. She looked up as Agnes strode over and opened it a crack. Ariana couldn't make out the words and raised her eyebrows expectantly when Agnes closed the door and turned. The girl was blushing a remarkable shade of dark pink as she walked back to Ariana.

"Well?" Ariana asked.

Agnes studied her hands and whispered. "My lord has returned. He says that he wishes to speak to you in his room. You—" Agnes faltered and her eyes flicked up for a second and then fell again. "That is he says…"

"What? What did he say?"

"He says you will not need me to accompany you." The girl wrung her hands and repeated, "He says."

Ariana smiled and placed a gentle kiss on the flustered girl's forehead. The girl looked up in surprise at the gesture and Ariana chided herself for being overly familiar. Then the girl smiled meekly and Ariana felt better about it. People were entirely too formal with each other in 1349. If she were forced to stay, she would try to break those barriers down.

"What are we to do, my lady? If you go, I fear he will ruin you. If you do not go, I fear he will punish us."

Ariana smoothed down Agnes's stringy wheat-colored hair. "It's very late and we have this whole side of the inn to ourselves. If I go to him, no one will see me."

Agnes wrung her hands nervously. "Will you go alone?"

"Yes, and you mustn't worry. I can handle him. You just go ahead to bed."

Ariana waved at her to do as she was instructed and then went to the door. She opened it and looked up and down the hall before stealing out of the room. She went to the next door and opened it, but she froze in the doorway at the sight of Morgan attending to Marcus who was in a tub full of steaming water.

"Close the door," Marcus said as he scrubbed his arms.

Ariana stepped in and closed it, glancing between the servant and his master. Morgan, to his credit, acted like nothing was amiss.

She realized suddenly why Marcus always smelled so much better than the other people in the fourteenth century; he was fastidious about bathing. She supposed it helped that he had plenty of servants and plenty of magic to fill tubs with hot water.

"You may go, Morgan. I will finish myself and call for the bath to be emptied much later."

"Aye, my lord." Morgan hurried to the door and exited without looking back.

"You will make us the scandal of London, Marcus."

"My servants would never breathe a word of what goes on between us. Come and scrub my back," he said, looking her over.

"What do you think of my new gown?" she asked as she strolled toward him. The dark hair of his chest was matted against the swell of his muscles. He looked altogether edible.

"Very nice. Take it off so you don't get it wet."

"What do you have in mind?" she asked softly.

"For you to join me in this tub."

She looked at the door. "Will we be disturbed, do you think?"

"Nay," he said and caught her wrist when she was within his reach. He lifted the wrist and kissed her palm, making her shiver. He looked up at her through his dark lashes and murmured against her skin. "All day my mind was preoccupied with this moment, the moment when I would be alone with you and could take my pleasure again. Undress for me."

She tried to draw her hand back, but he didn't release it. "You must let go of me if you want me to undress."

He hesitated as if he didn't relish letting go of her even for a moment. She could feel the heat gathering inside her. He placed a rough kiss on the inside of her wrist and then relinquished it.

She took a shaky step back and removed her clothes. The raw hunger in his eyes made her almost weak with anticipation. He'd moved so that he was kneeling in the water.

She stood still, admiring the way he looked with the candlelight reflected off his glistening body. His powerful erection rose from the dripping thatch of wet hair. He leaned forward and caught her upper arms, dragging her forward. His mouth latched onto her pert pink nipple and he sucked desperately. He gripped her buttocks and she found her belly pressed to the rim of the tub.

He moved to the other breast, and she let her head fall back as she enjoyed the sensations, his arms cool and wet against her sides, his mouth hot and wet around her nipple, the cool dry air circling her. She put a hand on his head and slid her fingers into the silken strands of his hair. He groaned at the touch.

Suddenly, he let her go and stood up. He towered over her for a split second and then lifted her and set her down so she was standing in warm water in front of him. He turned her so that her back was to him and then pushed down on her shoulders as he descended into the water. They were both on their knees and he leaned forward and bit the place where her neck met her shoulder.

She gasped and tried to pull away from the sharp sensation, but his arms captured and held her. She could feel his stiff cock pressed insistently against her back. His mouth fed on her, alternately biting and sucking. Hot burning pleasure and pain seared her skin. He cupped her breasts, pinching the nipples. She was helpless, and she liked it.

She whimpered, feeling moisture leak from her lower lips. "Marcus, please."

"Aye, vixen, tell me what you want," he growled.

"Inside me," she said between tortured breaths. "Please. I can't wait."

"Nor I," he groaned and pushed her forward. She grasped the rim of the tub, her body bent in submission. He cupped her sex in front and she felt his organ probing her cleft. She wanted him deeply planted there. She spread her knees wide, opening for him, her thighs bumping against the sides of the tub. He pushed forward until his thick length was imprisoned snugly inside her.

"Oh, God," she panted as he started to move. Water sloshed around her lower body. He held her hips and drove in and out. The warm water swirled and caressed her. She arched, dipping her breasts into the water as she pushed back against him.

He roared and the thrusts became more frenzied. Twice she buckled, and her body sunk deep in the water. He withdrew suddenly, causing her to cry out in protest. She felt herself being lifted out of the tub.

She dangled from his arms, water dropping from her limbs and splattering on the wood floor as if she were a sopping rag doll. He gently set her down and she flipped over onto her back, stretching on the floor, arms and thighs wide open and welcoming. She stared up at him as he positioned himself between her legs and drove deep inside the moist cavern that waited for him.

He lowered his body onto hers until she was almost smothered by the wet heat of his chest. She gripped his lower body with her legs, her bottom rising off the floor as he fought to withdraw so that he could plunge again.

She wailed as she came, but he didn't seem to hear. He continued to pummel her unabated until he finally roared and his cock jerked in a series of hard spasms. Thick warmth pooled inside her, and she felt her womb throb with satisfaction. Her body belonged to his. It was amazing and frightening. And absolutely right.

She turned her face, rubbing her cheek against his chest before she nipped his thick right pectoral muscle. He didn't cringe or pull back as she assaulted him with her teeth. Wanting a reaction, she bit him hard enough that she knew that even he would get a bruise.

"Are you taking your revenge?" he asked in the deep lush voice that she loved.

"Just reminding you that I'm here," she teased.

"I can assure you, my lady, it had not escaped my attention." He moved onto hands and knees. "Come let me wash you before the water is too cold." He picked her up and set her back in the bath. He climbed in behind her. She sat completely still, as if she were a compliant child, while he gently washed every inch of her.

When they finished, he took her to his bed and curled his warm body around hers. He spoke low in her ear. "I will take you to the king tomorrow morning. He asks me to ride with a small contingent of knights to Scotland to deal with some trouble there. It will not take me long. I would not be surprised if he invites you to stay at court until my return. If he does, you will do so. It will be the safest place for you while I am gone."

"What did you tell him about me?"

"I told him that you have no family that we know of and that you have no memory of your childhood. You were living for several years with a family on my lands. The clothes you wore and your speech when you arrived told them you must have been noble-born, but you had had a bad fever and the attempts to find your family were in vain."

"Did he believe that?"

"I can not say. Edward is no fool, but my assistance in the form of both coin and sword has been valuable to him. I think he will not trouble himself much to find the truth."

"Will I use Ariana as my name?"

"You were never at court, were you?"

"No."

"And your father... 'tis years since he was last there I think. Aye, we may use your name. I prefer that we do use your real name, for it will be recorded when we marry. I should not like to have a false name used for that."

"So the king wasn't bothered by you marrying a woman of no apparent relations?"

"If he was, he did not show it." She was quiet for a moment, thinking that things were moving forward at an alarming clip. Once she was married to Marcus, there would be no turning back. He would own her and he certainly wouldn't be inclined to help her leave him then. Was she ready to let go of the future? The way he looked, so utterly gorgeous, certainly made a compelling argument for staying, but would they really be happy when the heat of sexual desire cooled? Could she ever really be content living with so many limits on her life?

As if he knew her will's silent protest, his arm tightened around her possessively.

"I should go back to my room," she said. "It would not do for us to be caught together."

"Nay, it would not, but we are nearly betrothed, and I find that I do not wish to be without you. Sleep, my love, and I will awaken you before dawn."

Her small hand gripped his muscled forearm. "Marcus?"

"Aye?" he murmured. His mouth was close to her head and his breath brushed against her hair.

"Will you promise me something?"

"Aye. At the moment, most anything you wish, I expect."

"Will you promise to always treat me well, even if you tire of me?"

"I will never tire of you, Ariana. I could not do it when I wished to, so I certainly do not expect to now that I do not. But if it pleases you to hear it then have my assurance, I will never treat you badly."

"It's easy to think you'd never get tired of me when I'm twenty-four. One day though, I'll be older and your body won't crave mine the way it does now. Maybe you'll see someone younger that you want. Promise me, you'll take me back to the other time before you take up with someone else."

He was silent.

"Promise," she said, poking him in the ribs.

"Nay."

She pulled herself out of his embrace and sat up. "You won't make that promise?"

He rolled onto his back and folded his arms across his chest. "Nay," he said bitterly.

"So if you decide to take up with someone else, you just expect me to suffer in silence?"

He sat bolt upright, facing her, and she felt his fury riding on the air. "If I were inclined to betray you with another woman, I would not be the man who lies with you right now. A promise that I make tonight could have very little value to that man."

"You could still make it... to ease my mind."

"Why should I when you offend me, not only by your assumption that I will betray you, but also because you injure me with your lack of feeling?"

"My lack of feeling?" she snapped. "I don't think I could stand it if you were with someone else—"

"Aye, your pride would not endure it."

"That's right. Men aren't the only ones who have pride. I know this time tolerates very little of that in women, but *I* have been elsewhere, and I do have my pride. Indeed it is the only thing I have left to me at present."

He punched his fist into the bed, then leapt out of it. "Am I not allowed a little pride as well, Ariana? How do you think it affects me when you beg for promises that would separate us rather than those that would keep us together? You could have asked me for a promise that I would always be faithful, but you do not ask for that. Must you torment me thusly when I am so unable to defend myself?

"God grant me an enemy I can run my sword through," he cursed, clenching his fists at his sides. He looked at her with wild eyes. "I am weak with love for you. It brings me to my very knees," he snarled. He slashed the air with his hand and the floor beneath him split with a horrible cracking sound. He stopped and stared down in surprise at the seam created by the split. He shook his head and then looked up at her. His voice was low but tightly controlled. "It is a dagger that you thrust into my heart with your indifference. If you are wise, you will not attack me with it again this night."

"I am not indifferent to you," she whispered truthfully.

"Are you not?" he asked bitterly. "Forgive me if it does not thrill me overmuch to be second in your heart after that precious other life you had in the future."

She sighed and put her head in her hands. "I can't help what I feel." She tried hard not to cry, but the tears came anyway.

She felt him sit next to her and gather her into his arms. She could feel that his anger was gone. "I am sorry," he said in a low firm voice. "Forgive me, Ariana." He stroked her back gently. "I have no right to demand anything from you. I kidnapped you from a life that made you happy. It is understandable that you do not trust me. I have exposed you to naught but my selfishness and jealousy from the first moment I retrieved you. I have no right to you. I know it. But even as I say the words my throat tries to close and prevent them being said."

He took a deep breath and let it out. "Still, I will take you back. God help me, I promise I will. Only let me beg a promise from you first. Give me a little time. It is misery for me without you. Please stay with me until I can work up the courage to let you go. I could not bear losing you today, but, in time, I will prepare myself. I swear it."

"Yes," she said, wiping away her tears.

"What?" he asked.

"Yes, I'll stay for a while." She paused. If he could compromise, so could she. At the moment it wasn't even difficult since she couldn't think of anything in the future that she'd miss half as much as him. It was crazy to be so in love with him in such a short time, but there it was. "Maybe for a very long while."

He crushed her to his chest and kissed her deeply then he set her away from him. "Now tell me about the other place. I would know what you loved so much about that time. Perhaps I can create the like for you here."

"You're powerful, Marcus, but I don't think even you are that powerful," she said, taking in a sniffling breath. "Anyway, I'm tired of talking. I should get some sleep; I don't want to be puffy-eyed when I meet the king."

"There is a good deal of time until morning."

She rolled her eyes and lay back on the bed. "We need sleep, Marcus."

He sighed. "Aye." He crawled on to the bed next to her and curled her back against his chest. She slid her hand down and intertwined their fingers. As she closed her eyes, she felt his warm lips brush against neck.

"Are you very tired then?"

She smiled. "No, not very."

He turned her in his arms and looked into her eyes. "We are quite well suited," he said, pressing his erection against her belly.

She put her arms around his neck. "Why? Because you like making love to me and I let you do it often?"

"Aye," he said with a grin. "And because you've an appetite for it to nearly match my own."

"Is that possible, do you think?" she teased.

"As possible as traveling through time, I suppose."

She nodded. "Unlikely, but possible," she whispered before she kissed him.

✻❨ʗƆ❩✻

Ariana's gown was blush-colored and only minimally embellished, but very elegant. The real allure was in the cut of the fabric and the way it caressed her slim curves. Marcus had been stealing glances at her, and she guessed by the look in his eyes that he must have felt that his coin had been well spent.

She followed him through the labyrinth of palace hallways and didn't even hesitate when they stopped in an alcove. She looked up at him expectantly as he took her face in his hands. He kissed her slowly.

He looked over his shoulder to be sure that no one else was nearby and then he kissed her again with a dark hunger that bruised her lips. He leaned back taking a deep breath and looking at her for a moment. "There is nothing about you that does not bewitch me."

She smiled at him, tracing the line of his jaw with her fingertip. "Ditto."

"What?"

"It means that I feel the same way about you," she explained softly. "The king awaits," she added when he seemed inclined to steal another kiss and possibly more.

"Aye," he said, drawing her out of the corner.

They met a page in the last hallway who took them past the guards posted outside the door of the king's chambers. As soon as she stepped inside, she knew there would be trouble.

"Blackmoor," her mother's brother, Walter, said with a smile. "It has been too long." Then his smile faded. "Ariana?" He strode forward on long thin legs and stopped in front of her, peering with great interest at her face. "Richard de Causton's daughter, Ariana? Aye, it is. We had given you up for dead. Where have you been, girl?" Her uncle's sharp features converged with suspicion, and he turned his face to scrutinize

Marcus. "Explain how my niece comes to be in your company, sir."

There was a murmur of excitement among the group in attendance, and the king stepped forward. She only had a moment to think that Edward's brown mustache was far too long before the king turned to Marcus and said, "It appears that the identity of the lady has been discovered."

"So it would seem," Marcus said mildly. He shrugged broad shoulders. "I am steadfast in my intent, Your Majesty. Knowing her identity, you can have no objection to the match."

"She has been missing for years...stolen from her father's house," her uncle snapped in outrage. "She must be returned."

"I did not steal her from her father's house," Marcus said calmly. "And she is well beyond the age of consent. Certainly I will be happy to take her to visit her family, and they will be welcome at Blackmoor."

Her uncle whirled on his heel to face her. "Come, girl, speak up. Did the earl kidnap you?"

"Nay," she said firmly.

"Then what happened to you?" All the men in the room turned their gazes upon her. She struggled to remember the story Marcus had concocted.

"I had a fever, which stole my memory from me," she stammered. "I was living with a family."

"What family?" he asked.

She couldn't remember the names of the peasants with whom she was supposed to have lived. She glanced at Marcus, begging him to send her the names telepathically, though she knew that that was not one of his gifts. Nothing came.

The king narrowed his brown eyebrows. "You must remember the family," he said. "Blackmoor told me you lived with them for some years."

"I—" she stammered. "Forgive me. My memory is very poor."

"Poisoned," Walter hissed. "Or bewitched. No girl of a mere four and twenty years is feeble. Your Majesty, I entreat you. Return her to her family where no outside influence may work evil on her mind."

She felt a swell of power in the room, and it choked the breath from her. She turned her head instantly to Marcus, but he was focused on where her uncle and King Edward were standing together. They had lowered their voices and were talking over what should happen to her. The king had the power to take her from Marcus, to deny the marriage and betroth her to someone else if that alliance would gain him more.

Ariana could feel Marcus' rage and power building at the possibility. Her skin tingled. It was amazing that no one in the room seemed to feel the magic rising. A thick black mist gathered and floated toward the men. Her skin burned as if she were standing too close to a blazing hearth.

She felt Marcus's will; no man, not even a king, would stand in his way. She knew what was about to happen. She saw in her mind's eye the king and her uncle fall and then the guards running Marcus through with their swords. A desperate panic took hold of her. She had to prevent him from striking, but she didn't know how.

Marcus spoke. "Your Majesty, I have been your faithful servant for many years. This woman chooses me and I choose her."

"Aye, Marcus," Edward said. "We have known each other many years. And in these many years, I have heard rumors of strange occurrences in conjunction with your person."

"Am I accused of sorcery?" Marcus asked mildly, but she felt his underlying passion taking hold. To ask such a question was mockery and threat mixed together. Toying with the sovereign could only bring about his own destruction. Marcus raised his hand, poised like a snake to strike.

She could think of only one way to draw Marcus's attention from the king; she must draw it to herself. She fisted her hands and then opened her mind forcefully sending what power she had outward in a kaleidoscope to Marcus. At the same moment, she said his name and pretended to swoon.

As she fell, she tried to keep herself from wincing. No one was close enough to catch her, and she knew she would strike the stone floor very hard.

Marcus caught her. He must have flung himself forward and slid to land beneath her because her head was cradled in his lap.

When she opened her eyes, there was a sea of concerned male faces above her.

"Are you all right, my dear?" the king asked gravely.

"She is not well," her uncle murmured.

She was tempted to tell them that she was pregnant with Marcus' baby. That would certainly end the debate over whether they should be married. If she were pregnant, feeble or not, she and Marcus would have to be married. She worried though, about retribution. Husbands died in battle. Her family might decide to have their revenge and Marcus' land in the process. Her father could be ruthlessly practical at times.

Edward cleared his throat and looked her over. "She will rest, and we will summon her family. Lord Blackmoor will ride to Scotland as planned and upon his return, he will have my decision." So the king had found a way to use Marcus while still reserving the right to defy his wishes. Clever Edward.

They began to lift her away from him, but Marcus moved swiftly and held her body cradled to his chest as he stood. The king cocked an eyebrow, but allowed him to take her to her room with her uncle chaperoning the journey. In the bed chamber, she squeezed Marcus's hand as he started to back away from her. "Be safe," she said softly.

His face was silent thunder. "I shall return for you with all haste," Marcus promised her. She felt a distinct chill as he left the room.

Marcus' absence stretched for weeks, leaving Ariana sullen with longing. Her father, who had always been prejudiced against Marcus, was easily worked on by her uncle. They were determined that Marcus would not have her when he did return. She found the pair of them and her new stepmother tedious. When she'd been younger, her father had intended for her to marry his friend, Lord Darlinge, who was sixteen years older than she. Apparently while she was gone, Darlinge had married and been widowed by the plague. Her father seemed to think they would still make a good match despite her argument that she wanted to marry Marcus. She suspected her father's insistence had to do with a long-coveted parcel of land that he expected to get from Darlinge.

She had no idea what the king's decision would be with regard to Marcus' suit. He needed Marcus to suppress the conflicts within his kingdom, but an alliance with her father and Darlinge would also benefit the king. Of course, if Edward defied Marcus, the consequences for the king might be severe, monarch or no.

Ariana doubted that weeks without access to her body was going to bring Marcus home in good humor. Her dreams had become increasingly dark and erotic. She wondered if he were sending messages to her subconscious or if the dreams were the product of her own imagination. She couldn't deny that she missed him desperately. There was a dull ache in her breast that nothing seemed to ease.

Court should have been a good diversion for her attention, but it wasn't. It was peculiar and isolating not to be allowed to join the men as they discussed things like the primitive bank networks created by the Florentines. She wanted to play the prophet and tell them how international banking would evolve over the centuries, but she didn't. And their disdain for members of the merchant class who were using money to buy land and to move up within the societal strata infuriated her. To her mind, the meritocracy in America was far superior to any of the world's aristocracies, but she was not allowed to offer her opinion. *I am a stranger in my own land,* she thought countless times. Conversation with the women didn't interest her. They were consumed with gossip and fished for details about her past and the time she'd spent with Marcus. They sniffed scandal and were anxious to have the whole story. She did her best to avoid them, spending most of her time in her chamber or in the garden, waiting and wishing for Marcus, the only person who truly knew her, the only person she could talk to.

She was sitting quietly in the garden when she finally overheard that the Earl of Blackmoor was in the castle. She froze for a moment and then leapt to her feet. She crossed to the fluttering ladies who were talking. She pushed back an ivy vine and leaned close to where they sat on the white stone bench.

"Where is he? The earl, where is he?"

"In a private audience with the king," one of the women drawled softly.

She heard the echoes of their laughter as she ran to find Marcus. She didn't remember passing the halls that led to the king's chambers, she only knew that she raced to get there. She panted as she sat down on a bench across from the door to the antechamber.

She waited for what felt like hours and then the door swung open. She saw the people who were waiting to see the king. And then she saw Marcus.

She'd forgotten how big he was. He filled the doorway. He had weeks' worth of a black beard and his hair hung past his shoulders in thick waves. He looked like a menacing barbarian.

He stopped when he saw her and blinked. "Are you real or apparition?" he asked in his soft baritone. She hopped off the bench and into his arms. "Still light as a feather, but flesh despite that fact," he said with a chuckle.

"Is it good news then? Will he let you have me?"

"Nay," he said with a rueful smile. "He has found that stalling is a better tactic. While he delays in his decision, he may use me to his full advantage and placate your father and Darlinge. The king realizes, you see, that I will do anything that he commands to secure the right to marry you. Now he sends me to France."

"No!" she nearly shouted. She slapped his chest as if it were his fault. "No. You will not leave me here again."

He hugged her to him and whispered in her ear so that the guards could not hear. "Nay, I will not."

She looked up at him expectantly. He drew her down the hall and when they rounded a corner, he pulled her into an alcove. She waited for him to speak, but he just stared at her. "Well?" she asked.

"It feels an age since I have stood this near to you. Allow me to savor it for a moment."

She smiled at him. It was gratifying to know that she'd been missed too, but she only had a moment to bask in the thought before he swept her up in his arms and kissed her until she was half dazed. After he set her down, it took her a moment to focus on what he was saying.

"...I could not come for you because I could not sense exactly where you were without the magic connecting us. Take a bit of my power with a kiss that I may return at will and take you from this place."

"Yes," she said, grabbing a handful of his long hair and pulling his face down. She murmured the words and tasted his lips, his beard tickling her skin. Lust poured over her as he kissed her, and his power slithered deep into her body, stretching and filling her with crackling heat. She shuddered, thrilled at the renewed depth of their magical connection. *You are mine. I am yours. Forever.*

"At such moments, I know not if you be angel or maid. I know only that I would draw my sword on the devil himself for the taste of your lips."

She could not find her voice to tell him that she felt just as overwhelmed by the taste of him. He ran a hand over her cheek, their faces still close together.

"Let me die with your kiss on my mouth, and I swear I will not despair in death."

The thought that the king could continue to send him into battles where he might indeed be killed struck her like a hammer to the chest. She felt tears in her eyes, but blinked them away, determined not to let fear destroy her joy at seeing him. "I hope it does not come to that very soon. You are young, my lord. I think there is time yet for kissing without death hot on your heels."

He tipped his head back and laughed. "Forgive me, my lady. My heart runs away with me at the sight of you. I have known naught but trouble and swordplay for too long."

"Then kiss me again and remember that you are safe in my arms now."

"So much time spent at court, you sound like you are of this time again."

"Does that please you?"

"The manner of your speech matters little, but, aye, you please me…in the sight and sound and smell of you. And most especially the feel of you. That pleases me very much."

He pressed his lips to hers, and let his tongue explore her mouth. The kiss started soft, but then turned rougher with emotions so raw they made her tremble. The small invasion of her mouth was a promise, an echo of the ways he had already and would again invade her body given the chance. And she wanted him more than she'd ever wanted anything in her life.

There was a noise behind him, and he drew back slowly. She tried to hold on to him, but he extracted himself from her grasp with a soft laugh of delight at her reluctance to let him go. He looked over his shoulder and waved at the pair of young knights who were standing behind him.

"We will return the lady to her chamber," the light-haired one said.

Marcus turned and took a step toward them. He towered over them and looked at least ten years older than either of them, but they stood their ground with grave expressions.

"Marcus," she said, catching his hand as she stepped around him.

"Aye, my lady?" He looked from her face down to where she held his hand and then back to her face again.

"I missed you. Do not stay away so long again."

"I will do my best," he said and understanding passed between them. She would go now, with the promise that he would retrieve her very soon.

"Come, my lady," one of the knights said, taking her free arm.

"One moment," she said, trying to pull her arm from the knight's grasp.

"Nay, come now—" he began.

"Take your hand off her, boy, or lose it," Marcus growled.

The young knight puffed his chest out like a preening peacock. Marcus' boot caught him in the gut, driving him back. Her arm slipped free of the stunned knight's grip as he fell. He scrambled to get up, but found the tip of Marcus' sword on his chest, pinning him down.

Marcus' gaze swiveled to the other knight whose hand was on his own sword hilt.

"Draw that sword, and I will spill your blood," Marcus said with an icy calm that underscored his very serious intent. Marcus turned his head a fraction of an inch toward her and he winked. "Now then, my lady, your escorts have decided that you may take your time and speak to me for as long as you like."

She fought not to smile. She was afraid that if she and Marcus seemed to be laughing at them, the young men might decide that death was more palatable than ridicule.

"I only wanted to tell you one thing," she said, fighting to keep her voice neutral.

"Aye, go ahead."

"It is private, my lord. Bend down a little so that only your ear may hear."

He studied the knights as he bent his head.

"I love you," she whispered.

His eyes widened, and then he sheathed his sword in a single fluid motion. He turned to her and pulled her into his arms. She felt her feet leave the ground. He buried his lips in her hair, kissing her several times.

"Marcus," she gasped. Both knights had drawn their swords and were jabbing him in the back and flank.

He hugged her tighter to him. "Tell me again."

"You need to put me down," she said eyeing the pair of younger men who looked just as murderous as Marcus had a moment before.

"Tell me again first. These pups won't run me through for kissing you, for they would have trouble explaining to their king why his favorite instrument of death was stabbed in the back. I killed forty men at Crecy. He will not take my loss lightly when I have promised to kill double that number of Frenchmen upon my return to battle there." His voice was confident, and the knights stopped their prodding.

"My Lord, you will unhand that lady that we may escort her back to her chamber...for that too was an order from the king," the shorter, darker of the two knights said soberly.

Marcus grinned. "If you value my life, you will tell me again quickly. Your escorts grow impatient."

"I love you," she said softly.

His onyx eyes glittered with happiness. "And I, you," he returned equally softly. He set her on her feet then and took a step back in withdrawal. He placed his hands on his head as if to signify that he wouldn't hinder the young knights any further.

They eyed him suspiciously, waving impatiently for her to precede them down the hall.

"Soon," Marcus called after her.

She glanced back to see his brilliant white smile, framed as it was between the midnight black hair of his mustache and beard.

Marcus materialized at Ariana's bedside. The partial darkness didn't hinder him. Now that she was connected to him once more through his power, he could feel her and find her wherever she was.

She was still asleep and serenely beautiful. He stood over her for several moments, just feasting on her with his eyes. It gave him unmitigated joy to be in her presence. It also squeezed his heart because he knew it would not be for long.

Then, as if she could feel him too, she opened her eyes and focused them on him.

"Hello, Marcus," she said with a sleepy smile. She sat up slowly. "You're supposed to be on your way to France."

"The king agreed to let me have a few days of rest before I leave."

She rubbed her eyes. She was so small, so fragile. And yet she could withstand whatever his body offered. It amazed him.

"I want to go with you to France," she mumbled.

"Nay," he said with a short laugh. "Much as it drives me mad to have you away from me, even I would not take you to a battlefield."

"I want to be with you. I think I may have a talent for concealment. I concentrated hard and made a piece of parchment disappear for several minutes. You can teach me and protect me while I learn."

He shook his head.

She reached over and touched his arm softly. "It's not safe for me here."

"In what way not safe?"

"Darlinge comes often. The king insists that I see him when he comes."

Marcus waved a dismissive hand. "To placate your father and uncle. My help is more important to the king than Darlinge will ever be."

She looked down at her hands and he knew that there was something she wasn't telling him. A little curl of fear twisted inside him. He was afraid of nothing, save losing her.

He gripped her chin gently and turned her face up to his. "What more troubles you about staying at court?"

"You must promise not to do anything rash."

"You have my promise."

"I think the king is interested in me."

He raised his eyebrows. "In what way?"

"Twice I've been brought to him. He claims that he wishes to see to my comfort at court, but he could do so without giving me a private audience. It seems to me he could send someone to check on me."

Marcus frowned. She was right. Edward was quite practical and endlessly busy. He wouldn't bother to hold an audience with someone unless he so desired. On the other hand, Edward wasn't known for wasting his time in the wooing of innocent young women.

"What did the two of you talk about?"

She shrugged. "It was odd really. He asked how I was doing. I told him the truth."

"Which was?"

"That I missed you. That I was anxious for your return and that I was hopeful that he would agree to us getting married."

"How did he respond?"

"It was awkward. He nodded, but didn't really answer. He asked me questions about you. He wanted to know what you're like in unguarded moments. I think he admires you, but he's wary of you too."

As well he should be if he meets with you alone.

"He's not very good with women, I don't think. I don't find him charming."

"Kings and fighting men do not have much practice, I'm afraid. We are bound to disappoint."

"We?" she echoed and shook her head. "I don't put you in a category with him."

"No?" Marcus had never been considered charming any more than the king had.

"When I talk to you, you listen. I like being in your company."

That warmed his whole body.

"But the king is distracted. It's fairly clear that he doesn't think that a woman has anything interesting or important to say. During the second audience with him, I just stopped trying to make conversation. I sat there in silence, and so did he. And just when I was fighting the urge to roll my eyes and ask if I were dismissed, he squeezed my hand

and told me that I was not to tell anyone about our meetings. I haven't seen him since then, but the queen is leaving in a few days. And you go to France."

Anger tightened his muscles. Was Edward really trying to seduce Ariana? If so, Marcus would have to stop him, but there was no easy way to circumvent Edward's power while he was alive. *I may have to kill him.*

"We should leave this time. There's no easy way to defy him here," Ariana said.

He sighed. She had almost read his mind, though her solution was different. "I could protect you best by sending you back to the time I stole you from. Then you would be free of all the men who wish to imprison you," he conceded.

"Including you?" she asked.

He nodded and held his breath. He wanted her to forbid him to send her away.

"We should both go," she said, moving so that she was kneeling upright. Her bright eyes implored him.

"I can not live there," he said regretfully. Much as he wanted to be with her, there was nothing for him in the future. She'd told him nobility no longer ruled and that there were no knights left. A man could not even hire out his sword. Indeed, men did not even carry swords. It had taken him years to perfect his technique. To know that the weapons of the future were as foreign to him as some languages unsettled him. A great many things about her favored time unsettled him.

"Why not?"

"I would have no title or property."

"I didn't have anything when I went there. The—"

"You're a woman. A woman may rely on others for her keep. A man must make his own way."

"You could do it after you got used to things and learned how they are there. It's easy to make a living there, for someone who's willing to work hard. There are a lot of things you could do. And if you were willing to sell your mother's jewelry it would net you a small fortune. You'd have wealth to start out with." She swung her long soft hair over her shoulder and climbed off the bed. She moved close to him, her intoxicating scent reaching his nostrils.

He took a step back so that it would be easier to concentrate. "I do not belong there."

She smiled at him bewitchingly and tugged the shift up to reveal her shapely calves. "I thought we belonged together." She pulled the shift slightly higher to show her knees. "The king's set on sending you off to get murdered. My family's ready to marry me off to someone else. Back in the future we could be free. We could get married and live however we wanted. No one could demand you go to fight. No one could take me away from you. We could be together every night." She pulled the shift over her head, revealing her naked body to him.

His cock stiffened instantly. She stepped forward boldly and placed her palms against his chest.

"Think of it, Marcus. There would be no waiting for a king's blessing which may never come. Haven't you waited long enough to claim my body? All those years of trying to find me, wasn't that long enough?" She stretched her arms over her head. Her breasts rose a few inches closer to his mouth. "You could have me in your bed every night. You could do whatever you wanted to me," she whispered.

The blood roared in his ears, and he bent his head to take one succulent nipple between his lips. Ariana slid her fingers into his hair, stroking his scalp sensuously. His arms wrapped around her as if they had a will of their own, and he straightened up, lifting her from the floor. He suckled her hungrily until she was writhing.

Her sweet voice drifted to his ears, begging him to make love to her. His body screamed for him to comply. There was no use resisting, and he carried her to the bed and dropped her on it. He shed his clothes quickly, tearing things in his haste.

As he climbed on the bed, she spread her glorious thighs to welcome him home. He didn't hesitate. He took his phallus, heavy with blood and probed her moist slit with it. He found the entrance and sunk down into her body. For several moments, he didn't move. It felt so good to be inside her that he had to savor the sensation.

Then she struggled beneath him, trying to move her hips. He had her lower body pinned, and he smiled down at her. "Patience," he teased.

"No," she pouted and slapped his arms in frustration.

He grabbed her wrists and pinioned them above her head. She twisted furiously and he watched her face flush with the exertion and her breasts bounce as she struggled to free her arms. His staff grew longer and more rigid inside her.

Finally she went still, panting from the fruitless battle. "Damn you, Marcus," she snapped, her eyes glittering in the low light.

"Nay, vixen, no cursing. You must beg me for what you want. And very sweetly if you want the task done properly."

His teasing had the desired effect. She began to struggle again in earnest, and she cursed him vehemently. He laughed softly, bending to nip the peak of her breast. Her moan was louder than was strictly safe if they wanted to avoid discovery. He moved his mouth over hers to swallow the sounds she made as he started to grind his pelvis into hers. She continued to move beneath him as if she were something wild that needed to be tamed. It drove him to new heights of pleasure.

He groaned deeply as he felt her tight walls contract around him. He moved so that he could see her face as she tipped her head back and gasped for breath. He loved the way she looked, completely vulnerable in her ecstasy.

Moments later, he reached his own ecstasy, spending inside her hot folds. He collapsed on top of her soft body for a moment, enjoying the feel of her smooth skin against his.

He felt her try to move her head and he eased himself up and off her. He drew her wrists, which he was still holding, up to his lips and kissed one then the other and laid them gently on the bed.

She stared up at him. "I hope he's as beautiful as you are," she said.

"Who?"

"The baby we just made."

He froze and looked down at her belly as if it would be glowing or showing some other telltale sign. He shook his head at himself. He had known enough women to know that a woman could not feel anything as soon as this. He looked back at her face and arched a skeptical eyebrow. "You need not tease me, Ariana, with phantom infants. I will not leave you here unprotected."

She levered herself up on her elbows to look at him and smiled. "I know that. You couldn't see your face when I told you that I loved you, but I could. You'll never leave me, and I'll never leave you. Nothing will separate our two hearts. Not even a king." She spoke with such conviction. It took his breath away to hear her proclaim that they would be together forever.

He ran a hand through his damp hair and marveled again at her ability to surprise and overwhelm him. She was just one small woman, not particularly formidable. He could pin her to the bed as easily as take a breath, and yet she held his soul in the palm of her hand just as effortlessly. He marveled at the nature of love that it could make men and women partners in such an elegant dance where each partner controlled and pleased the other.

"And, by the way, I wasn't teasing you," she said.

He came off his palms, straightening up onto his knees and looked down at her belly.

"How do you know my child is in there?"

She placed her hand flat against her abdomen, just below the belly button. "I feel the tingle of your power inside me. It feels very much like when I took that wisp of power from you during the kiss."

He backed up on his knees and leaned down, face near her navel. He nudged her hand up with his nose and kissed the place where it had been resting. She touched the top of his head and twisted a lock of his hair around her finger.

"Hardly any men wear long hair in the future."

"If you prefer it shorter, I will cut it for you," he said, licking her lower belly.

"You will *not* cut it. I like it long."

"What of my beard? Shall I cut that? If not, I fear we may get tangled up down here," he teased as he rubbed his chin languidly over her mound.

She laughed. "You are very wicked."

He tilted his head down and bit the fleshy pad gently. She sucked in a breath in surprise. The sound of her gasp pleased him.

He moved his arms, pushing her thighs further apart. "Open for me. I would like to give my child a kiss."

"Marcus," she murmured in a breathless voice. He smiled just before he slid his tongue inside her.

❧✶❀✶❧

Ariana pulled the cloak tight about her shoulders and followed Marcus into the royal chapel.

"What are we doing here?" she whispered when she saw the priest and her father standing together near the altar.

"We are to be betrothed."

Her heart started to pound in excited anticipation. She studied her father's grim expression. Could it be true? "He agreed?"

"He did."

"What of the king?"

"He will agree also."

"Marcus, what have you done?" She looked up at his handsome face as he shrugged. He was as dark as the devil's own, and therefore not capable of looking truly innocent, but, at the moment, Marcus's face was open and agreeable...as if he hadn't had to use threats or violence to get his own way in the matter of their engagement. She narrowed her eyes.

"How did you convince my father?" she demanded.

His fingertips inconspicuously brushed the fabric of her dress over her belly, reminding her of the secret life she hid there. "Does it matter?" he asked.

She hesitated for only a second. Whatever he'd done to bring about the engagement, it was worth it. After all, her father looked perfectly healthy; Marcus hadn't spilled anyone's blood. And they *were* meant to be together. "No, it doesn't matter."

He led her to the priest who looked rather dazed, but he performed his part flawlessly. Marcus sealed the betrothal with a kiss and then a marriage gift. The fabric was soft and intricately patterned. Cloth was valuable, and this was more so than most, exotic as it was. Some merchant had traveled for weeks or months to bring it from some faraway place to England.

"It's beautiful. I love you," she whispered against his lips. Power arced between them, making her skin tingle from the inside.

Her father snorted. "I shall expect payment within a fortnight as you promised, Blackmoor. I trust you will not sample the goods and then say the cost is too high."

She gasped at the crude statement, but Marcus kissed the side of her mouth gently before turning his head to look at her father. "It is you who set the cost too low."

Her father's eyes widened at that, but Marcus turned from him and led her down the chapel's aisle and out the door.

"So we are promised," she said happily.

"Aye." He ran a fingertip along her jaw. "Your skin glows. The moon must be jealous of your radiance and the sun will soon follow."

"It must be the pregnancy," she whispered.

"Then I must keep you always with child." He strode to his horse and mounted it. He reached down and picked her up, setting her sideways in front of him.

"Will the king be angry about the betrothal?"

Marcus shrugged and rode out into the field behind the chapel.

"Now, what are you about?" she asked as he stopped the horse and slid down.

"I mean to sample the goods," he said, flashing a grin.

"What, here?" she gasped as he lifted her from the horse.

He nodded. "Why not? The morning sun is warm and high enough to give God a view of the union He blessed today."

"You best not mock God, Marcus."

"I certainly do not. I made my promise in His chapel, did I not?" He caught her arms and pulled her to him.

The kiss that followed made her mind fuzzy and her legs weak. He lowered her to the ground. Moments later, he'd moved her skirts up and slid into her, seating himself deeply. She purred in his ear, gripping his shoulders. It took less than a dozen strokes for the spasms to start.

As the passion ebbed and flowed, she heard a sound, something like the cracking of a twig. Had the horse wandered near? She grasped the back of his neck. "I heard something."

"'Tis my heart." He bent his head and pressed his lips to hers. His tongue thrust in her mouth echoing the invasion of his smooth hard erection. A few moments later she felt his warm fluids mixing with hers.

Afterward, they lay together still and spent until he finally adjusted his clothes and then hers. He stood and lifted her to her feet, kissing the top of her head. "There may be whispers at the castle. You will not let it trouble you."

"What whispers?"

"We were seen."

What? What! "The noise I heard?"

He nodded.

"Why didn't you stop when you heard them coming?"

"I arranged for us to be seen."

Her mouth fell open in shock.

"Betrothals are not necessarily binding except when the union is consummated. No one, not even King Edward, will be able to interfere now that I have had you and there are witnesses to it."

She slapped his arm. "You put the worst plotters to shame."

"I did what I must to keep you with me."

"You could have told me what you had planned."

"I was not sure you would have the nerve to go through with it."

She grabbed his hand and squeezed it hard, pinching the skin. He raised his eyebrows in surprise. "I'm your wife now. No more plans that you don't tell me about. We share everything from now on." He stared at her. "Promise me."

"Aye, but not because you are my wife," he said, putting her hand over his left chest. "Because you are my heart."

And you mine. She smiled and pulled him down for a kiss then shook her head. "We were seen making love in a field less than an hour after our betrothal. At court, they will think us consumed with lust and completely shameless."

"Aye. They have been trying to learn of my true nature for years. Today, they have their wish."

She laughed. "But you've dragged me down with you. We're a pair now," she said, walking over to the horse and running a hand over its sleek flank.

Marcus dropped a kiss on her head and remounted the horse. He took her arms and pulled her up in front of him, and they rode back to the castle at a full gallop. Ariana kept her head high and the wind in her face, feeling free for the first time in ages. She decided that love was very liberating and quite magical in its own right.

⁂

"I will escort Ariana to Blackmoor and then continue on to France," Marcus said.

Edward's eyes were steady and cold as they measured him.

"You mean to take her to Blackmoor before the wedding?"

"I do. She is already my wife."

"I had heard that," the king said, walking over to the table and taking up a goblet of wine. He took a drink. "You seemed quite anxious to make it so." A bit of amusement showed on Edward's face. "I trust from now on we will not have you frightening the field mice."

Marcus laughed. "Nay. I am done with fields."

"Except battlefields, I trust."

"Aye. As I said, I go to France as planned."

"Your young wife must be nervous about you leaving so soon. Are you sure it would not be better to leave her here? Court can offer distractions."

Their eyes locked. He wondered if Edward were baiting him. "She prefers to wait at our home."

"To worry alone?"

"Nay. She does not fear for my life. Ariana believes me to be indestructible."

"Touched as you are with the devil's magic?" Edward asked curiously.

"Nay, I do not believe that is what she thinks, but then I am newly married and she is a mystery still."

"A mystery and, yet, you risk much to claim her."

Marcus shrugged. "It is a love match. She is for me as England is for you."

Edward glanced out the window. "If that is so, then fortune has smiled upon you, my friend. Take your wife home."

❧〰(⁂)〰❧

Many weeks had passed since Marcus had left Blackmoor for France. The rigors and ravages of the battlefield had not left him free to use magic to visit Ariana's bed during the time away and she was on his mind constantly, though lately it was concern more than lust that made him wish to see her. As he rode home with his men, he worried that she was not well. One of his men had lost a wife in childbirth while they were fighting. Marcus had been thinking about that often since they'd heard. Normally such news didn't affect him, but now that he had a young wife of his own, who carried his child, he couldn't help but be troubled by it. He shuddered at his dark thoughts and shook them off. She must be well. If she were ill, surely she'd have drawn power from him to heal herself, and he would have felt it.

When he reached the castle, he dismounted quickly and hurried up the stone steps. "Ariana!" he called.

Joan stepped into his path. "My lord, you are home."

"Aye, where is my lady?"

"She is resting after tending the stable master's wife."

"My wife is well?"

"Aye. Only tired."

"What ails Cathy?" Marcus asked, wondering after the stable master's wife.

"She lost another babe and the fever left her poorly."

Marcus' heart nearly stopped for a moment. He did not want to hear about women losing babes or being consumed with fever from childbed.

"At first Cathy would not eat except when your lady sat with her. So she went to her every day. The girl, Cathy, is better now, but the lady, Ariana, needs her rest, so ye can just come with me—"

"Joan," Marcus growled. "I want to see her."

"And ye will not tax her overmuch?" Joan demanded.

"Nay."

Joan stepped out of his way. He liked to see Joan protective of Ariana. She had obviously won over the castle while he was gone. He wasn't surprised. It was impossible not to love his wife. He hurried down the hall to their bedchamber.

He found her sitting up on the bed with parchment and quill in hand. Her face lit up when she saw him, and she quickly discarded what she was doing in favor of coming to him. He caught her in his arms and hugged her to him.

"Are you well?" he asked.

"Yes. Are you?"

"Oh, aye. A few scratches from battle."

She lifted his hands to her lips and kissed them.

"Joan tells me that a fever swept through. I never felt you draw power from me to heal the sick. Why not?"

"There were too many. And I was afraid to pull power from you while you were in battle. I didn't want you to get distracted and maybe get hurt." She paused and looked at the floor, then sighed. "I'd better tell you before you hear it from someone else and rage at them. I was sick myself for a few days, but I'm fine. The baby's fine."

"You?" he murmured, feeling cold dread wash over him. "You should have drawn power to heal yourself. It would not distract me enough to endanger me," he lied. He would rather fall in battle than come home to find her dead. He never wanted her to hesitate to save herself at his expense. "You must promise me to always tend yourself no matter what—" His words trailed off as she shook her head.

"I can't heal myself. The power doesn't work that way. I can only help other people."

He swallowed hard. Healing was not one of his gifts. If she were to bleed overmuch or to get a fever in childbirth, she would slip away from him. He couldn't believe he hadn't thought to ask her about this before. He had just assumed she could draw power from him when she needed it to tend herself.

He had plenty of strength to give her, but it seemed that it would do them no good. His mind searched for a solution. He would not lose her. He cared for nothing else, save keeping her safe.

Then her talk of the future came to him. She had said that women survived the childbed there. He had resisted the idea of going to the future because it seemed unnatural for them to live there, but he could not accept her death in childbirth or from one of the many illnesses that swept through...

"Marcus," she said, softly touching his arm. "I am well."

"Aye," he said.

"So tell me what happened in France," she said with a bright smile.

"We won all of our battles," he said absently, looking her over. She looked hale. She looked beautiful.

"I wanted you to do well in battle, but maybe not that well. Edward will want to send you back over there while I want to keep you here with me," she said, sliding her hands onto his shoulders. She kissed him, making the thoughts fly from his head. "I missed you," she said.

He stared at her mouth. "And I you." He kissed her again. "Welcome me home. Then there is something I wish us to discuss."

Southern Italy in late summer was hot and sultry, but Marcus liked the breeze from the Mediterranean so he'd turned off the air conditioning and opened the bedroom windows overlooking the terrace. He set down his pencil, studying the sketch. Another big house. Each time he started a new design, he planned to draw something modest in size, but whenever he took pencil in hand he produced a mansion. A leftover addiction to grandeur from the days he'd lived in a castle, he supposed. Still, the intimacy of the places they lived in now suited him very well. There was really no need for places larger than four thousand square feet when there were no servants to house.

"What time is it?" Ariana mumbled.

He took a sip of the rich Italian burgundy and glanced over at his wife. Her diaphanous nightgown matched the billowing sheers that the wind was blowing into the bedroom. "Late."

"Then why am I awake?" she wondered.

"Because you slept through most of the day," he said with a slow smile.

"It's so warm." She moved and her full breasts strained against the front of the gown.

He licked his lips as his cock stirred to life. He stood. Her gaze was heavy-lidded as he pulled the white v-neck t-shirt over his head. He tossed the shirt on the desk chair and unzipped his jeans. He shoved them and the briefs he wore underneath down and off. His cock stood proud and ready against his stomach.

"Is that for me?" she teased.

"Who else?" he asked, walking over to the nightstand. He lifted the bottle of olive oil he'd put there earlier and dripped some into his hand.

"Olive oil?" she asked. Her eyes were open now.

"Certainly olive oil. We're in Italy," he said by way of mock explanation. He rubbed the oil up and down the length of his erection.

Her hand went to her swollen belly as if to protect their unborn child from its fiendish father. "Why do we need oil, Marcus?"

"Why do you think?" he asked, the edges of his mouth twitching up as he climbed on the bed.

"I'm still sore from the last time I let you."

He slapped her backside playfully. "You are not. That was a week ago."

"You're too big for that kind of sex. When are you going to accept that fact?"

When your protests turn sincere, he thought, but held his tongue.

"And," she added, "at the moment, I'm too big to be crawling around on all fours."

"You can lie on your back if you prefer," he said with a casual shrug. She was toying with him. They'd had every kind of sex that he could think of... or that he could read about. The twenty-first century was amazing; almost anyone could have a library full of books. In 1349, it hadn't been very long since parchment had been invented and books were scarce treasures. Now, they were plentiful, and he could learn anything he wished to know about, airplanes, architecture, electricity, war, history, and, of course, sex.

"Will you be gentle?" she asked.

"If my lady likes," he said amiably.

"Well, enjoy yourself. This is probably the last time I'll let you do it."

"As you wish," he said, suppressing a smile.

She moved onto her hands and knees. He slid the nightgown up, exposing her round bottom. Childbearing had made her curves fuller and more luscious. And the hormones made her crave sex almost much as he did.

He studied the picture she made from his vantage point. Her ripe belly hanging down, framed by her smooth thighs. Plump sex pink and puffy, glistening with excited moisture. And her buttocks twitching, hiding the tight rosette between them.

He gripped her cheeks and spread them. That movement alone made her sway and moan. He rubbed the tip of his cock back and forth over the ring, oiling it and applying steady pressure.

Her body trembled slightly as if fearful. His cock bobbed impatiently, her show of nervousness whetting his appetite. He pushed against her insistently until she relaxed. He gripped her hip with one hand, holding her firmly as he moved the dark purple, bulbous head inside. She whimpered.

He had only partially impaled her, but he waited. The ring was stretched taut around his thick cock. The sight of it turned him on as much as the feel. He slid his hand around her and rubbed the bud of her clitoris, making it stiffen and protrude past its hood.

"Oh God, Marcus," she moaned. "I can't." Even as she said the words she pushed back against him.

His eyes rolled back at the sensation of being held so tightly inside her body.

"Please," she cried, moving forward and then back, burying him inside her bottom. He took a deep breath, fighting the urge to thrust. He always let her set the pace in the beginning.

He crushed her clit against her pelvic bone until she was gasping and begging him to make her come. Her first orgasm always gave him license to move as he wanted. Caught up in her own pleasure, she spasmed around him, but never tried to resist him.

He thrust back and forth, very gently at first and then more forcefully as she pushed her bottom hard against him. His balls tightened as they pressed against her hungry sex. He pushed two fingers into her creamy vagina, gripping her in front with his hand even as he sundered her back hole.

She shuddered and sobbed, making all his muscles contract. She was so good at playing the reluctant innocent, coaxing him to dominate her. His scrotum burned and the flames licked up from stem to cock tip.

She cried out again, and the ring throbbed around him, pulsing like a heartbeat. He groaned, thrusting deep and gushing boiling seed into her.

He softened and slipped out, and she fell down onto her side, panting. He leaned over to kiss her and found that her lashes were wet with tears. His heart constricted with guilt.

"I'm sorry," he said sincerely.

She smiled and shook her head at him. "I'm fine. It's just intense."

"I won't do it again."

She laughed softly, sniffling at the same time. "Yes, you will."

"I won't if you don't want me to," he protested.

"That's the problem, Marcus. I will want you to. I like the way it makes me feel to let you have me that way."

He leaned forward and kissed her damp cheeks, savoring the salty taste. "I don't want to hurt you."

She ran a finger over one of the scars on his chest. "Sometimes a little pain is the price of something great." He glanced down at the scars. They'd faded for a while until she'd gone back to magical healing. Now she had more control over her power and she could draw some from him without opening wounds, but the old scars sometimes became red and ached when she worked. He'd decided that a little soreness was a small price to pay for healing people and for seeing Ariana so happy.

"I'm going to take a shower," he said.

She nodded, and he covered her up. He closed the windows and French doors and locked them, then strode over to the main door to the bedroom and unlocked it. He slipped into the hall and put the air conditioner on before returning to the master bathroom.

The cool shower felt good on his skin. He never seemed to get over the magic of turning a knob and having hot water spray out. He washed slowly and then rinsed for several minutes. Shades of heaven…having sex with his beautiful wife and taking a long shower afterward. He toweled himself off and strolled back out into the bedroom.

"Marc! Marc!" The insistent high-pitched voice rang out from beyond the door.

Shaking his head, he yanked on his jeans. He zipped carefully and then strode out of the bedroom, down the hall and into the nursery. He flicked the switch and flooded the room with light. In one crib, his eleven-month-old son was lying on his back, sucking his thumb and, no doubt, dreaming of Mommy, his favorite person. In the crib on the opposite side of the room, his black-haired two-year-old daughter tilted her head and chirped, "Marc."

He rolled his eyes and picked her up. "Not Marc. Daddy," he corrected. When she'd been younger, he'd taken her with him everywhere. She'd heard so many people call him Marc that she refused to call him "Daddy" as if that were not his real name, but some alias that she was too smart to fall for.

"Want it," she said, pointing to Cameron's bottle.

"That's your brother's bottle. You want your—"

"Want it!" Jessica snapped, holding out her hand. The bottle wobbled.

"Hey," he said in a low growl and carried her out of the room. He'd bound her powers, but not tightly enough. She had felt it when he bound them completely, and she screamed endlessly until he released them. She seemed to feel magic as well as her mother could. The trouble was that Jessica hadn't just inherited minor powers like Ariana's. She'd also gotten universe-cracking magic from him.

"Mommy, baby," she said.

He wondered wryly why Ariana got to be Mommy and he got to be Marc. "Mommy and the baby are sleeping. It's late."

"Wash machine?"

He chuckled. "Nay."

"Aye," she chirped, making him laugh harder. He'd gotten used to saying yes and no, but when she'd been learning to talk, he'd still slipped often.

He'd also been fascinated with the washer and dryer and had frequently taken her into the laundry room of their American house to watch the clothes get tossed about.

"Mommy, baby!" she called.

"Shhh!" he admonished.

"Mommy! Baby!" she screamed.

"Hey," he growled, frowning at her.

She giggled, sending her dark curls into a dance. She clutched his arm. "Mommy. Now," she added impatiently.

Once upon a time, grown men had cowered before his displeasure. Clearly those days were gone, he thought wryly.

He glanced at the bedroom door in surprise as it opened. Ariana stood, framed in a halo of light. Her hair was wet. She'd apparently taken a shower too.

"Mommy," Jessica squealed happily, thrusting her arms out.

"Hi, pumpkin," Ariana cooed, taking the squirming child from him. She kissed Jessica's cheek and carried her into the bedroom.

"Ariana," Marcus said.

"Yes?" she asked, taking the child over to the bed.

"We've had this discussion." He had a rule; babies who'd fled the womb weren't welcome in his bed since they prevented the exact acts to which they owed their existence.

"Uh huh." Ariana climbed into bed with the babbling toddler.

He leaned against the doorframe and folded his arms across his chest.

"Bed, Marc," Jessica chirped.

"Yes, come to bed, Sweetheart," Ariana encouraged sweetly.

He tried to be strong, but when his wife beckoned him again and offered him a kiss, he found his feet moving of their own accord. He lay down on the bed and accepted Ariana's soft kiss, swearing to himself that he wouldn't let them overrule him on the bed rule again. He'd have to lay down the law... unless of course Ariana widened her bright eyes in the way that always left him unable to deny her anything.

As sleep threatened to overtake him, his mind drifted to their first kiss and to even earlier when he'd first become aware of her. Fate had whispered to him, and he'd done as he was bade. He'd waited for Ariana for most of his life, and she had been worth the wait and more. The life they shared made him happy in ways he'd never dreamed possible. He ran a hand fondly over his daughter's hair.

"Sleepy, Marc," she said.

"Then go to sleep."

Ariana rolled over and looked into his eyes. She smiled at him. "When she falls asleep, you can put her back in her crib."

"Will I have a reason to put her back there?" he asked, reaching over to stroke Ariana's swollen belly. She put her hand over his, intertwining their fingers.

"Maybe," she teased. Her lids lowered, and she sighed contentedly.

"I love you," he whispered, and Ariana smiled as she drifted off to sleep. He watched her breathe.

Aye, Fate, there is no better matchmaker than you.

About the Author:

Alexa Aames likes to spend her free time reading, traveling, writing, and flirting. She has, thus far, not been on a time-travel adventure herself, but would be interested if anyone knows of a good tour. As this is her first publication, she is terribly excited to have readers and would be delighted to hear from them. She can be reached at alexa_aames@hotmail.com *or via her publisher, Red Sage.*

*Many thanks to publisher, Alexandria Kendall, and editor, Judith Pich, for giving writers the opportunity to tell diverse stories to the wonderful **Secrets** readership. And special thanks to David for being a good friend and this story's first reader.*

82

Night Heat

by Leigh Wyndfield

To My Reader:

In the heat of the night on an abandoned prison planet, monsters circle the camp, searching for a way inside. Only one man and his ragtag band of prisoners keep the compound secure. But when illness breaks out, he must find a Healer to save them all. Love and desire rule the daylight, while fear and terror rule the night. Hold on to your hats, dear readers, and let's go for a ride!

Chapter One

The raptors, that we've named Velopeds, are highly intelligent and seem to reproduce at an alarming rate. I have long suspected human flesh is an addicting meal for them, since they continuously spend their time and energy on the task of breaking into the prison.

Excerpt from Doctor Paul Lore's Notes

"Don't tell me you're reading the quack doctor's notes again?"

Jemma glanced up to see Silvy standing in the doorway. Big-boned and brawny, she had long, chocolate hair and a beautiful heart-shaped face. In the last two months, they'd become surprisingly close. Extreme stress had formed a fast bond.

"His research is fascinating." Jemma found her place in Dr. Lore's notes, an entry dated a month before the prisoner revolt. The doctor had been killed during the bombing raids the Inter-world Council had flown to try to put down the insurrection, which had occurred three days after Jemma's arrival on the planet. The raids hadn't been successful and after two months without any contact with the Council, rescue didn't seem too imminent.

The fact that the Council had decided to pull out rather than fight the revolt didn't make sense, especially since they had left behind eleven of their support staff. *Unless they think we are all dead.* Most of the guards had left right after the fighting started, but the unlucky eleven had missed the last transport out. Jemma had arrived just in time to see it blast off, having stopped to help an injured man along the way.

To occupy herself during the last two months, Jemma had engrossed herself in Lore's work on the Velopeds. "He says that he recommended building the towers and posting guards to shoot the raptors if they climbed over the first fence into no-man's-land. I didn't realize the Velopeds learned how to climb after the Council first built the prison here."

"Yeah, well, who knows whether they learned or not. They didn't, so we assumed they couldn't." Silvy shook her head. "We were so arrogant. The original team sent to build the prison let the raptors come straight into their camp the first night, and the beasts nearly eviscerated all of them before the few survivors could hide in one of the landing ships, until the morning sun chased them off. It still amazes me we have to resort to such antiquated strategies to keep them out, but they aren't like normal animals. They're death on two feet with wings." Silvy shivered, fear riding through her words.

Jemma couldn't help her fascination, the same one she felt when researching infectious diseases. "Dr. Lore wrote that he thought the raptors couldn't take sunlight because they have something similar to porphyria in humans."

Silvy narrowed pretty blue eyes that could stop a criminal in his tracks. She'd been here almost from the beginning and had become hardened by the stress of living on the planet. Only the Velopeds rattled her. "What in the stars is porphyria?"

"It's a deficiency of an enzyme in the blood. When someone with the disease goes out into the sun, they blister and burn and have all kinds of bad side effects from nausea to chronic pain." A thought struck Jemma that had her jotting a note to herself in excitement. If she could have access to one of the dead raptor bodies, there was a chance the Sem182Diagnostic could prove or disprove Dr. Lore's theory. Unless the Velopeds had a blood make-up that the Sem couldn't handle. She tried to remember any notation of the raptor's blood chemistry in Lore's notes, but didn't think he'd mentioned anything either way. The Sem would put all conjecture to rest.

She'd come to Prison Planet PP8800-1-21, known to the administrative staff as the Velopit, to test her new diagnostic equipment on the strange illnesses the planet struggled with on a frequent basis. The prison revolt had occurred before she could run her first blood sample. When the Council evacuated the planet, accidentally leaving some of the staff behind, her lofty goals of going down in history for her role in developing the Sem had been replaced by mere survival. They waited daily for the Council's return, barricaded in the old stockrooms they called the warrens to protect themselves from the hundred or so prisoners who now controlled the prison.

"Hello!" Silvy waved a hand. "Doctor, you in there?"

"Sorry. I was just thinking about one of Lore's theories. He really was a brilliant scientist."

"Yeah, well in person, he was an odd bird, always wandering around mumbling to himself." Silvy had been in charge of Chow, feeding not only the prisoners, but the administration, guards and staff as well.

Jemma had heard Silvy's opinions before on both the Velopeds and Dr. Lore and felt the notes tugging her attention back to them. "But his research is amazing. He catalogued the raptors' changes in behavior since the beginning. There are three years' worth of notes here. He even dissected several of them and has descriptions of their anatomical makeup." She scanned the tight, pinched scrawl, but saw no notation of a different blood chemistry.

"The Council should have blasted them to bits when they first decided to put a prison here." Silvy was a firm believer in two things: prisoners should pay for their crimes and the raptors should be annihilated.

Since Jemma's own race restricted behavior that might cause one Chosen to be separated from the other, she had never formed an opinion on prisoners before she'd arrived here. Crime was almost unheard of on her home planet, Trolen. No one would purposely be that Selfish. But she did have strong feelings about the raptors. The animals had been on this planet first. The Council had destroyed species all over the galaxies, just to annex more habitable land. She couldn't believe the arrogance, the crime of it all. "They are still living creatures, Sil."

"Yeah, living creatures that tear out your heart and lungs with knife-like claws, then munch them down for a snack." Her friend's gaze turned thoughtful. "Did you even have a chance to see one?"

Jemma could still remember her first glimpse of the beasts, the sight of three of them ramming their bodies against the electric fences. "The second night I was here, Zach took me up on one of the towers."

Zach Margorly had been the head of the guard staff before the revolt and was Silvy's lover. Jemma felt the odd twist of loss she always had in their presence. She tried to be happy for her friends, but their joy reminded her constantly that she would never find her own Chosen mate. She was ten years past the normal bonding period, which meant her other half had died. He must have, or he would have found her long ago.

"What's wrong?" Silvy touched her hand, showing the soft side others rarely saw.

She'd told Silvy about the loss of her Chosen in a roundabout way, saying her true love had died, but not betraying the secrets of the Trolen bonding ritual. Jemma hastened to reassure her before Silvy brought it up. "Nothing." She shook off the depression that had been plaguing her since she'd come to this planet and pointed to the book. "They're really not that far from humans physically. Different heart structure, but our lungs and nervous systems are the same. Their brain is bigger." Jemma could feel herself warming up to what had become her favorite topic. It was the only thing that interested her any more. Lore had done some amazing work. "And look at some of these drawings." She swiveled the book so Silvy could see it and flipped back to the doctor's sketches.

"They're hideous, aren't they?" Silvy pulled her hand away from where it rested near the book. "Black demons of death, moving through the night like wraiths, faster than a blink of an eye. By the time you see them, you're already dead."

Of course the raptors were dangerous, but Jemma was convinced the staff were turning the raptors into a myth more than the living beings that they were. To liken them to grisly specters seemed too much. She'd stopped arguing, though. "The details to these sketches are amazing. You can almost feel them standing in the room with us."

Lore had drawn them in black pen, fitting since the animals were midnight black, their skin a shiny leather that reflected the spotlights. Their bullet heads and leather wings sat on an almost humanoid shaped body. They were slightly bigger than a full grown human male.

Silvy shivered. "Gods, these drawings are terrifyingly accurate."

"There is something about the way he drew their faces. It shows their intelligence." It had taken Jemma several minutes of studying the pictures to spot what the doctor had done.

"Not to change the subject." Her friend nudged the book back towards Jemma, her voice filling with excitement. "But Zach asked me to Match with him last night." She fingered a pendant hanging from her neck made of two connecting circles.

Jemma forced a smile onto her face. "That's wonderful, Silvy." She skirted the examining table and gave her friend a hug. "I'm so happy for you!" Happy for her friend, but as much as she tried to stop it, the huge sadness she'd been battling the last two months threatened to overwhelm her. She didn't know why being on the Velopit caused her to feel depressed, but since the moment she'd stepped foot on the planet, she'd felt a nagging worry and sadness.

She brushed the amulet hanging from her neck beneath her shirt. The crystal was gifted to every Trolen female child at birth. The wise woman in each village performed the ceremony, capturing a small piece of her destined Chosen's soul and placing it into the stone. When the female was of age, she could then tell who she was destined to be with by the heat created in the crystal with his touch.

Her amulet had never warmed and it never would.

Silvy pulled away. "Are you crying?"

"Tears of joy, I assure you." Jemma swiped at tears she hadn't known were on her face. "I expect to be invited to the matching ceremony."

"You will be." Silvy's face glowed with joy. "When the Council retakes the planet, we're going to declare ourselves."

"If they come back." The words slipped out before Jemma could stop them.

"They will, Jemma. Zach promises it will be soon. He says the Council is too arrogant to leave a habitable planet out here unpopulated or to let a bunch of treasonous prisoners get the better of them."

Jemma nodded. "If that's what Zach thinks, I'm sure it's true." She pinched the bridge of her nose and told herself to grasp hold of her emotions.

"Are you really okay?"

"I just need a breath of fresh air. I think I'll go watch the sun set." She needed to escape before she ruined her friend's moment.

Silvy shook her head. "One of these days, you're going to be spotted by Bowhite's men. It's dangerous sneaking out alone and risk having some of the prisoners see you. Zach says they haven't come back since that first attempt right after the revolt because they don't think we have anything worth fighting for. We're fortified too well here to make it worth their while."

Right after the Council pulled out, a group of prisoners had attacked the warrens, but Zach and his men had easily held them off, entrenched in the better position. It would be almost impossible for Bowhite's men to get to them.

"We've been hiding in here for two months, Silvy. I think Bowhite would have come for us by now if he'd wanted to. He hasn't yet because we're insignificant compared to the dangers from the raptors he's fighting every night." Bowhite and the rest of the prisoners guarded the fences from the raptors as they attempted to climb into the prison each evening. It was a terrifying thought, but their lives depended on Bowhite's protection. If he and his men didn't hold the fences, Jemma and the remaining administrative staff would face attacks in the warrens. There wasn't much the staff could do but wait for the Council's return. Jemma smiled and patted her friend's arm as she hurried to the door, desperate to get away before the sadness welled up and she let more than a few tears escape. "Don't worry. I'll be back."

She slipped through the smaller of the two storehouses, winding her way through supplies stacked to the ceiling. The storerooms were filled with weapons and extra energy packs. If Bowhite had known the extent of the provisions they had down here, he wouldn't have left them alone. As she entered the larger storeroom, she could already see some of the piles of food had been depleted. They couldn't hide in the warrens forever.

At the door to the tunnels, she passed the first guard.

"Hi, Jemma," Simpson said, ducking his head a bit.

He was young, with sandy-blond hair and nice blue eyes and had a crush on her. As with every male she'd ever met, she felt absolutely nothing except mild friendship for him. "Hi, Simpson."

In a way she mourned the fact she couldn't reciprocate his feelings, but Trolen females were destined for either a life with their Chosen or a life alone. There were no other options.

"Be careful out there," he called from behind her.

She waved and side-stepped the first round of explosives set in the tunnels. Zach had rigged them more to warn if Bowhite tried to attack them than to do serious damage. There were two protective doors and five charges laid out along the tunnel. Plenty of advance notice if the prisoners finally decided to come for them.

When she reached topside, Jemma studied the fading daylight. Seeing that all was clear, she hurried to the nearby lake where the view of the sunset would be best. Hiking herself up onto part of the burnt out hull that used to be an administrative building, she settled in to watch. The sunsets on the Velopit were stunning every time. The sky molted into a bright orange, the clouds perfect dark shadows against the spray of exquisite beauty, all taking place over water turned red from a mineral that filled the soil on this planet.

It would be a gorgeous vacation spot. If not for the Velopeds.

All that stood between her and the raptors were two rings of electric fences and a hundred criminals.

Suddenly, the weight on her soul lifted and she smiled. Hope had always kept her going before and hope would keep her going now. Bowhite and his men would keep them safe. She had to believe that. Soon, she'd be back on Borrus, finalizing the Sem for release in more widespread trials. For now, she had the simple joy of a sunset to lift her spirits. With one last glance, she took in the beauty, ready to return to the warrens for as long as it took for the Council to come for them.

When she turned, swinging her legs over the other side to jump down, five men armed with blasters, knives and batons trapped her against the lake.

Chapter Two

As beautiful as this planet is, the danger far outweighs any gain we might possibly derive from it. Surely there are other places better suited for a prison?

Excerpt from Doctor Lore's Notes

She should run.

But what was the point? They'd easily catch her before she made the top of the tunnel. For a moment, she felt an odd feeling of relief, as if something missing had been returned to her, but she shook off the strange thought. She was usually quite grounded, but her emotions since she'd come to this planet had been bouncing all over the place.

Then fear caught her by the stomach, twisting her insides into knots and charging her internal fight or flight system to action. There were worse things than death. Being touched by strangers was an agony under normal circumstances, what would it be like if they forced her?

"Healer." One of the men strode forward with an easy stride, his body flowing over the ground with all the grace of a raptor.

The comparison wasn't lost on Jemma. She blinked away the glaze of fear. Whoever he was, he'd been blessed with a lushly frowning mouth and serious dark eyes. Thinner than the other four men, he had a wiry build that said speed and stealth. She wondered who he was and, more importantly, how he knew her.

"I'm Rip Bowhite." He nodded his head in an abbreviated bow.

She gave his muscled, well-proportioned body the once over, pausing to study his face in the fading light. It surprised her that the rebel leader appeared more like a commanding starpilot than a criminal. His features would have been starkly sexy except for the strain around his eyes and the harsh twist of his lips. An arrogance in his stance set him apart from the others, but otherwise, he was just a man. She had to remember that. Zach had once told her prisoners could smell fear.

She stuffed hers down deep and dragged on the professional attitude she used when Healing. "What can I do for you, Bowhite?"

He shrugged a long barreled blaster off his shoulder in a quick, graceful sweep, letting the butt hit the rock below his feet with a click.

She pulled up one knee to her chest to cover the small flinch her body made at the noise.

"We have need of your skills."

Blaster fire broke out along the eastern end of the compound where dark had already settled. Bowhite didn't glance in that direction but his eyes narrowed and he shifted, a cool roll of his shoulders. This was a man not easily swayed once he decided on a course of action.

"Sickness?" she asked, feeling a spark of interest. After all, this was why she'd come here in the first place.

"Half my men are down with some sort of flu."

"Just the men?" Something in the way he'd said it made her ask.

"Most are men. Only two of the thirty taken ill are women."

She hummed, her mind engaging completely for the first time since she'd landed on this planet. "Symptoms? Progression?"

"Everyone says they start out feeling tired with extreme dizziness and fainting. Then their body aches, then they begin to vomit." He put his hands on his hips. "They can't keep down food or drink."

"Dehydration," she murmured. "But mainly men. Why not more women?"

He shrugged.

"Any rashes? Sores? That kind of thing?"

"They had sores on their hands, but they went away after a few days, so it might be something totally unrelated. Some of them complained of having a sore throat and a headache, but that cleared up when the rash disappeared."

Immediately, her mind started clicking through possibilities. Women made up less than a fourth of the prison population. Maybe they hadn't been hit as hard with the disease due to numbers alone. She doubted that was the explanation. The discrepancy must come from the method of delivery. An air born illness would transfer more uniformly.

"What makes you think I'll help you?" Jemma rested her chin on her knee. She'd help, of course, but she thought she'd ask to remind them she was doing them a favor.

"If I lose many more men, I won't be able to defend the fences."

She nodded, tapping her dangling leg against the crumbling brick. If the fences were left undefended, they were all dead. "You have a point."

Staring off at the double ring of electrified wire, she imagined the Velopeds could feel their weakness and were creeping up in packs as the darkness rolled in. She wasn't anxious to go strolling into Bowhite's camp full of dangerous prisoners, but if they had an outbreak of an infectious disease, she had the tool to diagnose it. This was her chance to use the Sem182Diagnostic.

Well, no sense wasting any more time. She leaped down in one smooth motion.

The men surrounding her stumbled back, grabbing their weapons. Except for Bowhite. He stood rock still, watching her.

"I'll need to pack some diagnostic equipment and something to stop the dehydration." She marched towards the tunnels, her thoughts still turning over reasons the female population hadn't come down equally with the illness. A bacterium carried in the water should hit them in similar numbers as well.

"I'll come with you." Bowhite fell into step with her as if they had long been friends and strangely, she didn't feel the usual creeping sensation she had when she neared other males.

"Sorry, Bo. That's not part of this deal." There were things in the warrens Rip Bowhite couldn't see, such as all their supplies. Zach would string her up if she let Bowhite in.

"I think it is." His nice, deep voice vibrated through her body like the sweep of a feather.

"You'll just have to trust me." She stopped near the entrance and put a hand on his arm, ignoring the spark that jolted through her at the contact. "No worries. I'll come back."

He seemed to waver between forcing his company and letting her go. The internal war played out in his expressive dark eyes, which narrowed as he thought through his options.

She had a feeling that he didn't often hesitate to make a decision, and patted his arm in sympathy. "I'll be back," she said simply and jogged down the hole to the warrens.

⚜

Rip had been in trouble before, but he knew if his men started dying, the raptors would overrun the fences and kill off his rag-tag band of followers. They were like the Horsemen of Death in legends, almost invincible, their very presence signaling the end of life. Only a blaster pulse through their head would take them down.

He had every prisoner left on their feet in the guard towers or sleeping in shifts. If they lost any more manpower, they wouldn't be able to adequately defend the fences, yet here he was, putting his faith in someone he'd never met before and didn't believe for a moment cared about him or his people. One of his men had seen her watching the sun set the night before and had recognized her from when he'd been in Dr. Lore's infirmary, right before the Council had pulled out.

What did he have to lose? His people had to have a Healer. The situation couldn't be much worse and she had at least proved somewhat trustworthy when she'd returned when she'd said she would, carrying a small pack on her back.

His gaze drifted to the Healer's honey-blond hair, which was swept up into a messy ponytail. Loose pieces framed a strong face with sumptuous lips and deep blue-green eyes. Not beautiful, but pretty enough to be a problem.

Like himself, the men and women who followed him had committed crimes against the Inter-world Council, civil disobedience such as writing opposition literature and protesting policy too vigorously for the Council's taste, but life in prison had turned them hard. Since the planet had been abandoned, they'd been reduced to doing anything they could to stay alive. Even he had killed and would, he suspected, kill again—a far cry from organizing the protest rallies that had put him here. And while there were women enough to go around now that half his men were sick, the Healer was tasty enough to draw attention.

His request for her help put her under his personal protection. The thought pleased him on some level, and he allowed his body to move half a step closer to hers.

When she glided away, he caught her arm. Her gaze jerked to his and he felt again the surprisingly strong attraction between them he'd noticed outside the tunnels, where the few remaining administration personnel had barricaded themselves. He'd never even seen her before today, so how could he feel this way?

He'd gone without a woman for two years now, and he was probably just feeling the effects of it. He should take someone to bed. Soon. Maybe the Healer. He brushed her lips with his gaze, watching the flare of surprise cruise through her eyes. Something told him she would be different from the others he'd bedded. Soft, sexy, passionate. Right.

He yanked his thoughts out of his pants. His men needed him now. "Stay close to me, or I won't be able to protect you." He held her with the intense stare he sometimes used with his men. The one that said don't-screw-with-me.

She raised an eyebrow, but nodded. Not backing down.

He held her gaze for a second longer, then turned to enter the camp. "I'm surprised your friends let you come with me." He'd been worried they'd stop her.

She shrugged one shoulder. "I'm a Healer, Bowhite. I've given my oath to help when asked." Her gaze narrowed as they rounded a large pile of rubble and his camp was revealed.

The prison wasn't overly large, only the size of several starfreighters. Two months ago, it had consisted of fourteen buildings, an exercise yard and the no-man's-land, which ran around three quarters of the prison where it didn't back up to the lake. This ring was a large swath of barren land caged by two electrical fences. The prisoners had chosen to build temporary housing near the old Chow hall, since it was the only building standing intact after the Council's bombing raids.

He could feel the weight of people's stares on them, the rise of interest that followed their movement through the rows of hastily constructed shanties and tents his followers called home. Some of that interest was more than just curiosity. Some of it was sexual. He could smell it.

An odd possessiveness filled him, and a silent growl stretched his lips. He'd fight for her.

The realization gave him pause, but it was true. His instant attraction to her twined with the fact that she was their only chance at survival. He wasn't going to let anything happen to her. Circling her wrist with his fingers, he cuffed her to him.

When man after man had fallen ill, he'd had them moved to the Chow hall. The rains were coming soon, and it would be the one place that would remain dry. He led her in that direction, unable to stop himself from running his thumb over the pulse point in her wrist.

She stiffened under his touch. "What are you doing?"

He smiled, feeling his lips form into a predatory grin. "It would be best if you appear to be under my protection. This camp can be dangerous."

His followers consisted of fifteen women and a little under sixty men, only half of whom were well enough to work. The rest of the prisoners had died in the bombing raids.

They needed twenty people a shift working the fences and at least four or five to monitor the power supply and handle the rotations. He was already a few bodies short, pulling them from the day shift since the raptors only came at night. The Velopeds seemed to have an uncanny ability to sense their weakness, attacking the fencing in the early morning or at dusk when he was short-staffed. His followers had become more and more unstable as the stress of keeping the raptors at bay built. The illness that had swept through the camp had only added to it.

He pulled her to a halt as a thought hit him. "You could be at risk of catching this."

"I'm a scientist who works on diagnostic tools for every kind of disease known to man. I've been inoculated for a wide variety of viruses, bacteria and other nasties." She raised an eyebrow as if doubting his sudden concern.

He battled his reluctance to expose her, fighting the sudden and intense feelings he had about this woman, then forced himself to guide her through the double doors.

The Healer caught her breath. "Goddess," she whispered, staring down row after row of men and women. An even thirty of them in all.

He saw it through her eyes, the moaning, the smell of vomit, of impending death, which caught in the back of his throat, making him want to gag. They'd waited too long to fetch her. Already several men were hanging by a thread, unable to keep anything in their stomachs.

A professional mask came down over her features. "When did this start?"

He dropped her wrist reluctantly. "Two standard weeks ago."

She rotated the pack from her back to the floor, then began to search through it. "Mainly men." She hummed and met his gaze. "Why men?" He realized she was enjoying the challenge of the puzzle.

He shrugged, again having no answer for her. He'd wondered the same thing, but the closest they had to a doctor was a starship medic who'd protested the lack of salary increases a little too vehemently for the Council's taste.

"The rash. Was it blisters or bumps?"

"Blisters. They erupted, then went away." He'd watched his own hands daily for any sign of the rash, but it had never appeared.

"The pattern of the rash—was it covering their hands or only a small amount of random sores?" She brushed away a loose strand of the messy ponytail, drawing his notice to her graceful hands.

For a moment, he could almost feel her slender fingers brush his bare skin, and he had to tighten his hands into fists to keep from reaching for her.

"Covering their palms, sometimes the backs of their fingers." His voice came out only a fraction deeper, not enough to betray his inner struggle.

Snapping on a set of thin gloves, she pulled a face mask over her head, leaving it dangling around her neck. "How much time have you spent in here with them?"

He waved a hand. "So much I can't count."

She studied him. "From the beginning, right? You've spent time with the sick men since the beginning?"

"Yes." He saw where she was going.

"Have you gotten the rash?"

"No."

"Felt tired? Achy? Sick to your stomach?"

He shook his head. He'd been thinking the same thing. Why hadn't he gotten any of the symptoms? Some of his strongest men were here, flat on their backs, dying. In fact, everyone he usually relied on except his second in command, Jackson.

"Why not you, too?" She put his thoughts into words.

"I've asked myself that." He stared off into the room. "I've never been one to become ill easily."

"Maybe." She tipped her head and rocked lightly on her toes. "If you don't have it, it's probably not airborne or something transferred by casual contact. Let's go have a look then." She slipped the mask over her face and dug out a black, square box from her pack. From the way she lifted it, he could tell it weighed as much as a blaster, maybe more. She held it carefully, as if she thought it was worth her weight in balseems.

Hours trickled by. She examined everyone in the hall. Her hands were gentle, her voice soft, all of her earlier personality disappearing under a concerned, focused facade.

Rip didn't leave her side, not bothering to fight his desire to keep her in his sight. She took samples of saliva and skin, then drew out small amounts of blood. She fed it all into the box, watching the screen, her forehead scrunched in concentration. Then she pulled out some vials and injected each patient with medication. "It's for the nausea. If they keep down fluids, they'll be out of any immediate danger."

Finally, she took off her gloves and met his gaze. "Can we go somewhere to talk?"

He nodded, leading her outside into the moonlight. All three of the moons were full tonight, lighting the camp as much as the sun did, although everything shimmered in silver. Men and women swarmed a nearby fire, coming in from shift change to eat and rest. It couldn't have been worse timing.

Landis approached them before they'd taken two steps. "What do we have here?"

He was the best looking man in camp, but within the first weeks had bedded most of the women and ended up alone. His eyes lighted in interest as they moved over the Healer. Landis had been Rip's biggest problem lately, vying for his position as leader and generally stirring up trouble, as if he couldn't control himself. He seemed to thrive on the amusement of it all. People ringed around them, quivering excitement running through the crowd, as if the ex-prisoners sensed potential entertainment with Landis in the mix. Rip knew how to take care of trouble, but he couldn't fight each of his men one after the other if Landis ended up finally pushing the right button. Turning to the Healer, he found her gripping her pack, which held the precious box she'd used to collect samples from his men.

He made sure her gaze locked to his so she would see how serious he was. "Follow my lead, or we're both in trouble." Growling at her lack of fast response, he grabbed her arm. "Nod if you understand me."

Her eyes flashed to his, but he didn't see a hint of fear. "Your show, Bo." She glanced at his hand on her arm, her mouth turning down into a sharp frown.

He released her, then faced the circle, meeting every pair of eyes he could. "What we have here, Landis, is my woman."

Chapter Three

Originally, we thought the raptors couldn't climb the fences. They certainly can now and seem to relish doing so. We've never seen them swim, but I've warned the administration that it might only be a matter of time before the Velopeds spill in from the lake, which doesn't have any form of fencing at all to protect it. No one has listened to my warnings.

Excerpt from Doctor Lore's Notes

Everyone spoke at once.

Everyone but Jemma. She forced her mouth to close and narrowed her eyes. If Rip Bowhite thought she would hop into bed with him, he was mistaken.

Not that he wasn't good looking. He was, in a manly, arrogant kind of way. For a moment, she peeled away his clothes in her mind. He might be thinner than the others surrounding them, but he'd have muscles, she was sure of it. All that thick hair covering his head probably meant chest hair, too. She could almost feel it under her hands, silky skin over hard muscle with a dusting of hair on top.

Blinking, she shook her head. Obviously, she'd lost her mind to be ogling this man. She never had these kinds of thoughts about anyone. What was wrong with her? A high crime against the Inter-world Council had put him here. He was a traitor.

Not her type. Not her type at all. Although if she was honest, she really didn't have a type. Her previous experiences with sex had been an experiment to see what she missed out on by not having a Chosen. They hadn't been pleasurable.

"You haven't taken a woman before this," one of the men pointed out. Jemma could feel the tension building, humming just below the surface of the crowd.

Bowhite flipped a hand and his expression filled with mild humor. "That doesn't mean I didn't want one." He laughed, but Jemma could hear something forced under the surface that no one else seemed to notice. Bowhite was worried, which worried her. "I didn't take a woman to bed because I already had enough problems with all of you fighting amongst yourselves. The last thing I wanted to do was add to that."

"You think you can claim her? Just like that?" Landis snapped his fingers, his long, blond hair swinging ruggedly back from his face to show off handsome features.

Jemma would choose Bowhite over Landis in about three nanoseconds. Or faster. He was good looking, but her skin crawled worse than it usually did around other males.

Bowhite rested his hands on his hips, the action strangely aggressive, as if, by doing so, he showed Landis that he wasn't scared of what the other man might do. "Yes, I do think I can claim her." His voice came out a deadly purr. "She's a Healer, the only one left on this planet, and until she figures out what's making all of us sick, she's mine. After that, I'll personally escort her back to the warrens."

"That doesn't mean she wouldn't want one of us to warm her bed while she's here." Landis raised one eyebrow and gave her a charming smile that must have curled many women's toes.

Jemma figured she'd better make her preferences clear. She stepped in to press her front to Bowhite's back, suddenly realizing she wasn't taller than him. That was unusual. She was a tall woman, but she had to stand on her tiptoes to rest her chin on his shoulder, balancing herself with a hand on his waist. His whole body tightened at her touch, a zap of heat passing between them, then he relaxed.

"Just so everyone understands, my choice is Bowhite." Her words came out in a murmur, the tone sexual, even if she didn't intend it that way.

Rip's hand captured hers and pulled her arm tighter about his body, the action bringing her flush against his back. She gasped at the contact, her knees weakening as she realized what she was feeling was desire. Her hands spasmed on his shirt with the shock of it.

"This doesn't make any sense, Rip," said one of the men who'd trapped her. "You didn't even know who she was a few minutes ago. I had to point her out to you, but now I can see the heat coming off the two of you in waves."

"Love at first sight." Bowhite's deep voice rumbled under her arm across his chest.

Jemma agreed it was *something* at first sight. And whatever that something was, it concerned her. Badly. But not enough that she wouldn't take the protection he offered. The thought of being in the presence of any other man but him had chillbumps rising on her arms.

"Her choice. My choice." Bowhite's voice rang in the silence. "There's no more discussion here. Is there?"

Landis stared at her, his gaze considering, as if he wasn't used to women turning him down. "I'll be here when you want a real man, Healer." He shook his head in disgust and ducked into a nearby tent.

The excitement over, the remaining crowd drifted away.

Without looking at her, Bowhite dragged her through the sea of tents, then climbed up into one at the end of a row, which stood on a platform about waist high above the ground.

The tent was dark and he leaned down to turn on a lamp sitting on the floor, lighting the area with a dull glow. The prison still had power, since Bowhite's men had been able to keep several of the solar panels repaired, but this lamp ran off of some kind of fuel oil. She wondered if the power was being used solely for the lights in the Chow hall and the electric fences. Because she lived hidden in the warrens, she didn't know what shape the rest of the prison was in or the current state of their defense. The lack of power and Landis's challenge worried her. It seemed Bowhite's hold over his men wasn't as strong as Zach thought it was.

A narrow cot took up most of the space inside the tent, although there was also an overstuffed chair, obviously left over from an administrator's office, and a trunk that served as a desk. He pointed to the chair and sat on the trunk. "What's the diagnosis?"

She perched on the edge, excitement at using the Sem bubbling up inside her. "I used the Sem182Diagnostic to analyze the blood and other inputs. It's the latest technology available throughout the Interworlds, truly a breakthrough in modern medicine. Three days before the Council pulled out, I arrived to test it on the Velopit, but for obvious reasons didn't get to until now." She pushed her hair away, needing him to understand that history was being made here. When he didn't respond, she pushed on. "The Sem has the ability to diagnose seventy billion diseases, viruses, and bacteria and recommends treatment."

He didn't appear properly impressed. "Fantastic. So what did it diagnose?"

Jemma tried to remind herself that he was a layman, not another scientist, but her voice still came out with shades of annoyance in it when she said, "Fridincoccolosis."

"Fridincoccolosis," he repeated. He made a winding motion with his hand. "And that is what?"

Now was where the conversation would turn tricky, since even a diagnostic tool as amazing as the Sem had its limitations. "A bacterium." Jemma knew she was hedging, but she couldn't give him a more extensive explanation. She'd made a mistake leaving Xan Yang's medical reference back at the warrens. Without it, she was unable to research the illness and understand the ramifications fully.

"Which is treated how?" he asked, his voice slow and cautious, as if holding his temper in check.

"With a drug called Revostat."

He sighed. "Why do I have a feeling there is bad news here if I can just figure out the right question to ask?"

"I'll have to go back to the warrens to check but I don't believe we have any on this planet." She blew out a breath of frustration, anticipating his anger.

"So what's your back up plan?" The words were said with deathly calm.

"At this point, I don't have one." She held up a hand to stop the storm she saw brewing in his eyes. "But we can experiment with similar medications or generate our own compound. It might take me a few days, but we'll find a cure." She wasn't completely sure that was true, but hastened on to change the subject. "I'm more interested to discover why the women aren't contracting the disease at the same rate. By figuring out the cause, we can control the spread." In a way, this was intriguing, the chance she'd been waiting for, an opportunity to study a unique pathogen on this planet.

He leaned forward, his body coming dangerously close to hers. "Some of my men don't have days."

She refused to be intimidated by him. She was a Healer, a professional. No matter what, she would honor her oath to serve mankind and ignore the odd *something* between them. "Listen, Bowhite, your men are only in danger of dying from dehydration. Whatever this is, they aren't going to die from it any time soon, just from the symptoms."

"My best men are in there." His hand gripped the arm of her chair. "I don't want you leaving them to die."

"I would *never* leave someone to die." No matter how Selfish they were, she added silently. They were humans, even if they had made terrible decisions that left their mates alone. Regardless, all life was sacred to her. "The sooner I return to the warrens, the sooner you'll have your answer."

"That's not an option tonight." He suddenly backed away and dropped his head into one hand, pinching the bridge of his nose. He looked tired.

Dread rose up along her spine. "Why not?"

He exhaled as if attempting to rid himself of some of the tension he carried in his body. Meeting her gaze, one side of his mouth curled in a humorless smile. "Because I've locked down the camp. No moving at night anymore."

Fear squeezed her heart for a moment, before it began beating in double time. She knew why he'd restricted evening movement. "Velopeds have been inside the fence," she whispered.

He nodded his head once, the strain lines around his mouth deepening.

"How long have they been getting in?" Goddess, she needed to warn the others in the administration warrens. Zach had told them Bowhite's men were manning the towers, that they were safe. The prison encampment might be overrun. If that happened, it would only be a matter of time before the raptors made it into the warrens.

"Last night was the first time, although they've been getting over the first fence for a couple of weeks now." He dropped to his knees before her chair and caught her chin in one strong hand. "I need my men healed and back on their feet, or we're all dead."

She blinked once at his sudden move, swallowed, then cleared her throat. "I can't do anything except treat the symptoms until we have the proper medication." She ignored the burst of pleasure at the touch of his hand on her face. "I must go back to the warrens to save them."

Nodding once, he acknowledged he understood. Then he leaned in, his whole body intense lines of suppressed power. "What is your name?"

She tried to think, but suddenly his scent filled her mind, pushing out everything else. She couldn't tell quite what it was, something elusive and familiar. Within a heartbeat, her fear transformed into desire.

What had he asked? Her name. "Jemma." Her insides turned soft, the edges of her vision blurring so she saw only the man before her.

His fingers tightened on her chin. "Rip."

"What?" The small tent was filled with sexual tension so thick her breathing accelerated and her hand quivered on the chair arm.

"My first name is Rip." He brought his lips within an inch of hers.

"You chose me and I chose you. I want you to call me Rip while I make love to you."

His words drew her out of the fog of sexual desire. He had to be joking. She was not going to have sex with him. She opened her mouth to put him in his place, but his lips came down on hers. Lightly. Only a whisper-touch, the briefest puff of his breath.

Her hand landed on his chest to push him away, but the minute his tongue swept across her lips, she felt the amulet between her breasts heat.

No!

Everything suddenly became clear. She'd been depressed because somehow her body had known he was near. The minute he'd approached her at the lake, her spirits had lifted and she'd felt the best she had in years. She'd touched him freely and it had been wonderful, *because he was her Chosen.*

Her mouth returned the kiss against her will, her body leaning forward to increase the pressure between them. His scent curled around her, beckoning her to taste his skin. Wet desire flooded between her thighs. Her body thrummed with life, with longing. And now she knew why, knew why she'd been attracted to him from that first time he'd touched her outside the warrens.

Her Chosen. Her hands twisted on his shirt. She felt no joy at the revelation, only anger mingling with intense desire.

He'd condemned her to an existence alone. He'd been alive all this time, but had committed treason against the Council, landing himself in prison, thereby sentencing them *both* to a life of agony and desolation.

He had no honor. By the judgment of their people, he was labeled Selfish. He had committed an unpardonable sin.

Rage welled up, so strong, she pushed him off her with twice the usual strength. He fell onto his butt, hitting the trunk, clear surprise written across his face.

"How dare you!" Launching herself from the chair, she leaped around him. Screw the Velopeds. She wasn't spending a moment longer in his presence. He was the lowest form of Selfish slime and her Chosen. Wasn't that just her terrible, rotten luck?

She made it exactly one step before he grabbed her ankle and pulled her down. It happened so fast she barely had time to break her fall.

He was on top of her before she could catch her breath. "Listen." His voice was a growl in her ear, his large body pinning her to the platform.

"You cannot leave here. I won't allow it. Tomorrow I'll take you back, but tonight you have to stay in the safety of my tent. The Velopeds aren't the only thing that will attack you if you leave."

"Damn you." She wanted to rage at him, beat her fists into his face, but tears were about to come. She could feel them welling up in her eyes, feel the tingle in her nose. Dammit. She cried when she was furious, rarely ever when she was sad. And she *hated* the weakness. Venting her frustration and anger, she whipped her head to the side and sank her teeth into his forearm where he'd braced it beside her head.

He hissed in a breath, tightening his muscles so that her bite only broke the skin and stopped on the corded muscles below. He didn't pull away, but let her do it, then tugged lightly on her hair, so she'd meet his gaze. "That hurts," he said, his voice calm in the dim light of the tent.

She released him by degrees, cursing herself for exposing her body to his blood. It was probably carrying whatever bacteria his men suffered from and she'd swallowed a mouthful of the rich, spicy liquid. She refused to dwell on the fact Chosen pairs exchanged their blood and sexual fluids as a part of normal bonding. This man had lost his right to her when he put himself in a position to spend time in prison. And insult was added to injury when she realized he'd been put here for crimes against the Inter-world Council. What would a member of her race care about Council politics? Nothing!

"Care to tell me what's going on here?" Bowhite's voice was gentle and he sounded as if he spoke to a scared child. "You seemed fine a moment ago, more than participating in our kiss, and then you suddenly act like a rabid animal." He allowed her to turn onto her back under him, but kept each of her hands locked in his, holding his body out of biting range.

"I don't want anything to do with you, Bowhite." The tremble of desire in her stomach called her a liar. With a swipe of her tongue, she tasted his blood on her lips. She wanted him with a raging burn. No! She had a choice. She didn't have to bond with him.

To make a point to both of them, she jerked her knee up between his legs. He saved himself by quick reflexes alone, rolling to one side.

Cursing, he shifted, working his legs between hers to grind his thick erection against the apex of her thighs. "I do not know what in the Goddess has your panties in a twist, sweetness, but if you try that again, I promise you will not like the consequences."

Now she was ten times worse off than she was before. Closing her eyes, Jemma fought the need to arch into him, to strive for a release only he, as her Chosen, could give her. All the whispers, all the secrets she had heard as a girl flew through her mind. The things they could do to and for one another sexually would make her few previous forays into sex look like the waste of her time they had actually been. No other man could bring her to orgasm. She'd known that, but had tried anyway. After all, what did she have to lose? She'd believed her Chosen was dead. He'd had to have been, or he would have searched for her, would have found her.

She inhaled to find her inner balance, careful to draw the air through her mouth so she wouldn't end up with a head full of his scent. She knew why he smelled so good to her now.

When she opened her eyes, she found him staring at the hard peaks of her nipples. In slow motion, he raised his head, his nostrils flaring out, his chest heaving with the effort to control the ritual call screaming between them. His black gaze glittered as he rocked himself forward, his erection pressing her clitoris.

In a rush of blinding need, all her well-shored defenses crashed around her and Jemma rose up to meet his kiss.

Chapter Four

The Velopeds must reproduce at a staggering rate, since our constant killing of them hasn't seemed to put a dent in their population. Which begs the question of their reproductive preferences. Do they copulate freely like most animals? Or are they one of the few beasts that mate for life? The myth that some human races have predestined mates has long been a topic of discussion, but I doubt seriously the raptors could reproduce this quickly if they were restricted to only one sexual partner.

Excerpt from Doctor Lore's Notes

Need raged through his body, kicking him in gut, unlike anything he'd ever felt in his life. Raw desire, untamed and heady, like that first taste of liquor a boy drinks to prove to himself and his friends that he's a man.

Gods. His mouth still crushed to hers, he used one hand to brace his body while the other shook as he unbuttoned her shirt. He had to taste the nipples tenting the fabric, had to see what they looked like. It took every ounce of control not to rip and tear, but he didn't want to scare her with the blazing intensity of his passion for her.

Always before, he had wondered what was wrong with him. His sex drive had been so low, he knew he wasn't like other men.

It wasn't low now.

Breaking their kiss, he glanced at the bite mark on his arm. A thin trickle of blood ran down his wrist. Demon woman. He should be angry, but for some unexplainable reason, he'd liked it, liked seeing her mark him. He stomped down the urge to bite her in return.

He didn't know what had changed her mind, but he wasn't about to blow the opportunity.

Brushing the fabric apart, he took in the view. Small, firm breasts and tight, dusk-colored nipples. Perfect. A necklace made of a thin strand of woven metal lay between her breasts, ending in an amulet containing a large, purple stone.

With a groan, he captured her nipple in his mouth. Her breath caught in pleasure.

Oh yes.

She'd fought him before, but this desire between them was two-sided. He could hear her heart thumping in time with his.

He rolled his tongue across the tight bead, circling, then sucking lightly.

Her hands dug into his hair, and he paused to enjoy the scrape of her nails across his scalp. He'd never realized how good that could feel. His skin felt hyper-sensitive, his whole body buzzing with need, making everything that happened more intense, textures softer, warmer, the sound of her breath louder. Everything was just *more*.

He'd been in prison for a long time, been without a woman for even longer, but the way he felt inside couldn't be only from sexual deprivation. He had never felt this way before.

She tugged him to her other nipple. He obliged her by licking, then swirling around the bud.

"Jemma," he murmured, liking the sound of her name on his tongue. He captured her head so he could kiss her, the threat of her biting him again only heightening his desire.

Her breasts pressed into his chest as their lips and tongues explored and tasted. She may have been resisting a few minutes ago, but now she engaged fully in their play, wrapping her legs around his waist and her arms behind his neck.

He brushed his tongue into her mouth and lowered his chest onto hers. The necklace between them flared into a hot spark.

"Dammit!" He pulled back. "What was that?"

Her eyes narrowed, her body stiffening, as if he'd said the wrong thing. He let his weight fall heavier on her, prepared now so she couldn't try to knee him in the balls again. He captured the amulet in his right palm.

⚜

Jemma's stomach did a flip-flop. "You don't know?" Even to her own ears, the words sounded choked. How could he not? Everyone from their planet knew what the amulet was.

"It's some sort of religious relic?" Bowhite turned the purple crystal in his hands, so obviously taken with its warmth and weight in his palm, she felt an answering shudder through her core.

"Yes." How could he not know? Her mind whirled over and over with the question.

"Does it always give off heat like this?"

Of course he'd be attracted to it, Jemma realized. It had a piece of him trapped inside. "No." She placed her hand on his cheek so he'd meet her gaze. "Did you not grow up on Trolen?"

"Trolen? No. But my mother was from there. She died when I was a child." His brows drew down. "But how would you know that? Most people haven't heard of the planet, since few of their race ever leave there."

To tell him or not to tell him, that was the question.

Why keep it a secret?

Because he'll own you if you tell him, Jemma. He'll own you because he can. If the ritual is never completed, then you can retain your freedom. Do you really want to attach yourself to this criminal? One who is Selfish?

But he was her Chosen. She had to be with him.

Do you? Do you really have to or is it just what you've always been taught?

Bad things happened if you didn't find your mate. She tried to think with the firm press of his body between her legs.

Loneliness.

It wasn't a wonderful way to live, but she'd survived it for ten standard years, hadn't she? She could live without him. She'd already proven to herself that she could.

She was actually in a very fortunate position. She could get to know her Chosen and decide if she wanted him or not. If she didn't, she wouldn't tell him about the amulet. Being lonely seemed like a small price to pay if her other alternative was to bind herself to this man. Whoever he might have been on Trolen had been altered by growing up elsewhere. She didn't fool herself into thinking Bowhite was anything other than a dangerous criminal. He'd led the prisoners to revolt and ended up stranding them all here. This was not the behavior of a person she should trust her life to.

Her mind made up, Jemma shrugged and slid the crystal from his hands. "It's something everyone has on my planet."

He shifted his weight, drawing her notice back to the rock hard erection pressed into her belly. The benefit of finding him was she could finally feel what sex was meant to be like without trapping herself to him.

She rocked her hips, pressing herself up onto his stiff erection, and arched her body. Before he could capture the necklace again, she pulled him down for a kiss.

Distracted, he moaned into her mouth, then sat on his knees to pull his shirt from his body. A tanned, muscled chest rippled free of the cloth, making her ache to touch him. Lowering back down, he braced his hands on either side of her to keep from crushing her with his full weight.

She drew in a sharp breath, tasting his scent on her tongue. Despite the coolness of the air, sweat beaded his skin. Lean muscles ran the length of his arms, up across his chest. A light dusting of hair teased her bare skin, thickening as it ran down into his pants. He had small, dark, male nipples.

She stroked across his chest, fighting her need to rush. He rested on his forearms in a partial push-up, watching her touch his body with a patience that surprised her.

Of course he's perfect. He's the other half of my soul. He was built for me. It was a strange thought, one she'd never had before.

Overwhelmed, she placed a kiss on the muscle in his right arm.

His left hand captured her chin, tilting her head back so their gazes could meet. "No more biting, Jemma, or I'll bite you back."

The desire to bite him again raced through her so strongly, she almost whimpered, but she forced herself to nod, giving her agreement. If he took her blood, he would bind them together that much more. There were three stages that formed their ritual-bond, one of which she'd already decided to accept. She wanted the sex, but by leaving the other two rituals undone, she would allow herself the ability to walk away. Body, blood and mind. All three had to be complete before the ritual between them was solidified and their lives were irrevocably intertwined. Death for one would then mean death for the other.

He released her and she ran her mouth along his chest. His skin tasted like a Trolen summer day. Air so hot you could savor it in your mouth, swirled with sea spray and Merk, a summer herb with a spice-scented flower. The mixture was so heady, her head spun from a single lick.

Rolling them over, he gave her access to his body and she took full advantage, her hair falling free from its ponytail to brush across his skin. She'd never wanted anyone like this, hadn't been able to want anyone in this way. She straddled him, unbuttoning the top of his pants, then running her hands along his chest, enjoying the feel of hard male under smooth skin.

She dropped forward to taste his nipples, pressing kisses along his hairline all the way to the top of his pants. He didn't wear underwear. Licking just under the line of the waistband, she stopped at his hip and nipped his skin.

"Jemma." His tone wasn't light anymore, but dead serious. Warning her that time was speeding up and she wouldn't be able to linger much longer.

She worked up his body to kiss him again, rubbing her breasts back and forth across his chest, enjoying the tingle between them.

"I'm trying to let you set the pace, sweetness, but I'm afraid I'm close to taking back over. I want you badly." He softened the warning by brushing his fingers along her cheek.

Her heart skipped a beat. He was so very perfect.

Get a hold of yourself, girl. He might be perfect in bed, but he's a criminal and was raised without any understanding of your culture and you better keep your head on your shoulders, or you'll be the one who loses.

Dragging his fly apart, she pushed his pants over his lean hips to his boots. She pulled them and all his clothes off quickly. His erection sprang free, heavy and large, ready for her. She paused at the width, unable to stop herself from running her fingers along the underside of his cock for just a moment.

He watched her the whole time, not moving, but coiled on the edge of action. Every muscle on his body stood at attention in glorious definition. She wanted him to turn over, so she could see if the rest of him looked this good.

"Take off your pants, too," he growled.

She didn't like to be ordered, but she reveled in the fact that he craved her without even knowing she was her Chosen.

Sitting on her knees, she raised an eyebrow in challenge, then slowly undid the fastener at her waist.

His black gaze turned sharper, the heave of his chest increasing with the lowering of each button on her fly. Jemma drew it out, the power she had over him so exhilarating, her own pulse skyrocketed. To have this beautiful creature gaze at her with such total desire was a rush.

She slid her boots off, then her pants, then knelt to hook her fingers in her panties and strip them away. For reasons she didn't want to dwell on, she left the amulet around her neck, unable to bring herself to take it off.

Then she kissed up his inner thighs, inhaling his scent. Tasting her homeland. His erection was her ultimate destination, the large head begging for her lips, the bead of pre-come glistening in the dim light. When she made it to his hip, he flipped her on her back so quickly she could only gasp.

With his gaze locked to hers, he reached between them, grasped his hard, thick cock and guided it to her entrance.

If they were on their homeland, he would have said ritual words, words he didn't know and therefore couldn't say. A pang of almost physical loss rang through her as he entered her channel without them, but dissipated at the feeling of stretching. He was big, bigger than he'd appeared when she'd first seen him. Or maybe she was small.

"Tight," he murmured. "Not going to hold out long."

He pulled up so he could slip his hand between their bodies and rest his thumb on her clitoris, sliding in the moisture her body wept for him.

The tempo he set was fast, hard, and deep. Stroking in until his body met hers and he touched her womb. The crystal between her breasts sparked like a fire, increasing the pleasure, reminding her she was his, fated from the beginning of time. Pressure built. Too much. She arched into him, seeking release. "Please," she begged. "Help me."

His lips touched hers and something inside her snapped.

"Rip." She cried his name on the tide of her own release, shaking from head to toe as waves of pleasure rocked over her. Pleasure that was terrible and amazing and addicting all at once.

With a growl, he came, pulsing in time with her own contractions, their bodies fighting to match each other, to finalize the bonding, to mesh their souls and entwine them forever.

Her body shivered, peaking again for a quick burst of pure feeling that bordered on agony.

His hand slipped from between them to rest on the platform beside her head. He collapsed, pushing her back into the hard wood.

Outside a loud caw ripped the air, the sound strangely like a bird's. Dragging her way up from the haze of their lovemaking, she tipped her head, listening for the sound to come again.

When it did, Jemma knew it wasn't a bird.

Chapter Five

*The raptors are learning by trial and error how to work around
the latest security measures we've put in place and I am beginning to
wonder just how intelligent these beasts are.*

Excerpt from Doctor Lore's Notes

Rip raised his head with a jerk, every instinct going on full alert,
sloughing off the lethargy stealing through his body. He didn't want
to move and the need to let someone else deal with the raptors beat
inside him.

He wanted to keep his place inside Jemma's body. Cocking his head
to listen to the movement in the camp, he leaned on one elbow, his other
hand brushing idly across Jemma's face, the feel of her soft skin under
his calloused fingers pulling his attention.

The sound shattered through the air again, a sharp bleat, followed
by two quick chirps. Closer. Too close.

"They're inside the fence." Jemma's voice went breathy with
panic.

"Yes." He had to go. He was the best sharpshooter they had. It took
every ounce of discipline he'd ever mastered to part his body from hers,
but staying was impossible.

"Get dressed." He might have to stop their lovemaking long before
he was ready to, but he wasn't going to spend a second out of her presence. It didn't make sense that he felt this way, but he did. For whatever
reason, he *had* to keep her close. If Velopeds were within the compound,
he wasn't going to walk away with her alone and unprotected in his
tent. He pulled on his pants. "You'll come with me."

She sat, her hands shaking as she reached for her clothes. He pushed
them closer, pausing as she drew on the tan uniform shirt. Her movements were slow and supple, the natural grace of her body fascinating.
The play of the shadows concealed her skin, then revealed a quick flash

of her sex peeping between the bottom of the shirt as she pulled the edges together over her breasts in an unintended reverse striptease.

His cock throbbed back to life, pushing against his pants in fierce protest.

With a massive effort, he pulled on his boots. That major task accomplished, he watched for a few moments as her hands trembled so badly, she struggled to fasten her shirt. He dropped to his knee and pushed her hands away to take over the job.

Without fully understanding why, he drew the amulet to his lips and pressed a kiss on the crystal. It warmed as if it knew him. Then he tucked it beneath her shirt so she would think of him as it rested hot between her breasts.

Helping her to her feet, he handed over her pants, steadied her while she put them on and fastened her boots.

He had questions about the necklace, but they'd have to wait, along with his overwhelming need to have her again.

"I don't know why my hands are shaking so badly," she whispered.

He knew. She'd felt that same intense, hyper-sensation he had. It left his stomach rolling, but they didn't have time to deal with it now.

Grabbing his pulse rifle in one hand and her arm in the other, they left the tent at a run, dodging through the sea of shanties to the command center.

"Jackson," he called to his second in command before he'd even climbed the whole way to the platform that stood four man-lengths in the air. The three men in the tower popped to attention as he pulled himself through the trapdoor. "What's the status?"

Jackson handed him a set of field glasses. "We had problems earlier but stopped them at the second fence. I've scanned the whole no-man's-land and everything is secure now. I'll be dammed if I know how they're getting in." The man was a hulking, hairy giant and he'd been Rip's best friend since he'd landed on this waste of a planet two years ago. Jackson eyed Jemma with curiosity, but he wouldn't ask what she was doing in their command post. At least not in front of the other two men on the platform.

Rip studied the no-man's-land between the two fences that made a 270 degree ring around the prison. Nothing. Some of the trip wires had been sprung recently, lighting the warning flares, but no part of the fencing seemed damaged.

"We've got at least two of them in here, although I haven't pinpointed where they are yet."

Rip scanned the camp. He hated to turn on the spotlights, but they needed to see where the raptors were now that two of the moons had set, leaving the camp in shadows.

When the Council pulled out, they'd bombed several of the solar panels that supplied the prison with power. Rip had been fighting a losing battle to conserve enough energy to run the electric flares and fences, as well as the lighting in the Chow hall. He'd been forced to plunge the rest of the camp into darkness at night.

And now he'd waste precious energy on the spotlights. He had to do what he had to do. "Crank it up," he ordered. "Let's find them fast."

He jerked the rifle over his shoulder. They were running out of everything, including energy packs used in the blasters. It was a battle they would eventually lose, but he'd go out fighting to the death. Behind him, the generator whined as someone started it.

Hefting the heavy blaster onto his shoulder, he moved into the shadow on the far side of the lights. He felt Jemma beside him, but rather than finding her presence distracting, calm settled over his body. He met her gaze as he powered up the blaster, glad he knew where she was and didn't have the added worry of her safety. "We're almost out of ammunition." He said the words casually, then put the stock to his shoulder. "See them?" he asked Jackson.

"Looking," Jackson replied.

"Over by the tents?" Jemma didn't sound sure. Rip waited for Jackson's word.

A man's scream of terror tore through the camp, bouncing off the buildings, confusing the direction the sound came from.

Rip didn't take his eyes away from the sight. He'd have only a handful of seconds to fire and needed to be set to take full advantage.

"See them." Jackson's voice held the tension they all felt. "Twenty seven to the east, ten to the north."

Rip swung into position, the hours they'd practiced as a team coming into play. He saw the big, black creature as if it stood a hand's length before him, magnified by the sights on the rifle. He had to blow the head away to kill it. The raptors could take several blasts in the body and still keep going.

This Veloped was an adult, but still smaller than full size. The black, leathery skin glistened in the spotlight, the body as big as Jackson's, the wings retracted, the head an ugly bullet. The beasts couldn't fly, but they could glide for long distances. They liked to leap and hover before landing on their prey. Their claws were so long, he'd seen them penetrate a man's stomach and protrude from his back.

Rip exhaled and when the last drop of air left his lungs, he fired. He always blinked, just a quick reflex he'd honed down through years of practice to only a flicker, but the jump of the pulse rifle against his shoulder made the action unavoidable. The Council had trained him well when he went through the ranks of the starship command. The irony wasn't lost on him.

The Veloped took two staggering steps without its head, then toppled.

"Beside him, one degree to the east." Jackson's voice held no trace of tension now, but rather a thread of relief.

Rip turned and fired the second he found the target. He landed the blow, but too far down on the body. It slowed the retreating raptor long enough for him to shoot again to make the kill.

The pulse reverberated through the camp. "Any others?" he asked.

"I think we're clear."

⁂

Jemma watched Rip Bowhite shoot the raptors with the precision of a master. He'd been professionally trained and had obviously practiced for years. He'd shot their heads off from all the way across the camp and the second Veloped had been running away as well. What had he done before he landed in prison?

"How the hell are they getting in, Jackson?" Bowhite asked the huge man standing beside him. The two men were a study in opposites, Bowhite's lean strength against the overt power of the man beside him.

Without warning, Jemma's mind flashed to the moment Rip had climaxed in the tent, his hard cock pulsing part of himself into her body, a part she could even now feel inside her channel. It connected them intimately, even though they stood apart. She shut her eyes and took a steadying breath. Gods.

Boots made a hollow sound on the platform as someone walked across the wooden floor. She opened her eyes, knowing it was Rip before she saw him.

"I don't know." Jackson ran his hands through his hair, shaking his head at the same time. He was big and burly, a thick black beard covering his face.

"We better find out." In the center of the platform, Rip stared down at the map tacked to the table. "They can't be coming through the fences. They have to be getting in through the water."

"The Velopeds have always avoided water at all costs. I can't believe they'd start coming in that way now."

Rip tapped the map in obvious annoyance. "I've got to take the Healer to the warrens tomorrow so I'll take a look. Maybe something's happened over there, something that would allow them to enter the camp without going into the water."

Jemma stared, unseeing, into the dark of the camp, only partly paying attention to the conversation. She needed to figure out how the men were being exposed. Her safety and the safety of the other prison officials relied on Bowhite's team protecting them.

The Chow hall lights were on, or at least one light was. As she watched, the door opened and someone went inside.

Suddenly, she blinked, surfacing from her thoughts. Something had been wrong with the shape of the person entering the Chow hall. The shadow had been off. Too big. Too dark. "Bowhite," she whispered.

Then she dove for the ladder, dropping to the ground so fast that her hands were burned from skidding down the metal handholds. "One just went into the Chow hall," she yelled, stumbling off the ladder onto her knees before scrambling up and lurching forward.

"Shit," she heard him say behind her. "Stay here, Jackson. Leery and Drought, grab your weapons and follow me."

She ran as fast as she could, dodging between the tents, jumping a bucket near the campfire. It occurred to her that she didn't have a weapon. What she planned to do when she reached the building, she didn't know. She only knew that patients—her patients—were going to be slaughtered and she had to get to them. Now.

Bowhite overtook her, slamming through the door and sliding to a halt. He held a prison-guard issued blaster in his hands. The rifle hung down his back by the strap.

It had taken them minutes to arrive there. Only a handful of minutes. Maybe as many as five, but Jemma didn't think that long. What had happened during that time boggled her mind. A single raptor had caused destruction so great, it took her a few moments to even make sense of what she saw.

Rip started firing, both hands gripping the blaster, feet shoulder width apart. Controlled bursts. One-two-three.

One shot would have done, since the first pulse had gone through the Veloped's head, but he put two more in the body.

In the silence that followed, Jemma stared at the swath of red that ran down the center of the room. Behind her, panicked exclamations battled for answers as people gathered. Sick men yelled for help, but all she could do was count the dead. At least six lay unmoving, their chests torn open. She knew their hearts had been ripped out and eaten, as well as the lungs and other internal organs. So fast, so deadly, so much blood. In a blink of an eye.

For the first time, she realized why Silvy and the others hated the raptors so intensely. It was one thing to read about this kind of destruction in Lore's notes, quite another to see it up close. She found her voice enough to whisper, "Goddess above."

"So fast," Rip murmured from beside her, echoing her own thoughts.

They shared a moment of complete horror and accord, standing beside each other, separate from all the others.

Then the Healer in her snapped in place when an onlooker tried to walk around her. "What are you doing?" She stepped into his path.

"I'm going to help them." A man from the guard platform pushed her shoulder, frustration and anger swirling around him.

"You can't!" She placed her hand on his chest and watched rage gather in the man's eyes. "Listen to me. If you haven't come down with the disease, there is a chance you won't contract it. Risking exposure is not advisable. Bowhite and I and anyone he assigns will take care of this."

"I'll do whatever I want." The man grabbed her arm, but stopped in mid-motion when Rip's hand appeared on his wrist.

"I can't afford to lose any more men, Leery. So get out of here." He inserted his body in front of hers and his tone softened when Leery's hand released her arm. "We'll look after them. I know you're worried, but we're going to figure out what's causing this and find a cure. I give you my word."

"You better, Rip," Leery said, his eyes filled with pain.

"We will."

We, Jemma thought. She was now half of that whole and it made her stomach twist with both pain and pleasure.

Chapter Six

*Last night, I stood on the main tower and watched the Velopeds call
back and forth to each other from distant positions on the other side of
the fence. Could they be communicating a strategy for our demise?*
Excerpt from Doctor Lore's Notes

They worked all night to gather up the dead and stabilize the rest
of the sick.

Jackson led the effort to clean up the dead raptors, passing by with
only a tired shake of his head as he removed the Velopeds from the
Chow hall.

Rip carried the bodies of men to a makeshift funeral pyre, his hands
covered in gloves and his mouth protected by a mask at Jemma's insistence. He felt absolutely nothing, until he had to light the fire.

When the fire took and began to consume the men's bodies, Rip
turned to grab his knees, fighting nausea. These were men he'd led, men
he'd convinced to protest living conditions in the prison. Why hadn't
he learned the first time he'd led protests that the Council smashed
down those who spoke out against it? Anger swamped his mind and
guilt gnawed at his gut. How could he have been so stupid to make the
same mistake twice?

Flames licked up into the fading night. Soon the raptors would be
gone, hidden from the sun for the day and they would be safe once
more.

Bitterness and frustration burned him. Why had the Council pulled
out? Why had they just left? He had only organized a peaceful sit-in and
a petition at the prison, unlike the first time when he'd led a series of
protest marches that had turned ugly, erupting into days of skirmishes
with the Council guards and riots that raged through the Capital City.
Surely the Council wouldn't bomb the prison and pull off the planet
because of their mild protests? He'd had nothing to do with all the locks

failing. The warning alarms had blared into the air, then the Council ships had shown up, bombing the camp and evacuating the administrative personnel and guards.

Watching the bodies of the men he'd been responsible for burn, Rip fought a sudden urge to go to the Healer and hold her in his arms. Instead he said, "Let's have patrols spend the day checking the fences for breaches. I want to know how these bastards are getting in."

⁂

When the sun rose, Jemma and Rip staggered out into the daylight.

"I need to return to the warrens." She sighed and tipped her face into the sun, enjoying the simple pleasure of the light on her skin. They were safe from the Velopeds until the end of the day. That alone was something to celebrate.

"We'll go now." The deep vibration of his voice quivered across her body, replacing the brief contentment she'd just felt.

She squinted in the bright light to look at him. He rubbed his neck, the rifle still strapped onto his back, his clothes covered in blood, a blaster tucked into his pants. Exhaustion came off him in waves and she longed to help him, yet she had to go search through the medicine storage area. Her Healer duties warred with her sudden need to see that he rested and took care of himself.

"Why don't you get some sleep? I can go back to the warrens alone."

Tired black eyes turned to look at her. "We stay together. Period." His tone told her he wouldn't let her go without him.

She nodded, then remembered what she'd meant to ask him earlier. "Rip, what happened to the raptors you killed last night?"

"We burned them." He pivoted on his heel and marched away, his shoulders stiff and unyielding, warning her away from the subject.

She hurried after him. "Next time you kill one, I need to run some tests on it."

That got his attention, bringing him up short. "Why?" His face was a mask of anger.

It struck her that he was more impacted by last night's events than she'd realized. She longed to comfort him, but he seemed more like a caged raptor then her Chosen right now. "I just want to see why they can't go out in the sunlight, to test Dr. Lore's theory." If possible he seemed to become even angrier, his eyes narrowing into slits, so she rushed to add, "The more we know, the more we can protect ourselves from them."

He relaxed at that, blowing out a breath. "Fine." He strode off without a backward glance, leaving her to hurry after him into his tent.

Jemma was so tired, too dazed from the night's activities to reach for him, even though on one level she wanted to comfort him and reaffirm the bond of their flesh again.

The sight of his body as he changed clothes made her shiver, though, a delicate shudder that raced through her when he dropped the shirt, then his pants. Her knees went weak and she sank into the only chair.

For a moment, his gaze met hers and he stood naked before her, his eyes full of promises, his cock growing hard as she stared at it. "If we had time, you would be doing more than looking," he said, the words a promise.

She licked her dry lips, heat whirling through her. Stay on task, she reminded herself as the amulet between her breasts heated to a warm purr.

He drew on a clean pair of pants, then met her gaze. With her full attention, he stroked his fingers down his erection before tucking it inside. She swallowed, unable to stop the physical quake of lust that rocked through her. At the movement, he narrowed his eyes, while his hands opened and closed as if he fought some sort of internal battle. Then he turned to take a shirt from the trunk.

The spell binding her snapped, and Jemma leaned back in the over-stuffed chair, taking a shaky breath. Her body craved his now. She had seriously overestimated the strength of the bond that had formed from completing one of the three rites. There was a chance it came from proximity. They'd been working side by side for hours and he'd been touching her freely. Little caresses, his body brushing hers as he passed, his hand trailing up her arm as he handed her things she'd needed. And now he was blatantly provoking her.

"Up," Rip said, dragging her to her feet. "We leave now, or we'll end up staying here longer than we should."

She bent to pick up her pack which held her diagnostic equipment.

"Leave it." He stepped between her and the bag. "You'll be coming back here tonight."

"I can't promise to have the medication so quickly."

His face turned stubborn and he seemed to settle in, as if he planned to block her access to her bag for the rest of their lives if she didn't relent. "If you need to spend more time there, I'll return with you tomorrow."

Jemma realized he wouldn't let her out of his sight. Her first instinct was to argue, but instead she said, "Then let's go." She knew it was the mating between them that made him protective of her. Fighting it would be almost impossible unless she revealed their bond, and she wasn't ready to do that.

They set out. Her nipples were tight buds, scraping against her shirt. Moisture dampened her panties. The desire racing through her body had boosted her energy level and she had new strength to make the hike to the warrens.

She was so obsessed with her thoughts, she didn't realize he'd stopped at the water's edge until she stumbled into him.

He captured her with an arm around her shoulders, pulling her close against his hard, lean body, but his gaze searched the lake. The prison was built on a piece of land that jutted out into a huge fresh water lake. He scanned the fences that extended into the red, murky water. "They haven't been breached." He buried his face in her hair and inhaled. "How are they getting in, Jem?"

She resisted for all of a second before melting into his body. She trembled with a sharp joy at her childhood nickname on his lips. He didn't sound as if he was asking about raptors. He sounded intimate and sexy. "You think they're coming in through the water?"

"No. I'm not sure of anything." His hand cupped her cheek, then he stroked a finger around the shell of her ear. "Except that I want you. Badly." He shook his head. "Too badly. It's puzzling me."

She had a flash of guilt. He didn't know the bonding had begun and now he was lured to her. Snared by the need of their souls and bodies and minds to connect.

"Some strange chemical reaction," she whispered, her throat catching on the lie.

He gave a rusty laugh. "Yes."

A harsh need to make up for her deception flew through her. She sat, pulling on his hand until he dropped beside her, then she pushed him onto his back. She would satisfy him, but take nothing for herself. That would at least absolve her of the niggling guilt rising in her mind. "I don't think it was very nice of you to tease me as you did earlier." She slipped her hand from his knee to his groin.

He smiled with only one side of his mouth, raising his brows at her.

"You think I was teasing you?"

Jemma cupped the full erection straining below his clothes. "Weren't you?"

"I'm not sure I was teasing. I seem to lose control when it comes to you."

His desire burned as hot as hers, she knew, but he didn't understand why. Guilt and need filled her. Instead of meeting his gaze, she unfastened his pants and pulled his erection free.

His cock was framed by the edges of his pants, nestling slightly to the left of his stomach, the head bigger than the shaft, begging her to tongue the top. She obliged and licked the strong vein running up the shaft, up to the slit, where the taste of summer on her home world exploded in her mouth when she swallowed the single drop of fluid resting there.

She could have wept with the rightness of the taste. Instead she circled below the head, ringing it, only to circle back to lick the crease again.

"Gods. Jem."

Reveling in how good it was to please him, she took him deep in her mouth, holding the base of his thick shaft with her fist.

Up and down. She kept the pace painfully slow, knowing he'd get more pleasure this way.

His hands clutched at the grass beneath them, as if he was trying to hold still for her.

Then he sat up and stripped her pants and boots off in one swipe. It happened so fast, she could only blink. He pulled her onto his chest to straddle him, her head toward his feet. She stared openmouthed, her head craned over her shoulder to meet his gaze. "Bowhite?" What was he doing?

His hand landed with a playful whack on her upturned butt cheek. "Don't call me that, Jem, not when I'm about to do this." Tugging her body backwards, he parted the lips of her sex and licked her from one end to the other.

"Oh," she said. Never had she realized how good this could feel when the right man was doing the licking. "Rip."

He stopped and she groaned. "Feel free to return the favor, sweetness." She could hear the humor in his words.

She stared at his cock, wondering if she could think enough to both enjoy her own pleasure and give him his. She was game to try.

Taking his cock into her mouth, she suckled, then moaned as he added a finger inside her to the motion of his tongue. He groaned in return and she arched at the vibration on her clitoris.

Just the thought of what they were doing drove her desire higher, the tension building with a sharp jolt up through her body.

She tried to concentrate on his cock, tried to keep her mind where it should be—his pleasure. But it was hard to remember her earlier guilt when he added another finger inside her, mimicking the motion of her mouth with the penetration of his fingers.

Whimpering, a wave of pure desire flashed and she was gone, screaming her release, her lips still kissed against the head of his cock.

"Gods," he shouted and she had just enough time to take him into her mouth again before he came, shuddering below her.

They lay completely still, both breathing as if they'd run for their lives from a pack of raptors.

Rip still had his fingers inside her, the view of her sweet sex capturing his attention even after they'd both orgasmed.

Never, ever had he even considered that lovemaking could be this good. The other times he'd been with someone, he'd climaxed but was left with no satisfaction.

He was satisfied now.

Jemma ran her tongue over the head of his cock one last time, as if she enjoyed the taste of him, then rolled off his body into the grass. He followed her over, keeping his fingers lodged deep inside her.

She blinked in surprise.

In reply, he stroked his fingers out, then back in.

"Rip..."

"Yes, Jemma?" He stroked again, waiting. Propping himself up on one elbow so he could watch as he penetrated her, he inhaled deeply, oddly pleased at the shimmer of her desire on his hand.

Her pleasure meant a lot to him, maybe too much. His feelings for her were overwhelming, but he was willing to go with it. He'd found something special with Jemma and since it appeared that his time alive might be limited, he planned to enjoy himself as much as he could.

She didn't speak, just made a hum low in her throat.

Rip watched her swallow, her breath shallow as he added his thumb to her clit, stroking it in slow circles.

He took his fingers away and licked them. "You taste like magic, Jem. Spicy and rich." The taste of her made his cock harden painfully. He was ready for her again, so fast he couldn't stop himself from having her once more.

Moving between her thighs, he fitted his shaft into the tightness of her body and in deliberate pulses, worked his way to the hilt.

A powerful urge shook through him, words he'd never thought before bubbling up to the point he had to let them out. Framing her face, he pressed his cock to her womb and let the promise tumble from his mouth. "The raptors are getting into the prison, my men are dying and the Inter-world Council is never coming back. We could die soon, but I swear I will protect you with my life, with everything I have. Don't doubt it."

She made a small sound, as if her breath caught in her throat, but he didn't wait. He needed to seal his vow with a kiss and he did.

Then he moved, keeping his strokes deep and hard inside her, bringing them both to peak so quickly, all he could do was grit his teeth and groan.

She trembled around him, her contractions cutting off his orgasm before it could erupt, holding him back from release.

He growled in pleasure and pain, dropping his head to rest upon her shoulder. Without thinking why, he burrowed under the fabric of her shirt and bit her hard enough to break the skin.

Her contractions eased and he came, but then her body clamped down on him again. They repeated the crazy cycle until they both were spent.

His energy drained, he could only lick the blood away from her shoulder before falling into a deep sleep.

Chapter Seven

Nature always finds a way to right the balance, no matter how arrogant humans are to think they can tamper with her will.
Excerpt from Doctor Lore's Notes

Jemma woke by degrees, her body sated, her mind whirling in panic. They'd fallen asleep tucked into spoons together after making love, her body simply shutting down no matter how hard she'd tried to stop it. Rip was still wrapped around her, one leg and arm trapping her tight against him.

She didn't know how it had happened, but he'd said the binding words for the sexual part of the Trolen ritual. Oh, he hadn't said them exactly right, but the intent had been the same.

And then he'd bitten her, taken her blood!

Fear rolled through her body. Rip hadn't been raised within the Trolen culture, but the biological drive to mate drove him to act out the bonding process, saying the words without any instruction. The first ritual—the one of body—was complete. He'd pledged his protection. Words and fluids had been exchanged.

The second ritual—the one of blood—was half complete. Fluids had been exchanged. Luckily this time she had to say the words. She would have to be very careful not to pledge her protection to him. Part of her wanted to do so, but she knew it was only the strength of the bond influencing her. She needed to stay strong, needed to stick to her plan. Rushing into a lifetime of commitment, bound forever to a criminal would be madness.

The third ritual—the one of mind—involved an exchange of love. She had to offer him the return of his soul by giving him her amulet and he had to return it to her of his own free will, while pledging his love.

She was confident the rest of the ceremony would never be completed by accident. After all, she had to initiate everything that remained. But they'd gone much farther along the path than she'd ever intended.

Rip brushed her hair from her shoulder and ran a gentle finger over the bite mark there. "I'm sorry. I don't know what came over me."

She did. "We're even, Bowhite." She turned her face so she could peer back at him. "I'll heal." Although she wouldn't. She'd bear his mark until the day she died, as he would bear hers. What she needed, she decided, was answers. "Your mother died when you were a child?"

His eyes shuttered, as if he didn't want to talk about this subject. "Yes, when I was four."

"Your father was from Trolen?" Surely he couldn't be the product of a Trolen woman and a father from another planet, could he?

"I don't know where my father was from. I have no recollection of him. After my mother's death, I ended up living with her best friend on Borrus."

"You grew up on the Capital Planet?" She'd lived there for two years before she'd come to the prison, working on the Sem.

"Yes." He studied her, trailing his hand down her cheek. "Until two years ago when I was sentenced to prison."

They'd missed each other on Borrus. Barely. Had the Goddess been trying to pair them even then?

"What did you do to end up here?" She had to know, had to understand every part of him.

He rolled her to her back, the muscles in his jaw working with sudden tension. "You're full of questions."

"After what we just shared, don't you think I have the right to ask?"

He blew out a breath, seeming to concede the point. "It was stupid, really. I organized a peaceful rally to protest low wages on starfreighters, but during the march, the police came in and tried to stop it. Someone threw a rock." He gritted his teeth with anger that obviously hadn't left him in all this time. "That one rock started two days of riots. The Senators were furious, calling for the heads of the organizers on a platter." Dropping his head to her shoulder, he lowered his voice. "It wasn't worth it, but what has been done can't be undone. I was sentenced to ten standard years here in the Velopit."

He hadn't done anything that terrible. Relief ran through her. If they ever made it off this planet and completed the bond, he would need to curb his actions and learn not to be Selfish. Shaking her head, she realized she had been planning for a future together. It had to be the completion of the first bond that made her think such bizarre thoughts. She brushed his shaggy hair from his face. "You are a natural leader, Rip Bowhite."

"Not that it's gotten me any place but prison." He glanced at the sun, which was high in the sky. "We've managed to sleep through the morning and into the day. Let's go to the warrens so we can get back to camp before dark."

✧﹏(ⓒⓒ)﹏✧

"You'll need to wait here for me," she told him when they reached the top of the tunnel that would take her down into the warrens.

He shifted, his hand brushing his blaster tucked in his belt, and she knew he didn't want to let her go alone. "Why?"

She smiled. "You don't think we've left the entrance unguarded, do you? It might look like it is, but I promise you it isn't."

Thinking of Zach's security measures, she realized how strange it was that Bowhite had only tried that one time to penetrate the warrens. The two groups had simply co-existed. There were eleven guards and administrators, four of which were women. Bowhite hadn't even come to investigate.

"Why didn't you ever attack us?" she asked him.

He shrugged. "We knew when your supplies ran out, you'd have to come to us. Why waste the energy packs?"

She laughed at the simple explanation. "Why indeed?"

Slipping down the tunnel, she carefully stepped over the tripwire that would warn them if someone ever decided to visit without an invitation. As she walked deeper, she had a small attack of guilt at the lights they ran every day, all day that were strung along the walls. They were burning through precious energy that should be saved for the fences and the spotlights. She would need to talk to Zach about that.

Turning the corner, she stopped in surprise. The lights illuminated the hallway, showing clearly that someone had set off the second explosive.

"What happened?" she whispered. Then it hit her.

Bowhite had sent people here while she was with him. How dare he do that! She'd been wise not to trust him. Bastard!

She turned and marched straight back out to confront him. When she walked into the sunlight, she had to blink to find him sitting on a tumbled-down wall nearby. Without pausing, she strode straight up to him and grabbed the front of his shirt. "So Bowhite, what happened to the men you sent here?"

A strangled, surprised laugh escaped him, but he controlled his amusement enough to say, "What men?"

"Are you telling me you didn't send anyone here?" She watched his face closely. Their half-formed bond would make it impossible for him to lie to her without giving himself away.

"Here?" He squinted, his black eyes glittering in the sunlight. "I've got every man and woman still standing guarding the fences."

Not black. The deepest, darkest blue.

"They're blue."

"What?"

"Your eyes." She shook her head. Stay on task. Surely her urge to join her body to his wasn't returning so fast? "If you didn't send men, then what set off the explosives?"

"What explosives?"

She shouldn't tell him. The safety of the administrators depended on her keeping their secrets. "I should go back down." She turned towards the tunnel.

Rip caught her hand. "Jemma, I didn't send anyone." He stood. "I don't want you going down there without me."

She shook her head, fighting the dread welling up inside her. If Bowhite's men hadn't set off the explosives, who had? "I can't bring you with me."

They had a battle of stares which he won by fighting dirty. "Velopeds were inside the fences last night."

That possibility hadn't occurred to her. The warrens were protected, hidden. The thought of the raptors in the tunnels made her wheel around. Her friends. Her friends were down there. Silvy. Zach.

He whipped her back into his chest. "We go together." Framing her face with his hands, he gave her a small shake. "Stay behind me."

It was too late not to trust him. If the Velopeds had gotten into the tunnels, everything had changed. "No, you'll have to follow me down. The whole tunnel is a trap."

He drew his blaster. "Stay close, then. I want you to duck behind me as soon as we see movement."

They went at a crawling pace. She pointed out the first explosive as they passed it. Zach would just have to rewire it all if it turned out everyone was okay.

They passed the first guard location. No one challenged them. The eerie silence slithered up Jemma's back and had her breath panting from her lungs. Two other explosives along the way had been tripped.

"Look." Rip crouched down to point at a pool of black sludge on the floor.

Veloped blood. She shivered. They'd been here.

"I wonder if it died below or if they're still down there."

Rip growled and she knew he'd been worrying about the same thing. "We need that medicine bad enough that we'll have to keep going. I wish I didn't have you with me."

"You couldn't travel through the tunnel by yourself."

"I know."

She wanted to fight with him about his desire to keep her away, more to delay their progress than anything else. She was afraid. Afraid of what they might find.

On rubbery knees, she went on. "We're close now."

"Why didn't the explosives kill one of them?"

She didn't answer, too busy thinking about Lore's research. Stopping at the last explosive, she crouched down to peer at the trip wire, which still rested intact. They were learning. Fear scraped across her like an icy claw. She could picture the raptors watching for the wire after tripping the other three. Rip knelt behind her and placed a warm hand on her back. The action brought some semblance of calm to her mind, enough so she could stand and go on.

Three more turns and they'd be at the main door.

The first bend revealed nothing. She eased around the next, only to sigh in relief at the empty corridor.

One more to go.

What if the raptors were waiting for them? She pictured a group of black, leather-skinned, bullet-headed creatures crouching around the next turn. The thought was enough to cause her breathing to turn shallow.

A smell wafted around the corner, an odor so putrid, it singed her nostrils and had her hesitating. What was that smell?

"The explosives were mainly there to warn us you were coming and to try to scare you away more than anything else," she whispered, her heart in her mouth as she slowed to a stop. She could actually taste her pulse around the foul odor, her blood pounded so hard.

Rip sensed the importance of the next corner, pushing her to the wall. He swept around the bend, the blaster clutched in both hands.

Silence.

Everything, including Rip, was quiet.

She rolled off the wall and around the corner.

The door to the warrens hung by only one hinge. One of the two lights had been smashed, and this time there was a body. She couldn't even tell who it was. A man, she knew that much from the muscled legs and guard-issued pants. He lay on his stomach, blood pooling around him. The smell was worse here. His body was already breaking down.

She stared through the door instead of looking at him. He was too small to be Zach.

Unable to stop herself, she glanced back down at the body. A creeping sensation ran up her back as she spotted the sandy-blond hair. Simpson, the young guard who had a crush on her. Nausea rolled in her belly, but she fought it off, along with the pang of sadness.

Silvy and Zach had explosives and blasters. There was a large chance they were still living. Really, there was. The men and half of the women were guards, trained to use weapons. Silvy wasn't a girly-girl. She'd fight to her last breath.

Rip took a step forward to peer around the broken door, then glance back at her. "You still need to lead or can I?"

"I'll lead." Not because there were more explosives, but because she had to be the one who found them.

With hesitant steps, they made it to the main storeroom.

"Gods and Goddesses," Rip murmured, staring at all the supplies. Food, water, blankets, replacement parts, energy packs, all kinds of things rose up in stacks. Not nearly as much as had been there, but the stock piles were still impressive.

"We had to survive on something. Surely you thought about it?"

He let out a laugh. "No. No, I didn't think about it. I was too busy trying to keep my men from killing each other and keep the raptors outside of the fences to even worry about the group of you." His gaze wandered over the boxes, then landed on her. He waved a hand. "We'll talk about it later. Lead on."

She did. Through this warehouse and through the smaller one that made him mutter. Things were disturbed here, boxes knocked over, one door barricaded, then forced open, leaving two more dead men, neither of which was Zach.

What must the dead men have been thinking, stuck here in their final moments, unable to run? They were trapped. No way out. Raptors ripping down doors, forcing them farther and father back into the warrens, which had turned into their tomb. Two of the black leather beasts lay in the wreckage.

"Goddess," she whispered, her heart in her throat as she relived her friends' terror.

They pushed on, working their way back. In a side room, they found more bodies, bringing the count to five men and two women dead. Jemma knew in her heart they weren't Zach or Silvy, but it was hard to tell. Seven gone from the original eleven. Including her, only four people remained. Maybe.

Sadness prickled in her throat, making her pull in a sharp breath. Rip's body moved closer, sheltering her from the view, while he took her hand and gave it a squeeze. What would she have done if she'd left him above ground? His presence both comforted her and gave her the strength to stand upright when she wanted to drop to her knees and cry.

Before them, a door remained standing, slightly battered, as if something large had been thrown repeatedly against it. But the door still remained intact against whatever had tried to get in.

Her spirits buoyed. Jemma glanced at Rip, then tried the door. It was locked, so she knocked. "Zach? Silvy?"

No answer.

She knocked again.

On the other side of the door, the latch clicked, then the portal cracked open.

She expected Zach to greet her, expected to see them all huddled together.

The door swung open, pushed lightly from the inside.

She stepped back to avoid it.

Instead of seeing her friend's face, she had a moment, which stretched into eternity, to look at the giant monster standing in the doorway. Black leather skin reflecting a shimmer of light, the intelligent eyes watched her, tipping its bullet head to one side to see her better.

Then it chirped and raised its wings.

It was all over. She was dead. "Rip, get back!" She shoved him, hoping to knock him out of the way. He'd have a chance to survive while the monster ripped her apart. "Run! I'll buy you time."

The raptor jumped.

Rip grabbed her arm, hauling her back and firing at the same time. The blast, fired so close, hit the Veloped and it flew backwards into the other room.

Rip jerked her into a run, which had them both stumbling into the corridor, then into the smaller of the two storerooms. Raptor cries echoed behind them.

"We'll never make it," Rip yelled, hauling her to a set of boxes. "Climb, dammit! Climb."

They vaulted up as the raptors burst into the room. She knew they would struggle to follow since they were clumsy climbers, but while it would slow them down, it wouldn't keep them away for long. They learned so very quickly.

The boxes wobbled as the Velopeds slammed into them.

"There!" Rip pointed to a catwalk near the ceiling.

They scrambled, Rip reaching it first and pulling himself up and over the metal walkway.

The boxes trembled beneath her. Jemma had a single moment to meet Rip's gaze, before she felt the bottom give out.

She didn't want to die.

Launching herself upwards, she caught the metal floor of the catwalk with one hand.

For a single moment, she thought she'd be okay, then her hand slipped.

Rip caught her wrist, the snap of pain telling her she'd have a ring of bruises where his strong hand held on like a vise.

Dragging her up, they both collapsed backwards, gasping for breath.

Below them, a raptor chirped, the sound frighteningly like a song bird's warble. They rolled over to look down.

The pile had collapsed, burying one Veloped who tossed boxes across the floor as it worked its way out. Two others quivered in the entrance to the room. They called back and forth.

Knowledge slammed through her. "They're talking to each other, Rip." Other animals across the galaxies could communicate, but this was different. "Strategizing, organizing, following an acknowledged leader." Jemma's heart pounded. She wished Dr. Lore was here to see it.

Rip studied the stock of his blaster, then unhooked the rifle from his back and checked the gage. "So?"

She sucked in a breath. "So?" Irritation rippled through her. He couldn't be this ignorant and be her Chosen. "So, I'm not an expert in alien life forms, but I believe those are the qualifications one must meet to be a human equivalent being."

He pushed a button on the stock of his pulse rifle, then glanced up as if he'd just heard her words. "What are you saying, sweetness? That the Council accidentally invaded an alien-held planet?"

"That's exactly what I'm saying."

He shook his head as the ramifications of that flew through him. "But we're in Inter-world Council space. No aliens are allowed here."

"Considering we invaded their planet, I'm quite sure they don't agree with that." The Council and Senate had enacted laws barring the settling of alien-held planets since the Alien-Human Pact was signed on Borrus twenty years before. Heads would roll if news of this got out. Had this been why the Council abandoned the Velopit? Jemma's mind ran through the possibilities, warming to her theory of a bureaucratic cover-up.

A loud caw cut short their discussion, drawing their attention down to the raptors.

"I've got more than enough ammunition left to take care of these three."

Something else occurred to her. "Rip, it's daylight. What are they doing moving around?" Jemma stared down at them, a shiver passing over her body.

Chapter Eight

*Due to the thick skin on their hides, the Velopeds don't die easily.
The guards have started shooting them in the head if possible, since they
keep attacking even if they take blaster fire to the body. Their bones are
remarkably thick, their rib cage protecting their internal organs.*

Excerpt from Doctor Lore's Notes

Rip checked the pulse meter on the rifle. Nine shots left if he was
careful and controlled the bursts. About seven remained on the blaster.
Sixteen total. Minus two he'd need to save for them. He'd kill them
both before he'd let them be eviscerated alive.

He'd save four blasts, just to be safe. That meant he had twelve to
work with. It was enough, as long as these three raptors were the only
ones they ran into before he could dig out more energy packs from the
surrounding supplies. He cursed himself for not reloading earlier when
he'd had the chance.

Jemma seemed to think it was significant that they were fighting
aliens, but it only came down to one thing for him—kill or be killed. He
wasn't giving up without a fight, especially now that he had Jemma.

"I guess down here they're not exposed to the direct light." Jemma
lay on her stomach, peering over the catwalk. Her body was a tight line
of tension, her beautiful face filled with concern.

Even now, in the heat of fighting for their lives, he wanted her.
Badly.

And he'd have her, he promised himself, as soon as he took out the
Velopeds.

"Rip," she whispered. "They see the ladder."

She was right. The biggest of the three chirped excitedly, one clawed
hand pointing at the catwalk, then following its progress across the
ceiling to the ladder on the far wall.

"I know they're intelligent, but they can't be that smart, can they?"

She didn't answer, because neither of them knew.

Questions would have to wait. Rip stretched out beside her and sighted down the rifle. The Velopeds saw him, screeching as if they knew what the rifle could do.

He blew out his breath and pulled the trigger, fast. Faster than he'd like to, but the raptors' cries forced him to work at a speed that would lead to errors.

The smallest one slammed backwards. He didn't wait to see if he'd actually hit the head. He'd shoot again if the raptor rose from where it had fallen.

The other two raptors were lunging away, the biggest one climbing the ladder, the other darting toward the boxes.

Rip lost precious seconds finding them with his own eyes. If he and Jemma lived, he would have to teach her how to locate targets for him.

He took out the one heading for cover with a clear head shot, noting that the raptor already had part of its shoulder missing. It must be the one he'd hit earlier in the doorway.

"Rip! The ladder!"

Rolling to his side, he sighted on the big Veloped. It landed on the catwalk so hard, the grated floor shook, throwing off his aim as he fired. The raptor launched itself into a glide, eating up half the distance between them. Before it touched the catwalk again, Rip fired.

Its head exploded, sending bits of brain and black leather in all directions. Rip had a moment to think, *thank the gods its far enough away so we aren't covered in that,* before the raptor's body took another step forward. Jerking his rifle back into position, he watched it move as if still it wanted to kill them.

Then it toppled, landing hard on a set of boxes below.

He swung back to sight on the fallen Veloped he hadn't been sure he'd taken out earlier. It lay where it had fallen, no movement from its body to indicate it lived.

"Do you think that's the end of them?" Jemma's eyes were haunted. The look hit all the way to his heart.

"My gut says there aren't any more, that we're safe for the moment."

He would have her either way. *This is stupid, Bowhite. A hundred raptors could come in the room at any moment.* Then he'd be dead and so would Jemma. The need that streaked through his body demanded he touch her, no matter what the cost. If more raptors came into the room, he would stop loving her and fight them, but his gut said they were alone for now and his need screamed for him to fit his body to hers.

He set his rifle down, then placed the blaster beside it with shaking hands, feeling the adrenalin surge now that the immediate danger was over. Sitting up, he stripped his clothes, folding them into a neat pile while she watched with widening eyes.

He met her gaze. "I've got eight shots left, ten if I'm careful, before I'm down to two." He knelt on the metal floor and cradled her cheek in his hand. "I'm not letting us be torn apart by them, Jem. I'll kill us both before that happens." Sealing his lips to hers, he let the kiss be a gentle promise. "And I'm not dying without having you one more time."

"What if more come?"

"Then we'll fight them. Easy as that." It *was* as easy as that. Their position afforded them time.

Jemma opened her mouth, then closed it, her eyes narrowing with her own internal debate. He thought she might protest, call it the madness it was, but instead she pulled his head down to hers.

The kiss was urgent, eating at his mouth.

He thrust his tongue past her lips, then pulled away to tug off her shirt. *Slow down, Rip. Make this good. It could be the last time.*

Studying her body, he was amazed at how beautiful she was. Her honeyed hair had fallen down from the twist she'd had it in earlier. The sun-kissed ends brushed the tips of her ripe breasts. He trailed his fingers across her shoulder to run along the cord that still hung around her neck. She shuddered, as if he touched more than just her necklace.

"Rip," she whispered, stopping his hand before he could cup the crystal.

"Shhh." He placed the pad of his thumb on her lush red lips, then hissed in a breath when her tongue darted out to lave across his skin.

Jemma unfastened her pants, toed off her boots, then sat back to wiggle out of the constricting fabric. When she was naked, she raised an eyebrow, looking to him for the lead. He took a moment to enjoy the view, loving the sight of her small waist flowing into curved hips, down into muscled thighs.

He picked up one of her feet and kissed the instep. "So," he murmured, running his tongue along the bend of her ankle. "Would you really have taken on that raptor by yourself back there?" He nipped her Achilles tendon. "I think you would have," he said, answering his own question, running his mouth along her calf to swirl at the back of her knee.

He had never had someone risk their life for him. She had faced a raptor with her bare hands to save him. He almost choked on the love for her that welled up in his heart.

She arched off the catwalk, moaning from his touch.

"I owe you my life for that." Taking his time, he put his mouth on every part of her, suckling her fingers, licking lightly up her neck, tasting the tight buds of her nipples.

His woman, he thought, running one hand down along the outline of her body. She mewled, the small sound a signal she needed more than just this light petting. What she needed was something only he could give her. Only him.

Sudden need lanced through him, snapping his control, wrenching a growl from his throat. One part of his brain, the part that still retained its sanity, told him to calm down, to get a firm rein on his emotions. He squashed his rational mind, overcome by something so powerful, he struggled for breath around the force of it. Widening her legs, he slammed his cock home in one thrust, then grabbed her hair and twisted, so she had to meet his gaze.

Wide green-blue eyes blinked at him, filled with desire.

She was his! "Only me, Jem, promise it." The words came out so low, he didn't even recognize his own voice.

She nodded, her motion jerky and hesitant.

"Say it."

"Only you, Rip." Desire glazed her eyes and she lifted her legs, twining them around his body, deepening the thrust even more. He clenched his jaw and concentrated on not coming until she did, but he teetered on the edge. The pressure built and was enormous, a weight that made his whole body shake with the need for release.

Her body had gone tight, every muscle contracted and he knew she hovered on the edge.

"Please, Jem," he whispered.

She arched her back and her orgasm rocketed through her. It triggered his own, which blasted through his body like a starfreighter at liftoff. So very good, so perfectly wonderful.

Chapter Nine

I come back again and again to the puzzle of where the raptors go during the daylight.

Excerpt from Doctor Lore's Notes

Jemma brushed Rip's shaggy hair from his face, meeting his blue-black gaze.

When she'd pushed him out of the way of the raptor, she'd told him to run, that she would buy him time, *that she would protect him with her life.*

Without even meaning for it to happen, the second bond had been completed. She hadn't said the formal words. She'd done something much more powerful—she'd acted on the promise in those words. Inside her, the bands between their souls had doubled, signaling two of the three rites had been forged between them. Joy washed through her. She hadn't known how good completing the bonds would feel. Suddenly, she didn't want to ever let him go. He was hers. Or at least partly so.

It was time for truth. Time to tell him, because they were going to die. The raptors were inside the compound. The sickness had taken down most of his men. Time was running out.

"What, Jem?" He drew a line along her bare arm with one finger, stopping to brush her bruised wrist before capturing the crystal in his palm. It warmed to his touch, as always.

"There is something I should tell you." She shook her head, battling the pressure of her guilt and the ticking clock. "But we should go. We need to find Silvy and Zach, then we'll talk."

He nodded. "We also need to see if the warrens are secure, that there's no danger to the camp from here. Then we have to reach camp before nightfall." He fisted his hand around the amulet, before releasing it to sit up.

Relief at putting off the discussion blossomed through her. Yes, they had to get back to the sick men. They had to leave. "I'll tell you tonight." She sat up, pushing the guilt away. If they died without her telling him, well, she'd just have to face judgment before the Goddess for it. The conversation would take too long now.

He pulled on his pants.

On impulse, to make up for her lack of honesty, she took off the amulet and looped the cord over his head. She'd meant it when she promised she would only ever have him inside her and she'd meant it when she'd pushed him away from the raptors, risking her life to save his. Somewhere along the way, she'd changed her mind about this man, seen his worth, and she wasn't dying without showing him she cared.

It was in his hands. She ceded power to him, but she couldn't force the words of love from her throat, not when there were lies between them.

He started to take the necklace off. "It's your good luck charm. I'd rather you kept it."

Resting a hand on his to stop him from removing it, she shook her head. "No. It's yours. Please honor me by wearing it. At least until tonight."

"If it means that much to you."

"It does."

"Then let's go. We need to find your friends, the medicine and be back to camp before dark."

Her heart rose in her throat as they searched the remaining rooms. The three missing people were nowhere to be found. Dread rose up along Jemma's body, the tension of seeing room after room without them eating at her mind, until she wanted to scream.

Coming back through the storeroom, Rip restocked his energy packs, muttering the whole time about their stash of supplies. "At least I'm fully loaded again." He picked up two more blasters and tucked them into her waistband, before grabbing another for his own belt.

They moved on, but Jemma was worried. They only had Zach's office left, but the flimsy door wouldn't have kept the Velopeds out for long if Silvy and Zach had been caught there.

Rip went in first, rolling around the opened portal and dropping into a crouch. "Clear," he said.

When she entered, she saw that a set of cabinets had been pushed away from the far wall and a hidden door stood open.

"What's in there?" Rip kept both blasters drawn, his body tense as he moved to one side of the door.

"I don't know. I didn't even know there was a door there."

Rip ducked his head around a corner for a fast look, then went into the room. Jemma trailed him into a small foyer where another door, this one reinforced, stood open. Beyond it, darkness loomed, thick and black, but she could sense another room. The hair on her arms rose.

Pulling her back into Zach's office, Rip searched through the boxes until he found a thermo-flare. Cracking it to start the flame, he tossed the palm-sized light into the darkness.

Peering around the reinforced door, they saw...

"What is that?" Rip's voice echoed her own confusion.

"Caves?" she guessed. "Underground, natural caves."

The walls of the small cavern were smoothed from the passage of time, and the sandy, red floor showed clearly that something had been dragged to the middle of the room. Three tunnels sloped off in each direction.

"This is what must have caused all the sink holes on the planet."

"Did the raptors break into the warrens from these tunnels? Or did they come in over the fences?" Rip's black gaze glittered in the light of the flare.

Jemma motioned him back into the foyer to study the back of the reinforced door. "Maybe if it just locked with something simple, but do you think the Velopeds would be able to use a key?" She pointed to the padlock with the key still hanging from it. "Someone put an old fashioned lock on this door after the computer systems crashed."

"With the claws on their fingers, it would be impossible to unlock it." Rip shifted. "So one of the administrators opened it?"

She shook her head, wishing she knew what had happened here. "Zach wouldn't let anyone into his office. Only he comes in here."

"Zach Margorly? The Head Guard?"

"He and his Chosen—" she corrected herself quickly, "promised *match partner* are my closest friends." Other planets weren't blessed with mates, she reminded herself. She looked at her own, feeling a pang. It worried her that she hadn't told him about the bonding ritual. An odd thought hit her—what if he wouldn't want to bond with her? She staggered, struck by the realization that she'd never considered his feelings about their bond, only her own.

Rip caught her arm. "Are you all right?"

"Yes." She hurried to bring her attention back to the problem at hand, shoving the terrible thought to the back of her mind. "So Zach opened the door, but why? I don't think the raptors could force him."

"No." Rip studied the door, pursing his lips in thought. "What if he accidentally let them in? Maybe he didn't know the caves were here and when he opened the door, they rushed him?"

"But that doesn't explain what happened in the tunnel. The Velopeds were learning to avoid the trip wires. The last explosive hadn't been set off."

Rip met her gaze and held it. "Neither had the first."

Fear slithered up her skin. She thought they'd just learned to avoid the tripwire at the bottom, but what if the Velopeds had done it the opposite way and learned to avoid the explosives by the top of the tunnel as they went out? "Or what if they never made it out of the tunnel at all, but turned around and came back down?"

"Maybe they just missed the ones that weren't tripped? At least this explains how the raptors are getting into the camp. They wouldn't have to go over the fences. They could just walk through this door."

"Didn't you say the raptors got in two nights ago as well? There is no way the Velopeds were getting inside when I was here. I think I would have seen them roaming the corridors."

"Damn. You're right." He growled in frustration. "But look in the sand." He strode to the center of the cave, still holding a blaster in one hand. "However they got in, these raptor tracks are leading down the tunnels. Some of them, at least, left this way."

They stood in silence, Rip tapping his thigh with the blaster, while Jemma imagined the raptors right around the corner. Rip shifted, drawing her notice to his feet, where something sparkled in the light of the flare.

She crossed to pick it up, staring at the two interconnected circles on a black string.

"What is it?"

"Silvy's promise necklace. Zach gave it to her two days ago."

The sight of the necklace made Rip touch Jemma's amulet where it laid cold on his chest. He wanted it warm, resting between her beautiful, firm breasts.

"This means Silvy at least has gone down these tunnels." Jemma turned to the three, dark holes. "But which one?"

He caught her arm before she could dash away. "There is no way we are going down there this close to sunset, Jem."

"They're my friends, Bowhite. I'm not leaving them." A gleam of stubbornness that could only mean trouble sparked in her eyes.

"You can't help your friends if you're dead," he said simply, willing her brain to reengage and override her emotions.

"I can't just close this door and lock them down there."

Rip could see in the way she stood, her feet firmly planted, that they would be arguing all night if he didn't make a concession. "We go to camp for the night, then we'll come back in the morning." He carefully made sure he didn't promise to search for her friends. "Right now, we need to lock the door, find the medicine and figure out how in the hell the men are being infected. A lot of lives are at stake here, not just your friends." He said the last as gently as he could.

She closed her eyes and he could feel her internal battle. When she met his gaze again, she nodded.

Relieved that he wouldn't have to bind her up and carry her back to camp, he hustled her out of the way. Shutting the reinforced door, he hooked the padlock and took the key.

Chapter Ten

The Velopeds are learning all our secrets. Who is to say they aren't studying us as much as I study them?

Excerpt from Doctor Lore's Notes

Zach and Silvy are still alive. I feel it.

Repeating the words like a mantra, she led Rip to the makeshift infirmary she'd set up.

Inside the room, everything was just as she'd left it. Her half-finished glass of water sat beside Dr. Lore's notes, still open to where she'd been reading. Rip leaned in the doorway, a blaster in his hands, rifle slung on his back.

Ignoring her need to go to him for comfort, she began a thorough search for Revostat. She pulled out other meds she knew fought similar bacterium, lining them up along the table as she came across them.

Firing up her portable copy of Xan Yang's Medical Dictionary, she scanned for Fridincoccolosis, but the search came up 'no entries found.' She scanned for Revostat instead. Although relatively new, Yang had a notation. "Indicated for Voridified skin bacterium," she read out loud.

"Voridified?"

She shook her head, puzzled. "Bacterium which grows on animal skin that can also infect humans. Have you had interaction with the wildlife here?"

"We've been fishing, but otherwise haven't been hunting or interacting with any of the local animals." Rip paused. "Except the raptors."

Jemma nodded, thinking the same thing. "Has anyone been bitten by them or cut?"

"And lived? No. Once the Velopeds get close, you're dead."

Jemma shivered. Their earlier encounter with the raptors had been a near thing. She hadn't appreciated just how near until now. They were the first humans to get close to the Velopeds and live.

"Could we be contracting it through touching the dead bodies?"

"It's possible. I need to analyze one of the Velopeds to see if they're carrying it first." She stopped, considering. "If one person brought it in, could they infect the others through the rash or other exchanges of bodily fluids?"

"I take it you aren't really asking me that question, but are more talking out loud?" Rip asked, his tone dry.

She scrolled through Yang's to the section of Voridified skin bacterium.

Rip moved behind her, the bond between their bodies telling her he stood only a hair's breadth away, reading over her shoulder.

She reread the labels of the meds she'd line up, then scanned the view screen. "Looks like Meriostat is the closest. I'll bring all the stash we have and samples of the rest to test if that fails."

Rip reached around her to drag the small computer across the table so he could read it, too. "Could this have come from the dead raptors? We move them out of the camp or burn their bodies."

"But didn't you tell me they just started getting inside the prison?"

He growled in frustration. "I've had the men remove the ones we kill each night from between the first and second fences for weeks. It never occurred to me I should have had them wear gloves."

"You're burning them. That might release the bacterium into the air for all of us to breathe in." She lowered her head into her hands and tried to console herself that the raptors would eat her long before the disease killed her. They had enough meds to keep them all dying slowly if they couldn't clear it up completely.

"Can you cure it?"

"I plan to keep trying until I do." She shut Yang's down and threw it into a bag, then packed in the meds. Drawing the strings closed with a snap, she met his gaze. "From now on, no one touches the raptors without gloves and a mask." She shook her head, a half laugh escaping her. "This explains why the women aren't coming down with it at the same rate."

"Why is that?"

"Because even prisoners don't assign women to what they consider men's work. Your sexism has kept them healthy." She grinned.

His eyes narrowed. "If you're complaining, I can put you in charge of Veloped carcass removal."

Jemma found she liked his teasing. A strange, bubbling happiness zinged through her.

He caught her shoulders and kissed her on the tip of the nose. "We need to leave." He hefted one of the sacks. "Ready?"

She nodded, her emotions tripping over themselves. Lightness from their teasing. Worry for her friends. Fear of the raptors and finally, fear of his reaction to the fact that she had all but lied to him by not telling about their bonding. They were becoming friends as well as lovers. Friends didn't lie to one another. The minute they were safe, she would spill it all. Her stomach twisted with dread.

⁂

Since Jemma had put the amulet around his neck, it hadn't been warm. In fact, it lay against his chest almost like a chill, as if he needed to return it. For some reason, it nagged at him, like an itch in the middle of his back.

They were alive, but for how long, he didn't know. The Velopeds were smarter than he'd ever imagined; they were learning all the humans' secrets. Opening doors, climbing ladders, breaking into the Chow hall and attacking the sick. Hell, most likely the beasts were making them ill, killing them one way or another. And the caves—he wondered if they ran under the whole planet, allowing the raptors to travel where they wanted.

Rip gave the warehouse a cursory glance as they passed through it. He needed to remove everything they could use from here. It would keep his men armed and supplied for a while longer, but it seemed almost pointless when the raptors or sickness slowly killed them one by one.

It was as if they were merely treading water until they drowned.

He was reenergized now, though. Jemma made him want to live and live well, not just count the days until he died, as he had been.

They passed through the exit tunnel. He stopped her at the mouth to the outside. The sun sat low in the sky, the camp quiet in the pre-evening light. "I almost don't trust that they won't be out there. Every time we think we know their limitations, they change."

Jemma leaned against him. "I was just thinking the same thing. I need to see if the Sem can tell us what keeps them from the sun, as well as if they're spreading the bacterium. If it's a lack of enzymes as Dr. Lore thought, we'll know the daylight will always be safe."

"We kill ten a night, yet they keep coming."

"I wonder what their lifespan is? It would take years to grow to the size we see them, wouldn't it? And yet they seem to adapt so quickly, it's as if we're dealing with another generation every month that goes by."

The landscape was deserted so he stepped out, capturing her hand, as he covered their retreat with the blaster in the other.

They made good time back to camp, heading straight to the Chow hall.

Jemma grabbed his arm before he opened the door. "I'll do everything I can to cure your men, Rip."

"That's all I'm asking." He ran a finger down her cheek, already wanting her again with a fierce burn, his cock hard and ready.

She nodded, then ducked inside. They rested their sacks beside a table she'd been using as a desk.

More sick men had filled the beds since they'd been gone. Guarding the fences tonight would be tricky. Blowing out a breath, his gaze tripped over a familiar face. "Jackson." He shook his head, striding to where the other man lay on a cot. "What in the hell are you doing here?"

"Sorry, Rip," his best friend said. "I felt it coming on, but I couldn't seem to stop it." He held up his hands, palms out, to show the blisters. "I'm glad you're back to run the defense tonight. I'm too dizzy to stand for long."

Jackson had been his friend since the first day they'd come here. Two newbies, sticking together, defending each other from the scum that would shred them for amusement. "You led the group that moved the dead raptors last night."

Jackson nodded.

"We think they might be causing the sickness."

"You're kidding." Jackson's eyes narrowed and Rip knew he thought about the fact the Velopeds would kill them sooner or later.

"The Healer will run some tests to be sure."

Jackson glanced at her, then shot him a warning look. "You better watch her. She isn't one of us."

"She's mine, Jackson. I'll vouch for her." Rip couldn't believe the emotion that filled him at the statement, as if he'd claimed her. Since the moment he'd met Jemma, he'd felt as if chains made of the strongest alloy had started wrapping them tighter and tighter together. It seemed strange, actually, now that he thought about it, as if they'd each been waiting for the other. No. That couldn't be, could it? Yet his gut told him it was true. She didn't just turn him on. She made him utterly complete on every level.

"You aren't worried about her loyalties?" Jackson pressed his forehead, as if he fought the pain there.

"No."

Jackson raised an eyebrow at the sureness in Rip's tone.

Jemma appeared beside him, and Rip couldn't help but touch her, just a small brush of her arm. "Jem, you met my best friend, Jackson, last night in the tower."

She nodded, her professional mask coming over her face as she took in his condition.

"Jackson, this is my woman, Jem." Rip didn't bother to hide his feelings. She was his, period. Oddly, she didn't blink at his announcement.

"Nice to meet you, love," Jackson said, his voice all silver honey, as it tended to be when he spoke to the ladies.

"It's nice to meet you, too."

Rip pulled her back into his chest, unable to stop the possessive gesture.

Jackson had the nerve to wink at him. "Rip says the raptors might be giving us this." He held out his hand.

Jemma studied his palm. "The blisters could be a topical reaction to the bacteria, but the dizzy spells and nausea are more a reaction to the bacteria as it gets into the bloodstream. Still it's hitting fast. Faster than I'd have thought it would."

Rip could sense she was fading into her scientific mind. "About the medicine," he prompted.

She worried her bottom lip with her teeth. "I need to test out some antidotes on someone and Jackson, you might be a good person to start with. Since you just came down with the illness, we would see the effects of the treatment faster in you than the others."

Jackson met Rip's gaze. Rip shrugged. "It might not work. We don't have the exact medicine needed to heal you."

Jackson shifted. "Love, I would be honored to be your first." He grinned winningly, but the pallor of his skin and the sweat across his brow told them how he really felt.

Jemma prepared a syringe, injecting him with Meriostat. "We should see improvement or not within the next twenty-four hours."

Rip stepped closer to her and lowered his voice. "Night is coming and I have to get the fences ready. I would take you with me, but I know you have to be here. Whatever you do, stay inside the Chow hall." He tapped one of the blasters at her waist. "Know how to use this?"

She nodded. "I know enough to point and shoot."

"Use short, controlled blasts. I'll post some guards here as well." Bringing her close, he enjoyed the rub of their bodies for a brief moment. He pressed his mouth to hers, unable to leave without her taste on his lips. "We'll have to wait until the light of day to talk."

"Be safe," she whispered, her blue-green eyes filling with worry.

He stroked her cheek with one hand, pressing the crystal underneath his shirt with the other. "I plan on returning to you. Don't doubt it. I'd like you to take the crystal back for luck."

She stopped him before he could remove it. "No, Rip. Keep it until tomorrow. We'll talk about it then."

He nodded, reluctantly stepping away. The crystal lay dead cold on his chest. He had to battle the uncontrollable urge to feel it warm between his hand and her chest. "In the morning, then."

Chapter Eleven

The longer we stay, the more I think perhaps we made a mistake in coming here at all.

Excerpt from Doctor Lore's Notes

Jemma spent the night tending the sick and listening as blaster fire rang out in almost perfect twenty minute increments. What would Lore say about the timing? He'd probably think the Velopeds were purposely charging the fence for some well-thought-out reason. She shivered at the idea that the raptors were trying to distract the men in the towers in order to sneak into the camp through an unfound hole in the fences.

The sweltering heat in the Chow hall signaled the approaching monsoons. Sweat trickled down her chest, and Jemma longed to open the doors to ventilate the room. Unable to stand it another moment, she gave in to the urge to feel a breath of fresh air, just the barest hint of a breeze on her skin.

Sliding outside, she nodded to the men stationed to guard the doors. They were both tall and thick-shouldered, but the younger one fidgeted continuously with the strap of his pulse rifle.

She turned to stare at the night and breathe in the cooler air, enjoying her brief moment of peace.

The last hour talking to Jackson had showed her why her Chosen and he were friends. He was a wonderful charmer. Already Jackson's fever had gone down several degrees, so she had high hopes that her experiment would yield a solution. She was invested in these men now, no matter that she didn't understand why they'd done what they had to end up on the Velopit. She had to make sure she cured the men, but more importantly she needed to pinpoint the exact cause of what made them sick to begin with.

Leaning against the building, she thought about what she'd say to Rip when they talked in just a few hours. How would she explain the bonding ritual? How would she make him understand?

From several feet away, a shadow moved. Fast. Too fast.

She dropped to a crouch, but the shadow wasn't moving towards her. "Hey," she whispered to the guards at the door.

"We see them," one whispered back, raising his blaster. "Shit, they're gone!"

Blaster fire echoed from the towers directly across from her, as the raptors attacked the fences.

But they weren't just outside anymore. They were within the compound.

She had to warn Rip. "You two stay here. I'm going to tell Bowhite."

"Wait!" said the younger of the two. "Rip was very clear he didn't want you leaving the Chow hall."

She didn't give them a chance to argue. "Defend the men. I don't want another slaughter in there." And then she ran.

She'd never been a fast runner, but she was now. If she didn't get to Rip, they were all dead.

⁂

Fear smacked at him with an almost physical blow, freezing him for precious minutes.

Rip had been watching the eastern end of the no-man's-land, when a wire had been tripped on the western side. He hadn't turned, since he trusted his men to take care of their watch areas. That's why he'd seen them. While everyone's attention was caught on the western side, the raptors were slipping over the fence in the east. If he hadn't witnessed it, he wouldn't have believed it.

But why wasn't the second group setting off flares? There had to be a problem with the power to the tripwires. A short in the circuit that didn't allow multiple flares to light at the same time. The same thing must apply to the electric fences. His stomach twisted at the thought of their exposure.

The coordination it took was massive. The first group had to hit the fences to short out the circuits. Halfway across the camp, the second group used that crucial moment of power outage to climb over the fence.

He'd stood there, watching them replay the same scenario on the second fence. "Gods," he heard himself murmur, watching three Velopeds escape into the camp. They were dead. There was no way they could defend themselves indefinitely against a foe this intelligent.

The revelation shook him to his toes, leaving him standing there until he remembered Jemma.

"Fire up the spotlights," he barked. He had to kill every one of them that had made it into the camp.

"Spotlights? Why?"

"They're inside." Calmly, he took his rifle off his shoulder.

Leery cursed, lighting up the compound.

"Bowhite." Someone scrambled up the ladder calling his name. And he knew who that someone was.

Striding to the trapdoor, he opened it and hauled her inside. "What the hell are you doing here? You're lucky Velopeds didn't eat you for a midnight snack." He wanted to shake her for leaving the safety of the Chow hall. Fear and anger warred inside his gut. She'd been down there alone, in the middle of the gods only knew how many raptors.

Jemma blinked, then met his gaze, looking sheepish. "I guess you know they're in the compound."

He tightened his hold on her arms until she winced. "When I tell you to stay some place, I expect you to do so."

Her eyes narrowed and his insides jumped with desire. She was going to fight him. He could feel it, and it turned him on.

"I'm not one of your men, Bowhite." Her voice was velvet, sliding down his body like a physical brush of her hand.

He leaned in close to growl in her ear. "Listen closely, Jemma. You're mine and what's mine I protect above all others, including my men. If I tell you to do something, it's for your own safety. I promise you if you disobey me again and put yourself at risk, I'll chain you to me to keep you safe."

Jemma rose up on her tiptoes and placed a hand on his chest to steady herself. "And I'm telling you, Rip Bowhite." Her voice was a soft whisper that held a thread of iron in it. "If you think I was going to sit in that building while you were eviscerated by raptors, you don't know me at all."

Rip wanted to tear her clothes off and run his mouth over her body. They stood completely still in the moonlight, while he dragged in a breath to calm himself. Then another. Finally two more. One by one, he lifted his fingers from her arm, and spun to slam the trapdoor shut, enjoying the satisfying thud it made.

On the bright side, she was here with him where he knew she was safe. He caught her arm on his way by and tugged her to the rail. If he couldn't have her under him arched in orgasm, she could take Jackson's place as his spotter. "Every piece of ground is laid out on a grid."

"What?"

"Listen," he growled. "You're going to be my eyes, since you can't seem to stay where you're supposed to."

"Rip, I'm sorry."

"Don't be sorry, just be useful." He softened the words by stroking a finger down her cheek.

Her lids dropped to half-mast and she rubbed him back, but she nodded.

Straightening, he pointed, trimming his teaching to the bare essentials. "Tell me north, south, east or west as you see the raptors out there. Got it?"

"Yes."

He hoisted the rifle up, lining up with the sight.

She was silent beside him, but he could feel her searching.

In the stillness of the night, with the close heat that came before the rains, Rip felt the connection between them almost like a physical binding. He was attuned to her. Abnormally so, now that he focused solely on her and the world had narrowed down to just the two of them and his rifle. Every movement she made seemed to telegraph to him, even the smallest turn of her head.

So when she said, "Northwest," he had already known which direction she'd been looking, swinging the rifle towards the area of the camp to the left of the Chow hall.

"Move more to the north," she said.

He saw one, tracking it as it moved, fast, through the compound. Blowing out his breath, he fired ahead of the creature, anticipating the steps it would take as the pulse flew through the air. The raptor pinwheeled, headless.

"One right behind it."

He searched, just catching the Veloped as it turned to run the other way. Firing, he knew before the bullet hit he'd missed, and fired again. This time he connected, but didn't get the shot he needed to take it down. The third time, he did.

"There are three," he told her. "Find the last one."

"I'm on it," she murmured. "West of the Chow hall."

He'd felt her turn, knew where she looked as she looked there, the connection between them was so strong. This time, he didn't need three shots, but one.

Jemma didn't know who moved first, but when the last raptor fell, she found herself pressed into Rip's chest, her arms around his waist. She inhaled his scent, closing her eyes while he ordered his men to take over in the tower, warning them to come get him if the flares were tripped again that night. They checked on the men in the Chow hall, but it was as if she were in a dream. Her breasts were heavy with need, her whole body weeping for her Chosen. She needed him inside her, needed to reaffirm the half-closed bond. Her body longed to feel the weight of the amulet around her neck once more, but she couldn't accept it without coming clean about her deceptions.

She suspected Rip felt the bonding call just as strongly, since he never stopped touching her. Even as she checked Jackson's fever to find it had broken, Rip's hand rode on her lower back.

When they reached his tent, the sun was just cresting the horizon. She climbed the steps to the platform and turned. "We should talk." She didn't want to, but she also didn't want to keep the secret anymore.

He closed the distance between them. "Later."

His hand wrapped in her hair, pinning her head as his mouth crushed hers in a kiss that broke away her thinly held good intentions.

Yes, she should tell him about the Trolen bonding ritual, but now she needed to taste and feel his body with every inch of hers.

She clawed off his shirt, eating at his mouth. Without parting their lips, he grabbed her blouse and ripped it down the center. The fabric tumbled from her shoulders, pooling at their feet.

Always before there had been a level of caution in their lovemaking, at least on her part. She hadn't wanted to accidentally complete a part of the ritual.

But not now.

In this moment, she had to have his cock inside her, his lips on hers, his taste in her mouth. Everything. She wanted it all.

She scratched her nails into his back, breaking the kiss to run her tongue along his chest, lapping up the glorious taste of her home world and the man she loved.

Rip pushed her into the overstuffed chair and jerked her boots and pants from her body, while she fought to run her tongue along his neck. Her fingers wrestled with the fastener at his waist, wanting to free him. The moment she did, he turned her so she faced the chair.

Bending her at the waist, he curled around her body until her hands braced against the cushion.

"No, this isn't what I want." She wanted him beneath her, lying still while she fulfilled them both.

"I don't care," he growled, then reached between her legs from behind and tested her readiness with a stroke of a finger into her core. "Not this time, Jemma-mine. This time I want you fast." He slid in the wetness that had been building for hours, wrenching a moan from her. "Hard." His hand was replaced by something stronger. "And deep." He rammed home.

She screamed, part of her mind arguing that the whole camp could hear her, but the part that actually controlled her actions remained silent, letting her body react to his ministrations.

"I want you violently, Jem." He thrust, touching her all the way deep inside. "I want you always." He thrust again. "You are mine." And again. "I am yours." Their bodies crashed together as she scrambled to support them.

As he increased the pace, one of the hands holding her hips rotated between her legs so that it pinned her clitoris beneath a finger.

Whimpering, all she could do was arch her back and let him pleasure her. Her legs began to wobble as she felt herself cresting, so she rested her head on the cushion. "Please," she begged.

"Please what?" He was all demand, no thread of softness in his voice.

She was surprised at how much she liked this side of him.

Her body peaked like a wave crashing onto the shore in slow motion. The orgasm built those last few steps, topped the crest, then smashed to the ground.

Like the slow roll up the sand, aftershocks and secondary releases pushed through her. Vaguely she knew he'd come too, somewhere in the madness. She shuddered. He supported them both with one arm braced on the cushion below her, the other wrapped around her waist as they gasped for breath, the scent of their lovemaking twining around them.

As if she were a limp doll, he lifted her into his arms and sat in the chair, settling her in his lap.

Still unable to think, she snuggled into the warm cocoon of his body and fell asleep.

Chapter Twelve

Last night, raptors made it past the security into the camp, killing ten of the prisoners. This prison has become a feeding cage for them, if they can only get inside.

Excerpt from Doctor Lore's Notes

Rip came awake in the chair, sunlight streaming in through the slightly parted flaps of the tent, highlighting Jem's beautiful body in his arms. The cream skin beneath his hard, calloused hand felt like soft heaven. He stroked down her leg, curving around her knees to trail down to her delicate foot.

"How long have we slept?" she asked, her voice still dreamy.

He smashed her tighter to his chest as he rubbed his eyes. "Only a little while. It's still a few hours before midday." He wanted to have her again, but he knew they should talk about what was between them.

"Mmm," she murmured, stretching her body against his, distracting him. "Daylight. Too bad it can't always stay light to keep the raptors away."

Rip caressed her hip absently. "Last night, I saw how the Velopeds are getting in."

Leaning back to make eye contact, Jemma's tight rear end snuggled into his erection, making her gasp and desire spike through his body.

He tightened his arms around her, and a flare of heat sparked between them.

"Wait. Rip."

He stroked down her back to cup her buttocks, his attention on her body.

She tapped him on the shoulder, her face serious. "We need to talk first. Badly."

He sighed and released her rear end, placing his hands on the chair arms. It was hard to concentrate when all he wanted to do was have her. "Talk about what?"

"About the bond," she said, the words rushing from her mouth.

He tried to focus. "Bond?"

"Between us." She blew out a breath, wiggling as if she would leave his lap.

"Stay." He clasped his hands around her, not wanting her to leave him even to get dressed.

"Have you ever returned to Trolen?"

That got his attention. "No. Why would I?"

"Because then you'd know who you are." Exasperation laced her voice. "If you'd just gone home, you'd know all this and I wouldn't be stuck explaining."

His mother's face flashed through his mind. He tried never to think about her, since she'd ended her own life. First, his father died. Then his mother left their home to visit her friend on Borrus. There, she'd simply stopped eating and had wasted away. Rip had lost all memory of his sire, but he'd never forget those last agonizing days of his mother's life. No matter how much he begged, cried or pleaded, she wouldn't eat or drink. Within a week, she was dead. Just the name of his native planet made the old fear well up inside of him. "I feel like you're about to drop a massive surprise on me, Jem."

She touched the crystal on the cord around his neck. "When you and I were children, a wise woman on Trolen took a piece of your soul and put it into this crystal, so we would know the Goddess Chose us for one another."

Put a piece of his *soul* in her amulet? Rip's mind skittered around her revelation, trying to make sense of it. "Wait, are you saying we were *predestined* to be together? That we're what? *Mated*?" He couldn't stop the sharp laugh. "Mating is a myth. Everyone knows humans don't do that." Possession thundered through him on the heels of his harsh words. If they were mated, she would be his *forever*. He crushed away the fantasy.

She took a calming breath as if he irritated her. "Of course mating exists. Do you think someone just made it up? Every myth is based in truth. The people of Trolen keep the rituals a secret, so that others can't use it against us. Our greatest strength is also our greatest weakness."

"You say 'our' as if I'm one of your people." He'd been four when he moved to the Capital City on Borrus. Trolen had never been a part of him.

"Rip, just because you didn't grow up there, doesn't mean you aren't still one of us." She cradled the purple rock in her hand. "When we were twenty, we were supposed to find each other." Her blue-green gaze met his. "But you weren't there for me to find."

Rip struggled with what she was trying to tell him. What if what she said was true? "Part of my soul is in this amulet?" He tapped the crystal, then ran his thumb over it, since it had warmed to a pleasant heat in her hand.

"Yes," she said simply, as if that summed up everything.

"Jem." He wondered if he should laugh. Maybe not, looking at her serious expression that was turning stormy as she lost her patience.

"Think, Bowhite. Every time you've seen the crystal, you've been taken with it. Of course you would be, since it has a piece of you inside."

"A piece of me," he repeated. He was obsessed with the crystal, it was true. The desire to see her wearing it again had been on his mind since she'd given it to him, but before that, he'd been mesmerized by its warmth.

"It recognized you when you kissed me that first time we were here in this tent." She shook her head, her jaw going tense. "I couldn't believe it. I'd spent ten years of my life mourning your death and here you were, in prison." She spat the last word, as if it was totally distasteful to her. "For treason against the Council, of all the most stupid of things."

"Stupid?" he growled. Not that organizing protests against the Council had been the brightest move, but how else would change happen? The conditions aboard the starfreighters were abysmal, with not enough rations and half-pay penalties for the least infraction. He had to take care of his men. The Senators would never improve the laws without pressure to do so from the people they had promised to serve.

He shook his head. "Let's stay on track." The amulet was at the heart of understanding her, he could feel it. He stared at the crystal where it rested in her palm. "That's why it heats every time I handle it when it's around your neck, but then why doesn't it heat when I wear it?"

"It recognizes you as my Chosen. We must both be touching it for it to warm."

A thought hit him, turning his already reeling emotions even more turbulent. "I told you in my tent that first night that I didn't grow up on Trolen. You knew my mother had died without telling me anything, but you still kept all this from me."

"Yes." She raised her chin and started to stand.

"You aren't getting off my lap." It didn't matter how angry he was, he needed to touch her right now like a fire in his gut. "Tell me why." He knew she had a reason. He had enough faith in her for that.

"On Trolen, it is considered Selfish to do something that would send you to prison." Her eyes narrowed. "Selfish is the lowest form of behavior in our culture. Why do you think the people of Trolen rarely leave? They aren't just living for themselves; they're living for their bond-mate. As far as I knew, you had sentenced me to a life alone and grieving to commit treason against the Council, a government body the people of Trolen scorn."

She said the word selfish as others might say the word murder. There was something he was missing here, though. Something she still hid from him that he needed to understand. "You didn't tell me because I was selfish?"

She winced and glanced at her hands. "I wasn't sure I wanted to be bonded to you."

Pain lanced through him, the hurt like an unexpected slap, even though he didn't think he even believed in the concept of mating. He swallowed it down to ask more questions. "You keep saying that word. Bonded." He took her hand to comfort her, even though she'd hurt him. "What exactly is mate-bonded, Jemma?"

"It's a ritual Chosen couples go through to lock their souls together. It weaves a bond between them that is impossible to break. A bond of body, blood and mind."

"How is it completed?" A ripple of anger at her secrets ran through him, mingled with excitement. He knew instinctively they'd completed part or all of ritual, and with that realization, he believed her completely, down to the fact a part of his soul was trapped in the amulet around his neck. He'd felt their bond on the tower last night when he was so attuned to her, he could practically see from her eyes.

"Each is an exchange." She cleared her throat.

An exchange of body, blood and their minds. Pieces of the puzzle began to drop in place. "Blood." He fingered the bite mark that still showed plainly on her shoulder. "We bit each other."

"Yes." As if she couldn't help herself, her hand brushed his arm where a matching mark resided.

"And body?" He trailed a fingered from her shoulder to her luscious breast, knowing what she'd tell him.

"When we had sex, the fluids…" She didn't finish, shivering from his touch.

"And mind?"

"I gave you back your soul," she stopped.

"But that's only half of an exchange."

"To complete it, you must freely gift it to me." She laced her fingers together, then pulled them apart. "All the rituals have words that go along with them."

"So we haven't completed any of them?" He knew that wasn't true. The bond was there between them, he could feel it.

"Well, we've accidentally said them, or at least the first two."

He wanted her with every molecule of his body and now he knew why, but that didn't stop the anger. "Don't you think you should have told me about this when we began to complete the ritual?"

"I just wanted to have sex with you. I swear it, Rip. I didn't mean for all of this to happen, but at every turn, the words were said and the ritual kept progressing."

"You just wanted to have sex with me?" Now he was insulted. She was using him for sex? He curved his hand around her vulnerable neck and tried to rein in his temper.

Jemma closed her eyes and blew out a breath.

Rip watched the pain on her face and felt an answering pain in his own body, but ignored it. "Why?" He had to know, to figure this out. How dare she use him, when he loved her?

"Because," she said, opening her blue-green eyes. She didn't want to tell him, he could tell. "Because I can't orgasm with anyone else but my Chosen, and I wanted to feel what it was like that one time."

Forcing his face to remain blank, he hid the utter satisfaction that raced through his body. His woman, his mind roared. His, his, his. No one else could bring her to completion. "So you were using me?"

"As you were me!" Her whole body stiffened and she ripped his hand from her throat. "Don't you dare try to say you've had no choices, Rip Bowhite, because while I'm willing to take the starfreighter's share of this, I'm not the only person to blame here. The bond can't be formed without your participation."

He flung out his hand. "How could I participate in something I didn't even know was happening?"

"You wanted to have sex with me."

"Of course I did." He couldn't stop the half-laugh that escaped him. Who wouldn't want her? She was perfect in every way, made for loving.

She poked him in the chest. "And you pledged me your protection."

"I brought you into camp. You were my responsibility."

"You bit me, took my blood inside you."

He clamped his mouth shut. That still shook him. He hadn't wanted to hurt her, but he'd done it anyway. Guilt nagged at him for that.

She dropped her voice to a whisper. "Don't worry, Bowhite. The ritual can't be completed without your full cooperation, so you're safe."

"What are the consequences of the bond?" He knew there had to be some drawbacks. He'd felt the benefits and knew they must come with a price.

Her eyes darted away from him, then back, putting him on guard.

"Jemma," he growled.

"We... we can't be separated for long periods of time. It will be uncomfortable."

Okay, he could handle that. He didn't want her out of his reach anyway. This meant he'd have an excuse to keep her near him. "And?"

She tipped her head, back and forth, as if she had to make herself say the next words. "And if one of us dies, the other will, too." The words came out so fast, it took him a moment to decode them.

Dread spilled over his body. "What?"

❧⟨♡⟩❧

Jemma didn't know what upset Rip, but when the color drained from his face, she immediately cradled her body against his to comfort him.

He pulled her close and stayed silent, resting his head on top of hers. His hand stroked down her back. Finally, he shifted. "My mother died when I was four."

Her heart turned over. "I'm sorry, Rip."

Tilting her head, he met her gaze. "She let herself starve to death."

Jemma's breath caught. "No."

"Oh, yes." Bitterness rode in his words. "She didn't eat or drink. Her body shut down and she died a slow, horrible death. Right in front of me."

"Her Chosen must have died first." On Trolen, they had rituals attached with the death of the living mate. Everything was hidden in the shadows, the participants guided by the village wise women through the process. But Rip's mother had taken him off planet and had died unguided and unblessed.

"I have no memories of my father." His face was stone.

"Rip." She straddled him to hug him tighter, burying his head between her breasts.

"I don't know if I want to complete this ritual with you if it means that one of us dies like that, Jem." His hand stroked gently across her thigh. "I couldn't stand the thought of you suffering that way."

A sob escaped her. "It's okay," she whispered, although her heart hurt at the thought they might never complete their bond. Then she did the only thing she could. She ran her hands down his arms as she lowered her mouth to his.

Chapter Thirteen

Still, the sunsets here are beautiful. One can sometimes imagine lovers walking hand and hand on the lake shore.

Excerpt from Doctor Lore's Notes

Rip's whole body lit on fire with her touch, driving all other thoughts from his mind. "I want you."

"Yes," she breathed, her eyes closing, the word a moan.

He trailed a hand down her breast, amazed at how flawless and beautiful she was.

Her nipples peaked at the tease of his hand feathering along dusk-colored nipples, her breath catching at the sensation.

Their bodies knew what they could bring each other, knew now how amazing this would feel. The scent of her desire curled around him and he ducked his head to inhale the fragrance, running his tongue along her beautiful neck for good measure.

She kissed his cheek, her tongue darting out to lave across his skin. "You taste like our home world."

He pulled back to meet her gaze, kneading her waist as she perched on his lap. Resisting the urge to pull her onto his cock, he tried to ignore the heavy need spiraling through him to focus on her words.

"Like a Trolen summer day and Merk, which is a spice grown on our planet." She tilted her head to stare at him. "I won't ever miss it while I'm with you."

He realized what she was telling him. "You'll stay with me, even if I don't complete the ritual." His heart began to thud in double time, and it wasn't just that he had her naked and waiting on his lap.

She nodded, a small, sad smile tipping her lips. "The ritual is voluntary for a reason. Sometimes people do choose not to complete it. Even I was reluctant to tell you about it for fear of binding myself to you. But I would hate to give this up, now that we've found each other."

Running a hand down his bicep, she was distracted when he flexed the muscle there, returning to squeeze it, the motion slow and sexual, her important words forgotten.

He hadn't done it on purpose. He was just tightening his body from frustration more than anything else, but he found himself completely enjoying her obvious fascination with his body.

For some reason, her acceptance of their uncompleted bond bothered him. He didn't like it, even as he feared what would happen if the ritual was complete and one of them died during a raptor attack. They lived on the edge of death here. He wasn't condemning her to a horrific brutal death, like his mother had suffered, if he was killed first. He wouldn't do it, no matter how much he wanted to bind her to him.

"Thank you for understanding," he murmured, capturing her ear between his lips and licking along the lobe.

She shivered. "I don't want to lose you, Rip."

He framed her face in his hands. "I love you." It was the only thing he could say that would summarize his feelings.

She placed her hands over his. "I love you." Turning her head, she caught his mouth with hers and then they were lost.

He ran his mouth down to one nipple, then the other. If he didn't slow things down, this was going to be a fast coming together, a race to fulfillment like last night. He wanted to show her his feelings, not just take her body.

Kissing down her stomach, he spilled her gently onto the floor so he could part the lips of her sex, widening her legs to check how ready she was while he suckled on her clitoris. His fingers slid easily inside her, his cock throbbing at the taste of her desire and her readiness for him. He wanted her close to orgasm before he entered her, since he wouldn't last long.

She tugged on his hair to bring him up her body and he kissed his way up her stomach, pausing to capture each nipple before she grew frustrated enough to demand, "Now."

Smiling, he captured her lips, while she wrapped her legs around his waist. He wanted to build anticipation, wanted to make this last, but his cock slid inside her all in one motion and he had to grapple to retain his sanity. "That's why we worked so well together when you were sighting for me in the tower." He held still, rubbing his thumb down her cheek. "It was as if I could feel your thoughts." He trailed down between her breasts, down her wonderful stomach, until he found the bundle of nerves at the top of her thighs.

"Bonded couples often have the ability to anticipate each other."

"It's more than that. More than anticipation. It took Jackson and me months to come even close to what we had in the watch tower in only a few minutes." He increased the pressure of his thumb on her clit, knowing before she did it that she would arch and moan. Her legs trembled around him. "Can I feel it now between us?" He closed his eyes and found the feeling he'd had the night before.

He rocked inside her, paying complete attention to the strange bond between them, calling on it to increase her pleasure. He knew if he plunged deep and hard, he would hit a place inside her that would rocket her higher, so he did. All his focus was on the link between them, every particle of his being moving to bring her pleasure.

With a twist of his thumb timed with a deep thrust, he felt her orgasm roll through her, roll through him, the feeling so intense, he came merely from the backwash of her fulfillment.

Resting his head beside hers on the platform, he realized that the pleasure that jagged through him came from both their lovemaking and the bond that linked them together. How much more intense would it be if the ritual was complete?

✻ﾟﾟ(ʕ･ᴥ･ʔ)ﾟﾟ✻

"You promised." His mate was beautiful in the sunlight, wearing one of his shirts, since he'd ripped hers from her last night.

Rip sighed. He had. Dammit. He'd promised her they'd go back to the warrens.

"I'm going with or without you, Rip," she warned.

Before he could reassure her that she wasn't taking a step from his side for the rest of their lives, Landis laughed behind him.

"Trouble in paradise already, Bowhite?"

He didn't turn. "There is a possibility we'll get lost in the caverns."

She frowned. "I'm not leaving them in there, dead or alive."

"If you are tired of him baby, I'm your man." Landis' smarmy voice dug into Rip's spine.

"This better be worth it to you, sweetness, because to have even a hope in hell of finding them, we'll need to make a deal with the devil."

"Please, Rip." She touched his arm, her gaze pleading.

He realized, standing in the sunlight with his true love before him that he was in serious trouble. One pleading look from her blue-green eyes and he would kill himself to please her. Leaning down, he purred into her ear, "You're going to make this up to me later if we're still alive."

She nodded.

"On your back, your thighs spread, screaming my name."

Jemma hissed in a breath and shivered, staring up at him through honeyed lashes.

He let the exchange draw out for another sensual moment, then turned to make a deal with the devil. "Landis."

"Bowhite," Landis said, mimicking Rip's deep drawl.

Rip wanted to drive his fist through Landis' face, instead he smiled. "Today is your lucky day."

Twenty minutes later, he had a team of four other volunteers hastily gathered and they were heading back to the warrens. He'd had to promise Landis first pick of the storerooms to get the asshole's cooperation.

When they arrived at the warrens, Jemma worked them past the explosives and Rip rearmed his men from the stores.

"Lookie here," Landis said, spinning on a heel to stare at all the goods piled up around him.

"Work first, then reward," Rip growled, jamming a lightbeam into his stomach a tad harder than necessary.

Landis picked up a spray can of reflector paint. "Just in case." He grinned. "To mark our way out."

"I thought you said you were the best?"

Landis' mouth curved into a self-effacing smile, the first real expression Rip thought he'd ever seen from the man. "Even the best die eventually."

Rip nodded. "Bring the paint." He pressed the start button on a small timer he'd found, then led the way to the reinforced door. "Stay tight," he growled, reverting to his star captain days, when he'd had a team of men running his ship. Before his world had turned upside down, before he'd organized a peaceful sit-in to protest Council work conditions. "Beyond this door, the raptors are able to move about even though it's daylight, so keep close and don't accidentally shoot any of us."

He didn't think the men had any idea of what they were getting into, but he had a bad feeling crawling up his neck. He hadn't bothered to argue with Jemma about staying behind. As much as it burned him, he knew she wouldn't.

Unhooking the lock, he opened the door and threw in a thermo-flare.

The cave lighted to reveal emptiness. The tightness of his gut told him they wouldn't be alone for long.

"All right, Landis. Let's see how good a tracker you really are." Rip bowed to him mockingly.

Landis sauntered by. "I'm the best, Bowhite. Just ask anyone on Lack Sui."

"This isn't Lack Sui, asshole."

Landis aimed his beam on the floor, studying the sand, his face turning serious for the first time since Rip had laid eyes on him. He carefully worked his way across the room. "You're right, two or more humans were carried off from here by four Velopeds." He pointed to the tunnels. "Looks like they all exited through the middle one."

Rip fired up his own lightbeam. "Then down we go." He glanced at Jemma. "Stay close to my back."

She nodded absently, staring at the tunnel.

There was nothing left to do but go.

They walked, each footfall taking them farther from safety. Every time Landis stopped to paint a backwards arrow pointing to the way out, Rip looked at the timer. They'd gotten here about an hour before mid-day, giving them safely five hours before sunset to get back and bolt the door. They'd been down here for almost an hour. That meant they'd need an hour to return, which left them three hours to play with.

His instincts were screaming that they'd see action long before their time was up. He glanced at the four other men who'd volunteered to come, judging them useless for anything but firepower. As much as it killed him, Landis was his only experienced backup. He met the man's gaze as he finished another arrow. "We're getting close."

"To what?" Landis sprayed a curl at the end of the arrow, then met Rip's gaze.

Rip raised an eyebrow.

"Great," Landis groused. "What's the use of those supplies you bribed me with if I'm a gutted, rotting corpse?"

But under the grousing, Rip heard Landis' relish and he realized that Landis was someone who had to have a lot of responsibility to keep his mind busy or he'd make trouble for his own amusement. Instead of taking away his duties, Rip should have given Landis more to do. He promised himself he'd do so when they got back topside.

Rounding another corner, he ran into Landis who had stopped at the mouth of a large cavern. Landis ran his lightbeam over the room, highlighting hundreds of sleeping raptors. Fear crawled up Rip's spine, making movement impossible. Black balls of sleeping Velopeds dotted the floor several feet below them, allowing them a view of the room. A single raptor let out a frenzied caw, waking the rest.

"We're dead," Landis whispered.

"No shit," Rip muttered back.

Then Jemma rounded the corner and her lightbeam hit a patch of raptors. Horrendous screams rent the air when the light passed over their bodies.

The other men rounded the corner, their lights causing the same reaction. The floor was a squirming mass of agonized shrieks as the raptors attempted to flee from the light.

Rip grabbed the nearest lightbeam, flashing it on the advancing group of raptors who were sneaking up his flank. They hissed and spit, turning to run for the exit.

"Use your lights to keep them back," Rip yelled over the hideous noise.

Within moments, the room was empty.

The seven of them stood in shocked silence.

"These lights." Jemma clicked hers off and stared at the casing. "They must have ultraviolet properties in the light source." She glanced at Rip. "We are so lucky."

"Thanks for giving me one, Bowhite, you asshole," Landis said, flipping his lightbeam on and off.

He clapped Landis on the back. "Only the best for you, old buddy."

"Dick."

"Son of a whoremonger." They grinned at each other, finally coming to an understanding. When Rip opened his mouth, Jemma shushed him.

From far down the cavern, they could hear human voices yelling.

"Silvy," she called, and jumped into the room, right as Rip said, "Don't go down there."

He sighed. "You two," he pointed to two of the men. "Stay up here and watch out for the raptors. I'm sure they'll return. The rest of you, follow me." He jumped after her.

Running, he caught up to Jemma in a few strides. Behind him, he heard Landis muttering about fools in love.

It took time, but they managed to reach the pit without the Velopeds returning. Gazing down, Rip saw a woman and two men huddled in the bottom.

"How in the hell do we get them out? They must be twenty feet deep." Landis crouched to study the pit.

"Our shirts." Jem started to take hers off. "We'll tie them together and pull them out."

"Oh no, you don't." Rip stopped her by grabbing her arms, shooting Landis a warning look when he snickered. "We'll use ours."

"We might need hers," Landis said, fighting a grin.

"Strip, asshole." Rip pulled his shirt off. "If we need more clothes, we'll use your pants."

Landis laughed, handing over his shirt.

"Bowhite," one of the guards yelled. A squeal bounced through the cavern from across the room as the raptors at the doorway were hit by a light. "They're coming back."

Rip leaned down to help Jem tie the shirts together by the arms.

They lowered the makeshift rope into the pit. The woman grabbed hold and he and Landis pulled her up.

"Bowhite, they're coming through more than one door now," the two men at the exit yelled.

"Faster," Rip growled to the people in the pit.

When the woman reached the top, Jemma grabbed her. "Silvy."

They dragged out the first man without problems, but half way up with the last man, the shirts started to shred with an evil hiss.

Rip leaned down and yanked the back of Zach's shirt, hauling him up. Landis dropped the makeshift rope and caught Zach's arm when he was high enough up. The rope made of their shirts slithered into the pit.

Tugging the man to safety, they both glanced down. "Guess I know what I'll be taking from the storerooms first," Landis said, and Rip found himself finally appreciating his humor.

"Bowhite," one of the guards yelled, followed by more squeals.

"Let's go. Fast."

While Jemma helped Silvy, Rip noticed the administrative personnel were more torn up than he'd at first realized. Landis helped the other man while Zach limped beside them.

When they got to their escape route, the raptors poured through the entryways *en masse* and kept coming, even against the lights. Rip boosted the injured people, then handed Jemma up to Landis, who yanked her to safety. "Go, go, go!"

He grabbed onto the ledge, only to be hauled upwards by Landis.

"Get moving, dammit. I need you to lead us out of here."

"Why is it I'm never appreciated?" Landis asked, before racing off to lead the group. They made good time through the tunnels considering what bad shape the three admin people were in, but the raptors dogged their heels. The tight confines and the lights stalled the Velopeds but a long stretch loomed ahead.

It seemed like an eternity before they climbed into the last cavern.

"We're safe," Landis gasped, chugging in air from supporting one of the men for the run back.

Rip dragged Zach into the cavern, out of breath himself.

"Thank the gods," Jemma sighed as Silvy started to cry.

"Let's get to the other side of the door." Rip herded everyone forward.

The leading man through the door stumbled back, his chest slit from his throat to his thigh.

On the other side of the door, a loud caw sounded.

Chapter Fourteen

I, for one, plan to leave on the first available transport out of here. I've become sick of all this death.

Excerpt from Doctor Lore's Notes

Rip grabbed the blasters at his waist and shoved Zach out of the way. "Get out of the doorway!"

Jemma, who was in front of him where he thought she'd be safe, pushed people to safety.

"Guard our backs, Landis."

"Aye, cap'n," said he said, deadly serious for once.

Rip darted past the doorway to fire into the room. A raptor screeched, the sound a sharp yelp of pain. Rip dove behind the safety of the wall, hoping the Velopeds would come through the door so he could pick them off one by one. Scrambling claws sounded in the other room, but no raptors took the bait.

He met Jemma's gaze across the cavern, while Landis grabbed one of the lightbeams and covered the tunnels.

"I love you," Jemma lip mouthed.

He grinned, joy spreading through his heart, and rolled back into the doorway in a crouch, shooting indiscriminate fire to cover his entrance. The room was empty. "Damn." He raised his voice. "Everyone in here now!"

The group stumbled in, two of the men dragging the dead guard.

"Bring him with us. We'll bury him topside." They would need to clean out all the bodies that were down here, Rip realized, rubbing his neck. He strode to Landis and motioned him into the room so he could close the reinforced door and lock it.

"You're locking us in here with them," Zach said, his voice calm as Silvy retied a makeshift bandage on his leg.

"I'm locking hundreds of them out. We'll have a better chance if we cut the number we're dealing with."

"Who are you?" Silvy asked.

Before Rip could answer, Jemma said, "My Chosen."

Rip stood completely still, so many emotions crashing through him, he didn't know which one to concentrate on. He settled for simple joy. Jemma had announced her feelings for him publicly. He brushed his fingers across her cheek, smiling at her.

"We could leave the women here while we deal with the raptors." Rip met Jemma's gaze as he moved to the door, every part of his being wanting to keep her safe.

"I don't want to split up," she told him, and Rip knew she'd dig in and fight to stay by his side.

"Me either." Landis was serious again.

"Jemma, hand me a blaster," Zach said. He took the blaster and tucked it into his pants, then addressed Rip. "If we can make it topside, we'll be safe."

"Okay. Let's go as a group then." Checking the rounds he had left, Rip took the lightbeam from one of his men. "Landis, you and Zach take the rear again. We'll leave the dead here until we return tomorrow. We'll need to go as fast as we can."

He glanced back at Jemma and said inside his mind, *I love you.* Aloud, he said, "Stay tight behind me, Jem. I want to feel you at my back."

She touched her heart. "I'll be there."

And he rolled out the door in a crouch.

❧❧⟨♥⟩❧❧

Jemma stayed close to Rip, keeping him near so she could watch his back. By putting Landis and Zach on rear guard, he'd left the most experienced people far enough away that it was up to her to make sure he stayed alive.

They worked their way down the hall to the small supply room. Tension made them all keep their eyes glued to the doorways. The hair on Jemma's neck rose with the thought of Velopeds leaping from stacked boxes and gliding at her from behind.

"Maybe there aren't any raptors here," Silvy said, her voice filled with hope.

"We killed three in here yesterday." Rip's head rotated back and forth between the two doors ahead of them.

A physical feeling of dread walked up Jemma's spine and she touched his arm. "Rip, where are their bodies?"

He stopped and scanned the room. Boxes were still tumbled, a thick, black, oily substance covered the floor in three spots, but the dead Velopeds were gone. "None of us would have moved them."

"They were here when we went through earlier." Landis scanned the room, concern thick in his voice.

"If they're moving their dead that means there very well may be some here in the warrens now. We need to pick up the pace." Zach limped to a crate of blasters, tucking some in his belt and passing the rest out to the team.

Rip handed Jemma another blaster to replace the one she'd given Zach and grabbed two guard shirts from a nearby bin. He tossed one to Landis. "You've got me down to one shirt, which you're wearing," he whispered to Jemma, touching her cheek in a fleeting caress. Raising his voice, he told the others, "Let's go then." Turning, he led the way towards the larger storeroom.

"We need to get out of here now," Zach agreed, herding people forward.

They slid into the next room, Rip leading the way.

Nothing. They were alone.

Jemma let out her breath. After the crazy dash through the underground caves, they were going to make it out without any trouble. "You know," she said, unable to keep the revelation to herself now that they weren't in danger. "If they're hauling away their dead, it means they are definitely not animals."

"They're animals, Jemma." Rip met her gaze over his shoulder.

"Just like we are," Landis put in from behind her.

Jemma opened her mouth to argue her point when a shadow on a set of creates beyond Rip's shoulder suddenly rose up and flung itself into a glide.

A glide that would end with sharp claws impaling Rip's chest.

"Move," she screamed, then raised her blaster from her belt and fired. The action wasn't thought out, it wasn't preplanned.

The Veloped's head exploded and it dropped like a stone, tumbling from its graceful glide to skid into Rip's legs, knocking him down. Rip shoved the raptor away and stood.

Jemma gaped in horror at what she'd done. She'd killed a living, breathing, thinking being. A being who was cherished enough that others of his kind would come for its body.

She raised her gaze to Rip's, and knew the truth. As much as she loathed what she'd done, she'd kill anyone or anything to keep her mate safe.

He searched the room for more Velopeds, speaking to her in low tones. "Thank you." Black eyes glittered and she knew he understood what had just happened. "Mate." Scanning the shadows again, he called a warning. "Keep close. They always seem to hunt in groups so finding one means others are near. After we cross this storeroom, we'll be at the tunnel."

"Go!" Landis said. "I'll bring up the rear, but we should get the hell out of here while the getting's good."

They made it through the room at a fast clip, everyone going as quickly as they could.

The tunnel loomed before them and they began to jog. They were going to make it to sunlight. Jemma could feel it.

Behind them, a loud caw bounded along the walls, causing Zach to yell, "Faster!"

"Watch the trip wire," Rip warned, staying behind to make sure everyone got over it safely, then jogging back to lead them out.

Another raptor cried behind them as they made it to the explosive at the top of the tunnel. "Jump it," Jemma shouted to the others.

Down the tunnel, a raptor tripped the wire and the tunnel shook with the detonation, raining dust and debris down on their heads.

Herding everyone from the warrens, Rip and Jemma were the last two to burst into the sunlight.

They were safe.

Jemma turned to throw herself into Rip's arms, but he jumped back and held up hands. "I touched the raptor."

"We'll start you on Meriostat the moment we return to camp. Let me see them." She stared at his palms, shocked to see the blisters forming already. Concern welled up. "We'll cure this, Rip. I promise."

"I don't doubt it, Jem." He smiled and the need to pull him into a private place and touch him everywhere tugged hard at her mind. Leaning down, he whispered in her ear, "The moment we're alone, you're mine."

"I think we're going to have to risk a kiss." She rose up and pressed her lips to Rip's before he could protest.

Holding his hands out to the sides so he wouldn't accidentally touch her, Rip turned the kiss into a greedy exploration.

"All right, love birds, let's head out," Zach said, shaking his head.

The jokes at their expense continued as they trudged around a burnt out hull of a building, straight into a waiting throng of Inter-world Council troops.

Rip had hoped for this moment, but now that it was here, he had to stop the urge to fight.

They were rescued and he would be thrown into another prison—away from Jemma. He and his mate stood, their eyes locked in dread as they both realized what this new turn of events meant.

With their rescue, he knew he'd lost his woman, even as he knew she was saved from death. They were in trouble, because the small amount of time he'd spent away from her as she'd healed his men last night had been miserable. What would eight *years* feel like?

Every nerve ending in his body tingled with loss, every instinct inside him wanted to pull her close and kill anyone who tried to part them.

"Rip," Jemma whispered.

"We're saved." He could hear the anger in his words.

"No," she murmured.

"You'll be safe," he said, trying to calm himself with that thought as he watched the troops surround Zach, who'd gone out to greet them.

"Rip, we can't be separated." Her voice held the same panic that coursed through his own veins.

"I know." He wanted to curse, but checked himself. She'd be safe from the Velopeds, away from this planet. He had to remember that. Eight years wasn't forever. His heart stuttered at the agony of it.

"Rip." She turned to him, her face an urgent mask. "I love you."

"And I love you, Jem." He dragged the amulet over his head. "You have to keep this. They'll take it from me the minute I'm under Council control." He dropped it around her neck, unwilling to let his soul go to anyone other than his woman.

The moment he released the amulet onto to her chest, pain and dizziness stabbed through him, like a physical blow, knocking him to his knees.

Zach ran to them. "Jemma, what's wrong with him?"

"Rip," she whispered as she lowered him to the ground. "The bacteria. He shoved the raptor in the storeroom. It seems to be spreading through him faster than the others."

He felt her fingers at his throat, while he fought the urge to pass out.

Returning his soul to Jemma had somehow weakened him, allowing the bacteria to spread faster. He knew it in his gut.

"I need a scanner to be sure and ours is all the way in the prisoner's camp." Jemma's voice swirled around him as his vision closed in.

"Help me move him onto the ship," Zach yelled to two nearby guards. "Watch out," he snapped as they lifted him. "He's gone through hell."

Rip wondered why Zach didn't just tell the guards he was a prisoner, right before everything went black.

⁂

Jemma watched the ship's doctor do a complete scan of Rip's body, worried that the final bond had accelerated the disease in some terrible way. He had gotten sick hours faster than Jackson had, but at least this starfreighter had Revostat. He should heal quickly now that he'd had the injection. She checked his pulse for the hundredth time, finding it steady beneath her fingers.

"So few people survived," the Healer, Greer, murmured.

"Yes." Jemma curled her hand around Rip's, wishing he'd squeeze her fingers.

Greer shook her head. "The Inter-world Council should be ashamed that they pulled out, leaving you all there, but with the computer crash and all…" she trailed off.

Jemma focused on her. "What computer crash?"

"The whole prison system was attacked by a Trojan. Turns out some bigwig escaped from another prison by having a team take down all the systems in one swoop. You name it, it's gone."

"Back up tapes?"

"They're trying to restore them now but the process is taking them longer than anticipated. When it happened, they decided to pull off of the Velopit and come back when everything was up and running again, not realizing how long it was going to take. The Captain of this starfreighter convinced them to let him look for survivors since we were passing through this quadrant."

"They're not leaving the prisoners behind, are they?" Jemma's heart was stuck in her throat. Rip would be furious if they abandoned his men.

"No. The Captain's gotten a special waiver to offload them in the Omega system." Greer ran another scan. "He'll drop the remaining administrators on Borrus afterwards."

Jemma knew they thought Rip was a guard, but as soon as they had the records restored, he'd be discovered. "Why the Omega system?"

Greer shrugged, staring at the read out with a puzzled frown. "It's outside of the Inter-worlds. Dropping them without papers will bar them from ever reentering again. Since this prison was filled mainly with troublemakers against the Council, they figured they'd just dump them. They don't have time to mess around with minor offenses, since the whole prison system is in chaos across the galaxies."

Fingering the pack that held the Sem, Jemma had a moment to mourn the fact she'd never tested the Velopeds to see why they couldn't face sunlight. "Do you know what will happen to the raptors?" She had to ask.

Greer pushed a button on her hand-held and snorted. "Those animals have accomplished something no other planet has. The Council is giving up and abandoning the Velopit."

Jemma fought the smile that threatened to burst forth. Despite everything that had happened on the planet, she was happy to hear about the Council's decision. If Dr. Lore were still alive, he'd cheer for the aliens, too. They'd won. She knew they'd continue to win if the Council forgot the grim lesson they'd been taught.

The creatures had learned so much the Council didn't even know about. Zach and Silvy were convinced the raptors took them back to their underground home to study them. Maybe it was a good thing that the true cause of the Velopeds' sensitivity to light remained a mystery. She hoped the Council would forget the Velopit forever.

Greer handed over the scanner. "Look at this."

Jemma studied the read out. "Everything is normal except some enzyme levels, but even those aren't wildly out of range."

"His heart readout is fine."

"Does the Revostat usually act so quickly?"

"No, but maybe we caught him early enough. They'll need to check him out when you land on Borrus, run more tests." She took back the scanner and clicked it off. Rip stirred on the table. "There you go. He seems to be coming around." Greer checked his pulse. "Still, that's odd." She shrugged. "Ah well. I need to go treat the rest of the prisoners." Pushing the door open with her bottom, she winked at Jemma. "I'm sure your man will recover just fine under your healing skills."

Then she was gone.

Rip blinked up at her. "The Council arrived."

She leaned close to whisper, "Zach told them you're one of the guards."

"I feel like I've been sucker punched with a blaster stock." Rip tried to push up from the exam table to sit. Jemma balanced him before he fell, letting him rest his head on her shoulder. "What happened to me?"

"You touched that raptor in the storeroom." She leaned close to whisper. "I felt the third link bind us together when you placed the amulet around my neck, then you went down. I don't know what happened exactly, but I think the ritual's completion accelerated the spread of the bacteria."

He shook his head. "I didn't want to bind you to me. I just couldn't take the amulet to prison." Raising a bandaged hand, he ran a wrapped finger along her cheek. "If they figure out I'm a prisoner and not a guard, I'll be put back in prison."

Separating them. A physical pain lanced through him. Gods. They were in trouble.

"They're offloading all the prisoners in the Omega system instead of taking them to another prison. We'll need to debark there."

His stomach tightened. "But then you'd be banned from the Inter-worlds, banned from Trolen."

She shrugged a shoulder. "The important thing is we stay together, not where we live. If you remain on the ship, it will only be a matter of time before they figure out who you are. They lost all the prison files in a computer crash. Once the back-up is restored, they'll know, so we'll need to be gone before that happens."

Rip studied her face, searching through the emotions he could feel from her for any sign that leaving the Inter-worlds upset her. He found nothing but excitement, relief that he was okay and joy that they were together.

His mind clicked through possibilities. "We can find work on some of the new colonies. We'll see if Jackson and Landis want to come in on a mining venture. No one will even care who we are there." He braced himself on one hand, meeting her gaze. "Are you sure you want to stay with me, Jemma?"

She held up the amulet for him to see. "We've completed the ritual, Rip. We've both Chosen, for good or bad." She dipped her head and brushed her lips across his. "And I think it will be very, very good."

He nodded slowly, a grin stretching his lips. They would be good together. "Yes."

"We might have been destined to be together, but you chose me before you knew about the bond." She stroked a hand through his hair. The import of that hit him. He would never doubt his feelings, never have to wonder if he'd only bonded with her because it was predestined. He'd always know he chose her of his own free will. And she was his. His! Heart, body, soul. She'd pledged them all to him, just as he had to her. Elation poured over him. "I love you, Jemma-mine." He let his lips rest lightly on hers.

"And I love you." She licked his lips in a slow sweep, lighting a fire in his stomach. "Forever."

About the Author:

Leigh Wyndfield spends her time away from writing reading anything she can get her hands on, watching movies, and skiing or hiking, depending on the season. Unable to find romances that take place on other worlds, she started writing her own while working in the real world and obtaining her MBA from a top-tiered university. Installing software systems just didn't seem like any fun compared to writing, so she quit her job to create stories full time. Visit her website to learn about her other books at **www.leighwyndfield.com***!*

Ailis and

the Beast

❧〜⦅⦆〜☙

by Jennifer Barlowe

To My Reader:

Ailis and the Beast is a story about sex and appetite, and about how what we think we know is often just the beginning. I hope you enjoy it. Bon appetit.

Ailis bowed her head, letting her hair fall forward over her face. It made a curtain, black as night around her, and she imagined it was the walls of the *sh'rokk*. The priestesses would come for her soon, to take her to that sacred place for what would either be the first of three times, or else the last.

This final hour was afforded to her by tradition to be spent in solitude. She'd already said her farewells to family and friends, in the expectation that she might not see them again. She raised her head and looked through the doorway of the hovel. This was not her house, although it was made of the same reddish brown clay and a thick thatch for a roof. This hovel housed only the ceremonial trappings of the *koth*, the bride-feast.

Outside, the sun was setting, and Ailis rose up from where she knelt on the thick, woven rug so she could watch it. Her new white linen shift fell around her, pooling about her feet. Her hair hung dark and heavy with the silver ornaments woven into the strands. Small bells chimed softly as she moved.

The sun was gold turning red, streaking the floor of the valley with its last light. On either side of the clearing tall trees cast shadows, drawing the darkness closer as the sun sank down. In the last of the sun's fading light, the priestesses came.

They wore formless brown robes the color of the earth, with mantles the deep green of fir trees. Hoods covered their hair and shadowed their faces. Without a word, Ailis left the hovel and walked into the midst of them, letting them surround her and lead her down the thin path toward the *sh'rokk*.

It was a structure made of branches, bent and bound into a frame and covered with cloth. The limbs came from the evergreen trees that never died, even in the midst of winter. The fabric was as black as if it were dyed in purest midnight. No one entered here except the priestesses and the bride-feast.

Ailis repressed a shudder and stepped through the doorway. The floor was earth, swept until no grass or pebble remained. In the very center was the sacred stone, a white slab as tall as a man's waist, wide as an arm span, and longer than Ailis's modest height. At each of the four corners of the stone, a silver ring was set.

Knowing what was expected of her, Ailis walked to the stone and, careful not to snag the material of her shift, hoisted herself onto its surface. Lying down, she raised her arms over her head and apart. She spread her ankles as well, and waited while the priestesses bound her ankles and wrists to the rings with cloth.

For a brief moment, the priestesses stood in a ring surrounding her, then, still silent, they filed out of the doorway, the last of them letting the cloth flaps fall shut behind her.

Full dark had fallen outside. Ailis lay still. Her white linen shift was thin and did nothing to shield her from the roughness or the cold of the stone beneath her skin. Spring had only just begun, and the fading daylight had taken the last warmth with it. Inside the *sh'rokk,* a single candle burned in a shrouded lantern above the entrance.

Outside, bird song was replaced by the fainter sounds of the night's creatures coming to life, soft scuttles and the occasional beat of an owl's wings as it stalked the dark. Then those sounds too disappeared.

In the silence, Ailis strained to hear anything at all. Fear came for the first time. She'd been composed through the choosing, the ceremonial bathing and dressing, and the final anointment by the priestesses when they'd touched sacred oil to her eyelids. She'd let her sense of duty to her people be her armor from fear. But alone in this dark place, with her fate only a few steps away, she found herself seized by panic like a rabbit that finds itself snared. Her heart pounded. Her breath came too fast to feed her. Her vision darkened at the edges as she strained to raise her head.

The door flaps burst open as if blown by a gale. Ailis never saw the Beast enter, she only saw that he was there, a shadow darker than the other shadows, and huge, looming even as he crouched, the meager light behind him showing only the blurred outline of something monstrous—something that was far from a man, but was no animal she had ever seen.

Then there was the smell. It was solid, musk and heat, and something that reminded her of burying her face in the mulch of the forest floor when she was a child. The smell of it filled the *sh'rokk* so that it was hard to breathe without feeling that she took something of it inside her with each inhalation.

He made a low rumble that was too deep in his chest to be called a growl. Then he moved forward, hulking on all fours as he began to circle the slab. Ailis tried to turn her head to follow him, but found she was too petrified even for that small movement. She had only impressions of him, but no clear look. His size had made him seem like a bear at first, but the movement was more that of a monstrous dog. She felt the first touch of his fur, coarse, graze her bound hand as he brushed by, and she froze.

Above her head she felt her hair stir as he snuffled there, sniffing out her own scent. Something pushed hard against her head, nudging the way a dog will when it's seeking. There was a long inhalation, as though he would draw her in by the smell of her, then a rush of air blasted abruptly out again. Her hair was blown as though by a powerful wind, and her arms and legs strained against her bonds whether she willed it or not.

The Beast continued to move around her in a slow circuit, sniffing here, then there. Ailis fought not to scream. Whatever her fate was to be, she wouldn't dishonor her family by showing fear, although the Beast could surely smell her terror. She had no control over it. Would that in itself doom her?

The Beast stopped again at the foot of the stone. She strained again to lift her head enough to at least see him. Although the candlelight was faint, she could make out the silhouette as he stood. Even crouching he was huge. She could see that he was clearly not an animal, at least not any natural kind.

The stories said that the Beast was here before the forest, and before man or animal first came to the valley. He was neither of those things, but more than both.

He was covered in a thick pelt, although as she watched, it seemed to change in the flickering light, the hair longer, then shorter again as he moved. His head was wolf like, but the nose was too short for a wolf's, though far too long for a man's face. He stood upright, but still bent, as though his powerful legs were equally capable of carrying him on two limbs or running like an animal on all fours.

Her curiosity caught her, so that she was lost in her examination of this man-beast so close by. Then, without warning, he leaped, looming in the air over her—and Ailis saw her death—then landed with thunderous force on the stone between her spread legs.

She did cry out then, short and sharp, her terror no longer a thing that she could contain. The Beast crouched between her legs, then lowered his head, nosing the shift that covered her. His snuffling examination pushed the useless fabric aside, going straight to the core of her, and terror made her skin burn hot as she felt rough fur and a blunt nose explore ruthlessly at her most private place. Without warning his tongue licked out, wet and rough against her, and she screamed again in terror and a feeling she couldn't name.

He brought his head up then, leaning forward until he loomed over her, shoulders and chest obliterating the last of the light. She felt a sharp sting as a blade, no, one of his talons, traced a fine line of pain between her breasts toward her belly, fabric shredding away from her. She gasped for air as he raised his head over her breasts then brought it down, stopping just short of her skin. He breathed in, slow and deep, just above her newly opened flesh, and Ailis froze.

She lay perfectly still in her bonds, holding her breath, willing her heart to whisper. This would not be the last of her blood that was spilled tonight. The Beast would taste her. If what he found pleased him, her maiden's blood would stain the sacred stone. If not, then it would be her life's blood which would drench the white rock slab. She'd known this since the priestesses chose her. The Beast's tongue flicked out again, running up the length of the cut, lapping her blood into his mouth.

He reared back, still crouched between her bared thighs, and let out a guttural howl. Then he fell towards her, taloned hands striking the stone on either side of her ribs, and with a single, driving motion, plunged into her.

Ailis cried out in earnest. Relief that she would live was drowned out by the shock of pain that threatened to throw her from her own body. The Beast continued his motion undaunted, driving into her again and again with a single-minded ferocity that had nothing to do with thought.

Beneath him, her back arched up from the stone slab, her body straining of its own volition, a useless attempt to escape him. But as the onslaught continued, Ailis realized that her body moved without her will or guidance. And it wasn't to get away from the Beast that she rose and fell, but to meet him.

The first burning had changed to something else, just as hot, but within it there was another feeling—one that went beyond pain. As the Beast's body lifted her up, and up again, only the ties at her ankles kept her from leaving the slab entirely, and she clenched her hands against their bonds. Something coiled within her, something she was sure was as old as the Beast himself. Building until it filled her, pushing the breath out of her because there was no more room for it, it leapt to meet the

Beast, and in that joining, Ailis cried out not in pain but in the primal howl that had given birth to the forest itself.

When she'd screamed out the last sound in her, she found herself limp against her stone bed. The Beast stood at the entrance of the *sh'rokk*. It looked to her that he stood straighter than he had before, taller and less bent. He was silent except for the rough and regular sound of his breathing. His eyes met hers, and despite the dark, she could make them out this time. They gleamed a feral blue in the darkness. And there was an intelligence there that she hadn't seen before. He moved then, a blur of darkness, and was gone, the door flap stirring slightly at his passing.

Ailis lay back against the cooling stone. Her body hurt. She could feel the rough abrasions where the rock had scraped her skin, the cooling ache of her muscles from straining against the ties, and the raw warmth between her legs. She fought to still her breathing and her thoughts as the priestesses returned.

Still wordless, they draped her in fresh linen, even before untying her limbs, shielding her from the night's growing chill.

In the darkness a large shape ran through the forest. As it passed, birds did not take flight in fear. Deer kept their place next to the shallow watering hole. A grizzled badger stayed still on a fallen log. All of them marked the passage of the Beast, but none of them were alarmed. Their heads moved up to follow his progress the way they might note a sudden breeze.

At first he ran on four legs, then on two. Finally, he came to a stop in a clearing high on a hill, and there he stood still, looking up at the night sky. His thoughts were confused, his senses confounded, but as he looked up seeking answers, only the clouded sky met his gaze, and it offered no guidance.

He breathed deep, and the scent of her, still on his own skin, filled his nostrils. His hands moved, and he felt her limbs under them as though he still touched her. He tried to remember the sensation—tried to recall when, in all his days, he had felt something so pure. His pulse still thrummed with the rhythm of her heart, beating fast and furiously, so close to his.

The first night. He'd lived all his days with the knowledge that this time would come, but it had been meaningless to him because time had held no meaning. For a hundred thousand nights, time had had no substance. Now it was jarringly real. Three nights, he heard in his own head. Two more. The very idea of time was new to him, and he struggled under the weight of its alien import. How long, he wondered, would it take until the next night came, until he saw her again? It was such a foreign thought he had to stalk it in his own mind before he could bring it to bay.

And what would it mean, the second night? What would she see when she looked at him? What would he see when he looked at himself? The questions spun around him like moths until he finally brushed them aside and stalked to the edge of the hill. Below him, the valley stretched out a long ways before it gave way to deeper forest and then the plains beyond. Already he could feel the change in all of it. A sense of new vitality breathed through the land, racing wild through its earth and trees, the sky and streams, just as it coursed in him. All the earth felt the sense of anticipation and uncertainty that had come to envelope him. Not knowing what to do next, the Beast sat down on the edge of the hill and did something completely new to him.

He waited.

❦❧

Ailis dreamed. She knew she slept, but it didn't matter. In her slumber she sat outside in the sun on a woven mat with her mother. The two of them ground wheat into grain with stones, and the birds were singing.

"Mother," she began, "Why does the rain fall from the sky?"

Her mother, a woman with a thin, warm face and hair as black as Ailis's own, looked up at the cloudless sky. "There's no rain coming today child." There was a smile in her voice and, asleep in the hovel, a grown Ailis smiled in return.

"I know that," the child Ailis said with impatience. "But when it does come, *why* does it?"

"Because it is time." Her mother shrugged. "Because the land tells the sky that rain is needed, and the sky sends it to us."

Ailis frowned at this answer. "How does the land speak?"

"It has a voice." Her mother paused a moment to scan the trees that surrounded their valley. "There is one who speaks for it. He lives in the forest, but too deep to come out and be seen."

Ailis sat and contemplated this, her small fingers grinding the smaller stone against the larger. "Is he a man then? The one who speaks for the forest?"

Her mother shook her head, still working with her hands. "He is a Beast, but he is like a man. He came here before the trees, and the forest followed him."

"How can that be?" Her child's fingers lost their place as she sat still, working through this idea.

"It has always been." Her mother shrugged again. "The trees follow him because they are the same. They are his family, going where he leads. The wheat on the plains follows him too, and the fish in the river. Where he goes, life goes."

Ailis chewed at her lower lip. "Does no one ever speak to him?" she asked. But her mother only shook her head, not looking up from her work.

Ailis looked down at the partially powdered stuff on her stone. "Why is there less grain than last season?" she asked. And her mother exhaled with mock impatience.

"Because little girls have not *ground* any," she said. And Ailis began to work again.

"But why is there less wheat? Last year they brought twelve wagons of it. This year, there are only ten." She was determined to have some answer. It was in her nature. She'd once spent an entire day following a rabbit through the forest to see where it would go to sleep.

"There is less wheat because the land is tired. It's a long time since it's been fed." Her mother looked at her then, and her eyes looked sad.

But Ailis was distracted by this new idea. "What does the earth eat?" she asked.

"Many things," said her mother. "The leaves that fall from the trees, the sun that falls from the sky. But once in a great while, these things no longer sustain it, and the earth needs more. When this happens, the Beast comes forward on its behalf."

"Why does he come?" Ailis was fascinated.

"He comes to take a bride," her mother said softly. "He comes to make a child, and that new birth will fill the earth for many seasons to come, more than I or you will ever see pass."

"And is there less wheat because the Beast will come soon for a bride?" In Ailis's mind, she saw her sister's wedding when it had come a year ago with feasting and flowers hung through the trees, delightful to her child's eyes. "Will the Beast come soon?"

"He will come when the bride is offered," her mother said quietly. "And that will not happen until it is needed. Until the earth will no longer offer the wheat or call the rain. And even then, the Beast may not take her. She may not be to his liking."

"What would happen then?" Ailis asked, confused.

"Another bride would be offered," her mother answered. "But a year would have to pass before that could be. He won't come more than once with each turning of the seasons."

Ailis had long since ceased to grind the wheat. She peered up at her mother, contemplative. "If he may reject a bride, or many brides, why wait?" she asked. "Why wait until the grain is gone before offering the first?"

Her mother looked into her face then, and her expression was very tender. "Because the earth will be fed either way, darling Ailis," she said. "If the Beast won't accept his bride, then he will devour her."

The sleeping furs were musky and warm. Ailis stroked them absently as she came to wakefulness. The sun was still high in the afternoon sky. She could see it through the open doorway of the hovel. Rolling onto her back, enjoying the feeling of being alone, she stretched her arms over her head, pushing aside the furs.

Her body answered her with a sweet, sharp aching. Her limbs were heavy, but with a pleasurable exhaustion, like when she'd spent the day climbing steep hills and rocks to collect herbs. Her back was more sensitive. She could feel bruises forming where she'd been battered against the sacred stone, and the place between her legs was singularly tender.

Thinking of the night before, she felt something surge deep in her belly. It was like an echo of that stronger feeling—the one that had felt like a separate animal within her last night. Slowly she stood up, reveling in the feelings of her body, even the pain, because it meant she was alive. She had been offered to the Beast and he had accepted her as his bride, not merely as a feast. It could have gone differently, and thinking of it she shivered.

But then the terrible tension that had shadowed her mind and spirit shook loose and rushed away from her. Since the Choosing at the last new moon she'd been frozen inside. Now she felt herself thaw. Not only would she live, she would bring life into the village, and with it, into the land itself. She would give birth to the Beast's child, and to be certain of that, she would lie with him again for the next two nights. She shivered at the thought, and she walked shakily toward the doorway to distract herself.

She was not to leave the hovel until nightfall, but from where she stood she could see the trees, taller than they'd been yesterday. The sky was bluer and more birds flew in it. Somewhere she could smell meat cooking, and her stomach growled at the thought. She was ravenous.

The world outside seemed brighter, more vibrant. Was it only that she hadn't seen it yesterday because of the dread that had been on her? Or was the earth already stronger than it had been as a result of her union last night?

Watching clouds drift across the brilliant sky, Ailis let her thoughts wander. Her mother was long dead. She had not lived to see the seasons when the harvest was thin and so were the faces of the village children. She had not lived to see her daughter chosen from the other maiden girls of the village to be offered to the land—although she'd seemed to anticipate it on that long ago afternoon.

Ailis wished now that she could reach out to her mother. She wished that there were some way to tell her that it had come out all right. The land would have its fare, and Ailis would not die for it. She ran her hand down the rough clay of the doorway, and a single tear slipped down her cheek. Then she went back inside to wait.

At dusk again, the priestesses came. They looked as they had last night. No tell-tale movement betrayed them as any different. But Ailis sensed excitement in them as they led her again to the *sh'rokk*.

Again they bound her to the sacred stone, and this time the discomfort was greater since the stone pressed back at the bruises it had left the night before. There was nothing for it though, and the pain was small payment for her life and the continued life of her people. She breathed deeply and tried to force patience.

There was no sound that warned of his coming—only the absence of sound. It was as though the forest held still in respect as he passed. The curtain stirred and he was there at the entryway. It was dark, and Ailis could make out very little of his form. But as he came toward her she was sure he seemed taller, and he crouched less than he had the night before.

Inside the black fabric walls, the silence of the night continued. Ailis could hear her own breathing, but from very far away. Her heartbeat was so faint it felt as though she were listening to it buried a long way down beneath the earth. She strained her ears to hear some sound from the Beast, but there was none. He stayed perfectly still.

The silence became unbearable, and Ailis felt she had to speak, if only to know if she could hear her own voice, or if she'd been rendered suddenly deaf. "Why do you wait?" she asked, with no expectation of an answer. Her voice was breathy and tight, and as she spoke, something in the air seemed to ripple, like still water when a stone has been thrown. The feeling of pressure left the air, and the Beast took a step forward.

"Waiting means time. There is no time here." The voice was low and scraped from his throat like the milling stones had scraped against each other in her dream.

"You speak," she said, astonished, but he only nodded, seemingly not eager to repeat the feat. Instead, he stepped still closer. He towered above her, and she stared up at him in the near dark. His face was hidden in shadow, but beneath the layer of hair, she could see a chest like a man's, but impossibly wide, with shoulders to match. The hair of his arms was longer, coarser. He leaned forward, bracing himself with his arms while he lowered his head between her legs.

This was not last night's shuffling exploration. Instead he laid his cheek against the inside of one of her thighs and stayed there as though listening for something, or searching her scent. Finally he snorted and lifted his head.

He walked around the rock toward her head. He made no noise, and she was surprised that anything so large could be so silent. The air was heavy with the scent of him, but it wasn't an animal odor. He smelled like deep earth and sunlight, and Ailis felt herself grow heady with it. He stood still, just behind her head, and then she felt his hands cover each of hers. Fur and long fingers brushed the exposed skin of her wrists. There was a tightening of her bonds, then they were gone, shredded by his long talons.

"Sit up," he said, walking the rest of the way around the stone. He tore through the bonds at her ankles with careless ease, so fast it was a blur. Then he reached a hand toward her, and she took it hesitatingly. When his fingers closed around her hand, she couldn't feel any trace of his claws.

Upright and very close to him, curiosity overcame caution. Ailis leaned forward, peering through the darkness. His face was heavily shadowed, almost a silhouette in the light from the single lantern, still behind him. His eyes were the lupine blue she remembered, but when she tried to find the lines of his face—it was as though each time she thought she could see him, it turned out to be only a trick of the shadows.

"Do you want to leave this place?" She jumped again at his words. She'd only barely begun to adjust to the idea that he could speak at all.

"Where would we go?" Ailis asked, her gaze going to the covered doorway.

"Wherever you like," he responded, a smile slipping across his face. Or it seemed to. Ailis hadn't yet mastered the trick of seeing him. Looking at him was like trying to study an object through running water. She felt as though she was staring at a stone on the river floor while rapids obscured it. The idea decided her, and she said, "I'd like to go to the river."

He nodded. "Then we will." He held the door flap aside for her, but Ailis hesitated at the threshold.

"Is it allowed?" she asked. "For us to leave, I mean?"

He chuckled, and it was a deep, low sound, but strangely pleasant. "Who will stop me?" he asked. When she still paused, he continued. "They will not even see us go."

Doubtful, but not wanting to argue, Ailis stepped outside. The wind blew cool and empty. The sky was dark, clouds obscuring the moon. "Where are the priestesses?" she asked. She looked around, but they were nowhere in sight. From the speed with which they'd come last night, she'd imagined that they must wait near the *sh'rokk*.

The Beast came to stand beside her, his warmth holding back the chill wind as though he'd wrapped a cloak around her. A shiver ran through her that had everything to do with his nearness, not the wind.

"The priestesses," he said, calling her attention back to the moment, "are in another place, one with different rules."

She wanted to question him about his meaning, but he started walking, and she had to hurry to keep up, to stay near enough to him not to lose the shelter of his warmth. He led her across the clearing and into the forest's edge. As they stepped over fallen limbs, through piles of dry leaves, the smell of the forest seemed thicker than normal. The mulch underfoot was soft, like walking across piles of sleeping furs, and Ailis suddenly realized that she was barefoot. She'd worn no shoes to the *sh'rokk*, worn nothing but the white robe. She panicked for a second, imagining that her robe would be torn from brambles and stained with grass when the priestesses returned. Then she realized that not only did her clothing not catch on any stray sticks or stones, but her feet were unharmed as well. No sharp pebble stabbed her. No hidden roots reached up to catch her ankle. Instead, she moved through the forest as easily as she might make her way through a clear field.

Ahead she could hear the rushing water of the river. She knew there was no way they could have reached it this quickly, but there it was, just beyond the next stand of trees. Within moments they stood on the bank, watching the water rush by. The sky overhead was still clouded, so no moon reflected in the quick moving current. The trees grew close and overhung each side. She'd known this place since childhood. She'd come here to play, to fetch water, and to catch silver fish with a net. The river was very near to her village, and not at all close to the site of the *sh'rokk*. When the priestesses had come to lead her away, they'd walked most of a day to get there. Even without a moon in the sky to show the hour, she knew they shouldn't be where they were.

The Beast was still beside her, tangible even when he wasn't touching her. Somewhere over the river, two hills away was her village. Her people, friends and family, were there and going about their lives, probably all gone to sleep by this hour. Comforted by her memory of familiar places and things, she was less afraid.

She risked saying, "You aren't what I expected." She turned to look at him, and tilted her head far back.

He made a snorting sound. "What did you expect?" His head was a shaggy silhouette. She wished he would turn so she could make out a profile. Last night she'd thought his head was like an animal's with an elongated nose, but now she couldn't be sure.

"I didn't think you would talk," she said simply.

"I could say the same of you," he replied. They stood there side by side, both watching the water.

"Why did you bring me here?" she asked.

"Because you asked me to."

Ailis couldn't find any response to that.

Not looking at him as she spoke, she asked what she'd been wanting to. "Why don't you look like you did last night?"

He was silent so long she thought he might not answer. Then he said, "Are you so sure that I don't?"

She did turn toward him then. "Yes," she said without hesitation. "Last night you were more animal than man. You were a savage thing. You were frightening."

"And tonight, you're not afraid?" he asked.

"No," she said without thinking, then realized it was true.

He nodded again. "You were different last night," he said, and his voice was still low, but no longer sounded as if it echoed off stones. "You came to the stone as a sacrifice, innocent and ignorant." He turned away from her and she could see the side of his face, the shape of it. It was a man's face. "You're none of those things now."

"Do you mean that because I'm no longer a maiden, I don't see the same thing when I look at you as I did one day ago?" She shook her head. "That doesn't make sense."

"Have you ever traveled somewhere new for the first time?" He folded his arms across his chest as he spoke, facing out toward the river. "It's a long journey because you don't know when it will end. It's frightening because you don't know what you'll find. But then, when you've made the trip once, it becomes easier. Walk the same way twice, a dozen times, and it becomes familiar, part of you, an easy journey."

"Is that why it took so little time to reach this place tonight?" she asked. "Because it's familiar to you?"

He lowered his head, and she thought he might be laughing. But he only said, "Everything is familiar to me. There isn't a path that I don't know, that isn't my own."

Ailis pondered that. "So I no longer find you frightening because you're familiar to me now?"

"Just so," he said. "Last night you feared the unknown, and so I was frightening."

"That seems too simple," she said.

He shrugged. "Perhaps. You're different tonight in a number of ways. Not the least of which is that tonight you already carry the seed of my child. And so you and I are very familiar to one another."

Ailis's stomach clenched. Her breath caught in her chest. It was what was supposed to have occurred, but it was still a surprise to hear him say it with such certainty. "You're sure?" she asked, one hand going unconsciously to her belly.

"Oh, yes," he said quietly. "This is not a matter left to chance. I knew last night that you were to be the one, and I know tonight that you are carrying my son, just as I know that the river will rise when the rains come."

She turned his answers over in her thoughts. All her life, Ailis had been told that she asked too many questions. But for the first time she thought she had more answers than she knew what to do with.

"Do you want to walk?" he asked her, and she nodded her agreement. They walked upstream toward a patch of bushes that Ailis remembered sprouting berries when she was a child. They hadn't done so in years.

Perhaps this spring, there would be berries again. And in the springtimes after that, she could take her own son and teach him to pick fruit there. The idea was strange and familiar at the same time.

She looked down and watched her feet padding over the moss and wild flowers covering the forest floor. Her white dress was still clean where it brushed the tops of her feet. "Why don't I need shoes?" she asked. "Why aren't I dirty?"

The Beast—although the title no longer seemed to quite fit, she didn't have a better name for him—laughed softly.

"The forest is my home. So are the plains, the hills, the mountains. I'm the son of the earth. It knows me, and so I can pass freely where I like." He held up one hand to stop her next question. "You are my bride. Chosen by the earth's other children, accepted by me, you are my bride, and so you also go where you please." He looked at her sideways as they walked. "It isn't magic," he said, as though he'd known her next question before she spoke. "It's knowledge, understanding. It's the reason I chose you. I could smell the knowing in you, and that what you didn't know, you'd want to."

Ailis laughed then before she could stop herself. He turned to look at her, and she shook her head, still trying to catch her breath to speak. "I think that's the first time anyone's ever said they were glad of all my questions."

"Nothing else would have done," he said with humor in his voice. "But now I have questions. Tell me about your life, your family, where you come from."

At first, she wasn't sure what to say. The things he'd asked were so much a part of her, she wasn't sure how to talk about them. They simply were. Instead, she tried to imagine herself outside of her life, looking in, and described what she saw.

"My father," she began, "Is not yet so old he can't hunt large game. He laughs all the time, especially with my brothers' children. But he still misses my mother. She died ten winters ago."

Ailis remembered her mother taking a chill and never warming again, and she bit the inside of her cheek for distraction. "I still live in the central hovel with my father. My sister is older, and she's gone to live with her husband's family. As my brothers got old enough to take wives and start their own families, they've built their own hovels all around my father's."

She glanced at the Beast to see if this was what he wanted to know, thinking that he couldn't be interested in these details, but he only nodded, so she continued. "I have three brothers and one sister, all of them older. The youngest one is two years older than I am, and his second child was just born last full moon."

She wondered that the Beast could know every turn of every stone, as he seemed to, but not know any of this, and she marveled more that he should be interested in it. "There are thirty families in my village. We have fields nearby where the land is flatter, and there we grow wheat. Not so much in the last few years though. We hunt too, and fish, and gather wild plants that can be eaten. The village is between the river and the fields, so that neither is too far away."

He made a considering sound, but said nothing. He seemed deep in thought. When he finally spoke, it was only to say, "We should go this way," and to point to a faint path heading north and east of the river. She nodded and followed him. Their new route took them up hill, and the forest thinned out until it was only isolated copses of trees, and the ground became grassier. Ailis couldn't recall having been here before even though she'd thought she was familiar with the area.

He said, "Tell me about the priestesses."

They'd come one-quarter moon ago. The priestesses traveled between Ailis's village and two others not too far distant. They had a place of their own, but each winter they spent at a different one of the villages, sheltered from the worst of the storms. During winters they taught the old stories to the youngest children. They blessed crops and the sick, and they carried news between the villages. This year they'd brought the news that it was time to choose a bride for the Beast.

"All of the unmarried girls of age came forward," Ailis remembered out loud. "We gathered in the center of the village. The priestesses said that they'd already visited both of the other villages, and that there were no suitable women there. We stood in a line and waited while they walked in front of and behind us. It felt like they were looking for something, but no one knew what. I was the one they chose." She shrugged as she finished speaking, still turning over her own memory.

The Beast stopped walking then and turned to her. "There's something else," he said. "Something else about the choosing. What is it?"

He was so frank about it, that Ailis just answered without thinking about it.

"When we were standing there, in front of the priestesses, I was afraid. But at the same time, I remember wishing, *let it be me*." She'd barely let herself think about it since that day.

The Beast nodded, satisfied, as though he'd been expecting her answer. "That's what they were looking for." Ailis's breath caught at his words. It had never occurred to her that she'd had a hand in her own fate. The idea was exciting and frightening at the same time.

Distracted by this new idea, Ailis followed the Beast away from the river's edge. They walked uphill, climbing over rocks and tree roots as they went. Her thoughts turned inward and she no longer paid attention to where he led her. She stopped when he stopped, and looked up, surprised to see the mouth of a cave directly in front of them.

She looked around, trying to place their location. It was both familiar and not. Everywhere she turned looked *almost* like a place she knew well. Near the mouth of the cave were rings of mushrooms, growing in wide circles. The entrance itself was set into a hillside so that grass and wildflowers disguised the top of it. The Beast held out his hand to her, and she took it, following him inside.

Ailis was tense at first, not sure what to expect. She thought the cave might be cold, or the ground damp, but the cave was warm and dry inside, as comfortable as her hovel with the fire burning. It was dark, the little light from outside not crossing the threshold. She had to hold tight to the Beast's hand, and found herself staying close to his body, so as not to stumble in the darkness.

Their footsteps took them downwards; she could feel the slant of the passageway under her feet. It was stone, but covered loosely with sandy dirt that sifted between her toes as she walked.

Walking in such darkness, Ailis quickly lost track of both time and distance. She felt the cave wall brush her arm, and she stepped closer to the Beast, nearly pressed against his side, counting on him to lead her.

His arm was warm and solid. She could feel the play of his muscles under the skin. He still had that smell, one that was animal, but not. It made her stomach tighten as thoughts of the night before flooded her mind and then her senses.

She flushed at the memory and wondered if he could feel the new heat in her skin. Could he smell the desire that sprang to life in her when she imagined his hands on her again? She pushed the thoughts away and tried to concentrate on where she was putting her feet.

The floor turned level, and after a handful of turns Ailis realized that they'd entered a chamber. She could tell by the way the sound of their footsteps echoed back to them, and because the air was different, more still.

As she stood there, her eyes grew more adjusted to the gloom. There was faint light coming from somewhere above, thin shafts of illumination that drifted in pale rays from the ceiling.

The longer she stayed still, the more she could make out the space around them. It was a cavern about thirty feet in diameter. Rock teeth hung from the ceiling above them. The walls were rough, forming a loose circle around them. In the center of the stone chamber there was a wide pool of still water. The Beast led her to the water's edge.

"I have a gift for you," he said, surprising her. She looked up at him, but he kept his gaze on the water's surface. In the vague light, she thought that she saw him as a man, with long, dark hair hanging loose around his face, a mantle of leaves spread over his shoulders. Then the image was gone, and in its place was a man-Beast, like a wolf that had learned to walk on two legs. She almost recoiled, but forced herself to remain still. Whatever he was, he hadn't harmed her when he could have. He'd spoken to her in a way no one else ever had, touched her in ways she hadn't imagined. No, she assured herself. There was no harm for her here.

"Your gift," he continued, "is at the bottom of the pool."

She blinked, wondering if she'd heard him correctly. "You put it there?" she asked, confused.

"This is where it waits," he said. "Whether I put it there, or you did, makes no difference."

Ailis sighed, realizing she would get no clearer an answer. "Am I to wade in to get it?" she asked.

"You'll have to swim," he told her. She waited for him to continue, but that was all he said.

Ailis surveyed the chamber again, looking for some way to gauge the water's depth, but there was none. Sighing, she began to remove the linen dress she wore. It felt strange to undress in this unfamiliar place, in front of someone else's eyes. She knew it was foolish and girlish to think so, but as she uncovered her breasts, she blushed nonetheless into the darkness. When she'd taken off her clothing and left it folded on a nearby rock, she stood, naked, at the pool's edge.

Turning back to the Beast, she asked, "How did you know we would come here? You told me to pick the place we would travel to, but I might as easily have said 'the village' or 'the wheat fields' as 'the river'. So how did you know we would come here, to where this gift waited?" As she watched him, a bear stood before her, four hand spans taller than a tall man. He turned his head and opened his mouth and sharp teeth flashed a grin at the shadows. Then that image was gone again, leaving

Ailis to wonder if she'd ever seen it at all.

"All roads lead to the same place," he told her. And when he spoke he was a wolf, gray-furred and lean. "All roads take us to our own destinies." He had feathers, not hair, like those of a raven, shiny and black. "Don't you know that already?" he asked, his voice full of amusement, like the laughing call of the crow.

Ailis closed her eyes to keep from growing dizzy from watching him. She turned back to face the pool, and she felt him walk up just behind her. He put a hand on either of her shoulders. He bent down so that his breath stirred her hair. The chamber was already warm, but his body was so close behind her, it made the hair stand up on her neck and arms. At the small of her back—he was so much taller than she—his sex nudged against her bare flesh. Her nipples hardened, and the cave seemed suddenly very hot.

Emboldened by the surge of wanting deep inside her, Ailis leaned back against him, so that his manhood pushed against her heated skin. Her hips moved of their own accord, shifting to a rhythm she hadn't known until the night before. She felt his hands clench on her shoulders, then slowly he loosened his grip, pushing her gently forward. Disappointed, she took a deep breath, and stepped into the water.

It was neither warm, nor cool, but it was calming, especially after the upheaval she'd felt in the last few minutes. A few steps forward confirmed that this was not a shallow pool. She'd have to swim to reach the bottom. She'd have to sink.

Steadying herself, feeling the sandy bottom shift under her feet, Ailis took a deep breath—and dove.

Her first strokes were tentative, but then they grew bolder, as she carried herself downward by the strength of her arms and legs. In the absolute dark of the water, it didn't matter if her eyes were open or closed. She felt as though her worries, her fears lifted off her in the water the way her physical weight did. She thought of the Beast, whatever form was really his, waiting for her on the rocky edge above. She thought about her own wish to be chosen by the priestesses. Was that really all it had taken? Her wanting this? And, if so, why had she wanted it?

She began to wonder how far she'd come, and how long she'd been swimming. She'd lost all sense of distance. She couldn't breathe here underwater—but even as she thought it, she realized she didn't feel like she needed to. She hadn't once felt that she needed air since she'd begun swimming. So she kept going.

As she went further, she thought of what would happen in the days and months to come. She would have a baby. And by the very act of his being, the earth would grow stronger. That was what they taught in the stories. For generations to come, her people's children would live to see the earth give more each year; they'd see the harvest grow greater. She smiled at the thought. And for her part, she'd have a child—to raise and teach—alone. Would she keep her father's house? Would any man want her after this? Or be allowed to take her to wife if he *did* want to?

For three nights, she would be married to the Beast, but did that mean she would be alone for all the nights afterward? None of these questions had come to her before. She'd been preoccupied enough with the idea of being eaten alive, not living even this long.

Her chest was beginning to feel tight. Perhaps she needed air in this place after all. Her strokes faltered and she tried to see how far the surface was above her, but in the dark, she couldn't even tell if her eyes were open. Panic began to creep through her, and around her, the water seemed to grow colder. She thrashed her head back and forth, and was about to strike out for the direction she remembered being the surface, but then she saw something.

There was a prick of light in the darkness. It was small, but it was true light, not masked, or shadowed, or reflected. Drawn toward it, she continued deeper. As she came closer, she saw movement as well, then color. Fish, she realized with surprise. She'd found the bottom of the pool, and here there were hundreds, thousands of fish, all manners, moving together and alone. And there in the midst of them lay the source of the light, a gleaming, golden bracelet.

Ailis went toward it, marveling at its beauty. She picked it up after only a moment's hesitation. It was warm and smooth to the touch, the metal perfect and flawless. Somehow it glowed, casting light all around it. Holding it up, Ailis could see all around her with clarity. She saw fish of all colors, shapes and sizes. She saw strange animals that she'd heard lived in the open sea, but had never seen. And she saw other things that she'd never even heard described. It was beautiful, and Ailis was tempted to stay just where she was in this perfect and ordered place.

But then, she thought of the Beast waiting above. She thought of her village, and her father, and with a last look around, the golden bracelet in one hand, she set out for the surface again.

The journey back was easier. She felt lighter, as though she were rising on great wings back to the world above. Almost before she knew it, she'd cleared the surface of the pool, and she took in a great breath to be sure she still could.

The breath turned into a gasp.

In her hand, the bracelet still glowed brightly, and its light filled the cavern. Bigger than she'd expected, the walls of the cavern curved up to form a ceiling far above. The cave walls were covered with pictures. There were drawings like primitive stick figures, and elaborate illustrations painted in colors faded by age. The images climbed over the rock, giving life to the shadows and embracing the newly-come light. Ailis's hand shook as she waded back to shore, the bracelet held over her head.

She was so distracted looking at the cave, so full of rapt attention for the drawings there, that she did not at first see the Beast. And then, when she did, she almost didn't recognize him. Gone were the last vestiges of animal or monster. He was all long and wild dark hair, smooth skin, and pale muscle. His features were a man's, with a long and even nose, a wide mouth, and still the same piercing blue eyes. Over his shoulders hung a cloak of leaves, and they were all the deep green of springtime.

The cloak hung open, leaving the front of his body exposed. His chest was broad, and dark hair curled there, thinning over his flat belly, but bushing again lower down. There the coarse hair made a nest from which his manhood arose, naked and proud. Ailis's gaze caught there and she couldn't make herself look away. She'd felt his sex the night before, but that was different than seeing him. Looking at him now, Ailis felt her skin flush, despite the water still cooling on her body. There was a slipperiness between her legs that had nothing to do with the dampness from the pool.

She forced her gaze to leave his sex, instead looking down his long, strong legs where the muscles bunched, and she could imagine them holding him crouched above her. At the thought, her stomach tightened, as did something lower in her. She looked up and was caught in his stare. However human the rest of him appeared, his gaze was still pure animal. He looked at her as though he might devour her yet, and Ailis found herself wishing he would do just that.

He held a hand out to her, and she walked toward him on shaking legs. The arm holding the bracelet aloft fell to her side. As she approached him, he took off his cloak of leaves and wrapped it around her, even though the act left him completely naked. He looked not the least bit self-conscious of his nudity.

Standing in front of him, Ailis felt full of anticipation in a way she'd never imagined. He lifted her wet hair so that it fell on top of the cloak of leaves. He was much taller than she, the top of her head only barely coming to his chin. He lowered his face to just over her hair and breathed in, his breath stirring the strands at the top of her scalp. He drank in the smell of her, then stepped around her so that he stood at her back, his hands lightly on either of her shoulders. He spoke near her right ear.

"What do you see?" he asked. She looked at the cave wall in front of her. Wavering line drawings of men fled from a dark, threatening smear that reached for them with spiky hands. In the next scene, one of the man-drawings approached the dark thing with a torch held aloft. The image after that showed the man still with his torch, but the darkness had been transformed into a glowing orb with rays like the sun reaching all around. As she turned her head, looked above, below, and around the cavern, she saw the same scene acted out again and again in different styles. In some of the images, it was clearly a woman who carried the torch. In others she could see embraces between a woman and a Beast, or a woman and a man. She saw the seasons turn in the drawings, saw fallow fields grow fertile, and again and again, darkness transformed.

"I see us," she said. "Everywhere." She was so warm she was beginning to sweat. As though he'd read her thoughts, the cloak dropped away from her shoulders, leaving her bare. Even with the garment gone, his warmth still blazed behind her like the sun on the wall in front of her. His sex nudged against her buttocks, and his chest pressed against her back as he stepped closer to her. He felt enormous, and the tip of him was wet where it grazed against her flesh.

"You found your gift," he said softly. And his hand moved from her shoulder, dropping down to her breast. She shivered and tilted her head back to rest against his chest. His hand kept moving, squeezing, the pad of his thumb teasing her nipple.

Her hands clenched, and she felt the smooth, gold bracelet in one. "What is it?" she asked, then gasped as his other hand passed across her belly, fingers trailing through the hair between her legs.

"Insight," he said softly, and his tongue touched her ear, warm and wet. "The ability to truly see. I could offer it to you, but you had to claim it yourself." He bent then and she felt his tongue slide up her spine from the base to between her shoulder blades.

She tried to slide her free hand back behind her, wanting to feel him, to stroke him, but he pressed against her from behind so that their bodies were too close for her to reach him. His right hand moved to caress her other breast, pulling unapologetically at her nipple. His left hand dipped lower, sliding between her legs, slipping easily back and forth in the wetness there. The sensations inside of her continued to build, and she gripped the golden bracelet with one hand, and his thigh with the other.

He moved against her from behind, a steady, pulsing rhythm that pressed him against her again and again, but didn't penetrate. At the same time, his hand rubbed between her legs, fingers kneading the nub there until she was breathing in ragged gasps. Two long, wide fingers slid inside her so fast she didn't realize it was happening until it was done. She gave a sharp cry and her body reacted, clenching the invading members, muscles grasping and begging them to be still even as they continued to move inside her with that same steady pressure. Her knees buckled, but his arm around her waist kept her upright while he continued to stroke her from within, his fingers making a slow and thorough exploration.

She struggled against him even while her body cried out for him. She was still too new to this, and she hadn't yet learned how to accept this even while she wanted it. His fingers probed the core of her, still sensitive from the night before, and she thought she might die from the sensations that rippled from inside her, growing stronger and stronger. When she thought she would scream if it didn't end, he stopped, his fingers withdrawing as quickly as they'd entered. His member was still hard against her, pressing between her thighs, but then he turned her around to face him.

Half carrying her, he guided her until her back was against the rock wall of the cave. Gently, he took the golden bracelet from her, and slipped it over her hand and onto her wrist. Then, one of his hands wound in her hair, pressing back against the stone so that her head stayed still. His other hand slowly stroked her thigh while his head dipped and found one of the trails of water from the pool still running down her body. Starting just above her sex, his tongue traced the water up as though drinking from her body. His tongue ran over her belly, around her navel, up her ribs, and over her breast, stopping at the place where her neck and shoulder met.

He did the same thing again, and again, until all she knew was the rough touch of his tongue across her body. He released her hair then, and with one hand still pinning her hip to the wall behind, he pushed her legs further apart and his head moved between her thighs. She felt his tongue then, where his fingers had been before, and she cried out in confusion and pleasure. His tongue lapped at her opening, nudging and stroking the folds there. She buried her hands in his hair, trying to hold herself upright.

He laved the center of her with his attentions, then the insides of her thighs, and then he ran his tongue through her nether hair, pulling the individual strands. When he returned to her opening she felt pressure, then penetration, then he was licking along the inside of her. She struggled, legs trying to twist, but failing since he'd moved a hand to grip each of her thighs. Whether she squirmed to get away or to get closer, she could no longer tell. Her body was near panic with the cascade of feelings within her. If it didn't end soon, she was sure she would go mad. There was a terrible, beautiful pulling between her legs as he drew her into his mouth, hard, and she braced herself against the rough wall, letting herself flow into him, giving into the sensation.

Just as she thought that the terrible pressure building inside of her would be released, he ceased his ministrations. She slumped forward, but he caught her, keeping her standing as he rose again to his feet. Ailis gasped, trembling before him,

"Come," he said softly. Letting go of her slowly, he moved his hands to hers and drew her forward. Her gaze stayed on his, and she thought she could drown in that blue. She could look at the lines of his face forever and count herself lucky. And she wondered how she had ever looked at him and not seen this.

He led her back to the pool, the water lapping at both of their legs. She thought he would lay her down in the sand at its edge, but instead he lay on his back, head and shoulders above the water, the rest partially submerged in the shallows. He pulled her down so that she straddled him there on her knees. His sex rose between them, erect just in front of her and it was beautiful, slick and red and swollen.

She reached out to touch it, stroking lightly. He closed his eyes and tilted back his head, and she saw the raw need in his face. Seeing it made her own wanting spike, and she touched him harder, running her hand up and down the shaft until his breathing was as uneven as hers, and when she squeezed at the base, he cried out and her breasts ached at the sound.

At the tip of his shaft, a pearl of clear liquid glistened and, on impulse, she lowered her mouth, tongue going out to taste it. His hips reared up, and his body clenched. Thinking of his mouth against her, she lowered her head again and took him into her mouth. Her tongue whipped around his tip, two, three times, then she sucked hard and his rough-voiced cry drove her to do it again, and then again. All the while her mouth worked over him, she could feel the warm water of the pool lapping against her own sex as she straddled him there at the water line.

The feather light touch drove her until she finally released him to look into his face, his blue eyes darker with desire. "Please..." she said, not knowing what else to ask. His hands lifted her hips, guiding her over him. She could feel him nudging against her, and she sank gratefully downwards.

The touch of his fingers had been nothing. Now he opened her and entered her, stretching her around him. She sank down, and he pushed up, as far as he'd been the night before, and then farther yet. She felt a flash of fear as she wondered how far he might penetrate her. At the last she would have held back, but it was too late for that. Her own legs were too weak to hold her up, and she sank down until he filled her completely and her body pressed to his.

At first it was all she could do to hold still and remember how to breathe. He stayed perfectly still while she did, his blue gaze regarding her with burning intensity, his sex deep inside her. She gathered her strength to rise up a little, and the movement was glorious. But she realized that she felt empty as soon as he was no longer entirely within her. Experimentally she lowered herself again. There was pressure, but it felt good at the same time. Buried inside her, he touched somewhere that she'd been wholly unaware of before, and that place longed to be touched. By him.

She lifted again, then lowered, and as she did so her inner muscles clenched, and he arched against her with a groan. His hands seized her hips then, and his own began to rise and fall in an increasingly incoherent rhythm. She reveled in the feeling of him, and in the knowledge that he was as far from control as she. Again and again he found the core within her, and she found that elusive sense of release growing nearer until, with the suddenness of lightning, it struck. Her body went rigid, then slack, then rigid again, and she shuddered while below her he did the same. When it was over, she was slumped on top of him, arms draped around his neck, face buried in the rough hair of his chest.

His arms were around her, loose but strong. His eyes were closed, and his face was beautiful in its peacefulness. Ailis looked up, but the walls of the cave had gone dark again. Then she realized that they weren't rock walls at all, but the black cloth of the *sh'rokk*. The pool was gone as well. The Beast's head lay against the white of the sacred stone.

Confused, she pulled a little away, sitting up, and as she did so, his eyes opened. His arms tightened around her and pulled her back into his embrace. "We're back where we started," she said. "I don't understand."

He laughed softly, and the sound sent warm shivers down her spine. "We're a very long way from where we started," he said, stroking her hair fondly. "And you understand everything, darling Ailis. Some things you just choose not to look at yet."

Ailis turned her head to look around again. As she did, she saw the golden bracelet still around her wrist, and the realization dawned. "The *sh'rokk*," she said, brow furrowing as she worked it through. "It's the same as the cavern. It's what the priestesses have made to stand in for the real place." She looked at him for confirmation, and he nodded. "But why not just take me to the proper place to begin with?" she asked.

"Because they wouldn't know where to find it," he said, still touching her hair, looking at it as though it held the marvels of the night sky for him. "They likely don't even know it exists any more. But something in them remembers a little, and so they build this."

Ailis nodded slowly. She knew what the priestesses did not. She now knew things that no one else did. It was daunting and thrilling at the same time. He shifted, and she moved aside, half rising so he could sit up. Tilting her head up with one hand under her chin, he kissed her. She closed her eyes, giving into the safety and sweetness of his mouth on hers, his lips moving over hers. When he drew back she heard him say quietly, "It's time for me to go."

She smiled up at him. "But you'll be back tomorrow."

"I will," he said. Then he rose up, picking his cloak up from somewhere on the ground. He drew it over his shoulders, and with a last backward smile, he was gone.

Alone and happier than she could remember, Ailis sat and waited for the priestesses to come.

The Beast stood in the empty cavern. The light was gone, but he needed no outside illumination to see clearly in the dark. This place he knew with his eyes closed. He turned in a slow circle, looking at the drawings and paintings on the walls. Countless generations had made their own mark here.

He knew each one by heart. For almost as long as he could remember, these had been his only contact with the society of other men.

Sometimes, when he closed his eyes and pretended he still needed to sleep, he could remember flashes of living with people. He remembered houses, round and made of rushes bound together. He remembered the smell of cooking fires, and the laughter of children. Sometimes he went near the villages of men so he could hear those sounds again.

Very rarely, he remembered touch. The sensation would come to him sometimes, and he'd hold still, keeping the memory as long as he could.

The last two nights had obliterated his faint phantom memories. The first night he'd been so greedy for the contact that he'd been like the Beast the villagers named him. It was just as well they did since he'd long since forgotten whatever name had once been his.

That first night, he'd needed to be sure that she was the right one. But once he'd known, there'd been no holding back. A wealth of instinct, tradition, and need had fired his actions. It had felt like being struck by lightning, but glorious.

All today he'd lived with the expectation of what nightfall would bring. But tonight had been better than his imagining. Tonight she'd seen him; even at the beginning she'd known him a little. She hadn't been afraid, and she'd talked to him. It had been such a very long time since anyone had spoken to him.

The priestesses spoke to the earth in their chants and their songs. They spoke *of* him. But that wasn't the same as a woman standing before him, her eyes meeting his, her voice meant for his ears. He shivered at the thought and started to pace in his excitement.

She was the right one. She was smart, brave, and curious. He loved the way her mind worked, turning things round and round in her thoughts—her face so clear you could watch her thoughts pass behind her eyes.

It was necessary that she be intelligent, thoughtful. It was necessary that she be able to understand the things he showed her. Going through all the motions without really understanding why wouldn't be enough to fulfill what the earth demanded. And if he'd been wrong about her, wrong in his choice, it would mean another starving year, another freezing year. And not only for men and the children of men. The creatures of the land and air, the plants themselves would suffer if the sacrifice was not a proper one.

But he hadn't chosen rashly. He wasn't wrong. He thought about her standing pressed against him in the cavern. He remembered the touch of her skin, still damp from the water of the pool. That had been the greatest danger he told himself. If her wonderful curiosity had kept her at the bottom of the water—and it had happened with others, the drawings said so—then it would all have been ruined.

He walked to a still empty corner of the cavern. There he found the piles of ashes he'd left there—some black soot, others colored by the plants he'd burned, or the juices of berries. Dipping his fingers into one of the piles, he continued to work on his own illustration, his own history.

Surely the first pictures had been made by men. But men had long since lost the location of this place. And since then, there had been only the Beast—those who'd come before him to tell their own tales. He smeared a dark shape on the wall, seeing the way her hair looked.

He tried again, looking for the shape of her eyes in the image he made. How many before him had come here and done this same thing? Had any of them felt the way he did now? Had all of them?

He continued working, going faster, a little desperate to capture her properly. If he couldn't keep her, he could keep a little of her here. Perhaps the one who came here after him would appreciate his efforts.

Since he didn't need to sleep, he paid no attention to how long he worked. Finally he stopped and stepped away from what he'd done. Looking at his work, he felt satisfied, and a little sad. He'd finished his record of the last two nights. In them, he felt like he'd captured some small part of her beauty, her courage.

Holding onto that courage in his own chest, he turned to regard the backmost wall of the cavern. This wall stayed shadowed. It was the only thing Ailis had not been able to see earlier tonight. This wall told the end of the story, it told of the third night.

Looking at it, the Beast knew with certainty that this picture was always made the night *before* the last night. Looking at it, the wall of images, the Beast felt a tightness in his chest. If only he could hold onto her for the rest of time. If only the *second* night could be made to go on forever.

Resigned, he bent once more to dip his fingers again into the ash.

Ailis dreamed. And as she did, she realized that she had always dreamed, all her life, awake or asleep. It was this that had set her apart from the other girls in her village. It was this that had caused her mother to scold her fondly when she forgot to do her work, that had caused her brothers to tease her good naturedly, and her father to stand and shake his head perplexed. It was this that had led the priestesses to her. She knew that now.

Whatever the stories and songs said, there was more to the sacrifice than she'd known. After what she'd seen these last days, she doubted that the priestesses really understood what was involved either. It was strange to think that after a lifetime of regarding them with awe and respect. The priestesses were seventh daughters, all of them. The seventh-born daughter of any family in any of the villages was sent to be a priestess. When the land was kinder, there had been more of them. Now there were fewer children born, and fewer yet who lived past infancy, so the ranks of the priestesses had thinned along with everything else.

They still traveled from village to village, valley to plain to mountain, carrying the stories and songs and traditions that bound them all together. But there were fewer of them all the time as fewer girls joined them every year, and Ailis had wondered for a long time if they had also lost knowledge. Now she knew that they had. They were starving slowly, like everything else here. But that would change.

The last two nights, and the one to come, would restore the land. How that would happen, Ailis still didn't know. The Beast said that she knew everything, just chose what she would understand, but she didn't think so. After a lifetime of questions asked with impunity, why would she spare herself the same scrutiny now?

In her dream, she now stood on a hill. It was taller than everything else nearby, and from it she could see everywhere. She was standing in grass as tall as her waist, and the wind whipped it against her legs. Two children stood next to her, one on each side, clasping her hands with theirs. But the grass was so tall, and moved so much that she couldn't see them. Far away she could see the ocean, brilliant blue. She'd never seen its waters while she was awake, but it felt familiar to her now. She could see each fish in its waves, the sand on its beaches, and she knew them as well as she knew the lines of her own hands. To her other side she could see the mountains that stretched their tips skyward, but were still below her where she stood. She knew every up and down of them, each crevice and peak.

Someone was climbing up the hill toward her. She wore the dark, hooded cloak of one of the priestesses, but the nearer she drew, the more familiar she seemed to Ailis. She couldn't see anything of the other woman's face, but the walk was familiar enough that it was no surprise when she stopped a few feet away and pushed back her hood.

Ailis looked into the face of her mother, whom she hadn't seen alive in ten turns of the seasons. But the eyes were someone else's. They were the green of moss, the gray of winter shadows, and the rich brown of fertile soil. She smiled when she said, "Greetings, daughter."

Ailis dipped her head in respect, but raised it again to study the woman standing in front of her.

"You have questions."

It was and was not her mother's voice, but Ailis nodded anyhow. "Why have you been cold for so many years?" she asked. The answer came to her from her own thoughts at the same time it did to her ears.

"Because nothing is young forever. Nothing lives without change, including me. People are born, they live, and they die. I do the same. But when I've died, I live again."

Ailis nodded slowly while she let that settle in her mind. Then she asked, "Why do you need the sacrifice?"

"All life requires a sacrifice. It's only a matter of degrees." She smiled, and it was Ailis's mother's smile. "You'll understand that when it's your time." She nodded toward the two hidden children still holding Ailis's hands.

Ailis licked her lips and took a deep breath before asking her next question. "What will happen after the third night?" In her mind a riot of ideas had begun to populate. How would she live? Would she go to the cavern with the Beast? Would he stay with her in her village, come to her at nights? She held still, tense and waiting for the answer.

There was what felt like a long silence before the answer came. "Things will grow—crops, children, everything. The long waiting will be over..."

"I know that," Ailis said hurriedly. "I mean what will happen to me." But the other woman was drawing her hood back up, shadow falling over her face.

"That depends on you, on what you choose to do." She was turning around again, walking downhill.

"But what will the Beast do?" Ailis called after her. She wanted to follow, but the two hands in each of hers held her where she stood.

"He has fewer choices," came the answer as the woman grew smaller in the distance. "His promises were made before he was." Frustrated, Ailis cast her gaze around her and it seemed that everything was in motion, each fish, each bird, each lizard, all moving along their own courses until the buzz and motion of life itself drew Ailis out of her slumber.

It was nearly noon judging from the light outside. Getting up from her sleeping furs, Ailis went to the door of the hut and pushed the curtain fully open, not caring who saw. Her stomach growled, but otherwise she felt wonderful. She stretched, lifting her arms above her head, twisting and reaching. There were none of the aches or scrapes from the first night. In fact, when she felt gingerly at her back, the bruises there had vanished. She paced around the interior of the room, searching her body for some sign of physical strain, but there was none.

Ailis returned to the doorway. Looking out, she let herself be blinded by the sunlight, enjoying the way it dazzled her vision. Next she turned to look at the tree line beyond the clearing. Her eyes adjusted quickly, and she watched the shadows at the edge of the forest twist as the wind tossed the limbs of the trees. A different movement caught her attention. Small and furtive, a gray hare skipped at the base of one tree. Its head lifted, and its nose twitched to pick up the shifting scents. Smelling so many humans nearby made him nervous. They didn't often come to this valley. Ailis felt her own legs tense as he readied himself to spring. She searched for any sound out of the ordinary. Overhead she heard the telltale rustle that spoke of a bird, a large one, and thinking—hawk—she fled, powerful strides carrying her into the forest, the leaf-covered floor fairly flying by below her.

Ailis gasped, coming back to herself, still standing in the doorway of the hovel, in the middle of the valley. She could feel her heart pound with the rabbit's, racing from the danger of the predator hawk. And she knew just as clearly that the hawk was real, a genuine danger to the hare. The hawk had seen him well before the hare noticed the bird. In another few moments, the hawk would have struck, rushing down on the rabbit with fierce speed. The small animal had been right to run.

With a shock, Ailis realized that she knew how fast the hawk was, just as she knew what it felt like for him to shake his great wings out and fly, gliding on the currents overhead. She knew that he, like every other creature of the earth, was hungry, and had been for a very long time. What she didn't know was *why* she felt what she did. Was this yet another response to her experiences of the last two nights? Was she now so much a part of the world, that she could see it, share it, through the senses of the animals that lived in it?

Curious, Ailis stared into the forest at the far side of the valley. She thought of all the life the forest contained—animals, insects, birds.

Trees, flowers, and wild grass all grew together there. Standing apart from it all, she turned her attention there, and was rewarded by a wealth of heartbeats, pulses, steady dreaming minds, and wild, pensive ones. She could smell the mulch of the forest floor, feel it shift beneath her feet. She found she could think of anywhere and have a sense of what lived there and how. She shivered at the thought. This new gift was amazing, but also unexpected, and she wondered again what the next day would bring. Already, she'd seen so many changes, she could no longer guess what might come after tonight's joining.

She forced her thoughts blank and let the curtain fall back over the doorway. Still preoccupied, she went back to her sleeping furs and sank down until she was sitting there in the middle of the room. She wondered what would happen if she tried to imagine the Beast. Would she find him at all? And if she did, where? She wondered for the first time where he went when he left her, how he spent his days and the nights he didn't share with her.

The curtain opened then, and a young priestess entered with a pitcher of water, and a cloth bag with food in it. Wordlessly, she began to set out berries, a rarity these days, and bread. While she did, Ailis sat down again on her furs, still distracted. She looked to her wrist, and the golden bracelet was still there. She looked up and caught the priestess staring at it. As soon as she realized Ailis was watching, the girl ducked her head and continued with her work, cutting the bread into pieces.

Ailis examined her feet, looking for scratches, dirt, stains from grass—any indication of where she'd been the night before or what she'd done. But there was no trace. Nor was there any mark on her arms, or her legs which she raised her skirt to examine.

The last two nights were the most real she'd ever known, and yet they left no more mark than a dream. The golden bracelet was the only outward sign of where she'd been. The places she'd traveled to, the things she'd done were separate from the world that others saw. She knew that now. She turned her attention to her visitor, watching as the girl laid out dried fish along with the bread and fruit, then poured water from the pitcher into a cup. The girl had hair almost as dark as Ailis's own, but thinner. Her face was thin too, and it was obvious that it'd been a long time since she'd eaten a meal like the one she'd just laid out. When she realized Ailis was watching her, the girl tilted her head forward so that her hair fell over her face.

She murmured something, then scooted backward and began to sort out the ribbons and bells for Ailis's hair that lay in a tangle in a shallow, round basket where they'd been discarded at the end of last night.

The berries were tart but lush. The fish was divine. Ailis realized she was ravenous and had to make an effort not to eat too quickly.

As she tore a piece from the loaf of bread, still warm from the stone oven, she watched the young priestess. The girl went about her work, but her gaze kept slipping up toward Ailis, then back down again. Then a moment later, the girl would look again, as though unable to stop herself. Ailis was reminded again of the excitement she'd sensed from the priestesses last night as they'd escorted her to her second meeting with the Beast.

Ailis held out a piece of the bread. "Would you like some?" she asked. The priestess's head jerked up in surprise. She looked at the offered bread for a moment with longing before she shook her head and turned her attention back to sorting out ribbons.

"It's all right, really," Ailis tried again. "There's too much of it. I won't finish it all." She sat with the bread still held in front of her, feeling as though she were trying to coax a shy animal.

The priestess hesitated, then reached out and took the offered food. She sat on the floor opposite Ailis and began to pick apart the bread, eating slowly and with a relish that almost made Ailis laugh. She pushed forward some of the berries as well.

When the priestess seemed a little more relaxed, Ailis's curiosity got the better of her. "What do you see when you look at me?" she asked.

The priestess sat back and regarded her, eyes wide but thoughtful. She seemed to turn the question over in her mind before she responded.

"Two days ago, I saw a girl near my own age, frightened of what was to come, but brave enough to go." She paused and Ailis waited patiently for the priestess to continue. "You're different today. And yesterday was different from the day before." She seemed to search for the words.

"It's difficult to see you now."

Ailis started at the words.

"When I look at you," the priestess squinted at her, "you look like the same girl, but you seem older sometimes, or taller maybe. It's almost like you change while I'm looking. But that doesn't make any sense."

Ailis thought of the Beast's features, sliding over each other last night, before they went into the cave, before she entered the pool. She wished she could see what the priestess saw, and she peered into the other girl's eyes as though she might see her reflection there.

Something shifted. It was a feeling like losing her balance, but then finding it again. Only when she had, it wasn't her balance, but someone else's.

She looked out from the priestess's eyes. She knew her name was Caela, and that before she went to join the priestesses she'd lived in a village near a large lake. She was the seventh born daughter, but one of only four to live. She looked out, and Ailis saw her own face.

She knew the features from seeing them reflected in still water and in the darkened glazes of pottery. Her features were her own, but Ailis was surprised to see how much she looked like the memory she held of her mother. Dark eyes looked back at her from a pale face framed by dark hair. Her nose was long and straight. Her lips were thin and her mouth wide.

She looked older than she'd expected, or maybe it was just that she knew more than she had two days ago, and the knowledge was clear in her eyes.

Then she fell again, this time out of Caela's sight of her. She blinked once and opened her own eyes, looking back at the young priestess who regarded her with startled confusion.

"I should go," Caela said, glancing about her and standing up quickly. She went out the door, the cloth flapping behind her.

Ailis watched her go with a pang of loneliness. A week ago, she might have met Caela as friends. They were near the same age, and might have spoken easily together. Now they were a world away. Ailis knew that the girl recognized the difference in them, even if she didn't understand it. Ailis did though. Whatever path her life took after tonight, it would be different from that of other women.

She sat very still and let herself feel the grass blowing outside, and the sun on the rocks. Out in the trees, birds were leaping from branch to branch, and she could tell because she was a little more like the Beast was today. She was of the earth, and so she could feel it everywhere, including in Caela. Her loneliness was a small price for what she'd gained. Lying back on her sleeping furs, she wondered what new changes tonight would bring.

Night came, and with it a wild excitement that was new and dear to Ailis. The last two nights had brought changes, not only to her, but to the world as she'd known it. She shivered in anticipation of what new revelation would occur with this final night in the *sh'rokk*.

When the priestesses came, she met them at the door, eager and regal at the same time. She knew that they could not see her as she saw herself, or know the things that she now knew. But she felt a palpable awe from them even as they stayed their course as silent guides. It was in the way they bowed their heads, the way their eyes turned to her when they thought she wasn't looking, only now she was always looking. They couldn't know that she could see things now without needing to look, that the very air carried knowledge to her, and the trees knew her name.

It was power, she thought as she walked with them down the now familiar path. She was heady with it. Not power over other people. It was the power of knowledge, of understanding, and that was something intimate that she shared only with *him*.

They had reached the *sh'rokk*. The priestesses filed in, taking their places. Ailis went in and approached the stone, but a single priestess stood at its foot, waiting for her. She shook her head as Ailis hesitated, then she looked once around and the other priestesses, taking some cue from her, filed out.

Ailis stood, confused, the more so because of the sharp contrast with her recent sensation of knowing all there was to know. When the other women had left, and the door flap closed behind her, the priestess spoke.

"There are no bonds tonight," she said.

Ailis flushed, thinking that the priestess must know after all, what had transpired the night before.

"This is the final night," the priestess continued. "And so it is time." She reached under her dark green mantle and drew forth a long, bright silver blade.

In confusion, Ailis shook her head slowly. Did the priestess mean to kill her? Why had the wind not spoken to her of this? Why had the world to which she'd newly awakened given her no warning?

But the priestess made no move, only stood there, with the blade in her hand. Then she extended it, offering the hilt to Ailis. She reached out and took the blade. It was cold in her hand, and heavy. The blade was flat and narrow, as long as her forearm. "What is this?" she asked the priestess.

"It is the final night of the *sh'rokk*. Tonight, you will slay the Beast."

Ailis stared, uncomprehending at the other woman. "No," she said then. "That's awful. That's absurd."

But the priestess only shook her head. "It is what must be. What has always been." She reached out and laid one hand tenderly against Ailis's brow. "So young," she said softly. "But you will do what you must."

Then she stepped around Ailis. She hesitated once at the doorway, but then walked away without looking back.

Ailis stared at the knife in her hand. It was too unreal to be here in her grip.

She heard then, or more precisely, she felt the Beast's approach. Filled with horror, she flung the blade from her onto the ground at the back of the *sh'rokk*. Turning, she was in time to see his entrance.

He was beautiful, she thought. Tall, graceful, powerful—he was every good thing that any man had ever been, and more. His hair hung loose around his shoulders, his eyes were dark and deep as still water, and when he opened his arms, she threw herself into them without thought or question.

His arms went around her, wrapping her close, and she held on tighter, tears stinging her eyes. She couldn't possibly lose him. Not now, not at her own hand. There was no way the priestesses could make her hurt him, or that they could do him harm. She told herself this over and over, but still she was afraid. He stroked her head, running his hand down through her hair so that the bells jingled. He reached his hand under her chin, and tilted her face up to look into his.

"What's the matter?" he asked, smiling fondly down at her. In that gaze she felt safer, but when she tried to answer him, she could not. He ran his thumb down the side of her face. "Who is this girl?" he asked, teasingly. "I remember we made you a woman these last two nights. Why now do you tremble and look so frightened?" His voice was amused, and Ailis blushed at her own foolishness.

"It's nothing." She mustered her courage, searching out the confidence she'd felt earlier that day. "Only something one of the priestesses said to me. But it doesn't matter now." She embraced him back, letting her arms slide around his broad back, and laying her cheek against his chest.

"Good," he said. "I hate to see you upset." He put his hands on her arms, stepped back, and leaned down to kiss her. In the warmth of his mouth Ailis felt her worries slip away to be replaced with rising lust. Her need for him was tidal, and she felt it might drown her at any time.

When he released her, she stood still, eyes closed, to savor the feeling. But when she opened her eyes, she saw him walking toward the back of the *sh'rokk*. Before she could speak, he went unerringly to the place where she'd thrown the knife, bending to pick it up. He turned to look questioningly at her, and she froze.

He turned it over in his hands, from side to side, and end to end, examining it closely with a sense of curiosity. When he looked back to her, she stammered, "The priestess. She left it, but I don't know why."

"She left it for you to plunge through my heart," he replied matter-of-factly.

Ailis covered her mouth with both her hands in horror. "I never would," she said, willing him with all her heart to believe her. "I never would do such a thing."

"You have to," he said, and Ailis felt her blood run cold in her veins. She struggled against her rising panic to make sense of what he said, the sense of safety of only a few moments before evaporated. He went on. "This is the third night. We will make love. You will be fully initiated into the world, and then you will kill me. With this." He held the knife still in his hands, showing not the least bit of alarm.

The air froze. The world was silent. Then Ailis screamed. "No!" She shook her head violently, panic building in her breast, fear making her blind and numb to everything except the stabbing pain in her own chest as if that was where the silver blade had already found its home. He came to her and forced her still with his hands on her shoulders, then pried open her hands with his own to show the bloody tracks her nails had left there.

"There is no help for it," he told her softly as she stared at him, mute, through her tears. "Darling Ailis," he cradled her face gently in his hands. "The earth must be fed, in your blood or mine. This is how it has always been."

"Then let it be mine!" Her voice was a fierce whisper. Whatever her thoughts may have been when she came here two days ago, she knew now that her own death held no fear when weighed against a life without him.

But he shook his head again. "It's much too late for that," he said with a soft smile. "Your fate is set now. And your death would take more life than just your own."

Ailis wept in earnest at the words. She'd known, but hadn't truly believed until now. And now, what should have been joy was dust in her mouth. "There will be a child." she whispered.

"There will be two." As he spoke, he rubbed the pad of his thumb along her cheek, wiping away some of the tears that streamed down her face. "One for each night we have spent here." He leaned his face toward hers and softly kissed her forehead, and she sobbed the more for his tenderness. He went on. "The first son will be a leader of men. He will make more sons, and with each of them, the land will live again, and will know its children." He looked into her eyes. "The second son will belong in that other world. He will grow in the deep earth, and when he is grown he will leave you to live there, ageless, until such time as he is called to come and take a bride. This is how it has always been."

Ailis felt anger build in her, raging upward until it exploded. "Is this all there is then?" she pushed his hands away, stepping back and out of his reach. "Is this what it's all been for? So I can lose you, then bear two children and lose one of them as well? And all because the earth requires sacrifice to feed its maw?" She stalked away until the stone stood between them. "I won't do it. The price is too high."

He looked at her with sympathy, and it only enraged her more. "The earth doesn't nourish, it devours. There is no balance—all of it is a lie," she spat.

"When you came here two nights ago, you believed in it. Then, you were willing to die if that was what was required. Even minutes ago, you offered yourself again. Why then is this so unthinkable?"

"Because I'll die anyhow without you!" she cried. "Because when I came here two nights ago, I was ignorant, innocent. Only now you've given me knowledge, and that makes it unthinkable."

"And that makes it a sacrifice," he said softly. "That makes it a true, *willing* sacrifice, with full knowledge. And that is all the earth will accept."

Ailis broke then, her knees giving way beneath her. She sank down to the ground, leaning against the stone, sobs crashing like the waves because she knew that he was right.

She felt him settle down beside her and fold her in his arms, pulling her against him, and she let him because there was nothing else to do. And finally she clung to him because if she could not keep him, she would hold him as tightly as she could for as long as she could.

He stroked her hair soothingly and pressed his lips against her brow, then kissed the tears from her cheeks. When his lips covered hers she could taste the salt on them. She turned in his embrace so that she could wind her arms up and around his neck, taking in the warmth of him, the smell of him, the coarseness of his hair and the smoothness of his skin under her palms. She didn't know when the kiss turned from tender to passionate, but when he lifted her in his arms, she clung to him with an urgency that made her thoughts swim. He laid her down on the white rock. It felt like their bed, no longer hard and unyielding, but instead giving way beneath her, cradling them both.

He stripped the linen from her shoulders, uncovered her breasts, laid the heat of his mouth against her throat, and she moaned. Once, she stopped him, laying a hand against his chest. "If we make this moment last forever, the next will never come," she whispered. But he shook his head.

"The next moment always comes, whether you wait for it or run." He covered her then with his lips, and his hair, and himself, and she let herself be lost in the reality of him. If she couldn't have forever, she could at least give herself over to this timelessness.

She fell upwards into the heat of his mouth as he suckled her breast, his tongue, insistent. His hands slid over her body. At first his fingertips brushed her skin lightly, teasing and tantalizing. Then his palms pressed to her flesh, smoothing over the curves of her shoulders, her hips, and her thighs.

He stroked her body as though he would memorize it by feel. With each touch she felt more possessed by him, more part of him, and she reveled in it. Passion called her to him as sure as a voice. It named her his, and promised him to her in a way that death and time would never touch.

His sex rose between them, and Ailis reached for him, the last vestiges of self-consciousness left behind her. She held him, stroked him, breathed in the scent of him, as familiar now as her own. He moaned into her hair, his breath rushing against her heated skin. The sound and sensation drove her, and she lifted her hips to press against his length, starting the motion she knew would undo them both.

When Ailis had become pure fire, a blaze of need embodied, he slid into her and their bodies melded together. They moved as one, like perfect music. His hips lowered, hers took him in. She arched her back, and he lifted her higher.

She felt stronger than she'd ever been in her life, wrapped around him, and still her limbs trembled. She shook all over, as if she was cold, but the air around her was warm as a perfect day in spring. She could smell wild flowers, and her body shivered as though it would break apart. He lifted her up, holding her against him as he rose to his knees, her legs still wrapped around him, and she came undone, every sense filled past its limit.

She kept her eyes open so she wouldn't miss a moment as he followed her over the edge. His body strained and arched, his expression pure joy, and he kept his eyes locked to hers so she could watch them go liquid blue, so dark they spoke of hidden caves.

Finally, slowly, she unlocked her legs from around his waist so that she was kneeling in front of him. Their bodies were slick with sweat, and his hair mingled with hers to make a curtain around them both. She felt heady still with what they'd done. She was still gazing up into his eyes when he pressed the metal into her hand. She'd expected it still to be cold, but it was warm, and that made it somehow better.

"I don't want to," she whispered, as he guided the point of the blade over his heart.

"I know," he answered softly. She looked for some trace of fear in his face, but there was none to find. He leaned forward, even though it pressed the blade to his chest, until he could kiss her once, and Ailis pushed the blade forward, crying out when his warm blood spilled over her hands.

She pulled the blade back, and cast it aside as though that could somehow change what she'd done. His hands locked on her arms and he kept his eyes on hers as though he would drink the sight of her as he slid into darkness. Ailis gave a sob, and eased him down until he was lying on the stone, his blood running freely over it. She laid one hand along the side of his face, and he smiled, then closed his eyes, and his chest ceased its rise and fall.

She bent over him, her tears as hot as his blood, and she lowered her head until she could bury her face in his hair. "I love you," she said softly in a voice that sounded too weak and shrill to be her own. "Don't go." But he remained silent. Motionless.

There were no sounds. The air itself had gone still. The priestesses, the village, everything outside this place and this moment had ceased to exist. Then, very slowly, the sound of her own heart came back to Ailis's ears. Then, more faint, another heartbeat, echoing hers, matching its rhythm, and then a third. The Beast—how strange that she'd never learned or needed any other name for him—had spoken truly. There were two children; she could hear them clearly.

Then, as though from a great distance, she could hear one more heart beat. In her grieving mind, it made no sense. The sound seemed to come from miles away, but it was drawing closer. Around her, the air began to move again. Outside it howled, and her head came up to watch the walls of the *sh'rokk* whip fiercely against their ties. That other sound grew closer, as though it came with the wind, like a horse galloping fast toward them.

In a rush, it was there, washing over her and through her and she gasped at the force of it. Then the fourth pounding faded, back and down—and into the chest of the Beast. Ailis stared down, hardly daring to hope, and in that instant, his eyes opened. They fluttered, then found hers. Then he moved, gulping down air in a single rush and exhaling it again. Ailis's hand went to his wound, but it was gone. She brought her hand to her own mouth, covering it, trying to understand what she was seeing. He rose up a little and held his arms out to her, and she fell into them, crying all over again.

"How can this be?" she asked, as she held tightly to him. "I killed you."

"You killed something in me," he said, and his voice was different. It was still deep, still full, but some of the power was gone. It took her a moment to realize the difference, but it was a human voice now that she heard when he spoke. His next words confirmed it.

"What bled from me was the magic," he said, one hand going in wonder to his own chest. "It's gone back to the earth, to replenish it. And to wait." He moved his hand from his own chest to Ailis's bare belly. "To wait for its next heir," he said, and his voice was filled with amazement.

"Did you know this would happen?" she asked, still struck with the wonder of him, alive beside her.

He shook his head. "I knew of my dying. That was foretold from the beginning. The third night always ends in the death of the Beast. Before I knew you, I thought it no great chore, it simply was."

He raised his hand to cup her face. "And after I'd known you, I thought it no great price for the time we'd spent together. I would have welcomed a hundred deaths for each night in your arms. But I never imagined this greatest gift—a life to spend with you."

A life together.

Ailis's heart leapt at the idea, and she cried softly as she ran her hands over his face and his body, reassuring herself that he was real and whole. When she could speak without sobbing, she said, "So parts of all of this," she waved a hand in the empty air, "they're still a mystery?"

"I think they always will be," he answered. He looked deep into her eyes then, taking her hands in his. "Do you still want me Ailis, as only a man?" he asked.

Ailis only laughed and threw her arms around him.

The afternoon sun was full and bright, and Ailis had to shield her eyes with her hand as she emerged from the shadows of her hut. She smiled to see Varden coming up the path from the river. He raised one hand to show her the fish he'd caught. On his shoulders he carried their son, Bal. He waved at her, one small arm swinging happily through the air. Along the far side of the path, grass passed into forest. In the shelter of the trees, pacing his father, was their other son, Dermot. He came into sight one moment, then faded again into shadow the next.

Watching him, Ailis felt a pang. He was young yet. It was years before she would lose him, but she knew whenever she saw him that the day would come when he would walk into the forest and not return. But she didn't fear that time anymore. In truth, she feared very little. She had her husband by her side and—for now at least—she had two sons, both of whom would go on to fulfill their own destinies.

Varden walked the last steps to where she stood, and bent to kiss her, his tongue running lightly over her slightly parted lips. She smiled up at him, looking into his blue eyes. They were no longer the lupine blue they'd been when she'd first seen him. Since their third night together, they'd been the blue of deep water, brilliant, but still human. Dermot joined them, and Varden handed the fish he'd caught to his young son. Then he lifted Bal down from his shoulders.

Ailis stifled a laugh as he instructed them very solemnly in how to clean and prepare the fish for the night's dinner. "Be very careful you don't let him swim away while you're not looking," he instructed both boys with a wag of his finger. They burst into giggles when he made a swimming motion with his hand, imitating the fish speeding off through the air. "Now off to work with you both," he told them. "I have something to show your mother down by the river."

"Oh, do you?" Ailis asked with one eyebrow raised. He nodded at her and reached for her hand.

"I most certainly do," he said, leading her back down the path he'd come up.

"Do as your father says," she called back to her boys as she followed Varden. "And don't forget to gather berries for the meal, too." Both boys nodded distractedly at her, already about their task. She turned to follow her husband downhill toward the river, the path twisting several times along the way. They quickly lost sight of their home, and Varden picked up his pace, so that Ailis had to skip to keep up with him.

"So, what do you have to show me?" she asked as they approached the gurgling river. With a laugh, he wrapped her in his arms, gathering her up and off the path. He carried her easily into a sheltered grove of trees, hidden by leaves and branches from the bright sun. Laying her down on the thick green moss, he dropped down onto his knees beside her.

"Nothing you haven't seen before," he said with a mischievous smile. He bent to nibble her ear lobe. "But I thought we might appreciate dinner more with an appetite." He moved his attentions from the edge of her ear to the hollow of her throat.

Ailis started to laugh, but arched up against him instead as he caught the soft flesh of her neck and bit lightly, drawing the skin between his teeth. She breathed out in a hiss. His fingers worked at her clothing, undoing the ties that held her dress closed over her breasts. He freed them and immediately dipped his head to capture one nipple in his mouth, running his tongue over the already hardened point before sucking lightly. She moaned softly, encouraging him to do it again. He lowered his head, taking in more of her breast this time, wetting her with his tongue, heating her skin with his breath, before drawing back to let the soft breeze cool her. Both nipples were hardened pebbles by the time he uncovered the second.

She twined her hands in his hair as he ran his tongue along the bottom of her breast, then up along one side. He toyed with her with his teeth, tugging gently, drawing her nipple out, his tongue flicking along the tip like a cat's.

While he did, he pulled her clothing down so that the neckline of her dress, already loosened, came down around her shoulders, keeping her arms close to her sides, and baring her breasts completely. Next, one hand slid beneath her skirt, finding her bare leg in the folds there.

She kneaded her fingers into the muscles of his shoulders and the back of his neck. He still worked torturously at her breast, while his hand continued to massage its way up her thigh. Ailis felt heady with his attentions, dizzy with them. More than six years they'd been together now, and he still made her gasp at his touch, made her wet at the thought of him. Even now, his fingers were sliding back and forth between her parted legs.

She arched against his hand, pushing against him, begging for more, but his fingers only teased her, pulling at her bud as his teeth did at her nipple. She twisted beneath him until his hand left her entirely, going to his own breaches. His mouth covered hers, drawing her into a long deep kiss that tasted of salt and sweet, warm breath. She felt him lift her skirt over her thighs, felt the breeze against her bare body.

He shifted his weight so that he knelt between her thighs, then slid his hands under her buttocks, raising them slightly. She felt him thick and wet, pressed against her, and she groaned while he caught the sound from her with his own mouth, returning it with a deeper one. So slowly it was almost painful, he slid inside her. She would have bucked against him, but he'd carefully taken all her leverage from her, leaving her at the mercy of the pace he chose. What seemed an eternity passed until he was finally buried deep in her body. His breath coming raggedly from between his lips was her only indication of how great his own need was.

He drew back ever so slightly, before sliding forward again, and again, building a slow and steady rhythm. Ailis gasped as he coaxed the breath from her, making her feel at once light as air and heavy with pleasure. She could hear the river nearby and she felt swept away by her own current. Her own hands touched what they could reach, running over his ribs, her palms against the muscles of his stomach, fingers combing the thick, curling hair at the base of his sex.

He pulsed stronger against her, speeding up his strokes, and her body struggled to meet him. She felt him tense, his whole body going rigid with his need for release. But with a growl, he pulled away, out of her, and crouched gasping for air and control. Her whole body shuddered, so close to release. She began to struggle out of her dress, and he reached for her, pulling the fabric over her head so she knelt naked across from him, the crushed green moss and wild flowers fragrant all around them. With his hands on her shoulders he turned her around, then guided her back to him so that her back was pressed to his chest. He entered her again, this time from behind, so that she pressed against his lap.

Ailis let her head fall back against his shoulder, her eyes dazzled by the sunlight above them, filtering down through the trees. He pushed forward, up, and she pressed down. He slid a hand around her, letting it drift over her breasts and belly before coming to rest at her sex, exposed by her open knees. His fingers began to work at her then, rubbing against her in time with his strokes inside her. His lips found her neck, and his tongue joined the rhythm of his hand and member.

Her whole body strained against and into the pleasure that enveloped her. An overwhelming sweetness built between her legs, growing until it pushed the air from her lungs. She began to rock more fiercely against him, and in turn, felt Varden's own body move more violently, less controlled. She moved her hips in a slow circle, and he gave a low moan, his hips bucking recklessly against her. Behind her, she wrapped her arms backwards and around him, clinging as he slammed forward into her, and again, and again, and a final time before coming up off the ground, his arms pressing her tightly to him as she clung on.

She felt him come inside her, his seed spilling, and his body shaking. And in that moment of his completion, Ailis felt herself go over the edge as well. The sudden stillness after his fierce possession of her threw her into her own abyss. With a cry, she fell forward, his arms around her the only thing that kept her even a little upright. Gently he lowered her down onto the bed of moss, following her down, so that he could wrap himself around her while they both breathed in the warm, spring scent of the forest air.

"I love you," he whispered into her ear, and she smiled.

His arms fit snugly around her. For a little while longer they could stay here and rest together. Then they would rise and go to their home, and make an evening meal with their sons.

Leaning back into him, she answered, "I love you, too. My very own Beast."

About the Author:

Jennifer Barlowe is a southern California transplant who lives by the water with her husband and their dog. She likes good books and bad movies. This is her first erotic romance.

Soul Kisses

by Angela Knight

To My Reader:

I've always intended to do a story for Beth Chase, Val's little sister from *The Forever Kiss.* But it was obvious to me that Beth couldn't have just any vampire hero—he had to be something special. In fact, an earlier attempt to write Beth's story fizzled altogether because it wasn't right. This one is, mostly because I gave Beth not one hero, but two.

I've always wondered if it would be possible to get two alpha males to share the same woman, and I finally figured out a way. I hope you have as much fun with it as I did!

Prologue

Beth Chase leaned close to the canvas to add a dot of gold highlight to one painted brown eye. Stepping back, she tilted her head and studied the portrait she'd been working on for the past two weeks.

Her sister sat in a spill of white lace and seed pearls, her tall, handsome groom standing behind her in a dark and elegant suit. Valerie's big gray eyes glowed with happiness, and Cade looked downright besotted as he gazed down at her.

Beth decided she'd caught both likenesses pretty well. Except...the painting still needed something.

An idea struck, inspiring a wicked grin. She dropped her brush in the jar of turpentine and chose a sable one that was even finer. Humming under her breath, Beth leaned forward and added a tiny, delicate shape between the groom's painted lips—the barest hint of a fang. Not enough for a casual observer to notice, but her brother-in-law would spot it immediately.

Cade McKinnon, former Texas Ranger turned vampire, would probably laugh his ass off. What better gift for the couple's fifth wedding anniversary?

Her portable phone rang from amid the litter of paint tubes and brushes on her art table, jolting Beth from her artistic haze. She gave the phone a wary glance and picked up, hoping it wasn't Joaquin Ramirez again. She wasn't up to another creepy conversation. She really needed to get caller ID. "Hello?"

"What's wrong?" Val's creamy Atlanta drawl rang with instant alarm.

Beth winced. She'd set off her sister's Mommy alarm. "Nothing."

"Don't give me that—I know that tone. Something's bothering you."

Oh, hell, might as well come clean. Besides, she might need the help. "I've got an ex-boyfriend who's pushing a little hard."

"Are you saying you're being stalked?" Val's voice took on that God-help-anybody-who-threatens-my-baby-sister tone. "What's going on? What's he been doing?"

Now Beth was beginning to feel like an idiot. "Look, it's not that big a deal, really. I broke it off with this guy, and he's not happy about it. I can handle it."

The line clicked as Cade picked up the other phone. "You want me to come to Atlanta and have a word with him?"

It was a tempting thought. Five minutes with Cade and his psychic powers, and Joaquin would forget he even knew Beth. On the other hand, she hated the idea of turning to her vampire relatives to solve her problems. "I don't know if you noticed, but I'm a big girl now. I can take care of myself."

"We didn't say you couldn't, babe," Val said. "But back when I was a reporter…"

"…You wrote a story about a stalker who ended up killing his ex." No matter what the topic of conversation, Val had usually written a story about it.

"Not *a* story—more like ten or fifteen. Stalkers are nothing to screw around with."

"Look, Beth, just humor us," Cade said. "Tell us about this guy."

Well, Joaquin *had* gotten a little scary lately. "Not much to tell." Brooding, she rubbed at a spot of wet Cadmium Red on her jeans. "I met him at my gallery showing last month. He seemed charming enough at first—good looking, had this kind of Antonio Banderas thing going…"

"Let me guess—he's married," Val said.

"I wish. He might be easier to get rid of. Anyway, after we went out a few times, I started to suspect there was something nasty under all that charm." Needing to move, she began to pace her studio restlessly. "So a couple of days ago, I told him to get lost."

"Good," Val said. "When you get a psychic impression that strong, you need to listen to it."

Beth frowned. She'd never been comfortable with the idea she might share her sister's mental abilities. "I don't know that I'd call it a psychic impression, but he definitely freaked me out."

"Are you sure this guy isn't a vampire?" Cade was beginning to sound worried.

"Joaquin?" Oh, now there was a nasty thought. She shook her head. "Can't be. We went out five or six times, and he never gave any indication he was anything more than just a guy. A son of a bitch, but not supernatural."

"If he is a vampire, who knows what kind of game he's playing?" Cade said. "You're Kith, Beth. That makes you damn rare. There are vamps that'd go to any length to get their hands on a Kith female." Few people could survive being infected by the virus that caused vampirism. Vamps called those who could the Kith, as in "kith and kin."

By transforming a Kith, a master vampire could enslave him and use the new vamp's psychic powers to strengthen his own. Ugly as that enslavement could be for a man, a woman would suffer an even worse fate. Some vampires had very ugly tastes indeed, and would like nothing better than torturing a woman whose vampire powers could heal any injury. The possibility of falling victim to someone like that was terrifying. Beth had come far too close to it once before, when she'd been kidnapped by Cade's vampire sire, Edward Ridgemont.

"Boy, that's a disgusting thought," Beth said, grimacing. "Come to think of it, I haven't seen him during the day. That might be coincidence, though."

"Or it might not." There was a long, chilly pause. "I think I should come to Atlanta."

She sighed. "Maybe that wouldn't be a bad idea. I..." The doorbell rang, cutting her off. "Hold on a minute, there's somebody at the door."

"Beth..."

Carrying the phone, Beth walked out of her studio and down the hall to the apartment's front door. Automatically, she checked the peephole. "Oh, hell."

It was Ramirez, tall and elegant in a charcoal Seville Row suit, his gleaming dark hair flawlessly styled. Her heart began to pound. Could Cade be right? Was he a vampire? Licking her lips, she automatically checked the deadbolt. It was locked. That was something, anyway. "Joaquin, go away or I'm calling the cops," she called through the closed door. "I've told you I'm not interested."

"The problem is, my dove," he purred back in that thick Castilian accent, "I am."

"Too bad." Lifting the phone with a hand that shook, she turned to move away. "I've got to call the cops. Joaquin is at the..."

The door exploded inward with a crash. With a startled yelp, Beth whirled as Ramirez shouldered through its splintered remains. "Are you nuts?" She backed away, wondering nervously if he'd broken it with vampire strength. "Get the hell out!"

"I don't think so, my dove." He looked more cruel than handsome now, his hawkish face stark with hunger and feral anticipation. When he smiled, her blood chilled. He had fangs. Well, that answered that question.

Beth whirled to run, but Ramirez grabbed her before she could take another step. His grip sent pain lancing through her arms. She dropped the phone and went for his eyes with her nails. He hit her, a stunning backhand slap that sent her staggering back to trip over the coffee table. She fell, hitting the floor in a bruising tumble. Blackness crowded in.

The last thing she heard was Cade roaring her name over Val's frantic questions. "Beth? Beth, what's happening? Be…!"

Chapter One

The rope's coarse fibers had chewed her wrists raw, but Beth kept working at the knot. She thought it was beginning to give. If she could only untie herself...

The basement door creaked, sending light lancing into her eyes. She cursed silently. It figured the bastard would come back just as she was making progress.

"Missed me, my dove?"

"Not really, no." Beth squinted warily at the figure on the stairs. The liquid Castilian accent sounded like Ramirez, but the voice itself was deeper, rougher, and the man's hulking silhouette looked more like one of her captor's thugs. Ramirez had a whole pack of identical blonds working for him, apparently brothers. Not that it really mattered which one of them it was. They were all vampires.

Cowboy boots rang on the wooden steps as the vamp started down into her makeshift cell. Like his brothers, the Swede was a big man, beefy and broad-faced, with a round knob of a nose and greasy dishwater blond hair that hung to his shoulders. In contrast to his master's Savile Row suits, he wore jeans and a Budweiser T-shirt. He carried a length of white silk draped over one arm—a nightgown? She squinted at the fabric uneasily, wondering what he intended. The light from the doorway made her temples throb.

"Headache?" the blond asked with sugared sweetness. Appraising blue eyes flicked across her face. "You seem to be in pain."

"What do you care?" she growled, in no mood for false civility. The punctures in her throat were aching, and her mouth was sawdust dry. After he'd taken her from her apartment two nights ago, Ramirez had fed from her and forced her to drink his blood. He hadn't killed her—despite the myths, vampires weren't really soulless undead.

But he had infected her. Where viruses like HIV and influenza destroyed their victims in order to spread, this one was actually symbiotic.

In the long run, it would make her stronger and longer-lived—and better able to spread it, since it couldn't survive outside a host. By now the virus was already at work, reshaping her cells like something from a science fiction movie, altering bone and muscle even as it gave her a need for blood. In the final stages, it would render her comatose as it completed its work.

"A headache is one of the first signs of the Change," the blond said now in that liquid purr that sounded so much like his master. "In a few days, you'll be one of us—a child of the night. A vampire." Fangs flashed. "And my slave."

Her stomach clenched at the thought. "I won't be *your* anything—your master is the one who's Turning me."

He grinned, exposing those gleaming fangs again. "My dove, haven't you guessed? I *am* Ramirez."

He stepped into a shaft of light from the door. The master vampire looked out from the Swede's eyes, ancient and evil and supremely powerful. He'd possessed his fledgling—moved his consciousness into the man's body so he could use it like his own. Val had told Beth once that master vampires could enter those they'd turned because they shared a mental link with them. Five years ago, she and Cade had used a similar technique to defeat Cade's sadistic sire, Ridgemont.

Beth's eyes narrowed with sudden speculation. That kind of link wasn't an easy thing to establish. Cade and Val had only tried it because they couldn't defeat Ridgemont any other way. Why would Ramirez make the effort? Unless…"What's with the new body, Joaquin? Are you expecting company?"

That chilling smile flashed again as he reached down and snapped the rope binding her wrists to a ring in the wall. "As a matter of fact, I am."

Beth's heart leaped. Over the past two days, she'd tried desperately to contact Val's mind, praying she really did have the psychic abilities Kith were supposed to possess. There'd been no response, so she'd assumed she'd failed. But maybe…

"Cade and Val are on the way, aren't they?" Beth bared her teeth. "He's going to rip your head off your shoulders with his bare hands."

"Your vampire brother-in-law? I think not." Reading her expression, Ramirez laughed and jerked her off the cot so hard her dark hair flew. "Yes, I know all about your family. I checked you out thoroughly before I decided to take you. Don't get your hopes up."

Icy fingers clamped in her gut. "What did you do to them?"

He grinned mockingly into her eyes. "Sent them to Africa on a wild goose chase. They're busy fending off assassins by now."

"Assassins?" Beth's knees went weak. "What assassins? And what the hell are they doing in Africa?"

He smiled, obviously enjoying her fear. "I planted a clue or two indicating I'd taken you out of the country. Then I sent three of my Swedes after them. Assuming they make it back alive, they'll be too late to do you any good."

The thought of her sister in danger made Beth feel sick, but she hid it behind a sneer. She needed to get out of this mess before she could help her. "So if not Val and Cade, who are you expecting? A mortal enemy, maybe? Preferably one who's going to rip out your throat. I want to watch and cheer."

Rage flashed through his eyes and he lifted a hand. She flinched, expecting another of his brutal slaps.

Instead he stopped and smiled in a chilling stretch of the lips. "Oh, they're going to love you."

"Who?"

"The guests I went to so much effort to attract." He brushed a knuckle down her cheekbone and grinned when she recoiled. "I'm sure they'll enjoy taking the...bait."

Still smirking, he scanned the length of her body, his gaze lingering on the paint-splattered shirt and jeans she'd been wearing when he'd snatched her. Blood had since joined the smears of crimson, ocher and cerulean blue. Beth took a certain grim satisfaction in the fact that some of it was his. The resulting bruises had been a small price to pay.

"But I fear this is not quite the look we want." Before she could shrink away, Ramirez wrapped a fist in the front of her T-shirt and ripped upward, tearing it off her body in one effortless swipe. With a satisfied smirk, he dropped the scraps.

Beth stared at him as cool air touched her bare breasts. "You *bastard!*" Too pissed to consider the risk she was taking, she slammed a sneakered foot into his shin.

She didn't even see the return blow.

Stars exploded behind her eyes as she went flying. She hit the floor with stunning force and rolled twice before she came to a stop. Gasping, Beth lay still, aching cheekbone pressed to the cold cement as tears of pain stung her eyes.

The vampire approached. Blinking at the engraved silver tips on the toes of his cowboy boots, she licked at the blood oozing from her cut lip. Something cool and soft landed across her back. "Put it on," he ordered.

Beth lifted her spinning head to look up at him. Her heart was pounding, but she forced herself to ignore it and meet those cold, cold eyes. "Go to hell." When he grabbed for her, she fought him with swinging fists and kicking feet, too furious and terrified to consider the consequences. The second time her foot came too close to his balls, Ramirez drew back a hand and cuffed her viciously hard.

Blackness crashed in for the second time in three days.

"He's in there," Morgan Axton said in the mental link he shared with his cousin. He stared at the clearing in the moonlit Georgia woods where their enemy's house stood, its white wooden siding gleaming, golden light spilling from its lower windows. *"I can feel his power from here."* Ramirez's psychic stench put the match to the fuse of his rage, sent it sizzling along paths already well-seared by guilt and pain.

Crouching next to him in a screening shadow of the trees, Garret shot him a concerned look. *"You know he's probably riding another of his thralls. He never fights us in person if he can help it."*

Morgan shrugged. *"Doesn't matter. If we kill enough of them, he'll eventually run out of fledglings. And then we'll have him."*

"Assuming he doesn't get us first."

"We're not that easy to get." Drawing the great sword sheathed across his back, Morgan rose and moved toward the house. He could feel his cousin following through their mental link, a rapier in one hand and a dagger in the other.

Pop culture myths notwithstanding, it took a lot more than a wooden stake to kill a vampire. You had to either decapitate him or destroy his heart. A shotgun would do the job, but Morgan wasn't in the mood to kill Ramirez that quickly.

It had taken Elena a very long time to die. He intended to make sure her killer suffered just as much.

Cautiously, he studied Ramirez's latest lair as they approached. It was nothing more than a two-story farmhouse—white and nondescript, with a wrap-around porch and steeply pitched roof. Quite a comedown from the mansions they'd reduced to rubble over the past sixteen months. They were making progress in destroying Ramirez's little empire.

"I don't sense any booby traps," Garret began. *"We should be..."*

Morgan cleared the six steps to the porch in one long, low bound. Ignoring his cousin's curse, he rammed his booted foot into the door. The jam exploded into splinters with the force of his kick, and the door crashed in so hard it banged against the wall. He stalked through the doorway, sword held in a steady two-handed grip as he scanned for enemies.

Somewhere in the house, Morgan sensed Ramirez jerk to attention. He could almost feel the bastard's anticipation. "Yes, we're out here," he muttered under his breath. "Come and get it."

"Morgan, it's a wonder you don't get your idiot head blown off!" Garret snarled, charging in to join him, both blades glittering in his fists.

"Ramirez won't use a gun on me." Morgan moved warily down the foyer as his cousin followed. Every sense he had was on quivering alert. He could sense their enemy waiting. The bastard's psychic power field tasted like rot on his tongue.

A searing memory flashed through his consciousness—Elena's mind calling to his that last time, reaching out to him across the miles, begging him to save her. He'd tried—God, how he'd tried. He'd failed.

Now all he could do was avenge her.

Yet when they stepped into the farmhouse's shabby living room, the man who stood waiting wasn't Ramirez. Not physically, anyway.

"Ah—the Axton cousins come to call." The big blond Swede raised his broadsword with a practiced skill that shouted of their enemy. One look in his eyes told Morgan Ramirez had possessed him. "Welcome, *mis mamabichos.*"

"The only cocksucker I see is you," Morgan growled.

In contrast to Ramirez's habitual dark elegance, the thrall was broad-faced and beefy, with close-spaced blue eyes and greasy shoulder-length hair. He was obviously one of the brothers Ramirez had turned a few decades back. There'd been fifteen of them when this private little war started. Now, thanks to Morgan and Garret, less than half were left.

Two more Swedes guarded a dark-haired woman who stood in the corner. In contrast to the white lace nightgown she wore, a dog's choke chain bit into her throat, its leash clipped to a hook in the ceiling. A half-healed vampire bite marred her neck, while bruises shadowed her pretty face and slimly muscled arms.

Morgan glared at the thrall. "Did you ever meet a woman you didn't abuse, you bastard?"

Ramirez pretended to consider the question. "No, I don't believe I have."

Lifting his sword, Morgan snarled and started toward him. *"Free the girl, Garret. I'll take Ramirez's thrall."*

"It'll be my pleasure." Garret headed for her two vampire guards. *"Wonder where he's got his own body stashed this time?"*

"It can't be far. We need to finish this fast and find him." Morgan began to circle the big blond, who watched him with catlike interest. "Ramirez," he said aloud. "Raped anyone lately?"

"I have not had that opportunity." There was that faint, cold smile again as he flicked a look toward the bound girl. "Perhaps later."

"I don't think so." Morgan bared his teeth. "You'll be dead in ten minutes." He leaped, swinging his sword in a hard, flat slice at the Swede's head. The thrall threw up his broadsword in a parry. The two blades struck with a ringing clang and force enough to knock Morgan back on his heels.

Six hundred years as a vampire had given Ramirez a great deal of power.

Regaining his balance with a wrench, Morgan lunged at the Spaniard. Steel clashed on steel as the two vampires slammed chest-to-chest, muscles straining as each tried to break through the other's guard.

"You grow reckless, *amigo*," Ramirez told him in that infuriating Castilian purr. "It will be the death of you, I fear."

"Or you." Morgan shoved his opponent back a pace, getting room to circle and look for another opening. Swords rang as his cousin engaged the two Swedes, but he wasn't worried. Without their master lending them strength, Garret was more than a match for them.

At least, as long as they didn't get lucky.

Chapter Two

This situation just screams "trap," Garret thought, using both his blades to keep his opponents at a distance. If Morgan had been thinking clearly, he'd have seen it too.

Unfortunately, his cousin's capacity for logic had gone out the window when Elena was murdered. All he cared about now was killing Ramirez—or dying himself. Garret wasn't really sure which Morgan would rather do.

Flourishing his sword, Garret sent the two thralls into momentary retreat. They looked as nervous as a pair of foxes attacking a wolf. He could tell by the way they held their weapons that neither had more than a passing idea of how to fence.

Which was a damn good thing, since he needed to take care of them quickly so he could go looking for Ramirez's body. The Spaniard couldn't be far, not and maintain a mind link with that big blond thrall.

Unfortunately, killing the Swede wouldn't do a damn thing to Ramirez, which was why the Spaniard preferred to work through his puppets. Why chance Morgan's vicious rage when he could let somebody else do his dying for him?

On the other hand, if Garret could find and kill Ramirez's body, finishing the thrall would take Morgan about ten seconds. Nobody was better with a blade.

One of the Swedes danced in close, hacking at Garret's head. He parried with his rapier and spun, flicking his dagger to deflect the second vamp's thrust. Whirling again, he lunged at the first and drove his blade into thug's left shoulder. The vampire yelled and scrambled away as Garret danced around and blocked another attack from the second man.

His blade circled the vamp's desperate attempts to parry. But before Garret could shove the rapier's point into his opponent's heart, the first thrall came charging in again, forcing him to spin and parry.

This was becoming a pain in the ass. He didn't have time to dance, not with Morgan fighting Ramirez. His cousin was far too capable of some stupid, suicidal heroism.

Garret had already lost Elena. He was damned if he'd lose Morgan too.

❧∾⟨✦⟩∾❧

Standing very straight in an effort to relieve the pressure of the chain around her neck, Beth watched the two newcomers go after Joaquin's thralls. She'd seen Val and Cade practice often enough to know this pair was really good.

The one fighting Ramirez was just as tall and muscular as the big Swede, with effortless grace and strength in every swing of his broadsword. Like his partner, he was dressed in black—a long-sleeved knit shirt and loose pants tucked into heavy combat boots.

His soldierly appearance was enhanced by the sleek, short cut of his hair. The cropped style emphasized the aristocratic angles of his handsome face, with its deep-set black eyes, long nose and wide, sensual mouth. Striking as he was, though, there was feral rage in his dark eyes, and his snarl revealed inch-long fangs.

Ramirez is good-looking too, she reminded herself. *He's still a son of a bitch.*

The vampire's partner was shorter, leaner, built like a marathon runner rather than a heavyweight boxer. He wore his hair a little longer, in a curling, collar-length cut. A neat Van Dyke beard framed his mouth, its curving mustache giving him the look of a perpetual smile even as he fought for his life. Like his hair, the beard was a deep, rich brunet that made his green eyes look all the more striking in his narrow, foxy face.

He fought his two opponents with a sword and knife, both blades lighter and narrower than the clumsier weapons his foes used. He made the most of that advantage in lightning attacks that kept his foes scrambling.

The end came so fast, she almost missed it. The taller of the two thralls bellowed and lunged, trying to decapitate him with a wild swing. The brunet deflected it with a skillful parry and simultaneously plunged his knife into the man's chest.

The second thrall leaped for his unprotected back. Beth screamed a warning, but the brunet was already whirling, slamming his elbow into the man's face. As the thrall staggered back, the brunet drove his sword into his heart. The dying vampire hit the ground beside his groaning brother.

For a moment, the brunet looked down at his fallen foes, breathing hard. Then he reached behind his back and pulled something from a sheath at the small of his back. It was a hand axe.

One of the fallen vampires cursed and tried without success to rise.

The bearded newcomer glanced up at Beth. "This might be a good time to close your eyes."

Hastily, she obeyed, wincing as the first thrall screamed. The sound was cut off by a meaty thunk.

"No, please..." the second began.

"Sorry," the brunet said. "We can't afford to take prisoners Ramirez can possess."

Another choked, too-short scream. Beth swallowed hard and squeezed her eyes tighter. *Both those bastards tried to get Ramirez to let them rape me,* she reminded herself. *They don't deserve pity.*

"Hello, poppet."

Startled, she opened her eyes, jerking back as she realized the bearded vampire now loomed over her. She hadn't even heard him approach.

"I need to find Ramirez," he told her. He wore an expression of concern she didn't trust at all. "We'll free you when he's taken care of."

"Wait..." Beth began, but he was already striding from the room, throwing a worried look at his big, black-haired partner as he went.

The newcomer and Ramirez's thrall were still fighting, circling like starving wolves as they tested one another with skillful feints and lunges. Beth turned her attention to them, trying to ignore the dead vampires at her feet. She hoped like hell the black-haired vamp was as good as his bearded partner.

No matter what they did to her afterwards, if they managed to kill Ramirez, they'd be doing her a favor.

"How long has it been since I cut out Elena's traitorous heart?" Ramirez sneered. "A year? Or has it been two?"

"She was no traitor. She owed you nothing," Morgan growled. "And it's been sixteen months. I'd think you'd remember, since we've been wrecking your little empire ever since." He rammed his sword toward his enemy's chest.

Ramirez parried and retaliated with a whistling slash of his own, forcing Morgan to leap back. The master vampire pressed the attack, and Morgan retreated, beating aside each blow. "I remember she died begging for mercy, squealing like the *puta* she was."

"The only whore was your mother." Furious, he swung at Ramirez's head with such force, he felt the jolt of the thrall's block all the way to his shoulder. "And Elena died with her fangs in your throat, trying to rip out your jugular. *You're* the one who was squealing."

Ramirez's borrowed eyes widened as he retreated. "Now, how would you know that, *amigo*? ¡Ay! You were *in* her, weren't you? I thought she seemed stronger there at the end. She'd managed to reach you, even across so many miles. You gave her your strength!"

"Yes, you bastard, I was there." He bared fangs aching with the need to rip out his tormentor's throat. "I only wish she'd reached me sooner."

"How soon *did* you two link? Were you with her when I raped her?" His fangs glinted as he sneered. "Did you feel my dick?"

Morgan lunged with a bellow of rage, driving his blade at his enemy's heart. Ramirez tried to parry, but Morgan's fury gave him strength, and the broadsword smashed through the thrall's guard. Its lethal point drove into his chest with a wet crunch, and the vampire choked in agony.

"I was there, you bastard," Morgan gritted, bearing down hard as he twisted his weapon to destroy the blond thrall's heart. "I was there when you sodomized her, and I was there when you took her head."

"And soon I'll...take yours...too, *hijo de la gran puta!*" Ramirez spat in Morgan's face and fled the thrall's dying body. The man stared at Morgan in horror for a split second before his destroyed heart stopped and his knees gave way.

"We'll see, won't we?" Morgan wiped the spittle from his face and stepped back, jerking his sword free.

Eyes almost painfully wide, Beth stared at the dark-haired vampire. She could almost see the fury boiling off him.

Despite her fear, she also felt a twinge of pity. It was obvious he'd loved this Elena, whoever she'd been. It must have been excruciating being psychically linked to the poor woman during her brutal murder.

"Ramirez!" He whirled and stalked past Beth toward the nearest window. She flinched as he jerked up the sash, the glass protesting the rough treatment with a rolling metallic boom. "Bloody hell!" he growled, staring out across the moonlit woods. "The coward is running!" He lifted his voice in a shout. "Garret, dammit, he's gone!"

"What?" Beth dared, licking her dry lips. "Who?"

The vampire shot her a glittering look. "Ramirez. Must have had his body stashed in some kind of vehicle the whole time we were fighting. Now he's driving away."

She strained to listen. "I don't hear anything."

"You wouldn't. He's a good mile away." Raking a frustrated hand through his hair, he turned toward her. "But I can hear the engine, and I feel his power field fading. There's no way we can catch him before he's out of range." He stared at her a moment. Then, mouth tightening, he started toward her, purpose in his stride.

Despite herself, Beth cringed.

To her surprised, the vampire stopped in mid-step. "I'm not going to hurt you. I'm just going to take the chain off your neck. Doesn't it hurt?"

Beth swallowed, suddenly aware of the links digging into her skin. "Oh. Yeah. Yeah, it does. I'd...umm...appreciate it."

Painfully conscious of her bound wrists and the collar around her neck, she watched warily as the vampire approached and bent to examine the clasp. Warm fingers brushed her skin as he went to work on it.

He had to be at least seven inches taller than she was. Something hidden and feminine within her purred approval—of that impressive height, of the width of his chest, of the warmth of his fingers on her throat.

Oh, God, Beth realized, looking up into his face, *he's gorgeous.*

His eyes were beautiful, large and deep-set, the color of melted chocolate striated with honey and gold. His brows were thick and black, matching surprisingly long lashes. But there was nothing at all feminine about his lean, angular face or the width of his mobile mouth. His sensual lips tightened as he struggled with the clasp, and she felt her nipples peak.

Shame stung her at her own heated reaction. *Cut it out, Beth! The man is a vampire.*

He might not be soulless and undead as the legends insisted, but judging from the last ten minutes, he wasn't exactly a choirboy either.

Until this moment, Beth wouldn't have thought it was possible for her to feel attraction for any vamp. Cade was a good man, but his master had murdered her parents, and Ramirez had tortured her. As far as she was concerned, they were all evil until proven otherwise. Yet there was something about this vamp that was different. There'd been such grief in his voice for his Elena. Her inner romantic insisted that any man who loved a woman with such passion couldn't be a monster.

What was more, her body responded to him on a level beyond common sense. Even his scent was tempting—darkly male and sexy.

He looked up and met her eyes, and everything just…stopped. She was painfully aware of the warm brush of his knuckles on the upper curves of her breasts. With an effort she could almost feel, he tore his gaze away from hers. As if against his will, his eyes dropped to the cleavage displayed by the silk nightgown Ramirez had forced her to wear. He swallowed.

Beth wanted to step away, but even that seemed beyond her. Her traitorous mind produced a dangerous question. *How will it feel if he touches me?*

He straightened convulsively, then hastily did something to the collar's clasp. It came loose and he stepped back, dropping it on the floor. "Turn around," the vampire ordered hoarsely. "I'll get the ropes around your wrists."

Beth stared up at him, feeling as helpless as a bird hypnotized by a cobra. At last she managed to shake off his spell and turn her back with a jerk. Steel whispered as he drew his knife. Oddly, she felt no fear. Her instincts insisted he wouldn't hurt her.

He sliced the ropes with a single pass of his blade, then retreated a pace. Though common sense warned her to put more distance between them, Beth turned to him again.

The desire and guilt she'd seen on his face was gone now, replaced by a distant courtesy. "Give me your name and address. *Then you can nap while we take you home.*"

Listening to the emphasis he'd put on those last words, Beth realized he'd intended them as a telepathic compulsion, the kind few mortals could resist. "Sorry, I'm afraid that's not going to work. I'm Kith."

His brows raised, and his attention fell to the healing vampire bite in her neck. Suspicion hardened his gaze. "So Ramirez was trying to Turn you." He took a step back, eying her. "But why did he leave you here for us to find?"

Oh, God, what should she say? Would he kill her if he knew the truth?

He tensed, his handsome face hardening as menace chilled his dark gaze. Looking up at him as he towered over her, Beth realized her only hope was honesty.

"Actually, I suspect I'm bait."

Chapter Three

Morgan hated to admit it, but Ramirez knew how to bait a trap.

Beth Chase was tall and slim, with a delicately pretty oval face and big chocolate eyes balanced by an erotic mouth. Her dark hair frothed around slim shoulders, drawing male attention to the plunging V neckline of her silk nightgown and the sweet double curves of her cleavage. The whole damsel-in-distress effect was heightened by the bruises on her slender arms and the vampire bite purpling the long, slim column of her throat. She brought every one of his protective instincts to quivering attention. The problem was, his dick found her equally fascinating.

It was the first time Morgan had felt this kind of arousal since Elena's death, and he didn't like it. He didn't have time for women right now. Once Ramirez was dead, things would be different, but until then he had far too much to atone for.

Yet as the girl told her story, pacing the room in restless strides as she described her first meeting with Ramirez, Morgan was acutely aware of her. His gaze dropped to her swaying backside under the soft silk of her nightgown. When he inhaled, he breathed her scent, delicately feminine and spiced with arousal. She wanted him—wanted both of them—though he wasn't sure she was aware of it.

"She reminds me of Elena," Garret said in their link. He'd joined them after Ramirez had made his escape.

"Too thin," Morgan said shortly. Elena was a voluptuous seductress, not leanly muscular like this girl. Why the hell did she appeal to him so?

"But there's something about her..."

"She's a fighter. Elena was a fighter." That was all it could be.

Beth turned to face them, raking both hands through her long, tangled hair. Unable to hear their mental conversation, she was describing the events leading up to her abduction. "I'm not sure when Ramirez realized I was Kith, but after the gallery showing he started trying to romance me." As if unconsciously, her fingers dropped to gingerly explore the fang punctures in her throat. "We went out a few times, but I broke it off when I realized something about him made my skin crawl."

"You have good instincts," Garret told her.

"He reminded me of Ridgemont." She turned to pace again, the full silk skirts of her gown kicking out around her long legs. "He had the same kind of slick surface charm with something nasty underneath."

Morgan frowned. "Ridgemont?"

"Edward Ridgemont, my brother-in-law's sire. He kidnapped me a few years ago as part of a sick game he was playing with Cade and my sister."

Garret's brows rose. "Is getting abducted a hobby with you?"

Beth grimaced. "Does seem like I should have used up my quota. I mean, what are the odds that I'd be taken by vampires twice?" She sighed, shaking her dark hair back from her fine-boned face. "So this jerk—your jerk, I mean, Ramirez…"

"He's not *our* anything," Morgan growled.

"I hear that. Anyway, after I refused to see him again, he kicked down the door of my apartment and snatched me right in the middle of a phone call with Val." She stopped and stood staring at the floor, her mouth tight. "He brought me here, bit me, and forced me to drink his blood." Dark eyes brooding, she looked up at them again. "That was night before last. Last night I didn't see him at all—evidently he was off leading Val and Cade on some kind of wild goose chase, with a couple of assassins thrown in for good measure."

"That does sound like Ramirez." Garret frowned, contemplating his rapier and pulling a cloth out of his pocket. Slowly, he started wiping the drying blood from its length.

"My sister must be going nuts." She headed for the end table and the phone that stood there. "I'm going to try calling her again."

A sudden thought made Morgan frown. He shot Garret a look and asked through their link, *"Could Beth be working with Ramirez?"*

His cousin glowered at him. *"That's a bit paranoid even for you. Besides, if she was lying, we'd smell it."*

"Maybe. I'd feel better if we could touch her thoughts."

"Well, we can't. She's Kith, so she's shielded. We can't get into her mind, and we can't compel her the way we would an ordinary mortal. We're stuck with doing this the hard way."

Beth finished leaving a message on her sister's answering machine and dropped the phone back in its cradle. "Val's still not answering her cell," she said, worry plain on her face as she raked her fingers through her tangled hair. "What if Ramirez's killers have gotten to her?"

"Don't leap to conclusions," Garret told her, sheathing his rapier. "There are a lot of places on the planet that don't have cell service. Knowing Ramirez, he probably lured your sister to one deliberately."

"It's like Ridgemont all over again." She grimaced, then stalked to a chair and threw herself into it. "And he's bitten me." Fisting her hands in her lap, she stared into space, her expression fearful. "I'm going to become a vampire."

"No, actually, you're not." Morgan met those big brown eyes. It was best to be honest with her. "Considering the amount of time that's passed since he bit you, you should be a lot sicker than you are. That you're still relatively healthy means he hasn't drained enough of your blood, or fed you enough of his."

Hope lit her face, making him wince. "So I'm going to be all right?"

Garret put aside his weapon and moved to crouch at her feet, taking her hand in his. "No, sweet, I'm afraid not."

"What do you mean?"

His grip tightened on her hand. "It takes a great deal of the virus to change someone into a vampire. Ramirez may not have given you enough blood to turn you, but even a little is more than enough to kill you."

The blood drained from her face, leaving her milk pale. "How long?"

"That depends on your immune system," Garret told her. "You'll get sicker as your body fights the virus. None of us is really sure how it works, but Elena thought that in a partial transformation, the immune system begins attacking the victim's organs as the virus changes them. Eventually so much damage is done that everything starts shutting down."

Morgan rested a hand on her shoulder and met her gaze. "The only thing that would save you is if Ramirez completes the process."

She pulled her hand from Garret's and sat up straight, her expression grim. "At which point I'll be the bastard's slave. I don't think so. I can already feel him as it is, and I don't much like what I sense."

Morgan came to attention. "What?"

She shrugged. "Evidently we've already got some kind of mind link. Not all that strong—I just get impressions, not thoughts."

"What's he feeling now?" Garret asked.

"Smug."

The cousins looked at each other. "Yeah, that's Ramirez," Garret said.

"Could another vampire complete the Change so I wouldn't become a slave to Ramirez?" Beth asked, eyes narrow and thoughtful. Morgan had to admire her obvious determination not to give up. "My sister, maybe? She wouldn't misuse the power a link would give her."

Garret and Morgan simultaneously winced. "Feeding on someone tends to be a rather…sexual experience for vampires, Beth. You both might find it a little uncomfortable," Garret pointed out delicately. "Besides, she'd need to complete the process immediately, or your body will be so damaged you won't survive the transformation. And she's not here."

Beth grimaced. "I see your point."

Suddenly Garret rose from his crouch and turned to face Morgan, his eyes lighting with the excitement of a new idea. *"We could do it."*

Morgan stared at him, astonished. *"Are you out of your mind? I feel sorry for the girl, but I don't care to be linked to her for the next century or more."*

"Not even to kill Ramirez?" There was a speculative half-smile on his cousin's lips Morgan knew well from four centuries of combat with various enemies. Garret was cooking up a scheme. And those schemes had a way of working very, very well.

"What do you have in mind?"

Garret watched hope and angry guilt war in Morgan's dark chocolate gaze. He knew had to play this carefully. This girl could save them all, if only…he clamped down on his own emotions, knowing his cousin could sense them. *"If we Turn her and she retains that link to Ramirez, we could use it to track him down."*

A muscle ticked in Morgan's cheek. *"Or he could use her against us, which is probably his intention. In retrospect, I think it's more than a little suspicious that we happened to encounter the one mortal flunky who knew where Ramirez was hiding at this particular time. This could have been a trap from the very beginning."*

"Morgan…"

Anger sizzled through their mental link like heat lightning. *"The girl is right—she's bait. Why else would he leave a half-turned Kith for us to find, especially when he obviously tried to make her as appealing as possible?"* He jerked a thumb at her. She watched them warily, her pretty face cool with distrust. *"Look at that dress—hell, look at that cleavage. He might as well have hung an 'eat me' sign around her neck."*

Garret grinned. *"I've got to admit, I wouldn't mind taking a bite."*

"Except that apple is poisoned, cuz."

"How? How can he use her against us, if we Turn her? We'll be her masters..."

"We? For one thing, I've never heard of a vampire having two masters..."

"And I'll bet Ramirez hasn't either. He may be planning to use her against one of us, but if both of us Turn her, there's no way in hell he could overcome our control. Then maybe we could use her against him."

Breath held, he watched Morgan weigh the idea, consider its consequences. *"It might work,"* he said slowly.

"I appreciate the fact you guys saved my butt just now," Beth announced into the silence. "But I still don't know you from Adam's house cat. And I sure as hell don't know you well enough to let one of you change me into a vampire."

Surprised, Garret looked over at her. "How did you..."

She shrugged. "My sister and Cade have these silent little conversations all the time. I've gotten good at guessing the content from expressions. And in this case, it's not hard to put two and two together. I repeat, *I don't know you.*"

Garret ground his teeth in frustration. He hadn't expected opposition from her too. "Do you have some other option you haven't told us about? Considering that your vampire relatives are God knows where, and you don't know if you can reach them in time for them to save you—assuming they're still alive."

Her stricken expression made him feel like a bastard.

"Even if you can reach them, Ramirez is very old and very powerful," Morgan said. "Freeing you is not going to be easy. Do you really want to involve them in a mental battle for you that they may lose? If Garret and I work together to turn you, we'd have a better chance of breaking Ramirez's hold."

Beth frowned at him. "I had the impression you were against this idea."

"I was." Morgan turned to look at Garret. "But maybe it's time we all take a chance."

She went still. Garret could almost see her mind work behind those remarkable eyes, sense the warring fears vying in her: her fear of death against her fear of enslavement by two vampires she didn't know. Her eyes flickered nervously between them. Garret wondered if she was imagining what it would be like to be taken by them both.

Long fingers crept to the bite on her throat again, then dropped. She squared her shoulders. "Will you help me find Val and Cade? Help them defeat Ramirez's assassins?"

Morgan studied her thoughtfully. "Yes." He shrugged his shoulders. "Though we'd have gone after the assassins anyway. They're Ramirez's spawn. We can't leave them alive."

Beth took a deep breath, blew it out. "All right. If you save my sister, I'll do whatever you want."

Chapter Four

Morgan hadn't touched a woman in sixteen months. For the first years, he'd simply felt no desire, not with the memory of Elena's death so vivid. He'd fed, when he fed at all, on the criminals he stalked when the Hunger was on him.

In the past few months, he'd abstained because he hadn't killed Ramirez yet. It was the kind of quest that seemed to call for celibacy. Which sounded stupidly melodramatic, when Morgan actually stopped to think about it.

Now he realized he'd made a very big mistake. A mortal man could get away with celibacy, but for a vampire, sex was too closely tied to the need for blood.

The minute they'd decided to Turn the girl, the Hunger had woken. It had been all he could do not to snatch her into his arms, strip off that lace negligee, and take her right there on Ramirez's shabby couch.

Luckily Garret had realized how close he was and sent him off to get the SUV. Now they were on the way back to the house they were using as a local base of operations. Morgan was driving, mostly for something to do with his hands. Beth rode in the back seat. Every time he breathed in, her sweetly feminine scent seemed to wrap around his balls. He could hear her heartbeat, could almost taste her blood on his tongue. His fangs were aching.

"Are you going to be able to keep it together?" Garret asked in their link. *"This girl has been through enough as it is. She's not up to having you pounce on her."*

"I'm not a barbarian." He flicked on the blinker and made the turn into the upscale development where they had their temporary base. *"I'm not going to attack her."*

His cousin said nothing, not even *I told you so.* Garret had been warning him for months that he was playing with fire, but Morgan hadn't listened. He'd thought he could ignore the need.

So much for that bit of arrogance.

"Nice house," Beth said as they pulled into the driveway. "Is it yours?"

"Belongs to the president of some company around here," Garret told her as Morgan reached to punch the garage door opener. "We... ah...convinced him it was time to take the family on an overdue vacation. The kids had never been to Disney World. Can you imagine? All that money, and he'd never taken his children to see the Mouse. What's the point?"

Nobody did distracting small talk better than Garret. Morgan concentrated on parking. It required far more effort than it should have.

His dick was aching. So were his fangs, throbbing right down to the roots.

"Why not just get a hotel room?" Beth asked.

"Once Ramirez felt us enter the area, he'd start watching the motels," Garret explained as Morgan switched off the engine. "We'd end up getting ambushed." They opened the vehicle's doors, both men collecting their swords as they got out.

"So you commandeered some executive's half-million dollar house?" She was nervous. He could smell it in her scent. It made him want to snatch her into his arms again. Instead, he stalked to the door and unlocked it, carrying his sword in one hand.

Normally he would have held it open for her, but this time he didn't dare. He just headed through the kitchen toward the stairs to the bedroom, pulling his shirt off over his head with his free hand as he went.

※⟩(℃)⟨⅌

Beth stopped, her eyes going wide as Morgan threw his shirt aside and took the steps two at a time. His back was a broad wall of solid muscle, curving down to a tight, narrow waist. The artist in her instantly itched to sketch him. The woman wanted to touch.

Common sense told her to turn around and run.

With that musculature combined with vampire strength, he could probably rip three inches of plate steel in two like a bodybuilder shredding a New York phone book.

Beth licked suddenly dry lips and shot Garret a look as Morgan vanished up the stairs. "What's with him?"

Garret winced. "He...uh...hasn't been with a woman... in a

while."

She remembered Morgan's snarled conversation with Ramirez. He'd been linked with this Elena when the bastard had forced her, making him as much a rape victim as she'd been. That would probably explain why he had remained celebate.

But Val had told her vampires needed sex as much as they did blood, since they also fed on the emotional energy their partners produced during climax. "In sixteen months?" The words emerged as a squeak.

"He won't hurt you."

"Maybe not intentionally, but you guys don't *do* celibacy. I'm not…"

Garret cupped the side of her face, cutting off her spill of words in mid-babble. His hand felt large and warm, and his eyes were very green. "Poppet, I won't let anything happen to you. You're safe with us." His gaze was steady, confident.

She found herself believing him. "All right."

"That's my girl." He stroked a finger down the curve of her cheek and across her lower lip. "May I get you something to drink? You're probably about half dehydrated, between Ramirez feeding from you and the virus."

She swallowed, realizing he was right. "Yeah, sure."

Beth's fear had retreated by the time she downed a glass of ice water and he escorted her upstairs. They stepped into the sprawling master bedroom to find Morgan's pants slung over the back of an armchair. His sword lay across the chair's arms, while his boots had been flung in different corners.

"He's normally not this big a slob," Garret told her.

But her attention was riveted on the open French doors. Morgan stood on the balcony, his head back, his eyes closed, his sculpted body silvered in moonlight. His cock thrust from a nest of fine hair at his groin, angled slightly upward by the urgency of his lust.

Beth had never seen anything so male, or so beautiful. She ached to paint him just like that, though God knew she'd never be able to display that particular work in any gallery.

He's a vampire, her common sense whispered. *He hasn't had a woman in sixteen months. He's dangerous.* Yet Beth found herself moving toward him anyway, helplessly drawn even though she knew she was playing with fire. She had to touch him.

Morgan didn't look around as she stepped onto the wrought iron balcony, but he tensed like a wild animal.

Her heart was pounding.

He held very still as she approached to look up at him. God, he was tall and broad and built, muscle forming hard, tight contours in chest and abdomen, brawny arms and long legs.

His cock jerked once, reacting to her. Beth gazed at it, admiring the long, veined shaft, the flushed, plum-shaped head. His balls hung fat, covered in a ruff of dark hair. More hair grew in an elegant masculine cloud across his powerful chest.

Beth been with other men, of course—at twenty-three, she was hardly a virgin. But none of them had ever been like him.

She looked up and met his gaze. His eyes were wide, black, glittering with hunger. Beth could almost feel his desperate grip on control. Touching him right now would be a very bad idea

She had to do it anyway.

Beth licked dry lips. His attention jumped to her tongue like a cat watching a fluttering canary. Slowly, she reached out a hand and laid it on his chest. He jerked under her fingers. Beth had touched her sister often enough to know vampires weren't really cold to the touch, but Morgan felt fevered.

Greatly daring, she brushed her fingertips across the ridged muscle of his chest toward one flat male nipple. He watched her, his eyes burning. It was like playing with a tiger. He was handsome enough to steal her breath, yet she could also sense a dark, alien hunger struggling against his control.

"You're beautiful." His voice sounded hoarse, almost agonized.

"So are you." She looked away from those dark, hungry eyes to the tiny male nipple so close to her thumb. Slowly, she brushed across it. Once. Twice. Back and forth. Recklessly.

"Garret," Morgan gritted.

"I'm here."

Beth looked around to see Garret moving across the balcony toward them. He, too, had stripped naked, his body as splendid in its lean, elegant strength as his brawnier cousin's. His skin was a shade lighter than Morgan's, but his build was even more sculpted, each muscle in hard relief, pectorals and biceps and abdominals forming luscious contours under his velvet flesh. His body hair lay in a sleek pattern over his pecs before narrowing into an intriguing trail down his rippled belly, all the way to the thrust of his cock.

His sex was quite simply luscious—not quite as thick as Morgan's, but a bit longer, with a tempting upward curve over tight balls. Following the direction of her gaze, he looked down at his erection, then glanced up again with a wicked grin. "Like the scenery?"

Beth looked from him to Morgan, whose cock jutted with impatient hunger. She licked her lips. "Definitely. Though you're a little…intimidating too."

"I guess that's understandable, under the circumstances." Reaching for her, Garret threaded a big hand through her hair and tilted her head back. "But the last thing we want to do is hurt you."

She found herself believing him. As her fear drained away, she let herself surrender to his hot, slow kiss. Morgan rumbled like a hungry cat. His breath blew warm against her arched throat, just below her ear. Garret tilted her head to the side, giving his cousin better access as he kissed her hungrily.

In the back of her mind, a small voice whispered, *I can't believe I'm doing this*. But God, it felt so good. She'd been so afraid, but they made her feel both cherished and safe.

*But they're vampires!*the voice protested. She ignored it, too entranced by the feel of Morgan's lips pressing against the taut cords of her throat. Slowly, he licked a delicate burning trail down her throat and paused to nip, the tips of his fangs just barely raking. "That feels so good," she groaned.

"And you taste so good." Garret sampled her lips in teasing, sipping kisses that coaxed her into opening her mouth. His tongue slipped in once, a gentle flicker, then deeper and more slowly. She closed her eyes and moaned as sensation poured over her like warm honey.

Morgan's long fingers found the thin strap of her gown and brushed it off her shoulder. Cupping her breast tenderly, he brushed a thumb across her nipple, stirring it to a sweet, aching erection.

Garret turned her in his arms as his cousin stepped behind her, smooth as a dancer moving through choreography he knew and loved. She'd always thought being with two men would be a little clumsy— hands and shoulders bumping, a little wrestle over who did what, who kissed where. Yet the cousins made love like one smooth, seductive man. As Garret caressed her breasts, Morgan's hands slid over her hip and between her thighs, pressing through the silk to tease her clit. While Garret kissed his way down her throat, Morgan turned her head to gain access to her mouth. His tongue slipped between her lips as his cousin nibbled on the arched curve of her neck.

Beth groaned as they drew her between them, acutely aware of the firm bodies against her, of the tickling rasp of chest hair, of the warm, demanding thrusts of their cocks. She felt herself growing steadily wetter with every touch and kiss. "You're really good at this."

"We've had a lot of practice." Morgan's skilled fingers dipped between her thighs, caressing her through the silk. Garret was pinching both nipples, twisting delicately to send sweet curls of heat spiraling through her breasts.

"Are you ready?" Garret murmured in her ear.

She let her head fall back. Morgan cupped her throat in one big, warm hand, and she groaned. "Ready?" Her lips twitched in sudden humor. "I'm about to go up like the space shuttle."

"So are we," Morgan purred as Garret bent and slid an arm behind her thighs. Smoothly, he swept her into his arms and carried her inside, his cousin at his heels.

Panting and dazed, she hooked an arm around Garret's neck and gazed up into his face. He smiled down at her, the curve of his lips revealing his fangs. Over his shoulder, she saw Morgan's eyes blazing as his cock swayed with every long stride. "Liftoff," she whispered.

Chapter Five

Garret had turned out the lights in the bedroom so the only illumination came from moonlight spilling through the French doors. Beth got a spinning impression of gleaming wood and glittering crystal before Garret put her down on a massive king-sized brass bed. She sighed in surrender as the two men followed her down, surrounding her in warm, hard-muscled strength.

Big hands brushed her gown down to her waist. Hot mouths engulfed her breasts, tongues flicking across her nipples until she tossed her head, maddened by the sweet delight.

Garret's beard tickled her skin as he swirled his tongue over the peak he'd captured. Morgan used his teeth with gentle skill, raking slowly over the nubbin, alternating tender bites with deep, drawing suction. She moaned. "You make a really killer tag team."

"We do try." Morgan's fingers slid down her belly, paused to caress her navel. Dropped lower and slipped between her thighs. Beth caught her breath at the sweet penetration of a forefinger into her needy core. "She's wet," he growled, lifting his head from her breast. His voice had deepened with need until it vibrated. He probed deeper. "And God, so tight."

"And sweet," Garret said, cupping her breast, stroking his fingertips over her sensitive skin. "Don't forget sweet."

"You like this?" Morgan asked, and added another finger in a long, deep glide.

"That's putting it mildly." she gasped, her hands coming up to cup their heads. Garret's hair was just slightly finer, silkier, while Morgan's felt thick as it curled around her fingers like strands of coarse satin. "I've never been so hot in my life."

"That's what we like to hear. Give me your lips again," Morgan demanded, cupping the back of her head and lifting it so he could swoop down for her mouth. He kissed her as if he hadn't kissed her a few moments before, as if he craved her taste until he could stand no more. His tongue swept between her teeth in demanding strokes, swirling and tempting.

Enthralled, she didn't realize Garret had left her breast until he settled between her thighs. When he parted her, she sucked in a breath in surprise. The breath became a gasp as his mouth covered her, his tongue stroking through the creamy seam between her nether lips. She moaned against Morgan's mouth at the burning pleasure.

Morgan lifted his head to look down into her dazed eyes. His seemed to glow. He threaded his hand in her hair and turned her head so he could reach her throat for gentle, arousing bites along its straining length.

Beth arched her back, groaning, Garret's tongue dancing over her clit. One of his fingers stroked deep in her hungry core, the sensation teasing her nerve endings to vibrating attention. His beard brushed over her labia as he nibbled and licked.

"We're going to take you," Morgan breathed in her ear. He flicked his tongue across the tender lobe, sending a shiver skating down her back. "We're going to work our cocks right into this slick, snug little pussy of yours." He nibbled gently, then bent her head a little further back to deepen the arch of her throat. "And we're going to bite. I can hear your pulse beating. Right here." He pressed his lips to the leaping vein. "Waiting." He licked along the line of it. "For me."

The sheer hot arrogance of the statement turned her on even more. "You're a bad man, Morgan."

"He's not the only one." Garret drew her clit into his mouth and suckled fiercely, the pleasure jerking her spine into a bow.

"God!" she gasped. "He certainly isn't."

"Oh, yes," Morgan breathed. "Like that. Give it up to us. Don't hold anything back." His fingers found her nipple, plucked and strummed, sending another glittering thread of pleasure to join those Garret's bearded mouth spun between her thighs.

Beth twisted under their hands, her orgasm building with every luscious nibble and stroke. She grabbed for Morgan's brawny shoulder, needing to touch him, needing to anchor herself against waves of pleasure so intense they were almost frightening, each higher, harder than the last...

Her climax smashed over her, tearing a scream from her throat.

Beth's thighs were still quivering when Garret lifted his head and started crawling up her body, his green eyes locked fierce and hungry on hers. "Our turn now."

She grinned, her sense of humor surfacing through the waves of pleasure. "If you insist."

"Oh, we do." Morgan drew back just enough to give Garret room to cover her body with his. She moaned in pleasure as he settled over her, warm and strong. His cock brushed against her belly, a hot, demanding length as he caught her thighs in both big hands and spread her wide.

"And here we go," Morgan breathed in her ear as Garret braced himself on one hand and used the other to aim himself at her slick opening.

He entered her in one long, hard stroke. Beth gasped at the sensation of being filled so abruptly, so utterly. His green gaze met hers in feral demand as he made his first thrust. His cock felt delicious, long and strong as he worked it in and out in deep lunges.

"Like that, poppet?" he rumbled.

"Oooh." She whimpered as he drove in deep. "Does a cat like cream?"

He grinned, white teeth flashing in his dark beard. "I don't know about the cat..." *Thrust...*"...But I certainly do." Bracing his muscular arms on either side of her head, he worked his hips, grinding against her, pressing deliciously into her clit.

Half blind with pleasure, Beth wrapped her legs around his narrow waist and held on for dear life.

"Remember me?" Morgan murmured in her ear, giving her nipple a delicious twist between two fingers.

She closed her eyes and panted. "Believe me, you're not the kind of guy a girl forgets."

"I'm delighted to hear it." His lips brushed her leaping pulse. "Here's something to remember me by." His fangs slid into her skin just as Garret plunged all the way to the balls. The hot sting blended with the spear of pleasure, tearing a scream from her lips. Beth writhed, but his arms encircled her, holding her still as his cousin rode her in those luscious thrusts.

Garret grinned at her, white fangs flashing in his bearded mouth. "Nice, huh?"

"Jeeesus," she gasped. "You've got a gift for understatement."

"Among other things." Smiling wickedly, he rammed in a particularly deep thrust, circling his hips so his long cock twisted into her like a delicious screw, raking her flesh, pressing her clit.

Morgan's mouth worked against her throat as he fed, added hot sparks of pleasure-pain to the whirlwind of the second orgasm building in her belly. As if sensing how close she was, Garret started bucking his hips against her, grinding against her clit until her climax boiled up in flaming pulses. With a hoarse scream, she gave herself up to it as Garret thrust into her and Morgan fed, drinking in long, hungry swallows.

By the time Garret roared out his climax, they'd reduced her to boneless satiety.

Garret collapsed beside her in the center of the bed, panting. "Damn, girl, you're going to be the death of me before the week's up."

Beth groaned. "But what a way to go."

Morgan lifted his head from the bite he'd been bathing tenderly with his tongue. Black eyes glittered at her, wicked and lusty. "You don't imagine we're done, do you?"

"Oh, Morgan, I don't..." she began alarmed, but he'd already rolled onto his feet and hauled her into his arms. Before she knew what hit her, he had both her legs wrapped around his waist.

He reached down to aim his thick erection at her sex. Then he rolled his hips up and impaled her in one breathtaking plunge.

She whimpered. "Have a little mercy, would you?"

He grinned. "No." If anything, he felt thicker than Garret had, as his massive shaft tunneled into her swollen sex. She writhed, caught on the knife edge of pleasure-pain.

Before she could decide whether to protest in earnest, Garret rolled off the bed and joined them. "Mmmm. Need a little help with that, Morgan?"

He grinned, rolling his hips in another breathtaking thrust. "If it's not too much trouble."

Garret stepped up behind her to claim her nipples with both skillful hands. "Oh, it's no trouble at all."

"Glad to hear it," Beth managed, shivering at the pleasure. With a moan, she let her head fall back on his broad shoulder.

"Poor little Kith," he whispered, stroking and twisting the pink tips. "Trying to feed two randy vampires. Are we too much for you?"

She could manage nothing more than a moan with Garret teasing her breasts while Morgan's big cock worked deep in her sex. Her sated libido woke and purred approval.

Garret knew just what to do to make her arousal burn hotter, kissing and licking her ears as he stroked her breasts. Beth arched back in his arms, surrendering as the roller coaster of pleasure started shooting skyward again.

"That's it," Morgan growled, staring into her eyes as he ground into her. "Go with us. Let it come. Feel it build."

He was using those powerful arms to work her up and down on his shaft so hard, each entry sent spikes of pleasure up her spine.

As if that wasn't enough, Garret dropped his hand down under her backside, traced the slick flesh he found, and drove a long forefinger up her ass. The shocking double penetration snapped her head back. She howled, feeling Morgan hammering into her sex as Garret plunged that wicked finger in and out of her backside. The double penetration made Morgan's thick shaft feel even bigger.

Her third climax of the night surged out of nowhere, a dizzying firestorm that was, if anything, brighter than what she'd experienced a few moments before. Beth twisted, impaled on Morgan's cock, scarcely noticing when his cousin suddenly released her. Staring blindly into Morgan's handsome face, she saw Garret move in behind him. Jerking his cousin's head back by the hair, he plunged his fangs in Morgan's muscular throat.

Morgan shouted, stiffening. His thick cock bucked inside her and began to pulse as he came.

Garret lifted his head, revealing the bite in his cousin's neck. Blood welled from the double punctures. "Drink from him," he growled, his green eyes locking on her face.

Beth hesitated, shocked.

Morgan tangled his fingers in her hair, dragging her face down against the wound. Blood touched her lips, burning and intoxicating, like some alien whiskey. Gingerly, she licked at it, aware that Morgan had stopped thrusting as he held her, his big body shaking.

"More," he groaned.

With a soft moan, Beth closed her mouth over the wound and began to drink. Morgan jolted against her and started grinding his cock hard and deep inside her.

Drinking, blazing, she came, barely aware when he stiffened against her with a shout.

Beth lay still, floating in the sated aftermath, acutely aware of the two vampires. Morgan curled against her, while Garret sprawled on the opposite side of the bed in glorious nudity.

She'd never experienced anything like this in her life.

And it was only the beginning. They'd make love to her again and again until her transformation was complete. They'd make her a vampire, establishing a psychic link with her that she wouldn't be able to break for centuries.

Yet she felt no fear. Somehow, despite all logic, she no longer feared they'd misuse the power the link would give them. Both men were far too honorable than that.

But if she felt no fear of Morgan and Garret, she was less confident in the future. Ramirez was not going to give her up without a fight. That's assuming she managed to survive the vampire virus, which wasn't exactly a sure thing. It could easily kill her.

And even if it didn't, she'd have to adjust to becoming a vampire. She wouldn't have to sleep in a coffin, but she would have to avoid sunlight and drink blood.

On the other hand, she'd have the Axton cousins to comfort her. And judging from the past hour, they'd be one hell of a consolation. It would be really, really easy to fall in love with them.

If they all survived.

For the first time in months, Morgan felt almost at peace.

Making love with Beth hadn't been like their unions with Elena, when the three of them had shared one mind—each feeling everything the others felt. Every kiss, every caress, every slow silken thrust.

But it had come damn close.

For a moment when she taken his blood, he thought he could feel her in his mind. There was something bright and almost innocent about her spirit. Elena, as much as he loved her, had been a vampire for a very long time, far too much of it as Ramirez's thrall. There was plenty of goodness in her, but very little innocence. Her exposure to her master's evil had left a permanent shadow on her mind.

On the other hand, contact with Beth's mind felt cleansing, soothing pain he wasn't even conscious of most of the time.

A breathy little sound drew him from his reverie. He glanced over and found Beth sleeping, her pretty face relaxed and open. She exhaled again in a tiny kitten snore.

He realized he was smiling at her in besotted pleasure. It had been so long since he'd felt anything but guilt and anger, the emotion felt...strange.

What am I doing? The thought shot through his sweet lassitude like a bullet into a balloon. *I don't have the right to feel this way. Not after...*

A male fist suddenly punched him in the arm, jolting him out of his spiral into guilt. "Cut it out," Garret growled. "I'd like to spend five minutes *not* mind linked with a suicidal vampire. Just...enjoy it. Or at least shut the hell up so I can."

Before he could decide whether to get pissed off, Beth muttered something and rolled over, slinging one slim arm across his chest. She felt deliciously warm as her soft breasts settled against his chest.

With a sigh, Morgan closed his eyes and surrendered to sleep again.

Chapter Six

"Beth." The voice was soft, feminine, flavored with a trace of Castile. It drew her from the depths of sleep and into the dream.

Opening her eyes, she saw a woman standing beside the bed. The stranger's eyes were a dark, rich brown, but her skin was as pale as cream. Her face was a delicate oval under a mane of dark, curling hair, with a long, elegant nose and a lushly sensuous mouth. She wore a black gown that looked like something from the Elizabethan age, its bodice and skirts heavily worked with silver embroidery. Its square neckline framed full breasts, while her waist was as narrow as a boy's.

"You are beautiful," the stranger said in that musical accent. Her mouth did not move. Moonlight from the French doors poured through her translucent body, giving her a faint glow.

"I was thinking the same about you," Beth said. "You're Elena, aren't you?"

"I was." The dark eyes were very sad.

"Is this a dream, or are you a ghost?"

Elena tilted her head to the side. *"I did not think you skeptical moderns believed in ghosts."*

"My brother-in-law's sister became a ghost," Beth told her, sitting up to slip from beneath the covers. "I never met her, but I heard the stories. She fought for years to save Cade from Ridgemont."

"As I'm trying to save mis angeles.*"* The ghost moved around the bed, looking down at the sleeping vampires. Sadness darkened those remarkable eyes. She extended a delicate hand toward Garret's face, but her insubstantial fingers slid into his skin. She winced and turned away. *"Even in your dream, I cannot touch them."*

"So I am dreaming?" Glancing at the bed, Beth startled. Her body still lay there, stretched out next to the men, sprawled and abandoned in sleep. "I guess so." Just as Val told her years ago, these psychic dreams felt like reality.

The ghost drifted to the other side of the bed to gaze into Morgan's handsome face, so uncharacteristically open and unguarded in sleep. *"I could not touch your thoughts otherwise. Your Kith mental shields are too strong when you're awake. But asleep, your barriers drop, especially as the vampire virus begins to take hold."*

Beth frowned. "I wonder why the men can't see you? Abigail could appear to Val and Cade—even Ridgemont and his flunky Hirsch." She hesitated, contemplating the stories she'd heard about the thirteen-year-old girl who'd died as the Civil War ended. "Of course, Abigail was dead for a couple of decades before even Cade could see her. They assumed it was because he didn't become a vampire until he was almost forty, but maybe it took her that long to grow strong enough to make him see her. Or maybe she just needed to learn how to communicate with living people." She shrugged. "Either way."

The ghost looked intrigued. *"But in time, she could speak to him?"*

"She could even throw things. Apparently she had some kind of telekinesis."

Elena looked down at the men, longing naked on her face. *"To share my thoughts with them again...Especially Morgan."* She sighed. *"He fought so hard to save me, but Ramirez had hurt me too badly. Even with Morgan amplifying my power, Joaquin was too strong for us."*

"Why was Ramirez so obsessed with you, anyway?"

Elena crouched beside the bed to gaze into Garret's sleeping face, longing in her gaze. *"He was my master. He abducted me from the convent where I was a novice nun. He raped me, made me a vampire, and enslaved me. It took me two hundred years to break his hold, and even then, he swore to get me back."*

"You were Ramirez's slave for two hundred years? And you'd been a nun? Oh, God, that must have been..."

"Horrific." The ghost looked up. *"He would have killed me for daring to break free. So I took a ship to the New World, hoping if I ran far enough, I would be safe."* Her expression lightened, and she turned a smile on the two men sprawled together in masculine abandon. *"But my ship was attacked and boarded by English privateers. I, of course, immediately approached the captain, planning to compel him to release us. When my efforts failed, I realized both he and his first officer were Kith."*

The light dawned. "So you seduced them instead and made them your vampire bodyguards."

Elena drew a ghostly hand down Morgan's long, hard muscled body. *"I never expected to fall in love with them both. They stayed with me for four centuries, long after they could have broken my control. Not that I ever really exerted any."*

"And Ramirez kept hunting you all that time? I've heard of obsessive, but…"

"Only for the first century or so. Eventually he gave up and left us in peace." She sighed and rose to her ghostly feet. *"At least until I encountered him in Europe sixteen months ago. It so happened* mis angeles *were attending to our businesses elsewhere, and he saw he had a clear path to take me. So he did."*

Beth looked away from the pain on her face. If it hadn't been for Morgan and Garret, she'd have shared Elena's fate.

A sudden thought made her frown. Did the ghost resent her? After all, Beth shared a bed with her lovers now. "I'm sorry. Sorry about Ramirez and…" She gestured helplessly at her own sleeping, sated body. "This. If it matters, I'm only a means to an end. They don't really care about me."

Elena's lips twitched as though she fought a smile. *"I would not be so sure about that. And in truth, I do not begrudge you any love you find with them. I want them to find some happiness. My time in this life is over. I must go to God. But I cannot leave until I know they're safe."* She turned toward Beth, intent and earnest. *"You can save them. From Ramirez. From themselves. If Morgan doesn't take care, he will destroy them both. Garret will kill himself trying to save him."*

Beth spread her hands. "But I don't see how I'm…"

Sudden alarm flashed across the ghost's face, and she snapped around toward the closest wall, throwing up a hand to silence Beth. *"Shhh! Something is…"* Her eyes widened in horror. *"Beth! He's coming!"*

"What? Who?"

Then she felt it too. A wave of evil rushed toward them, malevolent and powerful. Beth whirled with a strangled scream of terror, meaning to wake the men.

Before she could take another step, Ramirez exploded out of the wall like a demon out of hell, his face twisted and savage. She tried to run, but he was already on her, sinking his fingers into her as if her skull was made of wet clay. As Beth screamed in agony, he dragged her around to face him. "Oh, no you don't, my little slut. I have plans for you!" His eyes blazed red as a demon's in the darkened room, and his fangs shone white, a good three inches longer than they should have been.

A nightmare. This has to be a nightmare! "Get off me!" Beth grabbed his wrist in both hands and tried to drag his fingers from her skull.

They only sank deeper, digging in like a tiger's claws as he bared those horrific fangs at him. "Did you really think you could escape me?"

"Leave her alone!" Elena cried, flinging herself at his back to pound at him. Her ghostly fists passed right through him. Ramirez didn't even seem aware of her, all his attention focused on his struggling captive.

The ghost floated upward, meeting Beth's frantic eyes over his shoulder. *"It is no good—I cannot touch him! You must fight him off, or he'll possess you!"*

"I'm trying—it's not doing any good!"

"Who are you talking to, *puta*?" Ramirez growled as she struggled to tear herself free. He dug his claws in deeper and dragged her inexorably closer to his gaping fangs. "Not that it matters. It's too late anyway."

She shrieked as he sank them into her face. Something deep within her ripped like silk.

Beth woke trying to scream.

She was back in bed next to the men. Ramirez was gone. *A dream,* she thought, relief flooding through her. *It was only a dream.*

Needing comfort, she tried to roll over and snuggle into Morgan's side, but her body wouldn't obey. Instead, she rose from the bed like a robot. Beth frowned, confused, and tried to sit down again, but her body kept moving, heading for the armchair where Morgan had left his sword. *What the hell is going on?*

"Me." The deep, accented voice was all too familiar. *"You're mine now, little bitch."*

"Ramirez!" She tried to scream it, but she couldn't move her lips.

"Did you really think Elena's dogs could keep me away?" Beth could feel his sneer. *"I sank my link in you so deeply it was easy to take your mind, particularly in sleep."*

Ice sliding through her veins, she could only watch as her body reached for Morgan's sword. *"No!"* She fought to turn away, to shout a warning, but she was firmly under the master vampire's control.

"Oh, yes. Why do you think I left you there for them to find? I knew they wouldn't be able to resist you, that you'd spread your thighs for them to save your own life. And once they slept..."

Her hands closed over the hilt of Morgan's great sword. It felt cold and heavy as she lifted it. Moonlight glinted off the menacing length of its blade as she carried it back to the bed. *"You can't just kill them!"* The thought filled her with panic. Heroic, funny Garret and brooding, handsome Morgan, murdered in their sleep—at her hand. She had to do something!

"Oh, but I can. And you can do nothing."

Maybe an appeal to his ego…*"What kind of honor is there in murdering sleeping men?"*

"These dogs stole my woman from me. They deserve nothing better." He planted her feet wide apart and lifted the sword over their heads. His voice rang in her mind, smug with satisfaction. *"I wonder if I can take both their heads with a single stroke? Let's find out."*

"No!" Desperately, Beth tried to reach the men with her mind. *"Morgan! Garret! It's Ramirez! For God's sake, wake up!"* They didn't even stir.

The ghost, maybe the ghost. *"Elena! Do something!"*

Ramirez sneered in her mind. *"Elena is dead, you stupid cow."*

Pop! The bulb in the bedside lamp exploded, showering a tiny rain of glass on the night table.

"What?" Ramirez's head snapped up in surprise as every light bulb in the room exploded in a volley of tiny pops.

On the bed, Morgan jerked awake, his black eyes opening, then flaring wide as he saw her standing over him with the sword. "What the hell are you doing?"

Ramirez swore and lifted the blade, preparing to bring it down and behead both men.

"Have you run mad?" Morgan threw himself off the bed and grabbed for Beth's hands before she could decapitate them.

Impossibly, she wrenched him airborne and flipped him toward the wall as if he weighed no more than a poker chip. He slammed hard against the wall, plaster cracking around his body as the whole house shook with the impact. Hitting the floor, he crouched, ready to defend himself.

"Morgan!" Garret woke and rolled out of bed. "What the devil is going on?" .

"Our little bedmate's developed a homicidal streak." Morgan pivoted to avoid her lunge as she swung the sword at his head, spitting vile

Castilian obscenities.

Garret grabbed her jerking her around to face him. "Beth, what the..."

"*Cabrón!*" She jabbed the sword at his chest, forcing him to leap away.

"It's Ramirez!" Morgan snarled, furious and betrayed as he closed on her. "He's possessed her." Which he shouldn't have been able to do with the kind of link he supposedly had—unless she'd been suckering them all along.

"*Si*, she's mine." Beth wheeled toward him, blade lifted. Morgan backed warily away, knowing Ramirez's possession gave her superhuman strength. "She was always my lover. She only pretended to hate me so you fools would take her into your bed."

Dammit, he'd believed her.

"*He's lying,*" Garret said in their link as he moved around behind the girl, getting into position. *"He wants to goad us into killing her."*

Knowing he needed to keep Ramirez's attention focused on himself, Morgan danced just out of range of Beth's blade. With an inhuman snarl, she sprang.

Garret swept out a foot, hooked her ankles and sent her sprawling. Morgan snatched her sword hand as she fell. Twisting ruthlessly, he grabbed the sword and jerked it away. She hit the ground on her hands and knees and snarled up at him. *"Me cago en tu puta madre!"*

The foul words in Ramirez's hated accent sent fury steaming through him. With a snarl, Morgan lifted the sword. Ramirez vanished from her chocolate gaze as he tensed to bring it down.

Then it was Beth looking up at him, horror in her eyes. She snapped into a ball and flung up her hands to protect her head. "Nooo!"

"Morgan, Ramirez is gone!" Garret snapped. "Back off!"

He hesitated a split second, his gaze locked on her as she huddled pitifully. His instinct was to spare her, but he no longer trusted his instincts. "What if she *is* working with him?"

"No!" she gasped, lifting her head. "He was lying! I didn't!" The terror on her face stabbed pain into his chest. Just hours ago, he'd watched pleasure fill those glorious eyes as he rode her.

With a disgusted mutter, Morgan threw the sword aside. Spinning on his heels, he stalked to the balcony doors, banged them open, and barged through, cursing himself, Ramirez and Beth equally.

Ramirez had ruined everything yet again

Chapter Seven

Beth looked up at Garret, eyes wide in her pale face. "He almost killed me! Even after Ramirez left, he almost killed me."

Garret sighed. "Morgan couldn't have hurt you even if you had been working with that bastard. He's not capable of killing a woman in cold blood. Why do you think I didn't jump him when he didn't drop the sword?"

If anything, she looked even more spooked, as if she was wondering about his trustworthiness too. Those big brown eyes seemed to take up most of her face.

Hellfire, he was going to have to start all over with both of them. Sighing, Garret extended a hand down to help her up. "Why don't you tell me what happened?"

Beth frowned at his hand warily before accepting it and letting him help her to her feet. She was shaking. With a sigh, he led her to the bed before her knees gave altogether. "Nobody's going to hurt you, Poppet," he told her as she sat down. "Just tell the story."

Still, she hesitated, studying his face before she finally began. The tale she told was so unlikely, Garret was staring at her in doubt and astonishment before her story was half done.

"You dreamed about Elena?" Morgan asked from the doorway.

Beth met his gaze with a trace of defiance. "Actually, I think it was her ghost. And it was more than just a dream. She was here. Maybe she still is."

"No, you were dreaming—Elena's no ghost." The words were flat and emotionless, but Garret could feel Morgan's pain. "She went to heaven." His tone left no room for argument.

Beth had more guts than Garret had given her credit for. "Look at the lamps, Morgan. Hell, look at every light bulb in the room."

Both men glanced over at the night table. Tiny eggshell fragments of glass littered the table and the floor around it. Another patch of glass lay on the carpet beneath the ceiling light. "It looks like they exploded," Garret said thoughtfully. "Every one of them."

"So?" Morgan demanded.

"That's what roused you. After Ramirez possessed me, I couldn't speak. I begged Elena to do something wake you. So she shattered the bulbs."

Morgan's eyes widened as he whitened. Garret shared his sick horror at the thought that their lover might be wandering as a lost soul. "No. She loved God. Why would He reject her?"

"No one was more devout than Elena," Garret agreed. "She endowed any number of schools and churches over the centuries. Hell, her foundation operates half a dozen hospitals all over South America."

He and Morgan had even converted to Catholicism at her insistence—not that it had taken much persuasion after they'd seen how much her faith meant to her. God had sustained her through too many years as Ramirez's victim. But there'd also been times her faith had tormented her as she struggled to reconcile it with the sensuality of her vampire nature. Had God turned His back for her sins, as she'd always feared He would?

"It's not that Heaven rejected her," Beth explained, frowning thoughtfully. "It's more that she feels she has things she must do."

Morgan relaxed slightly, but if anything, his expression grew more grim. "She must avenge herself on Ramirez."

"No, she wants to make sure you don't get yourself and Garret killed," Beth told him tartly. "She's afraid for you, Morgan."

He rocked back on his heels, his expression startled. Garret wanted to cheer. Finally, a crack in his suicidal obsession with revenge.

"But I failed her," Morgan said, his voice low and hoarse. "He raped her, cut out her heart, and I did…."

"Everything you could have done." If Beth still feared him, it didn't show in her level gaze. "Elena knows that. And after what happened tonight, I understand it too." She glanced away sharply, as if unable to hold their gazes any longer. "Ramirez just…crushed me. He took me over. There was…I couldn't do anything." Her voice broke.

"Believe me, we know just how strong he is," Garret told her.

Beth rose to pace, raking shaking fingers through her long, tangled hair. "I watched my hands pick up your sword, and I tried to stop, but I couldn't." She sucked in a hard breath. "He lifted it over your heads, and I couldn't even scream."

"It wasn't your fault," Morgan told her as she drew in on herself, covering her mouth with one hand. Tears welled in her eyes. "A master vampire can seize his fledgling through the link, and there's no way to stop him."

She squeezed her eyes shut as if fighting a scream, then dropped her hand and whirled toward them. Anger blazed up in her dark eyes, searing away the shame and fear. "I thought the whole idea of my sleeping with you was that he wouldn't be able to do that to me anymore. He got to me anyway! And you almost killed me!"

Garret winced. "We're not finished with the process, Beth. You have to be practically drained while we feed you our blood. Then when you drop into a coma, we form a deep link with you and…"

"He didn't do any of that!"

"He must have formed some kind of link with you," Morgan pointed out, "or he wouldn't have been able to get to you, even in your sleep."

She spun away and stood rigid for several long seconds, as if fighting some battle. At last she asked in a low, careful voice, "If you finish it, will you be able to break whatever he did and keep him from taking me again?"

"Yes," Garret admitted, "but it's going to take time."

Beth turned to face them again, a snarl on her pretty lips. "I will *not* risk him grabbing me again. Finish it now!"

"Poppet…."

"Don't 'poppet' me! You don't know what it was like!"

"I do." Morgan's voice was low and certain. "And we'll do whatever it takes to make sure he can't do it to you again."

As he shouldered away from the doorframe, Beth fought the instinct to back away. She remembered far too clearly the cold look on his face when he'd stood over her with the sword, considering whether it would be safer just to take her head. The fact that he'd just finished making love to her only made it worse.

When Morgan reached for her, she flinched. He arrested the gesture and lifted a brow. "You just said you wanted this."

"And you just came really close to taking my head."

His expression closed. "You would prefer Garret attempt turning you alone?"

Garret frowned. "I'm not sure I'll be able to counter Ramirez without his help." Then he shrugged. "But I'm willing to try if that's what you want."

The word "yes" hovered on the tip of her tongue, but then she remembered Elena's fierce love for Morgan—and the way his mouth had moved on her own with such trembling restraint. He'd been so hungry, yet he'd controlled it for her sake.

Squaring her shoulders, Beth stepped closer, looking up at Morgan "No. You can be trusted."

He smiled slightly. "Which isn't quite the same as saying you trust me."

Gathering her courage, she slipped her arms around his powerful neck. "But I'm getting there."

He bent his head and kissed her. It was a surprisingly sweet kiss for such a lusty man, with a hint of apology in its tenderness. She wasn't entirely sure whether he was apologizing for what he'd done or for what he was about to do. But he felt delicious either way, tall and warm against her.

And, despite everything, he felt safe.

Beth leaned into his strength, surrendering herself with a sigh. Gently, he drew her into a long, slow kiss that made her blood heat. At last he drew back and turned her in his arms, then took her chin in one hand and tilted her head to the side. Feeling oddly fearless, she offered no resistance. Velvet lips touched her hammering pulse.

He bit her fast, his arms tightening with practiced skill. Without the distraction of arousal, it hurt more than she'd expected, the pain sharp and aching. She couldn't suppress a whimper as Morgan began to drink. As if to offer solace, he stroked his hands up her body to cup her bare breasts. Gently, skillfully, he milked her nipples.

Then Garret was in front of her, going down on his knees. He parted her sex with two fingers and slipped the wet length of his tongue between them. Beth moaned, the sound blending with Morgan's deep swallows and the flick of Garret's tongue on her juicy flesh.

By the time they carried her to bed, her knees were weak from both blood loss and arousal. Morgan draped her lax body across his and sliced a thin cut across his chest with his thumbnail. He guided her head to the slice. She lapped at it dizzily.

When she finished, Garret bent over them and kissed her slowly before taking her throat. It wasn't long before she slid into unconsciousness on a long, dark wave of sensuality.

And blood.

Beth dreamed strange dreams. She was back in the basement where Ramirez had held her. It was dark, and thirst clawed at her. She begged him for water, calling through the high stone walls—hadn't they been cement before?—but he only laughed at her. His amusement rumbled through the stone.

Her mouth felt like cotton, and her lips were cracked and bleeding. She sucked at them, desperate for any moisture at all. It was cold, so cold. She could see her breath.

"She's dying." Garret's voice came distantly through the stone. "If we don't break through her psychic barriers, we'll lose her."

"I'm not so sure they're hers," Morgan said. "They feel more like Ramirez to me."

She dreamed they had pickaxes, and they were trying to cut their way through the wall. She could hear the ring of steel on stone. But just as she started to beg them to hurry, something…slithered.

Beth turned to look, but the room had grown enormous, and she could see nothing in the darkness.

There was a whisper of movement. Every hair stood up on the back of her neck.

A snake. There was a huge snake in the cell with her. "Morgan!" She tried to scream, but the words emerged as a hoarse croak. "Garret—there's something in here…."

"They can't hear you." Ramirez's voice, whispering out of the darkness. "I'm keeping them out."

The slithering sound was very loud now. Claws scraped on stone.

"I told you, you're mine." Lights flared bright and red in the darkness. Horror crept over her as she realized they were eyes—two glowing, slit-pupilled eyes, opening wide. "If I can't have you, I'll see you dead."

The dragon opened its jaws and shot a gout of roaring flame. Beth screamed and tried to scramble away, but she couldn't move. The fire poured over her in a wave of agony. She screamed, a howl of helplessness and despair.

"Beth!" It was Morgan's deep-throated roar. The stone wall exploded as if it had been blasted with dynamite, and he and Garret charged through. They were dressed in plate mail like medieval knights, the engraved steel shining crimson in the light from the dragon's fire. Yelling war cries, they leaped at Ramirez, heavy swords swinging.

But Beth could feel the flames licking at her. Dying. She was dying…

"No!" Elena appeared, glowing in the darkness like a star, determination on her sad and beautiful face. *"Mis angeles need you!"*

Small bright hands touched Beth's agonized face. A white mist rolled over her, magical and cooling, extinguishing the flames. She sighed in blessed relief as the pain drained away.

The ghost smiled. *"Ahhh! It worked. Bueno. Better, si?"*

*"Si,"*she rasped. Her throat ached from screaming.

*"Rest now,"*Elena said over the sounds of combat as Morgan and Garret drove the dragon off down the cave. *"You are safe. We've defeated him."* Her mouth tightened. *"For now."*

Garret rested a hand on Beth's forehead. Despite the sweaty tangle of her hair, her skin had cooled, her breathing slowing and strengthening out of that deathly rattle. "Thank God," he told Morgan. "The fever's gone. It just...dropped." Sitting up, he rested his elbows wearily on his knees. "Just in time. I'd thought we'd lost her for sure." Two days had passed since Beth had dropped into the coma, and they'd had to fight for her every minute.

"It was Ramirez. He did his damnedest to kill her."

Garret sighed and scratched his beard. It badly needed trimming. "He had his claws sunk deeper than I expected. He's one powerful son of a bitch." Putting a hand to his aching back, he stood and slowly straightened it. Too long lying in the same position took a toll even on vampire muscles.

"But Beth fought him anyway." Morgan said softly. "She never gave in. She's...more than I expected. Bright. Strong. You can almost taste it."

"Yeah." Garret looked down at her as she lay sprawled on her back. There were shadows under those big eyes from her illness, but even that couldn't dim the beauty of her oval face. He could feel her in the link now, even as deeply asleep as she was. "She's so different from Elena, and yet...they're a lot alike. I can't wait to meet that sister of hers." They'd touched Beth's memories of Val, tasted the love she felt for the girl who'd all but raised her after their parents died.

"Love," Morgan said aloud, reacting to his thought. He broke off.

Garret looked over at him, reading the confused tangle of his emotions, the blend of longing and guilt. "I feel the same way. It would be so easy to fall in love with her, but after what happened to Elena..." He glanced down at Beth, taking in the sweet, bare curves of breast and hip. The taste of her had been intoxicating. Sighing, he glanced at his cousin. "Except I'm not sure either one of us has a choice. Besides..."

Morgan finished the sentence. "...It may be a moot point anyway if we can't take care of Ramirez."

Chapter Eight

Africa was half the world away, but Ramirez still felt the last assassin die.

He swore viciously. Beth's wretched sister and her whore-son husband had proven more formidable then he expected.

Restlessly, he began to pace the bedroom, anger eating at him. Wrapped up in his furious thoughts, he was barely aware of the terrified gaze of the bound woman watching from the bed.

He'd made a mistake in sending his spawn so far away. Though Ramirez could sense when they died, he couldn't control them over distances so great. Which meant that the little cocksuckers had probably spilled their guts to this Cade McKinnon if he'd bothered to torture them at all.

Ramirez stopped to gaze out the bay window at the mountains that surrounded the last of his homes. Perhaps they hadn't even needed torture. They hated him, the ungrateful bastards, hated the way he'd been forced to sacrifice their brothers in his battle with Elena's spawn.

He had only four thralls left, nowhere near enough. Not considering that McKinnon's whore would no doubt tell Beth where he was holed up, and she in turn would tell her lovers. All five of them would then join forces to storm his mountain headquarters. And soon.

It was fortunate he'd foreseen this possibility. He'd already hired a team of mercenaries to defend him if it became necessary. One phone call and they'd be here, armed to the teeth. They were only human, of course, but enough men with enough automatic weapons would tip the odds firmly in his favor.

It might even be possible to capture Elena's cocksucking spawn and the girl they'd tried to steal from him. And then...

His dick hardening at the thought, Ramirez turned toward the captive who still lay huddled on his bed. Grinning into her big green eyes, he started toward her.

When Beth woke, her mouth felt cottony with thirst. She moaned, the sound emerging as a croak.

"Welcome back." Without being asked, Garret sat down on the bed next to her and presented a squeeze bottle of water to her mouth. She sucked at it with greedy desperation as he pumped a cool stream into her mouth.

"That's enough, he said finally, and pulled the bottle away. "We don't want you getting sick."

"Thanks," she managed, as the dryness receded a little.

Morgan walked over to join them. Both men were dressed again—jeans and a black T-shirt for him, Garret in chinos and a golf shirt. They looked so neat and clean, Beth was instantly aware of her own sweaty body. "Gah. I feel nasty." Not to mention hung-over. Her head ached, and when she tried to move, every muscle protested as if she'd just run a marathon. "May I have some more water? I'm still thirsty."

Morgan exchanged a significant glance with Garret. "I'm afraid it's not water you need."

Good God, she realized, *it's the Hunger.* The idea felt so huge and frightening, she had to joke. "I feel more like a three-day old kitten than a super-powered creature of the night." She managed a sickly smile. "I want my money back."

"Give it time," Morgan told her. "Once you...eat, you'll feel better."

"Thanks for saying 'eat' instead of 'feed.'"

"Actually," Garret pointed out, "you've drunk from us before. Several times."

"Yeah, but that seemed more like kinky sex than...this." She reached for the bottle again. He handed it over without further comment.

But as Beth put it in her mouth, the nozzle hit one of her canines. Pain stabbed her gums, and the tooth gave way. "Dammit!" she lisped, slapping a hand over her mouth as it tried to roll down her throat. Choking, she scrambled out of bed and headed for the bathroom, blood flooding her mouth.

Bending over the sink, she spat hastily. A crimson blob of blood hit the basin, along with the white wedge of a canine. Pain jabbed her again as another tooth came loose. She spat that one out too.

With a moan of disgust, Beth turned the taps on full and scooped handful of water into her mouth. Spitting it out, she looked up into the mirror and found the men standing behind her, watching sympathetically. "I guess this means I've got fangs now." She cringed. Her sibilants had acquired a distinct "th" sound. "Great. Now I'm lisping." Reluctantly, she looked in the mirror and opened her jaws. Her canines had been replaced by inch-long fangs.

"Oh, God," Beth whispered. "I'm a vampire. I'm really a vampire." Her eyes began to sting, and she ducked her head, turning away from the mirror.

Garret pulled her into his arms. "I know," he soothed, gathering her close. "It's always tough at first."

Tears rolling down her cheeks, she wrapped her arms around his warm waist. "I feel like such an idiot. I asked for this. I did. But..."

"You feel as if you've lost your humanity." Morgan rested a comforting hand on her shoulder. "You haven't. You're still the same woman you always were."

She lifted her head and gave him a watery smile. "I don't know about that. I can hear both your hearts beating." The double thump sounded like distant music.

Morgan smiled slightly. "So a few things are different."

"Too many things." Pulling back from Garret, Beth licked at the blood on her lips. It tasted far too good for her peace of mind. "I need a shower." She turned toward the tub and felt her knees give way.

Before she could fall on her face, a strong hand clamped around her elbow, supporting her. "Take it slow," Morgan said. "Your body has been through a lot."

"Maybe you should go for a bath instead," Garret suggested. "They've got a huge tub. Big enough for all three of us."

"Yeah?" Intrigued, she hobbled around the corner, feeling like an old woman with Morgan's supporting hand under her arm.

He was right, the tub was huge. Made of cream marble veined with pink, it was a good five feet across and seven feet long. The fixtures were gold, and the faucet was shaped like a swan, its neck an elegant curve. "That's not a tub, that's a swimming pool. Somebody has way too much money."

"Maybe." Garret bent to turn on the taps and flicked a switch, sending jets of water thundering into the tub. "But you've got to admit, it's got possibilities." Straightening, he pulled his shirt off over his head.

The sight of his lean, elegant torso made Beth's mouth feel even dryer than it was already. "Possibilities," she repeated. "Oh, yeah. Definitely."

Morgan chuckled in her ear, the sound wickedly suggestive. "Why don't you get in? We'll start exploring them right now."

As the tub filled, Garret toed off his shoes and stripped out of his pants and underwear, then helped her down into the water while Morgan undressed. It was deliciously warm, and the jets beat gently against her aching body. She settled down on the low seat and closed her eyes with a tired sigh. She felt so rotten, she wasn't even sure she was up to entertaining the Sex Gods.

Water splashed as they joined her, settling down in the water on either side. Strong male hands caught her by the shoulders and pulled her upright. "I'm going to wet your hair," Garret murmured. He eased her back until only her face remained over the bubbling water. When she sat up again, her hair clung to her back in long, wet strands.

Beth slumped as he spread something deliciously cool over her head, then started working it into a lather. A second set of soapy fingers caught her breasts and began stroking over her skin. She surrendered herself, eyes sliding shut, content to let them wash her. Distantly, she was aware of building arousal. It took her a moment to realize not all of it was her own. Her eyes popped open. "I'm feeling you," she whispered. "I'm feeling what you feel."

"Yes." Morgan knelt in front of her on the bottom of the tub. His soapy fingers found her nipples, pinched gently. Stroked. The pleasure made her catch her breath. *"And we feel what you feel."* This time when he spoke, his lips didn't move.

She'd heard his thoughts. *They were linked*, she realized. It was a staggering thought, being part of a union that had formed four hundred years before.

Beth breathed in, fighting a wave of panic. Becoming a vampire was terrifying enough, but this... It was too much. She felt as if she was losing herself.

She should have known they'd feel her fear.

"Shhh. It will be all right," Garret told her, stroking his soapy hands over her skin. "Concentrate on this." Now she could feel the anticipation thrumming in his mind. "And as sweet as it was making love to you before, it's going to be even better now." He drew her back against his chest and slid one hand down between her thighs. She moaned as he found her clit and circled it with just the right pressure. Her fear began to recede under the sweet onslaught of delight.

Morgan drew in a breath, his hot eyes shuttering. "I feel it when he touches you."

"Oh? How about this?" Impulsively, Beth reached below the bubbling water and found the jutting length of Morgan's cock. She closed her fingers around it. Both men inhaled sharply.

So did Beth. It felt as if her clit had suddenly grown incredibly long and thick. Delicate fingers brushed along it—her own. "Wow," she breathed. Gently, she began to explore, stroking her hand up and down Morgan's thick shaft. It bucked under her fingers, the echo of his pleasure making her groan.

With her other hand, she found his heavy balls and cupped them. It seemed she could feel them there between her own legs, as delicately sensitive as her breasts. The pleasure was dazzling.

Maybe there was something to be said for this mind link after all.

Fascinated, Beth cuddled his balls in one hand while she caressed the length of his shaft with the other. Running a thumb across his glans made them all gasp.

"Stand up," she said hoarsely. "I want to taste you."

Beth heard Morgan swallow as he obeyed. Water streamed from his brawny body, rolling down his braced thighs to drip from his flushed and eager cock. She leaned forward. Through the link, she felt the two men tense in anticipation as she opened her mouth. Sucking him in, she felt wet heat and the caress of lips and tongue around that huge, phantom clit. Beth stopped, just absorbing the sensation. Morgan murmured in incoherent plea.

Gently, carefully, she began to suck, swirling her tongue over the head as she closed her lips snugly around the shaft. The sensations echoing up the link seemed to burn in white-hot intensity, and she moaned. Even the movement of her own lips felt delicious, a tender humming around her phantom clit.

And beneath that, coming through the link, she could feel the men's enjoyment of both Morgan's pleasure and her own. Each lick, each nibble, each movement of her head elicited a wicked echo of erotic feedback. Each built on the one before, the pleasure intensifying, increasing with dizzying speed.

The orgasm hammered into them without warning. Morgan threw back his head and roared. Beth cried out around his cock as he shot into her mouth, the sounds blending with Garret's hoarse shout. Morgan's knees gave, and he fell back in the water with a splash, pulling his softening cock from Beth's lax grip.

For a long moment, they all just sat there, dazed.

Damn, I've missed that. The thought came from one of the men, but

Beth wasn't sure which.

Morgan lay sprawled against the rear of the tub, both brawny arms flung wide across its marble lip. His head was thrown back, and a thick vein throbbed beneath his jaw. In the silence, she could hear their three heartbeats. Beth wanted to press her mouth to that banging pulse, wanted to feel it throb against her lips just as his cock had. She moved through the water toward him as if in a trance.

He lifted his head and watched her come, his dark eyes knowing. He opened his arms. She went into them, her eyes fixed helplessly on his pulse. But as she started to bend toward his throat, a thought pierced the hypnotic haze. *What am I doing?*

"You know exactly what you're doing." It was Garret, moving up behind her as she straddled Morgan's brawny thighs. "You're taking what you need."

Blood, she thought. *He means blood.*

I'm about to drink his blood. Something in her recoiled at the thought, but the rest was lost in the first rise of the Hunger. She looked down at his throbbing pulse as need coiled in hot knots in her belly, demanding and fiercely alien.

As Beth lowered her head to Morgan's throat, she felt the men's anticipation rise. They wanted this as much as she did. Morgan tilted his head back and closed his eyes. "Now, Beth."

She licked her dry lips. "What if I hurt you?"

"You won't." Garret caught the back of her head and gently pressed her face against his cousin's neck. The Hunger clamored, demanding she bite. Her fangs ached savagely, sliding to full length in her mouth. She could taste her own blood. Hesitantly, she licked his throat. He tasted delicious.

Unable to hold back any longer, Beth bit down. Morgan gasped, his body arching under hers. She'd never heard anything as erotic as his groan of surrender. He liked the sting of her fangs in his skin.

Encouraged, Beth began to suck, but only a trace of blood rewarded her Hunger. Frustrated, she drew harder. Garret laughed softly and used his hold on her head to turn her back and forth a fraction. Morgan moaned. "You've got to widen the openings or you won't be able to get anything past your fangs."

Sure enough, blood began to flood her mouth as the cuts widened. It tasted delicious—burning and sweet, more like some dark liquor than the familiar salt and copper she'd known as a mortal. With a low groan of pleasure, she stretched out along his hard body, loving the way he felt, loving the way he tasted. As she drank in hungry swallows, Morgan reached up to claim her breasts with his skilled fingers, teasing her nipples, tugging and twisting.

Arousal spilled out of nowhere in a gout of flame, still fierce despite the mind-searing orgasm they'd just enjoyed. Beth ground her hips against his hardening cock, hungry to feel it thrusting deep inside her. Something slick and hard touched the lips of her sex from behind. "Will this do?" Garret asked in a velvet purr as he began working his way inside.

Fangs buried in Morgan's throat, she could only groan.

"I think that's a yes." There was laughter in Morgan's voice.

"Sounded that way to me too." Garret began to thrust in slow, seductive digs. Beth gasped against Morgan's pulse, loving both the hot pleasure of his cousin's cock and the way her slick inner sheath gripped him.

The delight was so intense, she felt seared. It poured into her from every side—the hot taste of Morgan's blood, the steady plunges of Garret's cock, the tight, slick heat of her own sex. And each sweet sensation made the pulses in her core strengthen and pick up speed. Until...

The climax hit like a blinding fireball, flinging her out into a long, endless tumble, the men roaring with her, so tangled she couldn't tell where she left off and they began. She'd never known anything so exquisite in her life.

When it was all over at last, the three of them lay still, enclosed in a sweet bubble of warmth.

It felt almost like... love.

Chapter Nine

Beth opened her eyes. She was snuggled against a broad male back. A brawny arm curved across her waist from behind. Body parts that obviously belonged to two different men.

Imagining Val's reaction to this—probably along the lines of "You go, girl"—Beth stifled a giggle. Then she grimaced. "Ugh." Her mouth tasted like the bottom of a bird cage. *I have got to brush my teeth.* Preferably before somebody woke up and wanted to kiss her.

The thought made her smile in a loopy kind of pleasure.

Propping herself up on her elbows, she realized the only problem with sleeping sandwiched between two handsome studs is that you couldn't roll out of bed without waking one of them. With a sigh, she flipped off the covers and scooted her way off the end of the bed. Morgan made a grumbling sound when she moved his arm, but neither man roused.

Throwing a look at the window, Beth saw the sun was setting in glorious shades of salmon and gold off beyond the trees that surrounded the house. It wouldn't be long until everybody was awake—and probably horny, if recent events were any guide. Better take care of the teeth while she could.

When she emerged a few minutes later tasting of mint, the men were still deeply asleep. Beth gave thought to waking them, then spotted the bedside phone. It was a good time to make another attempt at calling Val.

Scooping the portable off its cradle, she retreated back into the bathroom. She'd been out for a couple of days or more; she'd lost track of how long. With any luck, Cade and Val were somewhere with cell service again.

No such luck. Despite calls to each of their phones, there was still no answer. Frustrated, she decided to check her own messages. Maybe they'd left one for her. After calling her number, she punched in her retrieval code and listened to two messages from a gallery owner and her agent, both wanting to touch base on a proposed show.

But the next voice was Val's.

"Beth, pick up! Dammit, call me if you get this message." Val's usual easy drawl had morphed into a snap of frustration. "We've been going insane for the past week, chasing all over Africa trying to find where that bastard Ramirez took you. Cade finally got his hands on one of the bastard's vampire spawn, and we made the little prick talk. We've tracked Ramirez down to a..." The call ended with a loud *beep*! Her answering machine had cut them off.

Just as Beth was getting ready to tear out her hair, Val came on again. "Stupid machine. Anyway, the flunky said Ramirez plans to take you to his headquarters in the Georgia mountains. It sounds like the back ass of beyond. Cade and I are going to hit it, but I thought I'd call on the off-chance the bastard was lying about Ramirez having you. If you're not being held captive by Fang Face, leave a message on the cell and sit tight. We'll come to you...Oh, it's 3 p.m. Tuesday afternoon."

Shit. Beth wasn't even sure what day it was. She lifted her voice in a shout. "Guys!"

Morgan and Garret listened grimly as she described the message. When she finished, Garret asked, "Did you try the cell?"

"Called it before I got the message. No dice."

Morgan frowned deeply. "Mountains of Georgia." He glanced at Garret. "Didn't one of the staff dig up something about some property he owns on a mountain called Cherokee Leap in east Georgia?"

Staff? They had a staff? Before Beth could ask about it, Garret nodded slowly. "I think so. It was squirreled away behind half a dozen holding companies. I'll double check. It would be about an hour away, if I'm remembering the map right."

"Not far at all." Beth clenched her shaking fists anxiously. "And today's Tuesday, right? We could back them up, if you..." She broke off.

"We promised we'd help them, Beth," Morgan told her, reading her anxiety. "We meant it."

At that, she felt tight muscles relax in her shoulders. She blew out a breath. "Good. What now?"

It was Garret who spoke, his voice grim. "Now we get ready to fight."

The three of them dressed hastily, Beth putting on the jeans, T-shirt and undies one of them had picked up from a nearby mall sometime during her bout with the vampire virus. Then, as she fidgeted, Morgan and Garret put their heads together over a stack of paperwork they'd collected from various sources—deeds and financial records from a dozen states.

"It's his, all right," Morgan pronounced finally.

"Looks like it," Garret agreed. He glanced over at Beth. "After we started waging war against him, he began stashing his properties under holding companies to keep us from finding and destroying them. Luckily, Elena's foundation has a large staff that is pretty good at ferreting out that kind of thing. This place on Cherokee Leap is about an hour from here."

"So we can go now, right?" The thought of what Ramirez might be doing to Val and Cade in the meantime made her want to jump out of her skin.

Morgan looked up from the map with a frown. "Not so fast. We've got to draw up a battle plan, and you need a quick lesson in amplifying our powers before we leave."

Beth was already familiar with the latter concept. It was the same technique Val and Cade used to defeat Ridgemont, who had been far too powerful to take down any other way. By sharing her consciousness with Cade, Val had been able to use her power to increase his strength and speed, making him a match for his ancient sire. Except…"We don't have time for that, Morgan. Val told me how she'd had to work for days to learn how to merge her power with Cade. We need to get to Ramirez before he kills them."

"It's not going to do us any good to rush to the rescue if we get ourselves killed," Garret pointed out. "Besides, I think I can teach you how to merge your power with ours more easily than that. It's not going to take that much time."

"I certainly hope not," Beth said grimly. "Because we don't have it."

Wide-eyed, Beth lay on the bed as Garret slid in beside her. The thought of what he was about to do made anxiety coil in tight knots in her belly.

"It's not going to be like it was with Ramirez," he told her, reading her fear as he took her hand in his. "This isn't going to be a possession, just a sharing. I can show you what to do more easily this way."

"I know." Too bad such logic didn't seem to mean anything to her jangling instincts.

"This isn't going to work if you don't trust us." Morgan watched her from the foot of the bed, his sword in his hands.

She lifted her chin at him. "I'll be fine." It was an outright lie. Her fear was spiraling in intensity until she wanted to leap up and run out of the room. She kept remembering what it had felt like to look on helplessly as Ramirez used her body like a puppet.

Garret rose on one elbow and looked down into her eyes. "Look, if it scares you this badly, you can stay here."

That stung. "Sit on the sidelines while you risk your lives fighting for Val and Cade? Not likely. If I can help you rescue them, I'll do it." Taking a deep breath, she forced herself to meet his eyes steadily. She could feel his easy, confident strength, and it made something in her relax. *They won't hurt me. I can trust them.* "Let's get this done."

He smiled and lay his head back down on the pillow. "That's my girl." His eyes closed and his body went limp.

The next instant, Garret flooded her consciousness like water rushing past a dam. Where the touch of Ramirez's consciousness had been cold and reptilian, Garret felt warm as sunshine. *"Hello, poppet."*

It was impossible to remain afraid. *"Hello, yourself."*

He wrapped himself around her like a sunny cocoon. *"You ready to go visit Morgan?"*

Testing, Beth took a deep breath. Her lungs obeyed, and she relaxed still more. *"Let's go."*

"All right. Meet his eyes. That'll make it a little easier."

Morgan was standing beside the bed looking down at them. He caught her gaze with his hot chocolate stare. It seemed Garret's warmth intensified, and she felt him streaming toward his cousin, pulling her along. And...

She was standing beside the bed, looking down at Garret and a slim, dark-haired woman whose face she'd only seen in mirrors. Herself.

Beth almost lost her grip and tumbled back into her own body, but Garret caught her close in that wonderful warmth of his. *"Hang on, poppet."*

"Damn, this is weird." Beth said it out loud, but the words emerged in Morgan's deep voice instead of her own. She winced, realizing she'd taken control of his body. "Sorry."

"Don't worry about it. It's all part of the process of learning how to merge," he told her. His mind was a little cooler than Garret's, but there

was something pure and shining about it—a calm power she found far more attractive than she'd expected.

"Glad you approve." Morgan turned, planning to head outside where they could practice. They needed a little more room to work.... He stopped in his tracks, the sword dropping from nerveless fingers.

Elena stood looking at him, her delicate face transparent, her expression hopeful. At his flabbergasted expression, a pleased smile lit her face. *"I thought you might be able to see me once all three of you combined."*

Beth felt the shock roll through both men, almost shattering their mental link. Automatically, she clamped down, trying to hold them together. It worked, though she had no idea how.

"Elena," Morgan managed.

The love and pain the cousins felt seemed to batter at Beth, but she held on anyway. *"If we lose this connection, you won't be able to see her!"* They realized she was right and coiled tighter around her, reinforcing the link.

Morgan reached out a hand toward Elena. "I'm sorry. God, I'm so sorry." He said the words in a pure, rolling Castilian Beth wouldn't have been able to understand if she hadn't known his thoughts.

"You have nothing to be sorry for, my angel," Elena told him, drifting closer. She started to reach out to him too, then dropped her hand as if afraid. *"You did all anyone could. Ramirez was just too strong."*

"I'm going to kill him for you," Morgan said, then corrected himself without being prompted. *"We* are going to kill him for you."

Sadness touched her eyes. *"I want to tell you to forget him, but I do not believe he will allow it. You must eliminate him, or you will never be safe."*

"Was Beth right?" Garret asked, taking control of Morgan's vocal cords. "Did you choose to stay here for us?"

"Yes." She smiled slightly. *"Do not fear, my love. God has not turned his back on me."*

"Then go to Him." It was Morgan speaking now. "You've earned His peace."

"Not yet." Both men recognized the stubborn determination on her face. *"Not until I know that you are safe."*

"Elena..." Garret began.

"It will not be much longer, mis angeles. *There is but one thing I must do."*

Beth felt a hot sting in her eyes, and knew the tears were Morgan's.

Elena's face softened. *"Ah, my handsome angel, there is no need to grieve for me. My future will be a wondrous thing. I can feel it."* She moved closer to them, looking deep into their eyes. *"And so is yours. The three of you will know great love together."*

This time it was Beth who spoke. "Not until Ramirez is dead." She didn't even jolt at the sound of her own words in Morgan's deep voice. "Are Val and Cade safe? Do you know?"

Something grim flashed over the ghost's face. *"For the moment. But the danger is great. You must hurry. Let my angels teach you what you must know and make haste."*

Determination filled Beth, echoing in the minds of the two men. "We will. We won't fail you, Elena. We'll get Ramirez."

"I have no doubt of it." The ghost smiled and faded away. This time the pain Beth felt was as much her own as the men's.

"Let's begin," Morgan said, and headed out of the room with his great sword in his hand.

Chapter Ten

As the SUV climbed the winding mountain road, Beth's stomach crocheted itself into knots.

The cousins had been right. Garret had been able to teach her the trick of amplifying Morgan's power faster than she would have believed. It had taken barely one precious hour.

Then he'd driven them to Cherokee Leap at a speed no one would dare except a man with vampire reflexes and the ability to hypnotize highway patrol troopers. Even so, every instinct Beth had screamed they were taking too long.

She knew her instincts were right when she felt a sudden ripping pain in her guts. Val's voice yelled, *"Cade!"* It wasn't a sound Beth heard with her ears. She knew her sister had just been hurt.

"Stop the truck!" she shouted, and Morgan hit the brakes. As the SUV skidded to a halt, Beth swung open the back passenger door and leaped out. Garret opened his own door and grabbed her by the collar just before she could throw herself down the steep mountain slope.

"Ramirez's house is further up the mountain," he told her, hauling her back from the edge.

"But Val and Cade are down that way." She flung out a hand to point down the mountainside. Anxiously, she peered over the edge. Even with bright moonlight and vampire vision, she couldn't see them—but she knew they were there. "They're fighting. Somebody's hurt." She had no idea *how* she knew it. She shouldn't even be able to sense her sister, since Val hadn't transformed her. Yet she felt Val's pain and desperation all the way to her bones.

"You've got a blood bond," Morgan told her, joining them on the edge of the cliff. "Changing strengthened it, even though your sires are different."

"Good thing, too." Garret released her cautiously. "Lead the way—but try not to break your neck. Trust me, it would be damned inconvenient."

Beth nodded curtly and went over the edge faster than she ever would have dared as a human. Her sister's pain had subsided from that first scarlet agony to a dull throb, but she could still feel it.

Spurred by Val's desperation, she scrambled down the trail, leaping over half-seen obstacles, grabbing at saplings as she plunged downward in an attempt to control her descent. As she ran, the men bounded along at her heels. Garret's calm combined with Morgan's solid confidence, soothing her fear.

Suddenly a hand clamped down on her shoulder, dragging her to a stop. "I hear them," Morgan said. He gestured at a fallen tree. "Why don't you curl up behind that and ride my mind the rest of the way in? Nobody would spot you, and you'd be out of the line of fire."

"But…."

"We can move faster than you can, Beth."

He had a point. She scrambled over to the log and slid down behind it as Garret jerked a couple of nearby bushes out of the ground and piled them in front of the trunk to conceal her. Rearing up just long enough to meet Morgan's gaze, she sent her consciousness to him.

She didn't even feel her body slump back down to the leaves.

After that, everything was a blur as the two men ran hard, plunging down the slop with a reckless disregard for the trees and thick brush in the way. Beth was dimly aware of limbs slapping against Morgan's face, of the crunch of leaves under his running feet, of the weight of his great sword across his back.

Ahead they heard the thunder of gunfire and screams. *"Sounds like World War III,"* Garret said in the link.

"Cade doesn't fool around when he's pissed off," Beth told them. And if Val was hurt, he'd be really pissed off. She tried not to think about that.

"We're going to be up to our asses in cops," Morgan grunted. Though a vampire could psychically influence one officer, there was no way to control a gang of them. If enough law enforcement showed up, the situation would go to hell in a hurry. "We need to get this under control now."

Morgan abruptly slid to a halt at a cluster of trees, grabbing Garret by the arm as he skidded past. The smell of blood hung in the air, and somebody was yelling in pain just below. Beth was relieved she didn't recognize the voice.

Cautiously, the two men went to their knees and edged past the screening trees onto a stone outcropping. The mountain dropped off as if something had taken a huge bite out of it.

Below them, thirty or so men armed with rifles and handguns fired toward a stone formation fifteen feet further down and a good fifty yards off to the left.

From behind the rock came a muzzle flash and its accompanying rolling boom. Cade was giving as good as he got. One of the gunmen fell with a howl of pain.

"Good shooting," Morgan drawled.

"Cade's a hell of a shot," Beth agreed in the link.

Garret frowned at the rock formation. "Which doesn't alter the fact that he's pinned down. Other than that outcrop, there's no cover over there—not so much as a bush."

Morgan flashed him a grin and drew his sword. "Let's do something about that, shall we?"

His cousin shook his head and pulled his own rapier and dagger. "You know the old saying about taking a sword to a gunfight, right?"

"Yeah, but I love a challenge." With that, he stepped right off the edge of the rock.

It was all Beth could do not to scream as they plunged downward. She was sure Morgan was going to break his leg, but he landed as lightly as a cat leaping off a kitchen counter.

The nearest gunman spun with a shout. Morgan promptly ran him through. A quick twist of his wrist destroyed the man's heart, and he pulled the blade free, simultaneously kicking another thug in the face before he could get off a shot.

"Morgan!" The psychic shout made him whirl, simultaneously ducking aside. A .45 boomed, followed an instant later by a scream as Garret drove his dagger into the would-be killer's throat. The man fell, gagging on his blood.

"Human," Garret said in the link, snatching the pistol out of his hand before he even hit the ground. *"Most of this mob is human."*

"No surprise," Morgan replied, spinning to decapitate one of the three remaining Swedes with a slash of his sword. *"We've killed the majority of Ramirez's thralls."*

Beth said nothing, too busy trying to amplify his powers with her own. It was hard work—he was so damn fast anyway that she found it almost impossible to keep up with him as he leaped and slashed. But there were so many of them. And Ramirez was definitely not among them. *"Where the hell is..."* she began, frustrated.

She broke off with a gasp as a vicious knifing pain tore into her belly. Her belly, not Morgan's.

Beth! Morgan yelled, but it was too late. She'd lost her hold on him. Feeling her consciousness ripping away from his, she cried out, tumbling into the darkness...

Male bellows of rage and pain cut off as if God had flicked a switch. As Beth jolted in surprise, leaves crinkled under her back. She was back in her own body.

Heart in her throat, she opened her eyes...

Ramirez grinned down at her, his fangs very white in the moonlight. "Ah, you're back. Good. I would have hated for you to miss this."

"Bastard!" Beth drove her fist straight for his smirking face with all her new vampire strength. He batted her arm aside, then backhanded her with a casual brutality that made stars explode in her skull. Her head snapped back and hit the ground. Stunned, she could only lay helpless as he grabbed the fabric of her T-shirt and jerked. It ripped away, leaving her clad only in her bra.

"Guys!" she yelled with all her psychic strength. *"I need help! Ramirez has me!"*

"Hang on!" Morgan shouted in the link. *"I've got to take care of some of these thugs before I can come to you, or they'll take Garret and me apart while I'm gone."*

And if Morgan's body died, there would be no one to save her from Ramirez anyway.

Beth clawed for Ramirez's face as he grabbed the cups of her bra and snapped them with one pull. *"Hurry—I'll try to hold him off."*

Ramirez smirked, obviously enjoying her fear. "You're on your own, aren't you? My men have Elena's dogs leashed. Just as I intended." Straddling her, he reached behind his back and drew a stiletto.

Her heart stopped at the sight of that long, wicked blade, bright in the moonlight. She was dead—as dead as Elena.

No. She had to stall. Morgan and Garret would come. They wouldn't leave her to die. She had to believe that. "How did you find me?" With any luck, the bastard would want to brag.

Ramirez knelt and rested the knife against her cheekbone, right at the corner of her eye. She fought to hide her fear. "I was attempting to circle around and take your pretty sister captive when I felt you coming. I knew they'd use you to amplify their strength, so I followed our link right to your body."

Just what they'd intended to do to him. "Garret and Morgan broke the link you had with me."

"I let them think they had. The only thing that will break my hold on you is your death." He flashed his fangs and pressed the knife a little deeper against her skin. Its cold point stung. "Take heart, my dove. That won't be long at all."

Suddenly pain ripped up her arm, startling a cry from her lips.

"What happened?" she demanded in the link.

"Garret's been hit," Morgan's voice said. *"Arm wound. We're surrounded—if I..."*

"He's coming to help you," Garret said. *"Morgan, go!"*

"No!" Beth protested. *"You can't leave him if he's hurt."* Wounded, he wouldn't be able to defend himself, and if Morgan's consciousness had gone to her, he'd be vulnerable too. They'd both end up dead. Even if she survived, she knew she'd feel the ache of their loss as long as she lived. Better to take her chances. *"I'll take care of Ramirez!"*

"Like hell!" Morgan snapped. *"Just try to stall him on a few more minutes."*

Easier said than done, she thought, *looking up into the Spaniard's black eyes as he relished her fear.* "One of them was hit, wasn't he?" Ramirez purred. "Which one? Morgan? Oh, that doesn't bode well, does it? Outnumbered, surrounded...And you here with me, all alone."

"Go to hell," she snarled.

"I think not. I'm having far too much fun right here. Now what should we do first?" He pressed the point of his stiletto against her cheek. "Mmmm. You know, I think I have time to fuck you. But first, you need to learn who is your master." He wrapped his free hand around her throat and squeezed. Choking, she clawed at him, but he only smirked and squeezed harder. "I've always loved this part."

Beth bucked beneath him with all her vampire strength, kicking and struggling, but she couldn't break his hold. Her vision was beginning to gray.

"Play dead," Elena said suddenly in her mind.

"What?" She dug her nails in his face, but he didn't seem to notice, his gaze locked on hers, bright with vicious pleasure.

"Go limp and fall back. Fix your eyes. Now!"

It went against every instinct of her howling body, but Beth went limp.

Ramirez felt her body go lax. *Time to let her catch a breath*. Then he could start enjoying that lush little body of hers before he cut out her heart. He wanted her to suffer until her pain crippled Morgan with memories of Elena's death. If Ramirez played his hand well, the new wave of guilt would make the bastard easy prey. And with Morgan dead, Garret would be unable to mount a proper defense. Ramirez could toy with him as he pleased before going for the kill.

He started to relax his grip so the little *puta* could breathe. Instead her darkening face suddenly went white, and something seemed to move under her skin. Startled, he let go. As he stared, the outlines of her face seemed to change, taking on a ghostly overlay. With a sense of horror, he recognized that spectral face.

"*Ramiiiireeeez.*" The word rang in his mind.

Elena.

No. It was impossible. It was some kind of mental trick...

The ghost floated from the gasping body of his victim, glowing like St. Elmo's fire against the darkness of the forest. "*Yesss, Joaquin. It's me.*" He'd looked into those dark eyes so many times as he'd tortured her. There was no fear in them now, only an awful knowledge, an awful power. "*You'll be joining me soon. And I'll have my revenge.*"

Dropping his knife, Ramirez made the sign of the cross with a shaking hand. The superstitious terror of his Castilian childhood rose, choking him. He wanted to run, but his leaden legs wouldn't obey. "Get away from me!"

"*Look at what you did to me, Rammmiiiirezzzz.*"Her pretty face was darkening, decaying as he watched, rotting away from her skull in black globs. Skeletal hands seized the front of her gown and tore it open to reveal the beautiful breasts he'd once taken such joy in tormenting. Maggots burrowed in them now. "*When you took me, when you raped me, I was a nun. For this, Hell waits for you, Joaquin. For your many sins, you will burn.*"

※҉(♥♡)ঐ※

Beth's fingers closed around Ramirez's forgotten knife. She looked up into his terrified face as he shrank from whatever horrific vision Elena was creating for him. Her throat still ached savagely from his vicious grip, and she felt weak. But she knew this was the only chance she was likely to get.

She stabbed for his heart with all her strength.

Black, glittering eyes flashed down to hers, and his hand clamped around her hand the instant before the point reached him. "No," Ramirez snarled. "I don't know how you brought the little bitch back, but you're not taking me that easily."

But as he started to twist the knife from her fingers, power surged into her in a white-hot wave. In an instant, all her fear drained away, replaced with a glorious anticipation.

Her grip tightened convulsively, frustrating his efforts to jerk the stiletto away. "Let go," Ramirez gritted, drawing back his free hand and curling it into a fist as he prepared to hit her again.

Morgan's grin stretched her mouth. "No," Garret drawled, "I don't think so."

Horrified realization flooded Ramirez's eyes, but before he could leap away, they rammed the knife into his chest with all their combined strength.

He stared down at it, appalled. "No," he choked. "You won't do this to me!" He tried to jerk her knife hand away from his body, but he was no match for all three of them. With two quick jerks left and right, they ripped up his heart. He sucked in a breath and fell backward across Beth's legs.

Elena flashed into view above the body, glowing like a star with white-hot triumph. "Yeesss!" Her hand flashed downward and punched into Ramirez's butchered chest.

"What the hell…?" Beth began, just as the ghost began dragging something glowing and translucent from the vampire's body.

Ramirez's ghost writhed as Elena hauled it into the moonlight. *"What are you doing?"* he demanded in frantic Spanish. *"Release me!"*

Elena sneered into his face. *"In a moment, you son of a whore. Watch."* She pointed.

Beth looked in the direction she indicated and gasped. A…*hole* was opening in the air, a vortex of darkness from which leaped tongues of flame. The stench that rolled from it made her recoil. Sounds emerged, echoing screams of torment.

"Good God," Garret said with her mouth, "what the hell is that?"

Elena smiled grimly. *"Hell."*

Beth rolled free of the Spaniard's corpse and shot to her feet, backing hastily away, heart pounding. As she watched, Ramirez's spectral body was drawn out toward the flaming hole. Panicking, he clutched at Elena's hands, arresting his fall. She caught at his fingers, about to pry him loose

"*No,*"he gasped. "*Do not let me fall into that! I beg you! I loved you, Elena. I did!*"

The triumph faded from her face, and for a moment, she looked almost sad. "*You gave yourself to hell before I was even born.*" She wrenched her hands free. He clawed at her as he began to fall, sucked toward the flaming darkness. His panicked howl made Beth flinch.

Ramirez hit the vortex, sending dark flames leaping as he vanished. The vortex instantly winked out.

Beth swallowed hard, staring at the spot where they'd been. "Remind me never to piss you off."

Elena shrugged. "*It was not my doing.*"

Beth's hands were shaking. She fisted them and attempted a smile at the ghost, who still gazed into the spot where Ramirez had vanished. There was a kind of sadness and horror in the woman's spectral gaze. Beth said the first thing she could think of. "You seem to have the hang of the ghost business a lot better."

Elena smiled slightly. "*I did some praying. It helped.*"

"Elena." It was Morgan. He took a step forward in Beth's body, extending a hand toward her. "I…" He broke off. What could he say? *Stay with us?*

Elena looked at him and smiled, but there was sadness in those big, dark eyes. "*Ah,* mis angeles, *I wish I could, but….*" Her voice trailed off.

"But you've got somewhere else to go, too," Garret finished for her.

Elena's smile widened, became more genuine. "*Now that I know you'll be safe and well, I can go.*"

Something… chimed, a long, sweet note, high and clear, like the most perfect bell Beth had ever heard.

Elena turned and gazed upward, arrested. "*Oh,*" she said. "*Oh, yes!*" The sadness fell away from her and her face lit with pure joy. She began to glow a pure, incandescent white. "*I'm ready now. I'm coming!*"

"Goodbye," Morgan said softly.

She tore her eyes away from the sky and smiled at him. "*I'll be waiting for you, my loves.*" That charming grin flashed again, the one they knew so well. "*But take your time.*"

She began to glow, brighter and brighter, until Beth had to look away. When she looked back, Elena was gone.

Beth swallowed around the thick knot of tears in her throat. Before she could think of anything to say, Garret spoke, urgency in his voice. "We've got to go. Val and Cade need us."

"What? Why? What's going on?"

Then, in their combined memories, she saw what had happened. With Garret wounded, they'd been locked in a losing battle with Ramirez's mercenaries when Cade and Val had suddenly charged up the mountain and joined them.

Val had sensed that Beth was nearby and in mortal danger—and that the two strange vampires were somehow connected to her. She and Cade had volunteered to protect their helpless bodies while they amplified her strength with their own.

But though Beth was now safe, Cade and Val were still in danger.

No sooner had she grasped the situation than the two men let their minds stream back toward their bodies. With a huff of worry, Beth lay down in the leaves and followed them, intent on providing any help she could.

Chapter Eleven

"...you long enough," Cade was growling as Beth entered Morgan's mind. He stood over Morgan, glowering down at him. "Did you get to her in time?"

"We got her," Garret said. "She's fine. And Ramirez is dead."

"It's awfully damned quiet." Morgan got to his feet and looked around. They still stood at the base of the cliff where the attack had begun, but Ramirez's thugs were nowhere to be seen. "Where are the bad guys?"

Cade shrugged his broad shoulders. "They broke it off and ran about five minutes ago."

"Probably about the time one of the Swedes sensed Ramirez was dead," Garret said, sitting up. He put a hand to his arm and grimaced. "I'm bleeding like a pig. I'm going to have to get some sleep if I want to heal this."

"Tell me about it." Val was leaning against the cliff wall, one hand clamped to her side. Blood seeped around her fingers.

"Val!" Beth gasped, and strode over to her. Dropping to one knee, she pulled her sister's hand away from the wound, then looked up into her face. "How bad are you hurt?" It wasn't until she heard Morgan's deep voice speak the words that she realized she wasn't in her own body.

Val looked into her eyes and smiled, recognizing her presence. "Oh, there you are. It's nothing. Did he hurt you, baby?"

"No, the guys got to me in time." She examined the wound anxiously. "Are you sure you're okay? There's a lot of blood here."

"Watch where you're putting his hands, Beth." Cade eyed them coolly.

Just as she realized she was resting a large, masculine palm on Val's thigh, Morgan rose and stepped back hastily. "Sorry," he said. "She forgot."

"That reminds me," Cade said in a steely voice. He took a long step forward until he was nose to nose with Morgan. "You want to explain how you ended up making my sister-in-law a vampire?" Beth had never seen such an expression of cold menace on his face before.

Morgan stiffened, anger sizzling through him.

"Great," Garret observed dryly to Val. "They're going to start pissing on trees next."

"Uh," Beth said, interrupting Morgan and Cade's staring contest. "Why don't I just…go back to my body and get the SUV. We can check into a hotel and…uh, talk."

Cade gave her a faint, cold nod. With a sigh of relief at that wordless promise of restraint, she fled.

Dressed again in one of her new polo shirts tucked into black jeans, Beth sat on one of the beds in the hotel room Cade and Val shared. Somehow or other the three men had managed to avoid any serious testosterone-influenced bloodshed. Now Garret and Morgan had retreated to a room on the next floor while Beth told Val and Cade what had happened since Ramirez kidnapped her—with the possible exception of a few sexual details they wouldn't have enjoyed hearing anyway.

Cade was kneeling at his wife's feet as she sat on the other bed, cleaning the gunshot wound in her side. Thanks to her vampire metabolism, it was already well on its way to healing, and should be completely gone by sunset. "So how do you feel about these two characters?" he asked, moving to the sink to wash out the rag. "Because if you're not happy with them…"

"No, I don't want you challenging them to a duel—or whatever bit of mayhem you've got in mind," Beth told him tartly, helping Val to sit back against the headboard. She watched in concern as her sister closed her eyes, visibly pale from blood loss. "One, they saved my life—several times. And two…"

Val's lips twitched as she finished, "…They're cute."

"They also seem to be joined at the hip," Cade said, wringing out the cloth. "What are they, gay?"

Beth laughed. "Ah, no."

"That would be a 'hell, no,' judging from her tone," Val supplied.

"And since when are you a homophobe, anyway?" Beth gave him a teasing smile.

He glowered. "I'm not a homophobe. I'm just not sure I like this whole psychic threesome thing you have going."

Val was grinning. "He's afraid they're going to corrupt you."

Beth couldn't help it—she burst out laughing. "Okay, now that may be a legitimate concern."

Val's eyes widened. "You mean—both of them? At once?" Her tone dropped to one of reverent awe. "Damn!"

"Hey!"

"You know I love you, baby, but did you *see* those two? My God, Cade, the possibilities are endless."

There was a long, sizzling pause. "Are you implying," he asked at last, his tone silken, his eyes smoldering, "that you feel deprived?"

"And on that note," Beth said, rising hastily to her feet, "I think I'll leave you two alone."

She barely made it out the door before Cade pounced. Val's giggles and yelps followed her all the way down the stairs.

⁂

Garret and Morgan owned a mansion. It even had a name—Rosecote, a 160-year-old Gothic Revival that stood on the cliffs of Newport, Rhode Island. Built of hand-cut rose marble blocks, it had turrets and arched windows and a yard going white under a gently drifting snowfall.

Beth pressed her nose shamelessly against the passenger window and stared at it as they pulled up to the gates in an opulent Lincoln Town Car. "Rosecote's not as big as the Breakers," Garret told her, referring to the sprawling Vanderbilt "cottage" nearby, "but it suited Elena's romantic streak."

"Damn, this place must have cost a fortune!" Stunned and dazzled, she got out when Morgan parked. The men on either side of her, she started up the cobblestone walkway to the house's impressive entrance. "What do you guys *do*, anyway?"

He shrugged. "We run the charitable foundation Elena started a few decades back. We do a lot of work in South America, building schools, encouraging development…."

"…Killing drug dealers," Morgan added dryly as he unlocked the house's massive oak double doors.

"And now that Ramirez is out of the way, we can get back to work," Garret added, gesturing for her to proceed them into the marble foyer. "The foundation has a capable staff—they kept things on an even keel while we were…busy. But I'll feel better when I have things back in hand."

"Garret's the Chief Operations Officer," Morgan explained. "I'm the muscle."

Beth thrust her tongue in her cheek. "Somehow I'm not surprised."

He lifted a dark brow and gave her a look that suggested she'd pay for that crack in some particularly delicious way.

Garret took her on a breathtaking tour. Beth spent the next forty-five minutes gaping at gleaming antiques in rich dark wood, heart-of-pine floors, hand-knotted rugs, and an art collection that made her artist's soul soar. By the time they'd worked their way through all the bedrooms and offices and back to the living room, she was in sensory overload.

While they'd been busy, Morgan had started a fire in the sprawling fieldstone fireplace and piled cushions on the floor in front of it. She sat down on one of them and accepted the glass of wine Garret handed her.

"We thought we could convert one of the bedrooms upstairs into a studio for you," he said. "There's one with a gorgeous view of the ocean."

She stared up at him. "You want me to move in with you?"

"You are part of us now," Morgan pointed out, sinking gracefully onto a cushion by her side. He leaned onto an elbow and took a sip of his wine, then studied her over the rip of the delicate crystal glass. "Just as Elena was."

She put her own glass down with a clink. "I'll never be able to take her place, Morgan."

"No," he replied steadily. "You're different women. But that doesn't mean we love you any less."

Her eyes widened. "Love?" Her heart began to pound with giddy joy. There it was, out in the open—the emotion she'd sensed building between them from the moment they'd linked. She licked her lips. "Do you mean it?"

"Open your heart and see," Garret said.

Beth licked her lips and closed her eyes, reaching through the link. There it was. That sweet, silken connection, even stronger now, purer, like a web of warm golden light.

They loved her as much as she loved them.

"When did that happened?" she asked softly, awed.

A thought flashed through Morgan's mind: *The first time I saw you standing in Ramirez' house in that white gown, with a dog collar on your neck and courage in your eyes.*

A knot thickened in her throat. She swallowed and tried for a joke. "I didn't realize you were that much a romantic."

Morgan reached out and caught her behind the neck, pulling her into a slow, hot kiss that made her toes curl. He took his time, licking and biting at her lips, slipping his tongue into her mouth in long strokes, swirling and tempting.

When he finally let her up for air, it took her two tries to manage speech. "Okay, I take it back. You're definitely a romantic."

"Among other things," Garret breathed in her ear. Catching her chin in his hand, he turned her head and took her mouth in a kiss of his own. With a sigh, she settled back into his arms.

While his cousin made love to her lips, Morgan brushed up the hem of her shirt to expose her breasts. Hooking two fingers in the lace cups of her bra, he freed her tight, furled nipples. She sank back against Garret with a moan as he went to work teasing and nibbling the hard peaks.

Between Garret's slow, intoxicating kisses and Morgan's delicious assault on her breasts, Beth was soon wet and groaning. By the time Garret lifted her short leather skirt, she was slick and swollen with need.

He sent a hand down the waistband of her lace panties. Both men growled approval of the way her sex gripped his exploring fingers.

Hunger surged through Beth, dark and intoxicating. She pulled away from Garret and sat up to grab the edges of Morgan's blue cambric shirt. One ruthless jerk sent buttons bouncing and on the floor, and revealed his beautifully sculpted chest. "I want to see you," she whispered, and shot a demanding glace at Garret. "Both of you."

With matching hungry smiles, the men went to work stripping off their clothes as Beth hastily pulled off her own, until at last they were all naked in the warm firelight, hands stroking as mouths met in slow, teasing kisses.

Finally, as the heat reached a wicked peak, Morgan lay back on the rug and caught her by the hips. Reading his intention in his thoughts, Beth grinned approval. "Naughty."

Then she straddled his face and leaned down over the demanding curve of his cock. Taking it in hand, she angled it upward and began to lick in long, hot strokes.

Morgan's long fingers closed over the cheeks of her backside, spreading her wide as he went to work on her clit. Garret straddled her calves as she knelt and leaned down to lap between her juicy labia. The fiery sensation of two skillful tongues working her sex made Beth gasp around Morgan's cock. Shivering, she fed still more of him into her mouth and cupped his full, round balls in her hand. Morgan closed his mouth over her clit, suckling greedily as Garret slid his tongue inside her in long, slow strokes. She shuddered in pleasure, feeling the pleasure echoing between them.

It seemed she could almost see the pleasure glowing with incandescent heat between her thighs. Whimpering, she rolled her hips against their faces in maddened little digs.

As if intent on driving her insane, Morgan reached beneath her to find her nipples. He squeezed, rolled, twisted and milked until she shivered like a palsy victim.

Then, without any warning at all, Garret slid two fingers up her ass. She jerked convulsively at the hot pleasure-pain and cried out around the cock filling her mouth.

"Are you ready for us?" Garret demanded, corkscrewing the little hole with a ruthless twist of his fingers.

"God, yes," Beth managed, lifting her head just long enough to speak before sucking Morgan's cock back into her mouth. The pleasure that surged through the link was so raw and feral, it made her shake.

"Just wait," Garret told her, pulling away from her sex and taking his long cock in hand to aim it for her creamy cunt. He drove inside hard, knowing she was more than ready for it. She gasped around Morgan's big rod.

With a rumble of approval for her reaction, Garret hilted himself with casual strength. The breathtaking penetration might have hurt, but Morgan was still licking her clit with wicked skill. She felt nothing but pleasure.

"Very nice," Garret purred, letting all three of them savor the sensation of his cock buried so deep in her sex. Sliding his thumb up her backside, he gave her a long, slow pump and grinned at her mental yelps. "You've got a really tight ass," he told her, adding a second finger to stretch her wide. "I'm going to enjoy fucking it."

At the uncharacteristic crudity, an image flashed through the link—Beth, sandwiched between the two of them as they slowly screwed her fore and aft.

The idea made her eyes widen. "I don't think so!"

Morgan laughed against her sex and gave her a wicked swirl of the tongue. "Count on it, love."

With that, Garret started riding her in long, deep thrusts, pressing his way to the balls with each lunge. Meanwhile, Morgan punctuated the slow reaming with flicking licks across her clit. Her mouth stuffed full of cock, all Beth could do was groan. Between Garret's rod, Morgan's tongue, and his clever fingers working her nipples, she felt as if she was drowning in honeyed fire.

She had no idea who started to come first, but when it happened, the climax rippled through all three of them. Morgan's come pulsed into her mouth as Garret slammed to the balls and roared, his cry mixed with her own muffled scream of pleasure.

*"Ours!"*one of them growled into the link, fiercely possessive.

"Yours," she agreed breathlessly. *"And mine."*

The word rolled between them, bouncing back and forth between their minds, hot and satisfied and almost glowing with pleasure.

"Ours."

About the Author:

Angela Knight's first book was written in pencil and illustrated in crayon; she was nine years old at the time. But her mother was enthralled, and Angela was hooked.

In the years that followed, Angela managed to figure out a way to make a living—more or less—at what she loved best: writing. After a short career as a comic book writer, she became a newspaper reporter, covering everything from school board meetings to murders. Several of her stories won South Carolina Press Association awards under her real name.

Along the way, she found herself playing Lois Lane to her detective husband's Superman. He'd go off to solve murders, and she'd sneak around after him trying to find out what was going on. The only time things got really uncomfortable was the day she watched him hunt pipe bombs, an experience she never wants to repeat.

But her first writing love has always been romance. She read The Wolf and the Dove *at 15, at least until her mother caught her at it.*

In 1996, she discovered the small press publisher, Red Sage, and realized her dream of romance publication in the company's **Secrets, Volume 2** *anthology.*

Whatever success she has enjoyed, she attributes to the marvelous editors she's had over the years. David Anthony Kraft and Dwight Zimmerman at Comics Interview taught her the nuts and bolts of fiction writing. Alexandria Kendall of Red Sage encouraged her to believe in herself.

But that success would be hollow without the love of her husband, Michael, and her son, Anthony. Her parents, Gayle and Paul, have been unfailing in their support and encouragement. Her sister Angela, whose name she adopted, was her first and most helpful editor. The help of her friend and critique partner, Diane Whiteside, has also been invaluable.

With such friends and family, it's no surprise Angela Knight considers herself a profoundly lucky woman.

Visit her website at www.angelasknight.com.

Men you've been dreaming about!

Satisfy your desire for more.

*F*eel the wild adventure, fierce passion and the power of love in every **Secrets** Collection story. Red Sage Publishing's romance authors create richly crafted, sexy, sensual, novella-length stories. Each one is just the right length for reading after a long and hectic day.

Each volume in the **Secrets** Collection has four diverse, ultra-sexy, romantic novellas brimming with adventure, passion and love. More adventurous tales for the adventurous reader. The **Secrets** Collection are a glorious mix of romance genre; numerous historical settings, contemporary, paranormal, science fiction and suspense. We are always looking for new adventures.

Reader response to the **Secrets** volumes has been great! Here's just a small sample:

> *"I loved the variety of settings. Four completely wonderful time periods, give you four completely wonderful reads."*

> *"Each story was a page-turning tale I hated to put down."*

> *"I love **Secrets**! When is the next volume coming out? This one was Hot! Loved the heroes!"*

Secrets have won raves and awards. We could go on, but why don't you find out for yourself—order your set of **Secrets** today! See the back for details.

Secrets, Volume 1

Listen to what reviewers say:

"These stories take you beyond romance into the realm of erotica. I found *Secrets* absolutely delicious."

> —Virginia Henley,
> *New York Times* Best Selling Author

"*Secrets* is a collection of novellas for the daring, adventurous woman who's not afraid to give her fantasies free reign."

> —Kathe Robin, *Romantic Times* Magazine

"...In fact, the men featured in all the stories are terrific, they all want to please and pleasure their women. If you like erotic romance you will love *Secrets*."

> —*Romantic Readers* Review

In *Secrets, Volume 1* you'll find:

A Lady's Quest by Bonnie Hamre

Widowed Lady Antonia Blair-Sutworth searches for a lover to save her from the handsome Duke of Sutherland. The "auditions" may be shocking but utterly tantalizing.

The Spinner's Dream by Alice Gaines

A seductive fantasy that leaves every woman wishing for her own private love slave, desperate and running for his life.

The Proposal by Ivy Landon

This tale is a walk on the wild side of love. *The Proposal* will taunt you, tease you, and shock you. A contemporary erotica for the adventurous woman.

The Gift by Jeanie LeGendre

Immerse yourself in this historic tale of exotic seduction, bondage and a concubine's surrender to the Sultan's desire. Can Alessandra live the life and give the gift the Sultan demands of her?

Secrets, Volume 2

Listen to what reviewers say:

"*Secrets* offers four novellas of sensual delight; each beautifully written with intense feeling and dedication to character development. For those seeking stories with heightened intimacy, look no further."

—Kathee Card, *Romancing the Web*

"Such a welcome diversity in styles and genres. Rich characterization in sensual tales. An exciting read that's sure to titillate the senses."

—Cheryl Ann Porter

"*Secrets 2* left me breathless. Sensual satisfaction guaranteed…times four!"

—Virginia Henley, *New York Times* Best Selling Author

In *Secrets, Volume 2* you'll find:

Surrogate Lover by Doreen DeSalvo

Adrian Ross is a surrogate sex therapist who has all the answers and control. He thought he'd seen and done it all, but he'd never met Sarah.

Snowbound by Bonnie Hamre

A delicious, sensuous regency tale. The marriage-shy Earl of Howden is teased and tortured by his own desires and finds there is a woman who can equal his overpowering sensuality.

Roarke's Prisoner by Angela Knight

Elise, a starship captain, remembers the eager animal submission she'd known before at her captor's hands and refuses to become his toy again. However, she has no idea of the delights he's planned for her this time.

Savage Garden by Susan Paul

Raine's been captured by a mysterious and dangerous revolutionary leader in Mexico. At first her only concern is survival, but she quickly finds lush erotic nights in her captor's arms.

Winner of the Fallot Literary Award for Fiction!

Secrets, Volume 3

Listen to what reviewers say:

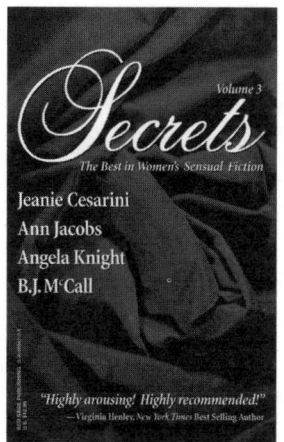

"*Secrets, Volume 3*, leaves the reader breathless. A delicious confection of sensuous treats awaits the reader on each turn of the page!"
— Kathee Card, *Romancing the Web*

"From the FBI to Police Dectective to Vampires to a Medieval Warlord home from the Crusade—*Secrets 3* is simply the best!"
— Susan Paul, award winning author

"An unabashed celebration of sex. Highly arousing! Highly recommended!"
— Virginia Henley, *New York Times* Best Selling Author

In *Secrets, Volume 3* you'll find:

The Spy Who Loved Me by Jeanie Cesarini

Undercover FBI agent Paige Ellison's sexual appetites rise to new levels when she works with leading man Christopher Sharp, the cunning agent who uses all his training to capture her body and heart.

The Barbarian by Ann Jacobs

Lady Brianna vows not to surrender to the barbaric Giles, Earl of Harrow. He must use sexual arts learned in the infidels' harem to conquer his bride. A word of caution—this is not for the faint of heart.

Blood and Kisses by Angela Knight

A vampire assassin is after Beryl St. Cloud. Her only hope lies with Decker, another vampire and ex-mercenary. Broke, she offers herself as payment for his services. Will his seductive powers take her very soul?

Love Undercover by B.J. McCall

Amanda Forbes is the bait in a strip joint sting operation. While she performs, fellow detective "Cowboy" Cooper gets to watch. Though he excites her, she must fight the temptation to surrender to the passion.

Winner of the 1997 Under the Covers Readers Favorite Award

Secrets, Volume 4

Listen to what reviewers say:

"Provocative...seductive...a must read!"
>—*Romantic Times* Magazine

"These are the kind of stories that romance readers that 'want a little more' have been looking for all their lives...."
>—*Affaire de Coeur* Magazine

"*Secrets, Volume 4*, has something to satisfy every erotic fantasy... simply sexational!"
>—Virginia Henley, *New York Times* Best Selling Author

Volume 4

Secrets

The Best in Women's Sensual Fiction

Jeanie Cesarini
Emma Holly
Desirée Lindsey
Betsy Morgan & Susan Paul

Provocative...seductive...a must read!
—Romantic Times Magazine ★★★★

In *Secrets, Volume 4* you'll find:

An Act of Love by Jeanie Cesarini

Shelby Moran's past left her terrified of sex. International film star Jason Gage must gently coach the young starlet in the ways of love. He wants more than an act—he wants Shelby to feel true passion in his arms.

Enslaved by Desirée Lindsey

Lord Nicholas Summer's air of danger, dark passions, and irresistible charm have brought Lady Crystal's long-hidden desires to the surface. Will he be able to give her the one thing she desires before it's too late?

The Bodyguard by Betsy Morgan and Susan Paul

Kaki York is a bodyguard, but watching the wild, erotic romps of her client's sexual conquests on the security cameras is getting to her—and her partner, the ruggedly handsome James Kulick. Can she resist his insistent desire to have her?

The Love Slave by Emma Holly

A woman's ultimate fantasy. For one year, Princess Lily will be attended to by three delicious men of her choice. While she delights in playing with the first two, it's the reluctant Grae, with his powerful chest, black eyes and hair, that stirs her desires.

Secrets, Volume 5

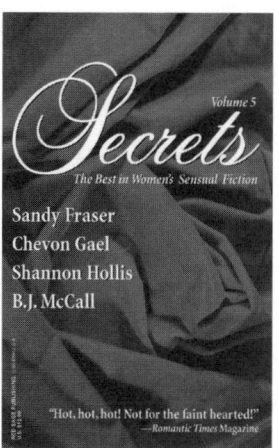

Listen to what reviewers say:

"Hot, hot, hot! Not for the faint-hearted!"
—*Romantic Times* Magazine

"As you make your way through the stories, you will find yourself becoming hotter and hotter. *Secrets* just keeps getting better and better."
—*Affaire de Coeur* Magazine

"*Secrets 5* is a collage of lucious sensuality. Any woman who reads *Secrets* is in for an awakening!"

—Virginia Henley, *New York Times* Best Selling Author

In *Secrets, Volume 5* you'll find:

Beneath Two Moons by Sandy Fraser
Ready for a very wild romp? Step into the future and find Conor, rough and masculine like frontiermen of old, on the prowl for a new conquest. In his sights, Dr. Eva Kelsey. She got away once before, but this time Conor makes sure she begs for more.

Insatiable by Chevon Gael
Marcus Remington photographs beautiful models for a living, but it's Ashlyn Fraser, a young corporate exec having some glamour shots done, who has stolen his heart. It's up to Marcus to help her discover her inner sexual self.

Strictly Business by Shannon Hollis
Elizabeth Forrester knows it's tough enough for a woman to make it to the top in the corporate world. Garrett Hill, the most beautiful man in Silicon Valley, has to come along to stir up her wildest fantasies. Dare she give in to both their desires?

Alias Smith and Jones by B.J. McCall
Meredith Collins finds herself stranded overnight at the airport. A handsome stranger by the name of Smith offers her sanctuaty for the evening and she finds those mesmerizing, green-flecked eyes hard to resist. Are they to be just two ships passing in the night?

Secrets, Volume 6

Listen to what reviewers say:

"Red Sage was the first and remains the leader of Women's Erotic Romance Fiction Collections!"

—*Romantic Times* Magazine

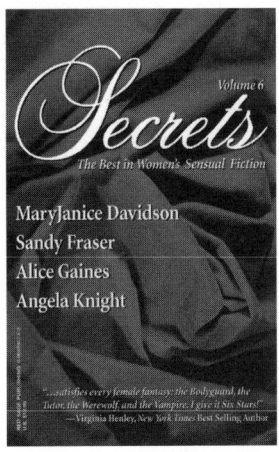

"*Secrets, Volume 6*, is the best of *Secrets* yet. ...four of the most erotic stories in one volume than this reader has yet to see anywhere else. ...These stories are full of erotica at its best and you'll definitely want to keep it handy for lots of re-reading!"

—*Affaire de Coeur* Magazine

"*Secrets 6* satisfies every female fantasy: the Bodyguard, the Tutor, the Werewolf, and the Vampire. I give it Six Stars!"

—Virginia Henley, *New York Times* Best Selling Author

In *Secrets, Volume 6* you'll find:

Flint's Fuse by Sandy Fraser

Dana Madison's father has her "kidnapped" for her own safety. Flint, the tall, dark and dangerous mercenary, is hired for the job. But just which one is the prisoner—Dana will try *anything* to get away.

Love's Prisoner by MaryJanice Davidson

Trapped in an elevator, Jeannie Lawrence experienced unwilling rapture at Michael Windham's hands. She never expected the devilishly handsome man to show back up in her life—or turn out to be a werewolf!

The Education of Miss Felicity Wells by Alice Gaines

Felicity Wells wants to be sure she'll satisfy her soon-to-be husband but she needs a teacher. Dr. Marcus Slade, an experienced lover, agrees to take her on as a student, but can he stop short of taking her completely?

A Candidate for the Kiss by Angela Knight

Working on a story, reporter Dana Ivory stumbles onto a more amazing one—a sexy, secret agent who happens to be a vampire.She wants her story but Gabriel Archer wants more from her than just sex and blood.

Secrets, Volume 7

Listen to what reviewers say:

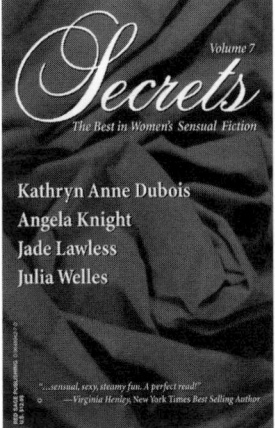

"Get out your asbestos gloves — *Secrets Volume 7* is...extremely hot, true erotic romance...passionate and titillating. There's nothing quite like baring your secrets!"
—*Romantic Times* Magazine

"...sensual, sexy, steamy fun. A perfect read!"
—Virginia Henley,
New York Times Best Selling Author

"Intensely provocative and disarmingly romantic, *Secrets*, *Volume 7*, is a romance reader's paradise that will take you beyond your wildest dreams!"
—Ballston Book House Review

In *Secrets, Volume 7* you'll find:

Amelia's Innocence by Julia Welles

Amelia didn't know her father bet her in a card game with Captain Quentin Hawke, so honor demands a compromise—three days of erotic foreplay, leaving her virginity and future intact.

The Woman of His Dreams by Jade Lawless

From the day artist Gray Avonaco moves in next door, Joanna Morgan is plagued by provocative dreams. But what she believes is unrequited lust, Gray sees as another chance to be with the woman he loves. He must persuade her that even death can't stop true love.

Surrender by Kathryn Anne Dubois

Free-spirited Lady Johanna wants no part of the binding strictures society imposes with her marriage to the powerful Duke. She doesn't know the dark Duke wants sensual adventure, and sexual satisfaction.

Kissing the Hunter by Angela Knight

Navy Seal Logan McLean hunts the vampires who murdered his wife. Virginia Hart is a sexy vampire searching for her lost soul-mate only to find him in a man determined to kill her. She must convince him all vampires aren't created equally.

Winner of the Venus Book Club
Best Book of the Year

Secrets, Volume 8

Listen to what reviewers say:

"*Secrets, Volume 8*, is an amazing compilation of sexy stories covering a wide range of subjects, all designed to titillate the senses. …you'll find something for everybody in this latest version of *Secrets*."

—*Affaire de Coeur* Magazine

"*Secrets Volume 8*, is simply sensational!"
—Virginia Henley, *New York Times* Best Selling Author

"These delectable stories will have you turning the pages long into the night. Passionate, provocative and perfect for setting the mood…."
—*Escape to Romance* Reviews

In *Secrets, Volume 8* you'll find:

Taming Kate by Jeanie Cesarini

Kathryn Roman inherits a legal brothel. Little does this city girl know the town of Love, Nevada wants her to be their new madam so they've charged Trey Holliday, one very dominant cowboy, with taming her.

Jared's Wolf by MaryJanice Davidson

Jared Rocke will do anything to avenge his sister's death, but ends up attracted to Moira Wolfbauer, the she-wolf sworn to protect her pack. Joining forces to stop a killer, they learn love defies all boundaries.

My Champion, My Lover by Alice Gaines

Celeste Broder is a woman committed for having a sexy appetite. Mayor Robert Albright may be her champion—if she can convince him her freedom will mean a chance to indulge their appetites together.

Kiss or Kill by Liz Maverick

In this post-apocalyptic world, Camille Kazinsky's military career rides on her ability to make a choice—whether the robo called Meat should live or die. Meat's future depends on proving he's human enough to live, man enough…to makes her feel like a woman.

Winner of the Venus Book Club
Best Book of the Year

Secrets, Volume 9

Listen to what reviewers say:

"Everyone should expect only the most erotic stories in a *Secrets* book. ...if you like your stories full of hot sexual scenes, then this is for you!"

—Donna Doyle Romance Reviews

"*SECRETS 9*...is sinfully delicious, highly arousing, and hotter than hot as the pages practically burn up as you turn them."

—Suzanne Coleburn, Reader To Reader Reviews/Belles & Beaux of Romance

"Treat yourself to well-written fictionthat's hot, hotter, and hottest!"

—Virginia Henley, *New York Times* Best Selling Author

In *Secrets, Volume 9* you'll find:

Wild For You by Kathryn Anne Dubois

When college intern, Georgie, gets captured by a Congo wildman, she discovers this specimen of male virility has never seen a woman. The research possibilities are endless!

Wanted by Kimberly Dean

FBI Special Agent Jeff Reno wants Danielle Carver. There's her body, brains—and that charge of treason on her head. Dani goes on the run, but the sexy Fed is hot on her trail.

Secluded by Lisa Marie Rice

Nicholas Lee's wealth and power came with a price—his enemies will kill anyone he loves. When Isabelle steals his heart, Nicholas secludes her in his palace for a lifetime of desire in only a few days.

Flights of Fantasy by Bonnie Hamre

Chloe taught others to see the realities of life but she's never shared the intimate world of her sensual yearnings. Given the chance, will she be woman enough to fulfill her most secret erotic fantasy?

Secrets, Volume 10

Listen to what reviewers say:

"*Secrets Volume 10*, an erotic dance through medieval castles, sultan's palaces, the English countryside and expensive hotel suites, explodes with passion-filled pages."

—*Romantic Times BOOKclub*

"Having read the previous nine volumes, this one fulfills the expectations of what is expected in a *Secrets* book: romance and eroticism at its best!!"

—*Fallen Angel Reviews*

"All are hot steamy romances so if you enjoy erotica romance, you are sure to enjoy *Secrets, Volume 10*. All this reviewer can say is WOW!!"

—*The Best Reviews*

In *Secrets, Volume 10* you'll find:

Private Eyes by Dominique Sinclair

When a mystery man captivates P.I. Nicolla Black during a stakeout, she discovers her no-seduction rule bending under the pressure of long denied passion. She agrees to the seduction, but he demands her total surrender.

The Ruination of Lady Jane by Bonnie Hamre

To avoid her upcoming marriage, Lady Jane Ponsonby-Maitland flees into the arms of Havyn Attercliffe. She begs him to ruin her rather than turn her over to her odious fiancé.

Code Name: Kiss by Jeanie Cesarini

Agent Lily Justiss is on a mission to defend her country against terrorists that requires giving up her virginity as a sex slave. As her master takes her body, desire for her commanding officer Seth Blackthorn fuels her mind.

The Sacrifice by Kathryn Anne Dubois

Lady Anastasia Bedovier is days from taking her vows as a Nun. Before she denies her sensuality forever, she wants to experience pleasure. Count Maxwell is the perfect man to initiate her into erotic delight.

Secrets, Volume 11

Listen to what reviewers say:

"*Secrets Volume 11* delivers once again with storylines that include erotic masquerades, ancient curses, modern-day betrayal and a prince charming looking for a kiss." **4 Stars**
— *Romantic Times BOOKclub*

"Indulge yourself with this erotic treat and join the thousands of readers who just can't get enough. Be forewarned that *Secrets 11* will whet your appetite for more, but will offer you the ultimate in pleasurable erotic literature."
— *Ballston Book House Review*

"*Secrets 11* quite honestly is my favorite anthology from Red Sage so far."
— *The Best Reviews*

In *Secrets, Volume 11* you'll find:

Masquerade by Jennifer Probst
Hailey Ashton is determined to free herself from her sexual restrictions. Four nights of erotic pleasures without revealing her identity. A chance to explore her secret desires without the fear of unmasking.

Ancient Pleasures by Jess Michaels
Isabella Winslow is obsessed with finding out what caused her late husband's death, but trapped in an Egyptian concubine's tomb with a sexy American raider, succumbing to the mummy's sensual curse takes over.

Manhunt by Kimberly Dean
Framed for murder, Michael Tucker takes Taryn Swanson hostage—the one woman who can clear him. Despite the evidence against him, the attraction between them is strong. Tucker resorts to unconventional, yet effective methods of persuasion to change the sexy ADA's mind.

Wake Me by Angela Knight
Chloe Hart received a sexy painting of a sleeping knight. Radolf of Varik has been trapped for centuries in the painting since, cursed by a witch. His only hope is to visit the dreams of women and make one of them fall in love with him so she can free him with a kiss.

Secrets, Volume 12

Listen to what reviewers say:

"*Secrets Volume 12*, turns on the heat with a seductive encounter inside a bookstore, a temple of naughty and sensual delight, a galactic inferno that thaws ice, and a lightening storm that lights up the English shoreline. Tales of looking for love in all the right places with a heat rating out the charts." **4½ Stars**

—*Romantic Times BOOKclub*

"I really liked these stories.You want great escapism? Read *Secrets, Volume 12*."

—*Romance Reviews*

In *Secrets, Volume 12* you'll find:

Good Girl Gone Bad by Dominique Sinclair

Reagan's dreams are finally within reach. Setting out to do research for an article, nothing could have prepared her for Luke, or his offer to teach her everything she needs to know about sex. Licentious pleasures, forbidden desires… inspiring the best writing she's ever done.

Aphrodite's Passion by Jess Michaels

When Selena flees Victorian London before her evil stepchildren can institutionalize her for hysteria, Gavin is asked to bring her back home. But when he finds her living on the island of Cyprus, his need to have her begins to block out every other impulse.

White Heat by Leigh Wyndfield

Raine is hiding in an icehouse in the middle of nowhere from one of the scariest men in the universes. Walker escaped from a burning prison. Imagine their surprise when they find out they have the same man to blame for their miseries. Passion, revenge and love are in their future.

Summer Lightning by Saskia Walker

Sculptress Sally is enjoying an idyllic getaway on a secluded cove when she spots a gorgeous man walking naked on the beach. When Julian finds an attractive woman shacked up in his cove, he has to check her out. But what will he do when he finds she's secretly been using him as a model?

Secrets, Volume 13

Listen to what reviewers say:

"In *Secrets Volume 13*, the temperature gets turned up a few notches with a mistaken personal ad, shape-shifters destined to love, a hot Regency lord and his lady, as well as a bodyguard protecting his woman. Emotions and flames blaze high in Red Sage's latest foray into the sensual and delightful art of love." **4½ Stars**

—*Romantic Times BOOKclub*

"The sex is still so hot the pages nearly ignite! Read ***Secrets, Volume 13!***"

—*Romance Reviews*

In *Secrets, Volume 13* you'll find:

Out of Control by Rachelle Chase

Astrid's world revolves around her business and she's hoping to pick up wealthy Erik Santos as a client. Only he's hoping to pick up something entirely different. Will she give in to the seductive pull of his proposition?

Hawkmoor by Amber Green

Shape-shifters answer to Darien as he acts in the name of the long-missing Lady Hawkmoor, their hereditary ruler. When she unexpectedly surfaces, Darien must deal with a scrappy individual whose wary eyes hold the other half of his soul, but who has the power to destroy his world.

Lessons in Pleasure by Charlotte Featherstone

A wicked bargain has Lily vowing never to yield to the demands of the rake she once loved and lost. Unfortunately, Damian, the Earl of St. Croix, or Saint as he is infamously known, will not take 'no' for an answer.

In the Heat of the Night by Calista Fox

Haunted by a century-old curse, Molina fears she won't live to see her thirtieth birthday. Nick, her former bodyguard, is hired back into service to protect her from the fatal accidents that plague her family. But *In the Heat of the Night*, will his passion and love for her be enough to convince Molina they have a future together?

Secrets, Volume 14

Listen to what reviewers say:

"*Secrets Volume 14* will excite readers with its diverse selection of delectable sexy tales ranging from a fourteenth century love story to a sci-fi rebel who falls for a irresistible research scientist to a trio of determined vampires who battle for the same woman to a virgin sacrifice who falls in love with a beast. A cornucopia of pure delight!" **4½ Stars**
—*Romantic Times BOOKclub*

"This book contains four erotic tales sure to keep readers up long into the night."

—*Romance Junkies*

In *Secrets, Volume 14* you'll find:

Soul Kisses by Angela Knight
Beth's been kidnapped by Joaquin Ramirez, a sadistic vampire. Handsome vampire cousins, Morgan and Garret Axton, come to her rescue. Can she find happiness with two vampires?

Temptation in Time by Alexa Aames
Ariana escaped the Middle Ages after stealing a kiss of magic from sexy sorcerer, Marcus de Grey. When he brings her back, they begin a battle of wills and a sexual odyssey that could spell disaster for them both.

Ailis and the Beast by Jennifer Barlowe
When Ailis agreed to be her village's sacrifice to the mysterious Beast she was prepared to sacrifice her virtue, and possibly her life. But some things aren't what they seem. Ailis and the Beast are about to discover the greatest sacrifice may be the human heart.

Night Heat by Leigh Wynfield
When Rip Bowhite leads a revolt on the prison planet, he ends up struggling to survive against monsters that rule the night. Jemma, the prison's Healer, won't allow herself to be distracted by the instant attraction she feels for Rip. As the stakes are raised and death draws near, love seems doomed in the heat of the night.

Secrets, Volume 15

Listen to what reviewers say:

"*Secrets Volume 15* blends humor, tension and steamy romance in its newest collection that sizzles with passion between unlikely pairs—a male chauvinist columnist and a librarian turned erotica author; a handsome werewolf and his resisting mate; an unfulfilled woman and a sexy police officer and a Victorian wife who learns discipline can be fun. Readers will revel in this delicious assortment of thrilling tales." **4 Stars**
—*Romantic Times BOOKclub*

"This book contains four tales by some of today's hottest authors that will tease your senses and intrigue your mind."
—*Romance Junkies*

In *Secrets, Volume 15* you'll find:

Simon Says by Jane Thompson

Simon Campbell is a newspaper columnist who panders to male fantasies. Georgina Kennedy is a respectable librarian. On the surface, these two have nothing in common... but don't judge a book by its cover.

Bite of the Wolf by Cynthia Eden

Gareth Morlet, alpha werewolf, has finally found his mate. All he has to do is convince Trinity to join with him, to give in to the pleasure of a werewolf's mating, and then she will be his... forever.

Falling for Trouble by Saskia Walker

With 48 hours to clear her brother's name, Sonia Harmond finds help from irresistible bad boy, Oliver Eaglestone. When the erotic tension between them hits fever pitch, securing evidence to thwart an international arms dealer isn't the only danger they face.

The Disciplinarian by Leigh Court

Headstrong Clarissa Babcock is sent to the shadowy legend known as The Disciplinarian for instruction in proper wifely obedience. Jared Ashworth uses the tools of seduction to show her how to control a demanding husband, but her beauty, spirit, and uninhibited passion make Jared hunger to keep her—and their darkly erotic nights—all for himself!

The Forever Kiss
by Angela Knight

Listen to what reviewers say:

"*The Forever Kiss* flows well with good characters and an interesting plot. ... If you enjoy vampires and a lot of hot sex, you are sure to enjoy *The Forever Kiss*."

—*The Best Reviews*

"Battling vampires, a protective ghost and the ever present battle of good and evil keep excellent pace with the erotic delights in Angela Knight's *The Forever Kiss*—a book that absolutely bites with refreshing paranormal humor." **4½ Stars, Top Pick**

—*Romantic Times BOOKclub*

"I found *The Forever Kiss* to be an exceptionally written, refreshing book. ... I really enjoyed this book by Angela Knight. ... 5 angels!"

—*Fallen Angel Reviews*

"*The Forever Kiss* is the first single title released from Red Sage and if this is any indication of what we can expect, it won't be the last. ... The love scenes are hot enough to give a vampire a sunburn and the fight scenes will have you cheering for the good guys."

—*Really Bad Barb Reviews*

In *The Forever Kiss*:

For years, Valerie Chase has been haunted by dreams of a Texas Ranger she knows only as "Cowboy." As a child, he rescued her from the nightmare vampires who murdered her parents. As an adult, she still dreams of him—but now he's her seductive lover in nights of erotic pleasure.

Yet "Cowboy" is more than a dream—he's the real Cade McKinnon—and a vampire! For years, he's protected Valerie from Edward Ridgemont, the sadistic vampire who turned him. Now, Ridgmont wants Valerie for his own and Cade is the only one who can protect her.

When Val finds herself abducted by her handsome dream man, she's appalled to discover he's one of the vampires she fears. Now, caught in a web of fear and passion, she and Cade must learn to trust each other, even as an immortal monster stalks their every move.

Their only hope of survival is...*The Forever Kiss*.

Romantic Times Best Erotic Novel of the Year

Finally, the men you've been dreaming about!

Give the Gift of Spicy Romantic Fiction

Don't want to wait? You can place a retail price ($12.99) order for any of the *Secrets* volumes from the following:

① **Waldenbooks and Borders Stores**

② **Amazon.com** or **BarnesandNoble.com**

③ **Book Clearinghouse (800-431-1579)**

④ **Romantic Times Magazine**
Books by Mail (718-237-1097)

⑤ Special order at other bookstores.
Bookstores: Please contact Baker & Taylor Distributors, Ingram Book Distributor, or Red Sage Publishing for bookstore sales.

Order by title or ISBN #:

Vol. 1: 0-9648942-0-3	**Vol. 9:** 0-9648942-9-7
Vol. 2: 0-9648942-1-1	**Vol. 10:** 0-9754516-0-X
Vol. 3: 0-9648942-2-X	**Vol. 11:** 0-9754516-1-8
Vol. 4: 0-9648942-4-6	**Vol. 12:** 0-9754516-2-6
Vol. 5: 0-9648942-5-4	**Vol. 13:** 0-9754516-3-4
Vol. 6: 0-9648942-6-2	**Vol. 14:** 0-9754516-4-2
Vol. 7: 0-9648942-7-0	**Vol. 15:** 0-9754516-5-0
Vol. 8: 0-9648942-8-9	

The Forever Kiss: 0-9648942-3-8 ($14.00)

It's not just reviewers raving about *Secrets*. See what readers have to say:

"When are you coming out with a new Volume? I want a new one next month!" via email from a reader.

"I loved the hot, wet sex without vulgar words being used to make it exciting." after *Volume 1*

"I loved the blend of sensuality and sexual intensity—HOT!" after *Volume 2*

"The best thing about *Secrets* is they're hot and brief! The least thing is you do not have enough of them!" after *Volume 3*

"I have been extreamly satisfied with *Secrets*, keep up the good writing." after *Volume 4*

"Stories have plot and characters to support the erotica. They would be good strong stories without the heat." after *Volume 5*

"*Secrets* really knows how to push the envelop better than anyone else." after *Volume 6*

"These are the best sensual stories I have ever read!" after *Volume 7*

"I love, love, love the *Secrets* stories. I now have all of them, please have more books come out each year." after *Volume 8*

"These are the perfect sensual romance stories!" after *Volume 9*

"What I love about *Secrets Volume 10* is how I couldn't put it down!" after *Volume 10*

"All of the *Secrets* volumes are terrific! I have read all of them up to *Secrets Volume 11*. Please keep them coming! I will read every one you make!" after *Volume 11*

Red Sage Publishing Mail Order Form:

(Orders shipped in two to three days of receipt.)

	Quantity	Mail Order Price	Total
Secrets **Volume 1** *(Retail $12.99)*	_____	$ 9.99	_____
Secrets **Volume 2** *(Retail $12.99)*	_____	$ 9.99	_____
Secrets **Volume 3** *(Retail $12.99)*	_____	$ 9.99	_____
Secrets **Volume 4** *(Retail $12.99)*	_____	$ 9.99	_____
Secrets **Volume 5** *(Retail $12.99)*	_____	$ 9.99	_____
Secrets **Volume 6** *(Retail $12.99)*	_____	$ 9.99	_____
Secrets **Volume 7** *(Retail $12.99)*	_____	$ 9.99	_____
Secrets **Volume 8** *(Retail $12.99)*	_____	$ 9.99	_____
Secrets **Volume 9** *(Retail $12.99)*	_____	$ 9.99	_____
Secrets **Volume 10** *(Retail $12.99)*	_____	$ 9.99	_____
Secrets **Volume 11** *(Retail $12.99)*	_____	$ 9.99	_____
Secrets **Volume 12** *(Retail $12.99)*	_____	$ 9.99	_____
Secrets **Volume 13** *(Retail $12.99)*	_____	$ 9.99	_____
Secrets **Volume 14** *(Retail $12.99)*	_____	$ 9.99	_____
Secrets **Volume 15** *(Retail $12.99)*	_____	$ 9.99	_____
The Forever Kiss *(Retail $14.00)*	_____	$11.00	_____

Shipping & handling (in the U.S.)

US Priority Mail:	UPS insured:
1–2 books .... $ 5.50	1–4 books $16.00
3–5 books $11.50	5–9 books $25.00
6–9 books $14.50	10–16 books $29.00
10–16 books $19.00	

SUBTOTAL _____

Florida 6% sales tax (if delivered in FL) _____

TOTAL AMOUNT ENCLOSED _____

Your personal information is kept private and not shared with anyone.

Name: (please print) _____

Address: (no P.O. Boxes) _____

City/State/Zip: _____

Phone or email: (only regarding order if necessary) _____

Please make check payable to **Red Sage Publishing**. Check must be drawn on a U.S. bank in U.S. dollars. Mail your check and order form to:

Red Sage Publishing, Inc.   Department S14   P.O. Box 4844   Seminole, FL 33775

Or use the order form on our website: **www.redsagepub.com**